# FRANCES HUNT'S BODY SHOP AND BONEYARD

*By*

Chad Darnell

To My Father: The last thing you said to me when I saw you
in your house, the house where I was raised was,
"Always remember who you are."

The last thing you said to us before you died was,
"See y'all soon."

We miss you and love you.

# Contents

# CHAPTER ONE

# HOT PEPPERS

Frances Hunt stood in the middle of Old Country Road, waving her phone high above her head, desperately trying to capture a signal. Steam billowed from the engine of her daddy's 1984 Ford pickup truck. Green antifreeze spewed from the radiator like a fountain at the recently closed Liberty Outlet Mall. She kicked a nearly bald tire in frustration and jammed a toe.

She stomped to the back of the truck, curled her fingers over the tailgate, and vigorously shook. "Don't you die on me too, you son of a bitch!"

It was a cold February morning in Liberty. The kind of Georgia morning where you're not sure if you need a down coat or tank top before leaving the house. The surrounding counties were hit with six inches of snow two weeks earlier, but the welcomed blanket of precipitation melted within days. Temperatures bounced back into the seventies by the weekend.

The phone died. "Dammit," she seethed under her breath. She ravaged the glove compartment for a charger, then remembered Kevin, her teenaged son, took it after buying a 2004 Saturn from a parishioner at their local Baptist church. The car had less than fifteen thousand miles on it, having barely been driven in almost twenty years. The previous owner passed away the previous summer in his sleep, and his wife had refused to ever learn to drive. When her children shipped her off to a nursing home, they happily sold the car to Kevin for peanuts.

Frances looked in both directions down the long, empty, deserted country road. *Which way to go*, she considered. One way led to Liberty's Main Street. The other led back to the family farm. Both journeys were about a mile and a half on foot.

It had been just over three months since Frances's life had been turned upside down by a series of chaotic events. These days, every move Frances made was intentional. She heavily weighed the consequences of whatever move lay before her. She considered how her maneuvers would affect the futures of not only Kevin but complete and total strangers. She had no one to talk to about the events that led her to this place. She took those feelings and memories and placed them in a box and placed that box on a shelf.

Not quite a hundred days earlier, Frances's mother, Birdie, and two of Birdie's childhood best friends, Sissy Stone and Delores Rogers, had arrived two hours early to the funeral of their dearly departed, Ruth Chambers. Ruth had borrowed a pair of black Michael Kors pumps from Delores a year earlier and had never returned them. Arlan Chambers, Ruth's husband, thought he had delivered the shoes, along with Ruth's favorite turquoise polyester suit, to the Lockhart Brothers Funeral Home. (The Lockhart Brothers Funeral Home had been in Sissy's family for generations, and she had worked there for almost fifty years alongside her brothers as a secretary, or as she referred to herself, "The Girl Friday.")

Convinced Ruth would be wearing the shoes in her casket until Jesus came back to rapture all of Liberty up to heaven, Delores insisted they snuck in before the service and switch out the shoes. Discovering the bottom door to Ruth's casket to be locked, Birdie was charged with pulling Ruth's body out of her final resting box, only to discover her arms and legs had been cut off and replaced with PVC pipe and realistic-looking plastic hands.

Hours later, Frances would learn Kevin was about to become a teen father to his very pregnant teenaged girlfriend. The baby mama in question, Brandy James, was what many called "trailer trash" and as mean as a rattlesnake. Under intense stress of financial woes (which would make her family homeless and farmless within weeks), Birdie's erratic behavior (a combination of depression and early stages of dementia), and impending grandmotherhood, Frances smoked an entire joint (which had belonged to poor, old Irene Bohanon before she died of brain cancer), and went along with the septuagenarians to search the Lockhart Brothers for a pair of missing shoes, under the cover of night. Should they have questioned/been more concerned with the fact Ruth's arms and legs had been cut off? Sure. But Delores bought those shoes in Las Vegas at the Shops in Caesar's Palace, and she wanted them back. Sissy had keys, so they weren't doing anything wrong. They were simply searching the family funeral home for a lost item.

Upon arrival, they discovered an old, beat-up van parked at the rear entrance of the funeral home containing dozens of Styrofoam containers. Before they could properly search the funeral home for the shoes, Oscar Lopez (who they would later learn was an escaped convict and super bad dude) appeared and took aim at the women with his double-barrel shotgun. A recent graduate from the Liberty Baptist Church self-defense course for senior citizens, Delores commandeered the gun away from Oscar, shotgun-whipped him, knocked him unconscious, and nearly beat him to death. Frances opened a Styrofoam chest in the back of Oscar's van, revealing the contents to be human body parts: arms, legs, headless torsos, and disembodied heads.

Frances and the women yeeted Oscar into the back of his van and drove him back to the Hunt family farm, where they duct-taped him within an inch of his life. Frances paced, Delores fanned herself, Sissy ate animal crackers, and Birdie (Liberty High School's class of 1964 head majorette) focused the shotgun on Oscar, daring him to move.

When he came to, Oscar explained in great detail how he was merely a transport driver for a human remains reseller, known only as "The Man." He claimed The Man had agreements with local funeral homes all over the South. The Man harvested dead body parts and sold them to hospitals, medical conferences, science labs, and universities. Disgusted yet completely engrossed, the ladies pushed Oscar for more details and stories of his scheming.

Twenty feet away and completely unbeknownst to everyone, Kevin was attempting to have sex with Brandy in the front seat of her daddy's Cadillac, parked right behind the Hunt family barn. When Kevin slipped, accidentally punching the car horn, a startled Birdie pulled the trigger, rendering Oscar Lopez very dead and very headless.

After answering the incoming call to Oscar's phone from The Man (asking for the ETA of his delivery), Frances determined the best way to get rid of Oscar's body was to deliver his headless corpse along with the rest of his haul. With Oscar's intended salary in hand, his van (and a single Styrofoam container The Man's goons seemingly missed at his warehouse) at the bottom of a lake, and all the evidence in the barn destroyed, Frances went to bed, believing she had successfully closed the chapter on what had been up until that point in her life, the worst day of her life.

But opportunity had knocked. Frances could not help but consider the idea of body snatching. She needed money. She needed a team. She would need an adviser, and as if sent from Jesus Christ Himself, Hector Ramirez, Oscar's woe-begotten former work partner, showed up on her doorstep, having tracked the van back to the Hunt family farm. Learning of Oscar's untimely unaliving, a very relieved and very happy Hector begged to come aboard as their "Butcher." Within days, the old lady gang and Hector had rented an abandoned bakery as their headquarters, cold-called potential buyers, and worked deals with other local funeral homes and crematoriums (who were already working for The Man) nearby. Frances became the face of the company, known as "Big Momma."

But not all secrets stayed buried. The rogue Styrofoam container containing a decomposed arm from the back of Oscar's van surfaced. Sheriff Ray Jackson's investigation led to the discovery the arm had belonged to recently deceased Liberty High football coach Dean Gilbertson.

As the object of Sheriff Ray Jackson's unrequited love for over thirty years, Frances was forced to feign interest in order to stay two steps ahead of him and his investigation. But soon, Frances began to question whether those feelings were completely pretend. Sheriff Ray Jackson was a good man. A decent man. But when Jackson told Frances he planned to exhume Dean Gilbertson's body, she dispatched Hector and Kevin to steal the casket from his mausoleum drawer in the middle of the night. The newbie tomb raiders couldn't chance Sheriff Ray Jackson investigating the funeral home and any late-night extracurricular activities once he discovered all of Dean Gilbertson was not entirely in that box.

Sissy's brother, Stephen Lockhart, went missing and presumed dead while on a cruise at sea. Sissy's husband, Carl, died mysteriously. Brandy had abdominal pains so intense she went to the hospital, only to learn she was, in fact, not pregnant and instead had a nine-pound teratoma growing inside her.

Brandy died several hours later while still in recovery.

A slip of Frances's tongue led Sheriff Ray Jackson to The Man's warehouse in Atlanta and to the discovery of Oscar Lopez's headless body. He realized Frances had manipulated him and lied to him. When he arrived at the Hunt family farm to question Frances, he found only Birdie, who, in the midst of her elderly confusion, confessed to killing Oscar. While Jackson searched the barn for evidence, he heard a shotgun blast from the house and discovered Birdie's lifeless body.

Frances would confront Jackson on the day of the funeral, and while neither showed their cards, they both knew he had confronted a mentally unstable woman. He knew Frances was somehow involved with the van at the bottom of the lake, Oscar's dead body, and the strange warehouse in Atlanta. He wasn't exactly clear how she was involved, but he knew her fingerprints were all over his investigation.

It had been nearly three months and yet seemed like a lifetime ago. Frances's life had become so consumed with death in the past few months that she felt like everywhere she turned was another dead body. She felt like she was a magnet for dead bodies. A dead body whisperer.

It had been nearly three months since she stepped away from most everyone in her life. She pushed her loved ones away and, instead, focused her life on serving complete strangers. It had been nearly three months since she had spoken to Sissy, Delores, Akasha, or Hector. Nearly three months since she had seen Sheriff Ray Jackson.

Frances was focused on starting a new life. She was focused on keeping Kevin alive and keeping pink envelopes out of the Hunt family farm mailbox. She was focused on her new business. In small-town America, it's nearly impossible to start over, but Frances Hunt was committed to shapeshifting into someone with purpose, integrity, and peace, even if it killed her.

A brand-new cherry red Mustang raced toward Frances, kicking up rocks and dirt in its wake, leaving a beige cloud on the horizon. Frances waved her arms over her head, and the car slowed on its approach.

The driver's window rolled down. "Ms. Hunt? Whatchu doin' out here all by yourself? You might get killed by a psycho killer or somethin'!"

Frances leaned into the window. He looked vaguely familiar, but she couldn't quite place him.

"Ms. Hunt, it's me! Clint Peppers!"

Clint Peppers and Kevin had grown up together but drifted apart in high school. Clint became Liberty High's star quarterback and a track star. He was awarded "Best Actor" for his role as "Stanley" in *A*

*Streetcar Named Desire.* He was crowned Mr. Liberty High School at the homecoming dance. He was a straight-A student, at the top of the class, expected to be the valedictorian in the spring, and had already received early acceptance into Emory University. The Peppers were one of the wealthiest families in Liberty. They were old family money with their family tree going back to the founding of Liberty in the early 1800s. Most of the Pepper men, including Clint's father, Joel, worked at their historic family law firm.

"Welp, I'd welcome a psycho killer at this point as long as they make it quick and don't drag it out," she said. This once string bean of a child, who used to eat frozen popsicles on the porch with Kevin, grew up to look like a Hollywood movie star. "Jesus, Clint. Have you been living in a gym?" She felt his bicep. "Are these real?"

"Yes, ma'am. Doing two-a-days."

"Don't call me ma'am."

"My momma would backhand me if I didn't respect my elders."

"Call me an elder again, and I'll backhand you myself."

"You need a ride?" he asked. "Looks like you're broken down. What seems to be the problem?"

Frances turned back to the truck, grabbing her purse from the front seat. "Yes. Yes, I need a ride. Thank you." She locked the truck doors. "It just stopped and blew up."

"I'd help you out, but I don't know much at all about trucks," he said, watching her round the front of his Mustang, climbing into the passenger's seat. "It's a good thing for you I came along. And it's my birthday, too! I turned eighteen today."

"So, you're legal now," she said, fastening the seatbelt.

"What did you say?"

Frances pulled the hair tie from her wrist and gathered her hair into a ponytail. "I said, you're legal now."

"I… Yeah. I mean, I can't drink for another three years." Clint gripped the leather around the steering wheel. "I ain't a virgin."

Frances snapped her fingers and pointed toward the road. "Drive, Clint. Drive."

Clint pulled away from the broken-down truck. Frances gave it one last look at the truck in the sideview window before turning back to Clint. "You've really grown up. You look like a…"

"Like a what?"

"I was going to say a man, but that sounds… You look good. You look real good."

"My aunt's an agent in Atlanta. She reps actors and models. She sent out some pics I took on my phone, and I booked an underwear campaign last summer. They were going to send me to Paris, but they found out I was only seventeen and… well, that was that."

"You booked an underwear campaign?" she asked.

"Yes, ma'am. I mean, Ms. Hunt. Mainly just jock straps and thongs and shit. But no Paris for me. It's for the best, I guess. I need to stay focused on school."

Frances laughed. Clint's head spun with a defensive, sad expression. "Why'd you laugh at me?"

"Oh, Clint, baby, I'm not laughin' at you. How did you and Kevin grow up to be so completely different?"

"I haven't talked to Kev in a while. Just different circles, I guess. He's a good kid."

She nodded. "Yeah. He's a good kid."

"I heard about Brandy and him. He doin' okay?"

"Not really. He goes and visits her grave every day. Brandy's momma and them don't want him goin' out there, but it's the church cemetery, so… What are you gonna do? They think he's creepy."

"Did they bury the… I mean, I know it wasn't a real…"

"No, it's a fair question. It wasn't a baby. It was a teratoma. I'm still not even sure what that is myself. But no." Her voice drifted off, and they continued to ride in silence. "Brandy's momma thinks it was a demon, and who am I to correct her?"

Frances pulled her phone from her pocket. "Can I charge my phone? It died."

Clint unplugged his phone and handed her the cord. "Dead car. Dead phone."

"Everything dies around me eventually, Clint. I'm the Angel of Death. Didn't you hear?"

After a long moment of silence, Clint offered, "They probably incinerated it. The teratoma, I mean."

"Yeah, yeah. They probably incinerated it," she agreed.

"I did some research on teratomas when I heard that's what she had. Sometimes, it's just hair and eyes and teeth. I heard they put Brandy in one of them fancy medical journals."

"Brandy James in a medical journal," Frances pondered aloud. Her eyes wandered to Clint's triceps cutting through his t-shirt. She leaned forward, turning up the heat. "Boy, it's like forty degrees outside. Why are you drivin' around without a coat on?"

"I just came from the gym. I take a pre-workout, and it always makes my body real hot."

"Why aren't you in school?"

"Half day because of my college prep classes."

"Lucky for me, you came along when you did."

"Oh, shit, I'm so sorry, I didn't even..." His voice dropped as he focused on the road.

"You didn't what?" she asked, suddenly concerned.

"I'm sorry. I need to work on my bedside manner if I'm gonna be a cancer doctor."

"You didn't what?"

"Your momma. I'm so sorry. I didn't even think to ask you." Frances didn't respond. "I'm so sorry. My dumb mouth. I'm just all like, 'your momma!' and that's gotta be the last thing you want to talk about."

"It's okay. I appreciate you askin'. Not many people do. She was sick. I wish I'd gotten her help. The help she needed. I thought we was doin' the right thing, but you just never know." She held up her hand, showing Clint a ring. "Momma got this when we drove out to Arizona on a cross-country trip when I was a kid. I can't even go into her room. Ain't been in since she... Sissy went in there and got out her jewelry box. I've been wearin' some of her pieces."

"Any idea why she did it?" Clint asked, slowly turning, checking to see if he had overstepped.

But Frances knew he was young and obviously had no idea the immense guilt Birdie carried from accidentally killing Oscar Lopez. "Nope. No idea. Guess we'll never know." Her eyes drifted down, catching the Liberty Raiders Football mascot on a keychain swinging near his thigh.

"Oh, Jesus, Clint. I'm sorry. Dean Gilbertson."

Tears welled in Clint's eyes. "Yes, ma'am. We miss him every day."

Frances punched him in the arm. "Boy, I done told you, don't call me ma'am."

Clint softly laughed as his face fell again. "He was the best-damned football coach this state ever did see. And you know none of us thought it was a heart attack that killed him."

Frances blinked. "Huh?"

"I mean, he was overweight and shit, but none of us think it was a heart attack that killed him. And then his body went missin'? Connect the dots." Then dramatically, "Follow the money."

*Follow the money?* Frances's mind raced. *Where is he going with this?* "What do you mean? What do you think happened?"

"He was murdered."

"Dean Gilbertson wasn't murdered. It was a heart attack. They even did an autopsy," Frances confidently responded with a deep breath. "I read that in the paper. Maynelle insisted on it."

"Maynelle Gilbertson *insisted* on it. Maynelle Gilbertson was screwing half the football team. I mean, I never... I mean, I wanted to, and the opportunity was definitely there—"

"Clint Peppers!" Frances shrieked. They stared at each other in silence, Clint occasionally looking back to the road to make sure he wasn't about to drive into a ditch. "You don't... You don't actually believe that, do you? How could someone have given Dean Gilbertson a heart attack?"

"Inject potassium chloride under his tongue. It won't show up in an autopsy."

Frances searched for words. "How would someone knock out Dean Gilbertson to do that?"

"Easy. He goes home every night after practice, has four beers, and passes out. Go in, move his tongue out of the way, get yourself a syringe, and boom. Dead football coach."

"You're talkin' like you know this is exactly how it happened," Frances said.

"One night, everyone was talkin' about how they'd get away with the perfect murder, and one of the math nerds suggested it, and that just got me to thinkin'."

Frances waved her hand. "He was fat, Clint. Natural causes."

"You keep tellin' yourself that, sister."

"He was real fat, Clint! I'm surprised they were able to…" Frances's voice trailed off.

"Surprised they were able to what?"

"Surprised they were able to get his whole body in that casket," she quickly responded, knowing damn well Dean Gilbertson went into that casket without his arms, legs, and probably a good fifty pounds around his stomach, thanks to Hector Ramirez's butchery skills.

Clint pushed further. "How would you do it? How would you get away with murder?"

"Snake."

Clint laughed. "A snake!? Where you gonna find a snake that can kill someone?!"

"We got rattlesnakes all out back behind our barn."

"But how you gonna get a snake to kill someone?"

"Not just one. Like a dozen. And then I'd put them in their bedroom so that when they go to sleep—"

"Your plan is to put twelve rattlesnakes in someone's bedroom!? You tryin' to kill a deaf person?! Because I hate to spoil it for you, darlin', but they gonna hear twelve little rattles goin' off!" Clint laughed. "I hope you don't ever plan on killin' someone because you'd make a terrible criminal!"

"Back to Maynelle," Frances said, changing the subject.

Clint nodded. "It's like the most messed up version of that old movie

*Clue* you ever did see. We're all in the showers after a game, and we all know someone among us done killed Coach Gilbertson."

"Ain't no high school locker room shower scene in that *old* movie *Clue*, Clint. And by the way, I saw that movie in a theater back in the day, and there were three different endings. You'd have to go buy a different ticket to watch all three versions." She narrowed her eyes on him. "But this don't make no sense. God give a goose, Clint. If y'all all are screwin' the wife, why kill Dean?"

"Because of the insurance money. He had a hundred-thousand-dollar life insurance policy. She probably offered to cut somebody in if they killed him. Then his body went missin', and people were sayin' it was devil worshippers. Ain't no devil worshippers in Liberty. Whoever came up with that story was just plain stupid."

"Is that right? You know, I think I heard somethin' about devil worshippers in Liberty," Frances quietly said, having been the exact person who started the very rumor of devil worshippers to throw Sheriff Ray Jackson off her trail nearly three months earlier. "What does his stolen casket have to do with his alleged murder?"

"It was either someone sending a message to Maynelle that they knew what she did, or she had someone steal his body, so the police couldn't exhume his body and check for signs he was murdered."

"Then why return the casket and leave it outside the cemetery?" she asked. "Remember? His casket was only gone like a few days, and then it showed back up."

"Because people are crazy, Ms. Hunt!" She punched him again. "What am I supposed to call you?"

"Your queen," she said, half-joking, half… *Clint Peppers* is *legal.*

"One of them football players killed him. And the fact is, we'll never know what really happened. And you wanna know what I think is gonna happen next? I think whoever killed Coach and stole his body is gonna shoot up the school! Cause they's crazy."

Frances sat mystified at the sweetly innocent and profoundly stupid thoughts flying out of Clint Peppers's mouth. "If someone killed Dean Gilbertson for the insurance money, they're ain't gonna shoot up the school. That's just bad business, Clint. This person is a sociopath, not a psychopath."

"If they killed Coach, that still makes them a psychopath! Psychopaths are dangerous!"

"Clint, I still believe it was a heart attack, but maybe you're right. Maybe it was some horny teenager who was obsessed with Maynelle Gilbertson's forty-five-year-old vag. Maybe she cut them in on the money. Maybe someone killed Dean Gilbertson by shootin' him up with…"

"Potassium chloride."

"Potassium chloride under Dean Gilbertson's tongue after he passed out from a few beers. That's a real nice story. Maybe *Dateline* will do a story on it." Frances slapped his bicep again, trying to be playful. "Call me ma'am or Ms. Hunt one more time."

"And now they can't even exhume his body anymore," he said.

"Well, I mean, technically, they can. They just have to slide him back out from his drawer," Frances said apathetically. Frances and Hector had considered the possible danger of returning Dean Gilbertson's casket back to Memorial Gardens. But having led Sheriff Ray Jackson to the warehouse in Atlanta and the discovery of The Man's body harvesting operation and the body of Oscar Lopez, they considered Dean Gilbertson's casket as one more road to lead Jackson back to The Man and, thus, further away from them.

In the past three months, Frances and the others had braced for the local news to report Dean Gilbertson's casket had mysteriously found its way back to Memorial Gardens, minus his arms and legs. But Sheriff Ray Jackson and the rest of the police department never released that information. No one was made aware the very late Dean Gilbertson was missing any of his appendages. In fact, no one in Liberty, nor the rest of the state of Georgia, was aware of any body harvesting operations and/or their subsequent investigations.

Life went completely back to normal in Liberty.

"He ain't in his drawer. You didn't hear? Maynelle had him cremated after his casket turned back up. And then she scattered him off Tybee Island, where they got engaged. You didn't see the pics on her Facebook?"

"No, I ain't been on Facebook since Momma…"

He pulled his phone from his right hip pocket. He opened the app and handed it to Frances. "Find her profile. But don't go scrolling through my photos on my camera unless you… Just don't scroll, okay?"

Frances took the phone, curiously glancing back at Clint. After finding Maynelle Gilbertson's profile, indeed, a few posts were beige-filtered beauty shots of her throwing Dean's ashes in the air at sunset. A flourish of "Live, Laugh, Love" in a decorative, sparkly font adorned each photo. "Damn, did she go out and hire a professional photographer to shoot all this?" she asked.

"Mark my words. That dumb whore had someone at Liberty High School kill Coach Gilbertson. And I'm going to find out who did it."

"She's not a dumb whore. She's a librarian."

"A dumb whore librarian about to get a hundred thousand bucks in life insurance." Clint gripped the steering wheel tightly. "Follow the money," he whispered.

Clint drove in silence for a minute as Frances scrolled through Maynelle's posts. "Where you want me to drop you off?"

"Huh?" Frances looked up. "Right. Need a mechanic. And a tow truck. Just anywhere up on Main Street."

"I'll take you to my uncle Humphrey. He'll take care of you."

They rode in silence for nearly two minutes until Clint asked, "So, you datin' anyone?"

Frances laughed. "Clint, I'm pushing fifty and live in Liberty. No. I ain't datin' anyone. You?"

"A few girls, but nothing serious. Too much homework in all my Advanced Placement classes. And with practice and volunteering down at the hospital on weekends, you know."

Frances nodded. "Yeah. That's a busy schedule. You volunteer at the hospital?"

"When I'm not tryin' to track down Coach's killer."


Frances and Clint arrived at Humphrey Rhodes's mechanic shop about ten minutes later. All three jumped into Humphrey's tow truck (Clint announcing, "I'm invested now!") and returned to the abandoned pickup.

"It's the engine," Humphrey said.

"The entire engine?! That sounds not inexpensive."

"I'm sorry."

"Well, how much is it gonna cost?" Frances asked.

"Honey, it's gonna be real expensive. There's nothing we can do for it. I think you're going to have to put her out to pasture."

Frances shook her head. "No. That's not an option. There have to be engines out there. Don't people rebuild them?"

"A new engine for this thing is gonna cost more than a good, used hybrid! Go get you one of them! Better gas mileage!"

"I don't want no damn hybrid!" Frances paced. "I ain't sittin' at a chargin' station once a week at The Pig to charge up my car. I ain't gonna have my son callin' me a liberal!"

"Dusty Dingle might have an engine," Humphrey suggested as he gently closed the hood of the truck. "You could check with him and see if he's got something I could work with. Elwood might be able to tune something if Dusty's got an engine. But honestly, Frances, it's more trouble than it's worth. I'll take your money because I could sure use it, but if I was you, I'd get me a new car."

Frances's brow furrowed. "Dusty Dingle. I know that name. Why do I know that name?"

"He used to be a friend of your daddy's. He owns that—"

Frances gasped. "He owned that used car lot!" Frances flashed on an old childhood memory, remembering her father taking her to a giant field with broken-down cars.

"Wasn't a car lot. It was a pull-a-part lot. You went in, picked the part you needed, paid Dusty, and left. Cash only. It was a car cemetery. A boneyard."

Frances blinked. The mental map in her mind landed on the location. *No… That can't be right… But it is.* "It was right behind the old Womack Bakery." Humphrey nodded, and Frances whispered to herself, "Oh, God."

Humphrey nodded. "Ain't heard a peep out of Dusty in a while."

"Me neither. I don't think he's still out there. That entire lot is all grown over. I took over the old Womack Bakery a few months ago.

It's like Romper Room for old folks," Frances groaned. "Dingle's lot is just weeds as big as Clint. You can't see anything through the brush. I completely forgot there was a house back there." She shook her head. "I plumb forgot he was back there. I don't know how I blocked that out of my head."

"You should at least go knock on his door. See if he's still alive. Tell him you're Buddy's girl. I'm sure he'll give you anything you want if he's got it."

Clint opened the door of Humphrey's tow truck for Frances. "Why don't you get out of this cold while we load up the truck and tow it?"

"Where you want it in the meantime?" Humphrey asked.

Frances shook her head in disbelief. She had to find a new engine. She couldn't let the truck die, too. "The farm. The farm's fine."


Humphrey delivered Clint and Frances back to Clint's Mustang at the shop before driving her father's truck back to the Hunt family farm. Frances wanted to go straight to Dusty's lot, hoping to find an engine as quickly as possible. And maybe if he didn't have the part, he knew someone who did.

Clint told Frances he would drive her to Dusty's. "Clint, honey, it's your birthday. You don't need to play chauffeur to me. It ain't that far, and Kevin'll be home soon, and he can pick me up."

"Get in the damn car. You ain't walking anywhere. You forget I'm invested at this point," he insisted. Frances relented, climbing into his car. "What's Kevin up to these days?" He smirked mischievously. "You know, when he's not visiting his dead girlfriend in the cemetery?"

*Stealin' dead body parts from funeral homes in the middle of the night and helping a Mexican and two old women sell 'em on the black market,* she wanted to say. "He's workin' for Sissy Stone down at Lockhart Brothers."

"Is he gonna make himself an undertaker?" Clint asked, surprised.

"I'm not really sure what he's gonna do. Right now, he's just working as a driver, pickin' up dead bodies after school and on the weekends."

"Dang, man. He really took a turn," he said softly.

"Delores Rogers is workin' there too now. One of Momma's friends.

She left the lunch counter down at the drugstore. She's the receptionist. They went all-in after Momma's death. And Ruth's death. And Brandy's death."

"Lot of people die around here."

Frances curled a finger for each death she could remember. Ruth, Oscar, Brandy, Carl, Birdie… She switched to the other hand. *Dean Gilbertson doesn't really count,* she thought. *Is that all?* "Sissy took over that funeral home after her brother went missin'," Frances said.

"Stuart Lockhart? But that was like years ago."

"You didn't hear? She lost the other one, too! Stephen. He went out on a cruise and never came back."

"How do you lose someone on a cruise?"

"Apparently, he fell out of his kayak. They think he drowned." *Stephen,* she realized, curling another finger. "So anyways, they all work there now."

A few minutes later, Kevin slowly pulled down the side road and past the old bakery and recently christened Birdie Hunt Memorial Recreational Center and Senior Fun Day Center. A very amateurish mural of brightly colored cartoonish old people filled the side of the wall."

"Dusty's is just back there." She pointed.

"That where you babysit old people?" Clint asked, motioning with his long neck. "Cute artwork. Did you hire Pennywise to do your painting?"

Frances pinched his arm and twisted. "That's where I babysit old people. It's basically an adult day center. Arts and crafts. Drew Ater comes in and does little workout routines with them. It's not a lot of money, but it keeps the lights on. Somethin' Momma wanted to do. You'd be surprised how happy and quickly their children are to unload their parents for a few hours a day. Bruce Underwood drives around, picks them up, and takes them home. He makes ten dollars a head."

"How many you got?"

"About thirty on any given day. Beats workin' down at the chicken plant."

"Maybe I ought to come work for you," he said with a grin.

As they rounded the corner of the building, Clint slowed down, taking in the overgrown weeds and brush of the Dingle property. "Dang, man. You think he still lives here?" Clint asked.

Memories began to rush back for Frances. How had she forgotten Dusty lived here? How had she forgotten Dusty Dingle had been friends with her father, and how had she forgotten running from rats the size of cheetahs in this lot as a child? How had she forgotten about Dusty's daughter, Ella? They used to play together until Ella moved away when her parents divorced.

The house was dilapidated, and most all the abandoned cars in the lot appeared to be rusted, with weeds and kudzu devouring them. There were a few cars covered in dust with painted numbers on their windshields, indicating Dusty might have been selling used cars as well.

"I don't think he's here anymore," she said, balling a hand into a fist. "I'll go make sure. Well, thanks for the ride," she said, climbing out of the car.

"I'm not lettin' you go in there alone. Psycho killers, remember?" Clint's eyes landed on the car cemetery. "Dang, man. That's a lot of old cars. He could sell them all for the metal, right? Bet he'd make a pretty penny."

Frances nodded. "I think he used to repair cars out here too. Like for collisions." Frances shook her head. "Basically, he'd just beat out the dents with a hammer."

Frances climbed the termite-infested steps and knocked on the door. "Be careful where you step. You're so big, you'll probably fall right through," she warned Clint.

There was no response from inside the house. Frances knocked again, harder, and the door opened slightly ajar. "Hello?" she hollered into the void. "Dusty? You in here?"

Clint grabbed her wrist. "You ain't goin' in there, are you?"

"Dusty Dingle is like eighty-somethin'. What's he gonna do? Gum me to death?"

She pushed the door and was met with some resistance. She pushed harder, walking inside, eyeballing a mountain of junk mail from the delivery slot. She looked around. Other than a thick layer of dust covering every surface, everything looked normal.

Clint stayed at the door. Frances turned back to him. "You comin' in? Psycho killers?"

"I'll cover you from here," he said.

A scent caught her nose. It wasn't a scent she was familiar with, but also something not unfamiliar. "Dusty? You good? You cookin' somethin' in here? Somethin' smells," she rounded the corner, stopping in her tracks. "Dead," she sadly lamented. Dusty Dingle sat in a rocking chair. "Son of a bitch."

Dusty Dingle was dead. Very dead. His face looked like a weathered football. Where his stomach once was, now a gaping hole. Skeletal, leathery hands clutched a remote.

"You good in there?" Clint called from the porch.

"Yeah, I'm good," she hollered back. "Hey, you want to see a dead body?"


Frances and Clint sat on the steps of Dusty Dingle's house. Clint chewed his cuticles while tapping his foot nervously on a step.

Frances gently placed her hand on his knee. "It's gonna be okay. He probably died in his sleep. Like three or four years ago."

"He was like... He was like a mummy! Like a real-life zombie in a horror movie! Like *The Walking Dead!*"

Frances smiled, remembering how Birdie used to call the show "*A Walking Dead*" and would always remind her Jerry Bright's nephew was an extra on the show. "Well, that's just make-believe. People die every day. That's just life. Death is natural." Frances held out her fingers and curled a seventh finger for Dusty. "You ain't never seen a dead body before?"

Clint shook his head. "I couldn't even go to Coach's funeral. I saw a dead body when I was a kid and had nightmares for years. Still do. Like why do we dress people up in their nicest clothes and pretend like they're sleeping? And then we take their nicely dressed bodies, seal 'em up in a really expensive box, and bury them six feet in the ground. Like, they ain't sleepin'! They can't breathe down there, sleepin' in their nice clothes in the really expensive box with their heads restin' on a pillow! That's just messed up. It's scary."

"A way to say goodbye. Pay your respects. Closure. Somethin' about just seein' a loved one's face for the last time. Knowin' that they are completely at peace," she offered. "But Dusty's soul is no longer in that body in there."

"You're sayin' Dusty Dingle's soul is trapped in that house now!?"

"We're all gonna die someday, Clint. And you don't hear about dead bodies coming back to life and bitin' morticians, do you? You never hear about instances where a dead body just sat up and started talkin', do you? No, you don't. There's no reason to be scared."

"How can you be so calm about all this?"

"You get used to it. You get real used to it," she repeated under her breath. "Wait, you volunteer at a hospital!"

"I ain't seen a dead body yet. I just help the nurses," he said. "I've been thinking maybe going to med school is a bad idea."

"Maybe you should just go off and just be an underwear model. A lot of money in that."

"I've been thinking about becoming a CIA agent."

Frances's head turned, hearing tires on rocks. She braced herself as she saw a sheriff's car slowly pull down the gravel driveway. It had been over three months since she had laid eyes on Sheriff Ray Jackson. Almost three months since she drunkenly punched him in a rainstorm behind the family farmhouse. Almost three months since she warned him to "Get the hell off my property. I never want to see you again. I know what you did."

The car pulled to a stop and parked. The door slowly opened, and out stepped Sheriff Wally Pembrook.

"Pembrook?" Frances asked, befuddled.

"Hey, Franny." He nodded, gently closing the door to the car, removing his own sheriff Stetson, as he meandered toward the house.

"Sheriff's car," she acknowledged, pointing to it. "Sheriff's hat."

"Yeah. Perks of the job."

"The job? Where's Ray?"

He shook his head. "Nobody knows, Franny. He gone."

"Gone? What do you mean, gone?"

"He packed up all his things and left. Left a letter of resignation. Ain't nobody seen or heard from him since. You didn't know?"

Frances shook her head and looked down at her shaking hands. She wanted a drink. She needed a drink.

"You okay?" he asked.

"Yeah. Just not every day you find a mummified dead guy," she said, standing up and wiping away the dirt on her jeans, giving Pembrook a half-hug. She waved her hand at Clint. "This is Clint Peppers."

Pembrook shook Clint's hand. "Everybody in Liberty knows Clint Peppers! How you doin', son? Y'all ready to go to state in a few weeks?"

"Yes, sir, I think we are."

"How's your daddy and them?"

"They're all good, sir."

Clint Peppers' perfection was beginning to annoy Frances. Pembrook's news about Jackson was upsetting her in ways that confused her. Once again, she found herself dealing with dead people. "Dead man. Inside. We good? You wanna take it from here? I'm gettin' a little PTSD out here right now, you know, with all of this," she said, waving at the yard and police car.

"Oh, sure, sure. Don't worry. Ben Camden and his boys should be here any minute now. I'll hang out. Y'all can take off."

"You don't need a statement?" she asked.

"Oh, sure. So… Why were you here? What did you see?" Pembrook asked, pulling a small recorder from his shirt pocket and tapping record.

"Daddy's truck broke down, and Clint's uncle thought Dusty might have an engine out there in the lot. Came here. Knocked on the door. It opened. I walked in. Boom. Dead man. We called you."

"She didn't scream or anything. Didn't even flinch. Just walked out and was like, 'He's dead,' and that's when I called you. She handled it like a boss," Kevin proclaimed. "It was so frickin' hot."

"Calm down, Sparky," Frances said.

"No, seriously. It was like you've been doin' this—" Frances put her fingers over Clint's beautiful lips.

"Stop talkin'." She waved to the overgrown car cemetery. "Don't guess no one's checked in on Dusty in a hot minute."

Pembrook walked inside, and Frances followed behind at a distance. "Door was unlocked," she offered.

"Nobody locks their doors in Liberty," Pembrook mused.

"True that."

He rounded the corner and found Dusty's badly decomposed body. "Lordy Jesus!" he hollered. "You know I'll never get used to dead people," he said. "Sad, ain't it? Probably had the house paid off. Utilities probably just got cut after he stopped payin'." Pembrook looked around the house and saw photos of a young girl. "He had a daughter, right?"

"Ella. She was a little older than me. Ain't seen her in thirty-something… Maybe forty-something years. The last time I saw Dusty was at Daddy's funeral, and that was over five years ago."

Pembrook folded his arms and leaned forward. "You doin' okay? How you and Kevin doin' after…"

*After your momma's death.* She knew what he meant. "I'm fine," she said.

"You don't have to be fine, Franny."

"Cooper down at the bank has been helpin' me probate the will and get all that stuff handled. He's been workin' on the side for me, helpin' me set up the business back there," she saved, waving to the bakery. "I just sign papers every few days and nod and smile. It's just a mess. Everything takes so long." Frances looked back to Clint in the doorway. "I guess we should leave you to it."

"Dusty probably fell asleep and never woke up. It's all good. We'll have Denny look everything over."

She nodded, turning to leave. "If you talk to Jackson, tell him I said hi."

Pembrook nodded. "Will do, but I don't think we's ever gonna see him again. He's gone completely off the reservation."

Clint stiffened. "Sir, just so you know, that's a racial slur toward Native Americans."

Frances pushed Clint out the door and back to the Mustang. He opened the door for her, and she climbed inside.

"This is not how I expected to spend my eighteenth birthday," he said before closing the door. He ran around and climbed into the driver's seat. "Where to next?"

Delores Rogers wheeled the decapitated head of an old woman over to Sissy Stone. "Don't this look like Josie Plunkett to you?" she asked.

Sissy raised the bodyless woman's eyelid with the tip of her gloved finger to reveal a cloudy brown eye. "Naw. Josie has blue eyes."

"That's right! She had the prettiest eyes."

"*Has.* Josie's still alive. Got a Christmas card from her. She's living with her daughter down in Vidalia." Sissy pointed to a scalpel on a rolling cart just out of reach. "Can you hand me that nine-blade?"

While initially reluctant to have anything to do with touching dead bodies, three months later was a very different story for Sissy Stone and Delores Rogers. Their new attitude came courtesy of a book gifted to each of them by Hector entitled *Fear Is For Losers.*

*Fear Is For Losers* encourages the reader to confront their fears. Shortly after Christmas, Hector insisted Delores and Sissy have an overnight, lock-in sleepover in the funeral home prep room, surrounded by uncovered dead bodies. The next morning, all their fear had vanished. Sissy gleefully begged to watch Hector remove the arms and legs from one of their descendants. A week later, Hector began teaching Sissy the art of butchery. Sissy took special glee in cutting up Liberty residents she didn't particularly care for or like in life.

"Why, this is just like carvin' up a turkey on Thanksgiving!" she joyfully exclaimed while working on Old Lady Nabors, who died in her sleep.

Delores and Sissy believed their new business was the Christian thing to do beyond the shadow of a doubt. They may be robbing Peter to sell to Paul, but Paul would take the resources and what he learned from Peter to save another life. They saw burials as a waste of valuable resources.

Did Delores and Sissy understand selling dead body parts and cadavers on the black market was terribly illegal? Absolutely. Did they care? Absolutely not. They believed they were doing the Lord's work.

Delores and Sissy were convinced they were doing more good than bad by supplying medical teams and universities with cadavers. There was a high demand. They believed society was better off with their mission in life. And now that The Man was out of commission and missing in action, business was picking up. With the spring quarter upon them, local colleges and universities would bring in substantial contracts.

Kevin sat in the corner, reading a book. Delores snapped, "Kevin, we need some help over here!" Kevin closed his Bible, bowed his head, and said a prayer, too quiet for anyone to hear.

Delores rolled her eyes. Hector quietly commanded, "Leave him alone."

In the days and weeks following Brandy and Birdie's death, Kevin had spent many hours in the Liberty Baptist Church cemetery and church parking lot. The Reverend Bill White (Juanita White's insufferable husband and pastor of the church) sat with Kevin one afternoon under an umbrella as the rain poured down upon Brandy's grave.

The Reverend Bill White asked Kevin if he was a Christian and if he had asked the Lord Jesus Christ to come into his heart. After a five-minute question-and-answer tutorial, Kevin was deemed "saved." Kevin decided from that moment forward that he was going to be a Southern Baptist minister, but he was too afraid to tell anyone for fear of them ridiculing his decision.

The Reverend Bill White worked with Kevin for an hour after school every day on scholarships and college applications. With no father in his life, the recent suicide of his grandmother, the death of his girlfriend and "child," a poverty-level homelife, and recently dedicating his life to Christ, Kevin was a shoo-in for religious scholarship money.

Also, The Reverend Bill White would need a new maintenance man at the church once Jethro Farnsworth retired in the summer, so he saw Kevin as an indentured servant he could tap into at a later date.

Delores sneered at Kevin. "Look, I love Jesus too, but I don't want you hangin' out with that Bill White anymore. He's just usin' you."

"Usin' me how?" Kevin fired back.

"To get to us. You know his wife and her friends, Edie and Queenie, are our mortal enemies, right?"

"You all go to Liberty Baptist!"

"That's because I'm old and I have to! I can't change my church membership at this point. Too much paperwork."

"Why don't you go to Wheat Street Baptist?" he asked.

"Kevin Hunt! I ain't goin' to no Black church! Black church is all day! At least you white people get Jesus done before all the tables are taken down at the Golden Corral." She huffed her chest and moaned, "Tryin' to send me to Black church just because I'm Black. That's racist, Kevin!"

Hector wheeled the heavy mechanism that lifts bodies from the worktable into a casket over to Kevin. "Don't listen to them, little man. You do you."

"I just think it's weird," Sissy added.

"I have a calling," Kevin insisted.

"God ain't callin' you to the ministry. God is callin' you to help us with *this* business. What we are doin' *is* God's work. We are savin' lives."

"By desecratin' dead people? Lyin' to people who think their loved ones are goin' in the ground to enjoy an eternal rest till Jesus calls them home?"

"Their soul is already in heaven!" Delores decried while pointing to the ceiling. "Ain't that your company line?"

"Ashes to ashes, Kevin," Sissy said, waving the nine-blade in his face. "Dust to dust."


Duane Brown had never met "The Man" in the flesh, so when Donald Dobkins arrived at the Brown and Brown Crematory, inquiring about a potential cremation for a loved one, he was blissfully unaware he was offering coffee to 141 Corona's former head boss and the ringleader of the entire southeastern operation.

Duane Brown also didn't notice when Donald Dobkins slipped Rohypnol into his Trenta Caramel Ribbon Crunch Starbucks Frappuccino.

When Duane Brown woke hours later, he was lying on his back, naked, with his hands and legs tied to steel rods. He turned his head to the left and right, realizing he was lying on the conveyor bed of his own cremation machine.

"Help! Help me!" he screamed out in terror. "Where are my clothes!?"

Donald dragged a step stool up across the crudely laid cement floor. The stool squealed with an ear-piercing screech, like nails on a chalkboard. Donald climbed the stool, staring into Duane's terrified face.

"I never liked you," Donald lamented. Donald turned to Duane's employee, handing Big Jerome a hundred dollars. "Thanks for your help. I can take it from here."

"Are you sure I can't watch him die?" Big Jerome pleaded.

"I like to work in silence," Donald stated.

"You're… You're…" Duane sputtered, realizing in horror.

Donald leaned into Duane's ear and softly whispered, "I'm The Man."

Big Jerome spat in Duane's face. "See you in hell, you pathetic loser. Tell your momma I said hello." He walked out.

Duane squirmed on the cold slab. "What is wrong with you!? Why did you tie me up?! What do you want?!"

"So many questions," Donald said, picking up a small, cordless electrical saw from the tray next to the table. He squeezed the trigger twice for dramatic effect, then brought it down on Duane's fingers, slicing them off one at a time.

Duane screamed in pain as his entire body convulsed from shock. Two of the digits bounced onto the ground, rolling under the stool.

"There was a woman," Donald started, but Duane cut him off.

"She calls herself Big Momma! She works with a Mexican! I only met her once! She's a mean bitch! The Mexican's even meaner! Just let me go! I'll give you whatever you want! I have money!"

"What's her real name?" Donald groaned.

"I don't know her real name! Check my phone! It's under Big Momma! You can see for yourself, The Man! No one around here uses their real names! Y'all are like a bunch of comic book characters!" Duane struggled to look over his protruding stomach to see his hand tied near his waist. "I can't feel my fingers! Did you cut my fingers completely off!?"

Donald squeezed the trigger again. "Did you know in order to biopsy a testicle for cancer, they make an incision right here," he said, placing the blade of the saw just above Duane's public hair. "They call this area the bikini line. You like to wear bikinis, Duane?"

"No! No, I don't! Please—"

"They cut right here, then reach down inside of you and pull the testicle completely out of the scrotum. They check it out. Biopsy it. If it's just a benign tumor, you can keep your balls and save the testicle." Donald whispered, "But tumors can go rogue. And sometimes it's better just to cut it out before it can become a cancer."

"I'm telling you the truth!" Duane insisted. "I swear! I don't know her name! If I knew it, I'd tell you! My loyalty is to you!"

"See, I think you're a liar, Mr. Brown, you ballless piece of shit. I'm almost sure of it. I think you're a pathological liar. Why are you protecting this woman? Where does she live?"

"I don't know! I swear! I didn't want to know too much!"

"Do I look particularly stupid to you, you fat fuck?" Donald revved the saw twice more near Duane's crotch.

"I swear!" Duane squealed. "My phone! Check the videos on my phone! The security cameras! You can see Hector's van! Maybe you can track that!"

Duane closed his eyes, trying to suppress his rage. *So, it was true.* Donald was almost certain Hector had deflected and was working with "that woman," but now he had proof. "That bitch calls herself Big Momma, yet you know Hector's real name?"

"I've known Hector for years! You know that! You sent him to me!"

"That's right. I sent him to you. And you cut ties with me and began doing business with her."

"I'm sorry! It was a better deal! I'll go back! I'll give you any deal you want! Name your price!"

"Catch up, Shamu. There is no business anymore, thanks to those two. I'm on the run from the law because of those two."

"Please! Just let me go! I can help you! We can partner up! We can take her down!”

“You can't help me.”

“Then what do you want?!”

“Revenge.” Donald quickly plunged the sawblade into Duane's groin, scooping Duane's testicles out with his small hands and slicing them off with a saw.

Duane screamed in the most agonizing pain he had ever felt. Donald pulled Duane's jaw open and shoved the testicles into Duane's mouth, wiping the blood on Donald's chest.

Donald hopped off the stool and sauntered to the controls for the cremation chamber. He pushed the simple, red "start" button and watched as the door to the crematory swung open and the conveyor belt slowly rolled Duane into the body of the retort. He watched as the door quickly and loudly clanged shut.

Outside the machine, Donald rifled through Duane's pockets and found his phone. "Son of a…" He sighed, realizing he needed Duane's facial recognition to open the phone or go through just shy of one million combinations. "What's the pass code!?" Donald shouted at the large metal door.

Sadly, all Donald could hear was the sound of Duane choking on his own testicles, gagging through his screams, as the flames roared to life, heating the vessel to eighteen hundred degrees, engulfing his body.

And that was the end of Duane Brown.

---

# CHAPTER TWO

# COME AND GET ME

Ella Anolik managed to look twenty years younger and twenty years older at the same time, thanks to filler, Botox, and the very expensive facelift she bought herself for her fortieth birthday nearly a decade earlier.

Ella Anolik was born almost fifty years ago at Liberty Hospital. Two years later, Frances would be born in the same delivery room by the same doctors and nurses.

Clary Dingle was only nineteen years old when she gave birth to Ella. Dusty had just turned thirty. They married six months into her pregnancy. Clary wanted a divorce well before her water broke.

Clary worked at The Corner Lunch Counter and Drug Store with Delores in the early seventies. There, she met Tim Turner, who owned a franchise of truck stops throughout the Southeast. Tim would always stop by the Counter for lunch on days he swung through Liberty while traveling to visit his truck stops.

One day, Tim asked Clary if she wanted to see his brand-new Alfa Romeo. Clary turned to Delores and announced, "I'll be right back." But she did not return. Hours later, Delores grew concerned and called Dusty to see if she had walked home. Officially a missing person, Delores called the police. A week later, Clary resurfaced, calling Dusty and demanding a divorce. She married Tim in a Las Vegas wedding chapel a year later.

When Ella turned eight years old, she went to live with her Aunt Josephine in Augusta. Josephine married a stockbroker, and they led a very well-to-do life. Josephine always wanted a child but was unable to carry a baby to term. While Josephine and her husband never officially adopted Ella, they treated her like their own. They also knocked Ella's country accent clear out of her mouth. Josephine spoke with a pretentious transatlantic accent (perfected from years of watching classic movies) and insisted Ella not sound like a hillbilly in her house and around her friends.

Ella was showered with toys, dolls, ponies, and piano lessons. An excellent student, she was accepted into Harvard Law School in the late eighties, graduating at the top of her class. She moved to New York City, where she met a doctor, had two perfect children, and made law partner before she was thirty. Ella and her husband owned a townhome in the West Village (just a few doors down from Sarah Jessica Parker) and a weekend beach property in Sag Harbor.

With her children in college, Ella planned to retire within the next five years.

"Just dump him in a cardboard box and throw him in an empty hole," Ella said, sitting across from Delores and Sissy. "He looks like a deflated football." She scoffed. "He actually looks better now than when I last saw him. How is that even possible?"

"Surely your father deserves a proper burial," Delores claimed. Dusty Dingle's corpse was not usable for resale, but no reason for him to not have a full dog and pony show burial in their most expensive casket, The Cadillac. Delores noticed Ella's shoes when she walked in and quietly whispered to Sissy, "This chick got city money, honey."

Ella cut off Delores, waving her index finger. "Box, hole," she said. "I tried calling one of the crematoriums, but they never called back. The guy at the bank recommended you guys."

"Anolik. Is that Middle Eastern?" Sissy asked.

"It's Israeli."

"Are you Israeli?" Delores quietly asked.

"My husband is," she said. "I married a man who is Israeli."

"Is that Jewish?" Sissy asked.

Ella pursed her lips. "Are we done?"

Delores glanced over the form attached to the clipboard. "I knew your daddy growing up. He was a real nice man. And I used to work with your momma before…" Delores's voice trailed off as she looked to Sissy to save her. "Before you came into the world!"

"Neither one of them wanted me. I was lucky my aunt got me out of this hellhole." Ella spread out the creases in her vintage Chanel skirt.

"By any chance do either one of you know Frances Hunt?"

Sissy and Delores shared a quick glance. "Why do you ask?" Sissy asked in a slightly high-pitched voice.

"The police said she found his body. I used to play with a Frances Hunt when I was a kid, and I can't imagine there are two Frances Hunts in Liberty. Has to be her, right? I was just curious why she was out there at his place."

"Frances Hunt found him?" Delores asked. "Is that right?"

"Frances Hunt found him?" Sissy repeated.

"Just curious why she was out there. That's all."

"You know, that is a real good question," Delores mused. "Why was she out there? Makes you wonder. She was probably tryin' to rob him."

Sissy and Delores had not spoken to Frances since December. They were furious she had left them with their new business after the first delivery to Athens State. Frances kicked them out of the bakery building, taking over the lease for her senior citizen initiative. Sissy and Delores wanted to expand to the growing market demand, and they needed Frances as their face and their leader. Instead, their operation with Hector and Kevin was small potatoes to the potential it could have become in the Southeast. There was a very high demand, and some clients were squirrelly when dealing with Sissy or Delores over the phone. Sissy and Dolores were afraid of someone swooping in and stealing what little business they had managed to grow.

"Just curious," Ella stated.

"She still lives out on the family farm. Her momma died last year." Sissy leaned in, whispering, "Shot herself."

"You should go visit her," Delores offered. "She's probably working today. She runs a program for old people out near your daddy's place. The old Womack Bakery."

Ella nodded. "Sheriff Pembrook mentioned she was renting it." Ella beamed. "I used to love that place. Mrs. Womack used to give me free cupcakes right out of the oven because I was poor." Ella's face dropped. "Because I didn't have a mother, and my father owned a junkyard," she said, remembering with a deep sadness. "And she would always make me go to Vacation Bible School in the summers. We would drink Kool-Aid out of little paper cups and wear daisy butter cookies like they were fancy rings." Ella looked down at the massive rock on her ring finger, the gift from her husband on her wedding day. "At least I was fed."

"You still go to church?" Delores questioned.

"No. I don't have time for make-believe. I do charity galas instead. You can drink."

"Don't let Frances's son hear you say that. He'll strap you down and make you ask for Jesus to come inside you," Sissy insisted.

Ella snapped her Birken closed. "He's at the morgue. Box, hole. Don't care where you dump him." Ella checked her watch. "I'm off to meet with the bank again and catch a flight back tonight. Just send me a bill. Thank you. And obviously, no rush."

She walked out.

Sissy turned to Delores. "She didn't even look over the prices. Charge her for the Cadillac and all the bells and whistles. That's a woman that goes to eat in places where they don't print the price on the menu."

"Why do you think Frances was out there at Dusty's?"

"I don't know, and I don't care. Frances Hunt is dead to me."

Frances leaned against the wall in the back room of the Birdie Hunt Memorial Recreational Center and Senior Fun Day Center, watching Nakoya work with a dozen senior citizens molding clay. Three months earlier, ten dead bodies were prepped in this exact same room for Athens State, and today, it served as a community center for old people.

Unbeknownst to Frances, Nakoya had been Donald Dobkins's right-hand woman at 141 Corona for over five years. Unbeknownst to Frances (*and* Donald), Nakoya had been secretly working with Sissy's brothers, Stephen and Stuart Lockhart, to launch a new international body brokerage company, which would rival 141 Corona. Unbeknownst to Frances (and *everyone else living in Liberty*), Stephen and Stuart Lockhart were both very much alive, not at all dead, and living in Europe, having faked their deaths.

Unbeknownst to Nakoya, Frances was the very woman who had inadvertently shut down the entire operation in Atlanta. When Frances suggested the handwritten "141 Corona" on the side of Oscar Lopez's van might be an address, Sheriff Ray Jackson set his Waze app to the location and discovered the remains of Oscar Lopez inside the warehouse. After the fall of 141 Corona, Nakoya moved to Liberty to live with her sister (and Frances's new best friend), Akasha. Nakoya told Akasha her job at "the bank" had dissolved. While she waited for the next move from the brothers Lockhart, she worked for Frances at the center.

Nakoya liked working with old people. She liked watching their eyes light up when they made a mug or an ashtray from clay or a small bracelet with beads.

Frances trusted Nakoya. Nakoya tolerated Frances.

The bell above the door in the lobby jingled. "Be right back," Frances announced aloud as she walked into what had been the bakery storefront, now a converted sitting area with a small area for coffee and a tray of cookies.

"Frances? Frances Hunt, is that you?" Ella asked, removing her Prada sunglasses.

Frances nodded, not placing the very tall, clearly city girl standing in front of her. "I am. Who're you?"

"It's me! Ella Anolik!" Ella threw out her arms, expecting Frances to rush into a tight embrace. "Anolik, formerly Dingle! We used to play together! Right?" When Frances didn't move, Ella dropped, "You found my dead father, right?"

Not big on hugs, Frances tentatively approached and gave her a hug from a distance with two pats on her back. "Ella, I'm so sorry I didn't recognize you. You look so—"

"I've had a lot of work done. Thank God you didn't recognize me! This cost a lot of money," she said, waving her hand about her face and body. "The sheriff told me you found him out there," Ella motioned behind Frances, indicting her father's land behind the bakery.

"I'm so sorry. I wasn't breaking and entering," Frances said. "I was lookin' for an engine for my truck."

"Better you than me! I haven't spoken to that man in decades." Ella eyed Frances up and down. "Frances, I think it's been since I was a senior in high school since I last saw him. He called my aunt's, and we had a quick chat, and that was it. Never heard from him again."

"I'm sorry."

"I'm not. I have a great life. So great! I've traveled all over the world. I'm a lawyer. I've made millions of dollars. I have two amazing children. My husband fulfills me sexually. I sit on the boards of a dozen non-profits. I'm going to be retiring in a few years." Her eyes shifted. "But the deceased left everything to me, so now I'm stuck with that dump back there and trying to get rid of it as quickly as possible."

"I'm sorry."

"Stop saying you're sorry! You didn't kill him!" She laughed.

"No. That's true. I did not kill him." Frances motioned to the two folding chairs by the coffee pot. "You want some coffee?"

Ella took a seat and crossed her legs. "I can't stay. I just met with the bank. Oh, you know him! He speaks so highly of you. Cooper Delaney?"

Frances nodded. Cooper Delaney had become one of Frances's closest friends since the death of Birdie. Not only had he set up their initial body harvesting business accounts and subsequently shifted all the paperwork for Hector, Sissy, and Delores, but he also helped her set up the paperwork for the community center. He didn't ask questions when the others were continuing a bakery with cash coming in, and yet, no product to be seen. Cooper had convinced himself they were drug dealers, selling off medications from dead people. Otherwise, why were they all working at a funeral home?

"Cooper's the best. I couldn't do anything without Cooper. He set me up with this place."

"I have a business proposal for you."

Frances sat up a bit taller. "Okay, but I got my hands full with this place at the minute."

"Got a dollar on you?"

Frances shoved her hands into her pocket and pulled out a coin purse, squeezing it open. "Four quarters work?" she quizzically asked.

"Who uses quarters anymore?"

"Old people."

Ella held out her hand, and Frances dumped them into her palm. "Great. You just bought yourself all that property and everything on it."

Frances's jaw dropped. "Huh? No."

Ella stood up. "That was a business transaction."

"No, I can't—"

"I'll be in touch with Cooper. He'll do the contracts. I just don't want anything to do with this place anymore. You understand, right?"

"But Ella… What about the house?"

"Call Goodwill and tell them to take whatever they want. Rent it out. Burn it to the ground. I don't care. And you should do pretty well with the scrap metal back there, right?"

"I mean, I guess, but Ella, that was your daddy."

"No, he wasn't. He was a sperm donor. And now he's dead."

Frances shook her head, taking in the news. "Ella, I can't."

"I give to charity all the time! Think of it as charity!" Ella insisted, oblivious to her condescension. Ella gave Frances a hug. "Just call Cooper if you need anything. He has the number to my attorney in New York." Ella shook the four quarters in her hand, then dropped them into her bag. "A deal is a deal. I really must go. I fly back to New York tonight, and you know how bad the Atlanta airport is."

She gave Frances a quick hug, curiously touching Frances's hair.

"What?" Frances asked.

"I just realized I could have ended up like you." Ella walked out the front door. Frances went to the window and watched as a chauffeur opened the door for Ella.

"What the frick?" she whispered.


Hector pulled his van to the rear of the Brown and Brown Crematory just after ten o'clock. Kevin was exhausted from a long week in school, helping at the church, and working in the funeral home.

"I don't want to be doin' this anymore, Hector," Kevin flatly stated as Hector turned off the ignition.

"Just think of it as money for college," Hector suggested.

"It's wrong. You know that. And the Bible says—"

"Kevin, I can't do Jesus right now. No offense," he said, climbing out of the van.

Kevin followed him to the back of the van as Hector retrieved a gurney. "I want to be a preacher one day. What am I supposed to tell my congregation about this?"

"Everyone loves a good redemption story. Or maybe, I don't know… *don't* tell them, Kev." Hector shoved the gurney toward the side entrance and unlocked the door. "Jesus raised people from the dead. Jesus literally came back from the dead. Mary went into his tomb, and he wasn't there—"

"Mary wasn't sneakin' into our Lord and Savior's tomb to chop off his arms and legs to sell to Judas!"

Hector heaved open the heavy metal door, flipped on the lights, and pulled the gurney to their usual refrigeration unit, designated by Duane Brown for Hector's pickups.

Hector had not heard from Duane in almost four days. Sissy and Delores had an order for various body parts in Florida, and they still needed three full cadavers to fulfill the request. Hector checked the three refrigeration units. All were empty.

"Son of a bitch," Hector muttered under his breath. His eyes traced the room. Everything looked normal, but something felt off.

Kevin narrowed his eyes on Hector. "What's up? You got a look."

Hector searched the room for cameras. "Something's not right. I can't say what, but something's off."

"Off, how?"

"Duane hasn't texted me in days." Hector began opening and closing the other refrigeration units, which were normally off-limits to Hector. They were empty as well.

"So, we drove all the way out here for nothing? He's probably just on vacation. This was a waste of time. And I've got to study."

Hector walked into the office hallway, turning on the fluorescent overhead lights. He arrived at Duane's office. Everything looked normal. A whiff of something caught his nose. Something burned.

Hector's head spun to the smell. An old coffee pot with badly burned coffee was still on. He unplugged it from the wall. He looked back to the desk. One cup of coffee sat in front of the visitor chair across from Duane's desk.

Hector walked around Duane's desk and saw the remains of Duane's Trenta Frappuccino overturned on the ground. "Oh, no," Hector whispered, backing out of the room.

Kevin stood in the hallway, raising his arms as if to ask, "Well?"

"Let's get out of here."

Hector wheeled the gurney out of the cremation room and back outside. Kevin followed. "What is it? What did you see?"

Hector shoved the gurney back into the van and slammed the doors. He grabbed his phone from the cupholder, considering for a long moment, before stating, "Siri, call Duane Brown."

Kevin grunted, throwing his arms up. "What!?"

"Something's not right here. I can't tell you what, but…"


Donald Dobkins stood over the body of Imelda Weathers, watching the blood drain from the dozens of small holes in her body. Every time she screamed in pain, he stabbed her again.

*My loneliness… is killing me…*Donald's head spun. "What the…" Somewhere in the embalming room, Britney Spears began to sing. His eyes landed on his own suit jacket, resting over the arm of a chair. The screen of a phone lit up through the lining of his breast pocket.

Donald dropped the knife and raced to the phone. He wiped Imelda's blood on his pants as he picked up Duane Brown's phone. He charged the phone nightly in the event someone called. With an incoming call, he could finally open the phone with one small swipe of his finger.

**"Hector Calling."**

"That little motherfu—" Donald slid his thumb across the screen and answered. His voice dropped an octave. "Hello, stranger."

Hector gasped, too scared to speak. He knew that voice.

Donald could barely contain his excitement. "I can hear your breathing, you overgrown, uncut enchilada. I thought you were dead. I was genuinely concerned for you. I thought that country bumpkin bitch had killed you too. What's new?" Donald waited for a response. "Tell your Big Momma I'm coming for her. And when I find her, I'm going to cut out her heart. And when I find you, I'm going to—"

Hector ended the call. His head dropped, clutching the phone.

"What?" Kevin asked.

Hector threw the phone against the crematory wall. Hector motioned with his head for Kevin to get in. "Call your mother."

"Hello?" Donald asked, shaking the silent phone. "Guess we're done." With the phone unlocked, Duane went through the phone to turn off the security settings, keeping the phone unlocked.

He scrolled through the contacts on the phone. He found her number. "**Big Momma.**"

"Hello, poppet," he whispered with glee.


Frances saw "**Duane Brown Calling**" on her phone. "F that," she said, quickly declining the call.

Frances sat at the kitchen table, eating a turkey sandwich with potato chips. The grandfather clock in the living room clicked and clacked in time. The house was oddly peaceful. Oddly quiet. In another month or two, the nightly symphony of crickets and cicadas would fill the yard.

"**Kevin Calling.**" She quickly answered the phone. "Hey! Why are you calling me? You never call. Are you okay?"

"It's Hector—" Hector shouted at the phone holder, throwing the van into reverse.

"Is Kevin okay!?"

"I'm right here, Mom," Kevin said.

"The Man has Duane Brown's phone."

Frances's phone beeped with an incoming call, and the Caller ID read: "**Duane Brown Calling.**"

"Why is that evil Hobbit calling me from Duane Brown's phone?" she asked.

"Unclear, but he mentioned something about hunting you down and cutting your heart out of your chest," Hector said.

"Beg pardon?"

"Mom, you need to get out of the house right now!"

"Can one of y'all go back to the beginning and catch me up?" she ranted as she began pacing around the kitchen.

"We came to Brown and Brown to do a pickup. Duane wasn't here, and something felt off. When I called Duane's phone, The Man answered."

"So, they're working together now?" she asked.

"I saw a knocked-over coffee cup in the office and…"

"And you went all Jessica Fletcher?"

"Who's Jessica Fletcher?"

"Jesus, Hector. I don't want to be involved in any more of your dead people stuff anymore! I told y'all! I'm through! I'm out!"

"He thinks you destroyed him."

"I *did* destroy him. Didn't you get that memo? And it wasn't my fault. It was an accident! An accidental destruction of everything in his world. Like a drunk hurricane!" Frances took a breath. "Kevin, don't you have homework to do?"

"I've been tryin' to study for my Algebra test, but Hector is makin' me work late."

"Hector, get him home right now. This is bull crap."

Hector shot a look at Kevin. "It's a Friday night!"

"You don't know me!" Kevin lashed.

"He said he was going to cut out your heart!"

"Well, he's gonna have to use a pole vault just to get to my chest. Get Kevin home right now."

"Aren't you scared?" Hector asked.

Frances laughed. "After everything I've been through in the past three months, you think Donald Dobkins scares me?"

Hector shook his head. "You should be scared, Frances! That's not normal!"

"You're talkin' to me about normal!? You chop up dead people for a livin'! I'm at least tryin' to make somethin' of my life. Get Kevin home. Drive safe." Frances hung up. She quickly rushed to the back door and locked it. She ran into the living room and locked the old deadbolt that was installed by her grandfather. (Probably great-grandfather.)

"No one locks their doors in Liberty," she hissed under her breath as she raced back into the kitchen, ripping open a drawer and sizing up all the kitchen knives. She went through knives on a block next to the sink and grabbed the largest butcher knife, tapping the tip of her finger on the point of the blade. She stabbed it onto her mother's cutting board for good measure, yanking it out with such force that she almost toppled to the floor. "This must be how that Laurie Strode feels every dang Halloween."

The knife wasn't going to be enough. The Man could have a gun, and she wasn't about to be the broad who brought a knife to a gunfight. She slowly turned, looking out the back window to the barn in the distance.

"Ugh," she quietly lamented to herself. "You can do it, Hunt. Put on your big girl panties."

Frances turned on the porch light, staring into the dark backyard. The moon cast a dim, gray wash over everything outside. Frances unlocked the door and quickly ran to the barn, throwing open the barn door and turning on the lights.

Her eyes scanned the barn. She had not been in the barn since her big Thanksgiving feast when she and Kevin stored the tables and chairs in the barn loft. She gripped the knife tighter, making her way to her father's old work bench. She crouched, moving several buckets of decades-old paint and boxes of rusty nails and screws. She reached into the back of the shelf, retrieving a long, brown box with the word **"Evidence"** stamped on every side.

She placed the box on the bench and grabbed the same utility knife she had used months earlier to cut the duct tape off Oscar Lopez's bound, lifeless body. She cut through the yellow police tape and opened the box, exposing Oscar Lopez's shotgun. The same shotgun Birdie had used to accidentally liberate Oscar's head from his shoulders. The same shotgun Birdie had used to end her own life.

Police protocol was to return personal effects (like a gun) following the closed investigation involving a suicide. Pembrook had called Frances and asked if she wanted the gun returned. Worried they might run a serial number and discover no one by the last name "Hunt" had ever purchased the gun, she gratefully asked him to return the gun, as it "Had belonged to my daddy."

Buddy Hunt was an avid gun owner while he was alive. Frances gave all his guns to his fishing buddies after his death. But she kept his ammunition.

Frances raced up the stairs into the barn loft, ripping away a large tarp covering several foot lockers Buddy had used while he was in the military. She unbuckled the locks to the largest case and opened the lid, revealing rows and rows of small cardboard boxes containing numerous bullets and shotgun slugs.

Frances grabbed a single box and slammed the locker shut.

Frances hated guns. Buddy took her hunting as a child because he wanted a son. She purposefully avoided shooting quail during their hunts, even though she could blast a skeet with the skill of an Olympian missing one eye and an astigmatism in the other.

She gently placed her hands around the barrel of the gun, feeling its weight in her palm. "Huh," she wondered. It was Delores who had commandeered the gun away from Oscar at Lockhart Brothers. It was Birdie who had accidentally pulled the trigger in the barn. It was Kevin who had taken care of the gun during the clean-up. Frances realized this was the last thing her mother had held in her lifetime. It felt cold and heavy. It felt delicate. It had taken the lives of at least two people. Possibly more.

She remembered taking the gun from her mother's hands after Birdie accidentally shot Oscar. She remembered having her own prints on the gun and was momentarily worried she might be charged with his murder, even though her actions put her at the bottom of the list of accomplices. She remembered hoping they *would* arrest her just so she could get three square meals and not have to worry about any more bills. Prison felt like a destination spa vacation.

A tear rolled down her cheek, and Frances quickly wiped it away with the back of her hand. With the precision of an experienced marksman, she popped the gun open, dropped five shells into the tube, and slammed it closed.

She stood and single-handedly pumped it. "Come and get me, little man."

Delores and Sissy were waiting in the Lockhart Brothers parking lot when Hector and Kevin arrived in the van. Sissy extinguished her cigarette on the ground the moment she saw headlights pull into the gravel lot.

"I can't believe you picked up smokin' at your age," Delores lamented. "Smokin' is gonna kill you!"

"Well, I guess that would just be horrible for my family and my husband," she dryly whined. "Oh, wait."

"What about me?!" Delores insisted.

"You should pick up smoking, too. I bet Cooper could write it off as an expense."

"Just because you've given up your will to live does not mean I have! I have big plans down at the Liberty Little Theater, and I want you to be alive for my opening night."

"Better hurry. I'm up to half a pack a day."

Hector and Kevin opened the back of the van and pulled out a body on a gurney. "You're going to have to call the buyer and tell them we only have the one body, and we weren't able to get more."

Sissy peered inside, seeing the second empty gurney. "They're expecting four!" Sissy screamed.

"Well, they're getting one!" Hector shot back. "You need to work harder to find more sellers! I'm just the butcher! Not Mission Control!" He sniffed the air. "Are you smoking?"

"That's a personal question."

"Can we talk about my mom!?" Kevin interjected. "What are we gonna do!?"

"The Man doesn't know where your momma lives," Hector said.

"Why do you think he has Duane Brown's phone, huh?" Kevin pushed. "And why were you all suspicious about that drink and things not feeling right at the crematory?" Kevin reached into his pocket and pulled out a shriveled-up mass. "And I found this while we were in there, and I didn't want to say anything to upset you while you were driving, but…". He showed it to the group.

"Is that a finger!?" Sissy screamed.

Delores leaped back nearly two feet. "What are you doin' with a finger in your in pocket, you little freak!?"

Hector took the digit from Kevin's hand. "You found this? Why didn't you say something earlier!?"

"It was near that machine that turns dead people into crispy critters," Kevin said. "And like I said, I didn't want to upset you while you were drivin' because Hector, you're a terrible driver."

Hector waved the finger in Kevin's face. "Never, ever, pick up dead body parts that don't belong to us! This is evidence!" Hector examined the finger. "This is bad. The Man did this."

Sissy sighed. "Maybe it belongs to someone they was burnin' up, and it just fell out of the oven. You people are so dramatic. Y'all are jumpin' to conclusions. We need bodies, not theories."

"I'm going home," Kevin said, shouldering his backpack and heading toward his Saturn, parked in a visitor spot. "And I'm not comin' in tomorrow."

"We need to make a plan—" Hector started.

"I don't care!" Kevin screeched slowly. "I'm goin' home to take care of my momma! You guys figure this shit out yourselves! I'm just a kid!"


"We ain't goin' nowhere, Kevin!" Frances swore as she paced the living room floor, stomping along the hardwoods as she clutched the barrel of the shotgun with one hand and the hilt with the other.

"Put that damn gun down!" Kevin demanded for the tenth time since arriving home and in the crosshairs of his paranoid mother. "You gonna accidentally pull the trigger and blast me into the middle of kingdom come!"

"I will not!"

"I'm sure Grandma thought the same thing before she popped off on old Oscar."

Frances rested the gun against the fireplace. "I mean, like, how can he find us? He don't got no leads. Just because he's got my phone number—"

"Can't he like cross reference it or somethin'? Like put your phone number in an internet search and find your address?"

"No," she said, snapping her fingers. "That phone is registered to the LLC, and we're usin' the bank address for all the company business," she said, slightly relieved, remembering the paperwork she signed with Cooper.

"So, he's gonna go to the bank and start showin' your dang picture around! We need to call the police."

"And tell them what, Kevin!? A little person is out to kill me because I accidentally helped shut down his illegal body harvestin' operation!?" She grabbed the gun from the fireplace. "That's what this thing is for." She began pacing the floor again. "At least we're gettin' real good at gettin' rid of dead bodies." Frances pointed to the stairs. "You need to go to bed."

"What about you?"

"I'm fine." She snapped her fingers and waved him away.

"*Fine*," Kevin sneered. "Sure. Don't die." He went to the stairs. "I mean, you can't die. I wouldn't know what to do. About literally anything." He ran up the stairs.

Frances went to the deadbolt, unlocked the door, and slowly pushed it open. She grabbed a heavy parka from the coat rack, walked out onto the porch, and sat in the swing.

It was freezing. She slung her arms through the sleeves and softly rocked back and forth as the rusted swing chain made a horrifying screeching sound. She looked out into the dark and spooky yard, watching the shadows twist and turn on the ground.

"Come out, come out, wherever you are, Donnie."


Donald Dobkins sat across from Cooper Delaney. Donald's feet were nearly a foot off the ground, and he was extremely annoyed.

The bank was only open until noon on Saturdays, but they were always packed with people who couldn't get away during the week to handle their business. Cooper was agitated by the small crowd forming in the lobby and motioned to the security guard to cut off any more morning stragglers from entering.

Cooper turned his attention back to the little person in front of him. "Big Momma?" Cooper laughed. "No, sir. I'm sorry, we don't have anyone here in Liberty that I'm aware of by that name. She sounds like a mob boss with that name! What did she do?"

"Can't really talk about it. It's an ongoing investigation."

"Is she big like 'tall' or big like 'fat'?"

"She looks good for her age. Medium build. Long brown hair." Donald pushed a scrap piece of paper across Cooper's desk. "This phone number. According to the internet, it belongs to Heavenly Cupcakes LLC. The address is"—he waved his arms around the bank—"here. There is no Heavenly Cupcakes anywhere in Liberty. I need to find this woman. It's important."

Cooper stiffened slightly, but not enough for Donald to notice. "You're looking for a woman, and all you have is an address and the name, Big Momma?" Cooper palmed the scrap piece of paper. "Sir, this is a bank, not the information desk at Epcot. Even if I knew what you were talking about, I can't just give out personal information for our clients."

Donald slid a hundred-dollar bill across the desk. Cooper raised an eyebrow.

"Mister, unless you're planning on opening an account today"—he pushed the bill back to Donald—"I'm going to have to ask you to leave my establishment and send you on your way."

Donald snatched the bill from the desk and hopped off the chair. "I'll find her," he said as he walked to the door.

"And I wish you the best of luck with that! Have a blessed day!"

Cooper watched as Donald walked out the front door of the bank, the top of his head bobbing past the storefront windows as he walked along the sidewalk.

Cooper flipped the paper over and immediately entered the number in a search engine. "Don't be Frances… Don't be Frances," he said as the screen searched.

**"Hunt, Frances."**

Cooper grabbed the phone receiver and dialed Frances's number. She answered with a "Hey, Cooper."

"Franny… You in danger, girl."


Sissy smoked a cigarette, watching Hector pace in the embalming room.

"This is bad!" he groaned. "If The Man shows up in Liberty—"

"We kill him, Hector. We kill him, and then we have another body," she said, exhaling a long stream of smoke. "I wish that little turd would. I wanna see what he looks like."

"You've never seen him?"

Sissy threw up her arms. "When would I have seen him?"

"You shouldn't be smoking in here."

"Why? Am I gonna kill someone?"

Hector pointed to the body lying in a body bag. "What about her?"

"What about her?! She's already dead."

"The body count, Sissy. We need three more bodies."

"Oh, we can't use her. Young mom. Died of…" she lowered her voice and whispered, "Breast cancer."

"What?" Hector asked, not hearing her.

Again, she whispered, "Breast cancer."

"I can't hear you."

"Breast cancer!" she loudly whispered.

"Why are you whispering? Who's going to hear?"

"You don't say that word out loud in the South, Hector."

"Breast?"

"Cancer! Jesus Christ, Hector. Are you slow!? Were you dropped on your head in your village when you were born?"

"I was born in Texas, Sissy."

"Were you dropped on your head in your village in Texas?"

Hector unzipped the body bag and looked inside.

Sissy stood on the other side of the body. "Christopher's embalming her when he gets back. He's taking some continuing education classes down at the community college."

"The technology doesn't change, Sissy—"

"I don't care what he's doin', Hector. He don't ask questions, and he gets the job done. I'm a little grateful he told me he was doin' classes. He could just as easily have said, "I'm gonna watch my soaps all day and see you when I do. He knows somethin' is goin' on, and he playin' stupid. Leave him be."

"We should find another embalmer," Hector stated.

"This is my family funeral home," Sissy said. "We can't just let anyone in here."

Delores knocked on the door and stuck her head in. "There's…" She paused, waving her hand at the thick smoke in the air. "You ain't supposed to be smokin' in here!"

Sissy raised an eyebrow with a "What do you want?"

"There's someone to see us. And maybe this is a total coincidence, but…"

"But what?" Hector asked.

"It's a… I'm not supposed to use the word 'midget,' right?"


Donald Dobkins sat across from the terrified plastered smiles of Sissy and Delores in the wood-paneled office of the Lockhart Brothers.

"You have a family member you want to bury?"

"I have someone I want to bury, that's for sure." Donald looked around the office. "I heard about Stephen Lockhart." Donald sneered to himself. How could he have been so naive? How could he have been blind to the fact that all roads led him here? Why didn't he start here first?

In the past three days, he had murdered four funeral home undertakers, seeking information on Big Momma, when it was suddenly and painfully obvious "her" origin story had started here.

How had he forgotten Oscar and Hector were scheduled for a stop at the Lockhart Brothers Funeral Home the night Oscar was murdered? How had he forgotten about Stephen Lockhart going missing in the days leading up to the raid? She probably killed him, too!

Donald stared into the terrified faces of Delores and Sissy. *They know something.* Donald realized he was going to have to play it cool in order to find his "Big Momma." He was going to have to play the long game. *But he was close.*

"I'm sorry, I didn't catch your name," Sissy squeaked.

"I didn't throw it," he whispered with a stern look before bursting into laughter. Delores and Sissy jumped. "It's Melvin. Melvin White."

"Oh! Melvin! You're a Melvin!" Delores exclaimed with relief and excitement, clapping her hands. "Do you know Juanita White? Y'all related?"

"Please tell me Juanita's the dead person you want to bury," Sissy begged.

Donald paused, pivoting his story. "Don't know a Juanita."

"Too bad," Delores said.

"We went to school with her. She's the Devil," Sissy insisted. "She's married to Bill White. He's the minister down at our Baptist church."

Delores cleared her throat. "So, your name is Melvin White, and you would like to plan a funeral for your…"

"My… mother."

"I am so sorry for your loss. And would this be an open or closed casket funeral?"

Donald looked around the office. "My momma used to mention a man who owned this place. He had a brother too, right?"

"Hence the Lockhart Brothers!" Sissy beamed.

"Where are they now?"

"Dead. Both of 'em," Sissy said, making a sign of the Cross.

"I thought you were Baptist."

"You can't be too safe nowadays, amiright?" she snapped.

"They're both dead?"

"You ask a lot of questions, mister."

"I'm just making conversation," he said. "Both dead," he mused. "That's wild. What happened to them?"

"Stuart went on a hiking expedition, and Stephen drowned at sea."

"And they never recovered the bodies?"

"They did not," Sissy impatiently stated.

Delores put her hand over Sissy's folded hands. "Sir, I'm sorry. Sissy doesn't like talkin' about her dead brothers."

*Brothers!?* Donald leaned in closer, looking at the business card on the desk. "Your last name is Stone."

"I changed it when I got married."

"How's your husband?"

"He's dead too—" Sissy started.

"No, he's not!" Delores said with a loud laugh, slapping Sissy's hand. "Sissy Stone! Your husband, Carl Stone, is alive and well and is probably wonderin' where his dinner is at!"

"Oh, that's right," Sissy said in a terrifyingly menacing tone that made Delores and Donald sit-up a little taller. "I just think of him as dead. You ever think about people as just dead, Mr. White?"

"I do."

"I'd like to invite you to church tomorrow," Sissy said.

"I think we need to plan Mr. White's momma's funeral here—"

"You know, I think church could do me some good, Mrs. Stone. Momma always wanted me to get saved."

"We can baptize you too! We do it on the third Sunday of every month!" Sissy boasted.

"What about your momma—" Delores started to ask before Donald cut her off.

"She can wait." Donald extended his hand to Sissy. "Mrs. Stone, I must say it was a pleasure to meet you. I feel like you see me."

"Oh, I see you."

"Where is your momma's body right now, Mr. White?" Delores

asked, completely confused by what was happening before her eyes. *Are these two fools flirting, or are they about to kill each other?* "Coroner's office. In Fort Lauderdale."

"Oh, she didn't die here?"

"No. Alligator thing. She would want to be buried here," he said, without ever taking his eyes off Sissy.

"So, it's a closed casket?" Delores said, slightly exasperatedly.

"No," he said, taking Sissy's hand. "I want to see her."

"Christopher's good, but he's not a sorcerer, Mr. White," Sissy said breathily.

Delores stared at Sissy and Donald. "Great, so church tomorrow! Liberty Baptist! It's the big one in the square. What's your momma's name so I can call the coroner down there?"

"I'll see you tomorrow, Ms. Stone," Donald said, gently squeezing her hand.

"I look forward to it. And it's our church capital campaign, so bring your checkbook."


"That's him!" Hector exclaimed, pointing at the security surveillance footage of the office, where Sissy, Delores, and Donald had sat only two minutes earlier. "What are we going to do!? The fox is in the hen house! This is—"

"Kill him," Delores insisted. "We gotta kill him!"

"We're not gonna kill him," Sissy stated. "We're gonna turn him."

"Beg pardon?" Delores said.

"We can use him."

"He literally said he was going to cut out Frances's heart out of her chest, Sissy!" Hector screamed.

"He's got contacts. He knows all the buyers. He knows all the sellers. He doesn't have an office. He doesn't have resources. He doesn't have a job. We bring him in and make him work for us." She turned to see their stunned faces. "What?"

"You done lost your got-damned mind, Sissy Stone!" Delores

shrieked, fanning herself with a file. "You damn coo-coo for Cocoa Puffs!"

"We are not bringing him in!" Hector insisted.

"You want to call the police? We can't call the police." Sissy said. "He knows we know somethin'. That's obvious."

"Obvious how?" Delores asked.

"He wants to bury his 'momma?' Like his 'Big Momma?' He knows we're connected in all of this. He might not have connected all the puzzle pieces just yet, but he's got all the pieces," Sissy said, lighting a cigarette. "We're bringing him in. Making him an offer he can't refuse. We can offer him a new base. We can expand. He needs us way more than we need him. He ain't gonna turn on us."

Sissy exhaled a long drag, then narrowed her eyes on Delores. "You missed something in there," she said, waving back toward the office. "He said, 'and they never recovered the bodies.' Stuart and Stephen." She took another drag. "I didn't say anything about them not finding their bodies."

"Why would he make a deal with us if we knows we were the ones who caused his downfall?" Delores asked.

"What makes you think he knows we're connected to Frances? We never laid eyes on him. He'd never laid eyes on us until today. For all he knows, Frances is workin' by herself."

"And what about Frances?" Hector asked. "What do we tell her?"

"We ain't tellin' Frances shit," Sissy stated. "Frances Hunt abandoned us. We ain't friends with Frances Hunt no more." Sissy took a long drag. "We're bringing-in the little person."

Hector cleared his throat. "And if he refuses?"

Sissy flicked an ash into a coffee cup. "Then we kill him."

# CHAPTER THREE

# THERE'S A STORM COMING

**"** This tropical storm comin' out of the Gulf of Mexico is supposed to hit Liberty in our late mornin', just before noon! Everybody be careful out there! They are predicting power outages and heavy rain, so I hope y'all are all stocked up on bread and milk at this point! If not, you might be plumb out of luck!"

Frances turned off the radio in Kevin's Saturn. "I'm so sick of hearin' Jerry Bright's voice. Momma used to love him. She loved listenin' to the obituaries every mornin'."

Kevin's Saturn slowly rolled around the back of the Catfish Cabin, coming to a stop in the gravel lot. Frances sat in the passenger's seat, holding a can of mace in one hand and a switchblade in the other.

"You really need to reconsider your stance on guns, Momma," Kevin insisted.

"I ain't gettin' no gun," Frances said. "Donald Dobkins comes at me, I'll spray him in the face with this," she said, holding up the mace, "And I'll slit his duckin' throat and stab out his beady little eyes with this," she said, snapping open the switchblade.

"Momma, stop using the word duckin'."

"Hurt people hurt people, Kevin. We use only bad words when we don't have any power."

Kevin rolled his eyes. "I liked you better when you were sneakin' shots of liquor out of your syrup jar."

"Your grandmomma hated it when I cursed. It's the least I can do to honor her."

Frances scanned the employee picnic tables at the rear of the restaurant. She checked her watch. "Cooper'll be here any minute. You head on to church."

"You sure? I can wait." Kevin said, glancing at the flickering digital clock on the dash, realizing he was already late for morning choir practice.

Frances closed the switchblade against her thigh. "You got a date with the Lord Baby Jesus," she said.

"It's our big, annual capital campaign today! We're raisin' money for our new steeple. You should come."

"What's wrong with the old steeple?"

"It's old, and the wood's chippin' off. We got birds up in it. It's rottin'. We need our new steeple to be big and beautiful to attract more people to join the church so we can save 'em."

Frances shook her head in dismay. "Kevin, I've got an actual goblin tryin' to kill me right now, but you go be with all your little church friends and raise lots of money for Jesus. And if you think to remember, maybe you can ask the big guy upstairs to save *me*? You know, someone who actually needs savin'."

She opened the door and slid out of the car. Kevin grabbed her arm. "It ain't like that," he begged. "It's just they might make me a deacon soon! And Reverend White has done so much for me already."

"Welp, hopefully, The Man don't come lookin' for you after stabs me to death and cuts my heart out. Hope he don't got a thing for young boys." She slammed the door and pounded her fist on the roof twice, signaling for him to leave.

Kevin's Saturn slowly drove away. Frances dug into her purse for a piece of nicotine gum. Frances made the choice to quit smoking on New Year's, and so far, had managed to not have a single cigarette in well over a month.

She shoved her hands deep into the pockets of her black leather duster. She heard a new set of tires in the distance and turned to see Cooper's Escalade round the corner from the other side of the building, slowly parking alongside her. He rolled his window down. "Hey, baby. You lookin' for a date?"

Frances ran around, hopped inside, and closed the door. "Well?"

"Frances, I'm not your lawyer."

"I'm aware."

"You don't need to tell me what's going on, but I can surmise something strange is afoot here at the Catfish Cabin."

"The less you know, the better."

"Did you kill someone?"

"Cooper! What a question!" She swallowed hard and locked her eyes on him, carefully choosing her words. "*I… didn't kill anyone.*"

Cooper gasped. "Oh, good Lord! It was that Sissy Stone, wasn't it?!"

Frances sucked her teeth and cocked her head. "The less you know."

"Are you tryin' to tell me Sissy Stone was involved in the death of your momma?"

"No! Nothing like that! That was definitely a suicide."

Cooper turned up the heat on the dashboard, shaking his head. "You mean that was an accidental death."

*Accidental death?* Frances jutted her jaw to the side and firmly repeated, "No, Cooper, that was a suicide."

"The police report claimed it was an accidental death, so it has to be true. You hear me? It has to be true."

Frances folded her arms, adjusting herself in the seat. "What in the hell are you talkin' about, Cooper?"

"Sheriff Jackson filed your momma's death as an accident."

Frances suffered from what she presumed to be a momentary bout of vertigo. She tightly shut her eyes, trying to stall a migraine. "Ray Jackson filed a false police report and said my momma accidentally shot her face off?"

"It…" Cooper paused. "You never saw the police report?"

"Stop talkin'. Nope. I don't wanna know. I don't need to know. I don't want that image in my head."

Cooper nodded. "Okay, but if anyone ever asks you about it, your answer is it was an 'accidental death,' got it?" He waited for her to respond. "Got it?!"

"Got it! Geez."

He waved an envelope in front of her. "If the death had been ruled as a suicide, the insurance company… Oh, Lordy… You have no idea, do you?"

"Cooper, spit it out."

"Remember when you asked me to set up your business with insurance?"

Frances nodded.

"That included life insurance. For all the employees."

"And I'm sure that dental will come in real handy for Kevin Hunt once all his teeth start fallin' out from cavities."

"Birdie, your momma, was an employee."

Frances shook the envelope. "Okay, sure. I mean, she didn't do anything, but whatever."

He handed her the envelope. She slowly opened it and pulled out a check.

The check was in her name in the amount of one million dollars.

A blast of lightning shot across the sky, seemingly hitting very nearby. Frances jumped, screaming. Her eyes went back to the check, blinking several times.

"Cooper! One million… dollars!? Is this dollars or like pesos!?" She shook the check in his face. "Dollars!? Like US American dollars!?"

"Like US American dollars. I told you to trust me."

Frances stared at the check, not able to breathe. Not able to speak. Not able to move.

Cooper patted her hand. "And now you have all that land and the property back behind the bakery, too. And I'd estimate that to be worth about half a million as well."

"A-half-a-million US American dollars!? How is anything worth that much in Liberty!?"

"Frances, that property is sitting on over fifty acres. Including…" Before he finished his sentence, she realized what he was about to say. "The old Womack Bakery. Turns out The Womacks and The Dingles were in the moonshine business together back in the day. And the Womacks unloaded the land to The Dingles because of some tax issues back in the eighties. So, now you *own* the bakery as well."

Frances took a deep breath and slowly exhaled, still reeling from shock. "Wait. Who have we been payin' rent to the past four months?"

"Already on it. Looks like that real estate agent was pocketing all the money owed to Dusty. Apparently, he hired them back about seven years ago to represent the bakery property, and they didn't have any takers until you four came along. She claims she was just saving the money until she could get in touch with him."

Frances looked back down at the check, her hands shaking. Tears started to well in her eyes. "Cooper, I don't even know what to say. This is the best day of my whole entire life!" she said as tears rolled down her cheeks. "It's like Momma used to say. 'The Lord giveth.'"

"I know it'll never bring your momma back. But hopefully, this will help a little." Cooper let her have a moment, then gently placed a hand on her knee and asked, "Changing subjects for a moment. I'm asking this in the kindest way I know how, and I want us to enter into this conversation with as much love and light as humanly possible. But why the holy mother of fudge was a little person in my office asking about you, and why do you call yourself Big Momma? Because there's something about that milk that just ain't clean."

"Nakoya! I'm leaving you if you're not in the car in the next thirty seconds!" Akasha hollered up the stairs to her sister from the living room. "If you're going to come to church with me, you have to be on time! I'm not going to have them white people turning around and saying, 'Oh, look, it's CPT.'"

"What's CPT?" Nakoya asked, rushing into the kitchen with her pumps in her hand. "And I'm ready!"

"Colored People Time."

"Kash, no one says 'Colored People' anymore."

"You've been in Liberty almost three months. You need to meet more white people."

"I work with white people every day! And most of them racist old prunes think Nixon's still president!"

Sissy leaned against the hood of her dead husband's Suburban, smoking a cigarette in the church parking lot while staring at the dark clouds swirling above her. She exhaled a long drag of smoke and quietly declared to herself, "This is the good life."

Delores spotted Sissy as her Crown Victoria turned into the parking lot. Delores honked the horn, rolled down the window, and loudly scream-whispered while pointing at the cigarette, "Put that out, Jezebel! You're in the parkin' lot of the Lord's house!"

Sissy raised her middle finger to Delores.

"Well, Sissy Stone, as I live and breathe!" droned a shrill, Southern accent behind her. Sissy turned around to see Edie Trussell flanked by Juanita White and Queenie Masters. All three stopped dead in their tracks at the sight of Sissy's cigarette. "Are you smokin'!? At your age!?"

Queenie Masters dramatically waved her hands, coughing loudly, and bellowed, "Oh, help her, Lord! You know secondhand smoke can kill!"

Sissy blew a long stream of smoke in her direction. "Not dependably."

"I hope y'all baked somethin' yummy for the bake sale," Juanita said, raising a cake pan with great pride. "We have to raise lots of money today for the steeple!"

Delores opened the trunk of her car, waving her hands over a large basket of homemade cookies. "Of course we did. We're Baptists. Not monsters."

Queenie continued coughing, practically hacking up a lung while stepping away from the group. "Oh, I just can't take her smokin'! My great-granddaddy died of smokin'!"

Lightning shot across the sky. Everyone yelped, looking skyward. "Relax, Queenie. You ain't gonna die today," Sissy hissed. A thunderous clap exploded in the distance. "Or maybe you will. Who can tell?"

"Fortunately, I'm bathed in His blood," Queenie announced as the three Witches of Liberty marched toward the church.

"I'd like to bathe that bitch in her own blood," Sissy grumbled. "I wish she'd die. All three of 'em would just die."

Delores yanked the cigarette out of Sissy's hand and stamped it with the heel of her orthopedic shoe. Sissy scoffed. "Them things are expensive!"

"Sissy Stone, I'm tired of this act of yours. You need to straighten up and get right with Jesus."

Lightning flashed again, followed by a loud clap.

"Something's comin', Dee, and I don't think it's Jesus," Sissy said with a glint of glee as she grabbed the pie from the backseat of the Suburban. "There's a storm comin', Dee. There's a big old storm a-comin'."

Delores turned in a huff and waddled toward the church. "Stick to the plan, Meryl Streep. We got a goblin to catch."

Hector scrunched down in the front seat of his van with a clear view of the steps of the church. Rain began to pound the windshield. He turned up the heat and turned on the windshield wipers.

The plan was simple. Hector, Sissy, and Delores would get The Man in a public setting (preferably the bake sale after church in the fellowship hall) and discuss the terms of engagement with the option of "bringing him in." They didn't tell Kevin any of the details for fear he would tip off Frances, and God only knows what she would do.

If The Man refused to fall in line with their plan, Sissy planned to poison his fruit punch with the ornate poison ring she recently purchased at Trade Day from a lovely goth girl named Vesper.

Inside the church, Kevin sang along with the other thirty members of the Liberty Baptist Church choir, dressed in their heavy, velvet crimson choir robes. They loudly wailed (mostly in tune) over the church organ, which always boomed louder on the last verse with a tempo no one could follow. "At the cross, at the cross, where I first saw the light, and the burden of my heart, rolled away!"

Donald Dobkins stood among the congregants in the packed sanctuary. Several parishioners tried to steal looks at the small man who had joined them as a visitor on this day of worship and fundraising (or "fun-raising," as the committee deemed it). Some believed he was the wealthy family member of a congregant from the big city. Many had offered a "Hello!" and a "Welcome to Liberty Baptist!" For a few who had never ventured far outside the county, this was the first time they had ever seen a little person up close and personal.

Donald craned his neck, searching for Sissy and Delores, who were in the fellowship hall next door, setting up for the after-church bake sale. Donald sang along with the choir, reading from the hymnal. "It was there by faith, I received my sight…"

Outside the church, Akasha and Nakoya raced up the steps, clutching their umbrellas for dear life as the heavy rain and wind kicked into high gear. Lightning flashed again.

"They're already at the message in song! We're so dang late! You made me late!" Akasha lamented, trying to hold onto her umbrella with one hand and keep the scarf around her hair from blowing away in the wind with the other.

"I think Jesus will forgive you, Akasha! It's kind of His thing."

"He will, but them old white people won't!"

Edie, Juanita, and Queenie stood in a row near the front of the church. Juanita lifted her arms into the air and swayed as the spirit moved her to the end of the song. "And now I am happy all the day!"

"Be seated," the Reverend Bill White instructed, taking the pulpit as everyone slowly lowered themselves onto the hard, old wooden pews. "We at Liberty Baptist ain't afraid of a little rain. Can I get an Amen!?" The entire congregation responded with an enthusiastic, "Amen!"

"We at Liberty Baptist ain't afraid of a hurricane or a tropical storm or a tornado because we know God is watchin' from above. God has placed his hand right over this church, and God is gonna protect us, or God is gonna take us all home to glory! Can I get an Amen!?"

*KA-POW!* went a loud, thundering clap outside as Akasha and Nakoya threw open the doors to the church. Everyone turned to see the late comers. Akasha kept her head down while Nakoya enthusiastically grinned and waved her way down the aisle.

Donald Dobkins did a double take, squinting. *No… it can't be.* Nakoya didn't see Donald as she shook the rain from her umbrella, following Akasha down to the center aisle toward the front of the church. She offered a quiet, "How you doin'?" to a scowling, elderly white woman.

It had been just over three months since Donald had fled 141 Corona, leaving Nakoya to sound the alarm, forcing her to put into motion the company-wide exodus and quickly pack all the evidence. Donald never reached out to Nakoya, and she never reached out to him.

Donald stepped into the aisle. "Nakoya?" he whispered.

Nakoya looked up, seeing Donald standing in the aisle. She froze. Was she in danger? She felt like she was in danger. She knew Donald was insane. What did he know? Did he know she had been secretly, actively working against him for months before the raid? Did he know she had been involved in orchestrating a hostile takeover, which was inadvertently thwarted when the police showed up?

Did he know she purposely left Oscar Lopez's body behind in the warehouse, knowing his fingerprints were on it and the tarp? Did he know she had purposely set him up to get him out of the way once Stephen and Stuart's coup was in motion?

*CRASH!* went another clap of thunder outside, shaking the entire church.

*Girl, run!* screamed a voice in her head. Nakoya spun around and ran back up the aisle, slamming her entire body into the heavy metal bar on the door with all her weight. The wind outside ripped the door backward with such force that it nearly flew off its hinges.

The sound of the door banging against the outside wall made Akasha (and everyone else in the church) jump and turn. *Where's Nakoya?* she wondered, as she saw a little person run out of the church.

"Let us pray," offered a very perplexed Reverend Bill White.

Nakoya raced into the parking lot as the wind blew harder and massive amounts of rain hit the concrete. The wind nearly knocked her to the ground.

A gust snapped the air, slamming the large wooden door shut just as Donald raced down the steps.

Everyone inside the church gasped, turning again to see the closed doors. Edie's eyes narrowed on Akasha, shooting judgmental daggers.

"What!?" Akasha mouthed over Bill's prayer.

"CPT," she sadly lamented. "CPT."

Racing through the parking lot, Nakoya rummaged through her purse, wrestling out a small handgun.

"Nakoya!" Donald shouted over the thunder, lightning, and pounding rain. "What are you doing here in Liberty? Why are you running away from me—"

What happened next happened in seconds, but it felt like an eternity and in slow motion for both Donald and Nakoya.

Donald froze in his tracks. Before Nakoya would turn around to aim her gun at his forehead, he (wrongly) concluded that Nakoya had been working with Big Momma all along. After all, it was Nakoya who had relayed the news to him about Stephen Lockhart going missing. It was Nakoya who had told him about the raid on Memorial Gardens. *Nakoya* was the mole. *Nakoya* was the rat.

No. Wait.

It was worse.

Nakoya *was* Big Momma.

Nakoya had clearly been running her own game, right underneath him the entire time and using "that woman" as a decoy. Donald had been looking for the wrong woman.

It was Nakoya all along.

"You… bitch!" he howled from the bottom of his soul. He clenched his fists in tight balls as veins popped out of his neck and forehead. His face turned beet red with rage. Every muscle in his body tensed in a fury.

At that exact same moment, a bolt of lightning pierced the clouds from the heavens, striking Liberty Baptist Church's historic steeple atop the church.

Nakoya spun around, aiming the gun at Donald's forehead. "Go all the way back to hell, you tiny malevolent ghoul!" she screamed, shaking the outstretched gun. Before she could pull the trigger, the lightning-struck steeple burst into thousands of pieces, sending debris in all directions. Even more surprising? The wood steeple, which had been in desperate need of repair or replacement for years, was covering *another* ornate steeple made of brass.

The twenty-foot brass steeple careened downward, with sparks and traces of lightning still circling the metal, casting a large dark shadow over Donald. It seemed to fall so slowly, like an Acme anvil, plummeting toward an oblivious Wile E Coyote. Enough time for Donald to turn and see the crucifix as it soared directly over him.

But not enough time for him to move. Just enough time for him to calmly say, "Well, shit."

*SPLAT.*

Hector, having watched the entire exchange play out from the moment Nakoya burst through the doors of the church, leaped out of his van, racing toward Nakoya.

"Nakoya!" he screamed through the deafening rain and wind.

Spooked to hear her name being shouted behind her, Nakoya turned and instinctually fired a single shot.

Hector spun once, falling to the ground, hard, face down.

Akasha screamed.

Nakoya spun, aiming the gun at her sister.

"Nakoya, drop the damn gun!"

Ten seconds earlier, the exact moment the lightning hit the church steeple, the three hundred congregants inside the Liberty Baptist Church all screamed, all leaping to their feet as their entire church rocked on its foundation.

"It's Jesus!" a terrified Edie Trussell screamed, leading the charge to the doors of the church. Edie slammed her hands onto the old metal exit bars of the doors and almost bounced backward as the doors did not budge.

Others followed suit, some even ramming their shoulders into the doors. The doors to the Liberty Baptist Church were stuck, jammed from the outside, due to structural damage from the lightning hit on the roof.

"Jesus wants us to stay inside!" Queenie Masters shrieked with joy, clapping her hands. "Jesus is going to open up the roof and take us all home!" she screamed, jumping up and down. "We're all going home today!"

"I hope no one's afraid of heights because Jesus is about to rip open this roof, and we're all about to soar up into the heavenly skies, all the way home to Jesus!" the Reverend Bill White cried out to the crowd, shoving his way down the center aisle, and lifting his arms to the sky alongside Queenie. "We're probably gonna fly right up through the eye of the storm!"

Indeed, the roof began to open. By flames. Smoke filled the

sanctuary as the entire congregation stood in silence, waiting for Jesus to appear. Congregants began coughing, quietly moving to the sides of the sanctuary as pieces of the ceiling began to fall, crashing to the floor.

"It's the fire and brimstone!" Queenie shrieked, pointing to the actual fire on the ceiling as it collapsed. Queenie began to sing, raising her arms skyward. "Sing the wondrous love of Jesus! Sing His mercy and His grace! In the mansions bright and blessed, He'll prepare us a place!"

Kevin raced out of the choir loft to join her, as everyone else in the church pews ran for sides of the church and down the aisles closest to the exits near the front of the church. "When we all get to heaven, what a wonderful day of rejoicing that will be!"

Screaming, crying, terrified congregants burst through those doors while others smashed out stained-glass windows with the bases of microphones from the choir loft. The Reverend Bill White looked around at the intense chaos and whispered to himself, "Screw this," choosing to flee the burning building and impending ride to heaven through the roof.

Queenie and Kevin continued singing, "When we all see Jesus, we'll sing and shout the victory!"

"Queenie, get your boney little butt down here right now!" Edie demanded, having made her way to the front of the church with the rest of the crowd.

"Second verse!" Kevin joyfully cried.

Flames engulfed the center of the ceiling. Edie pushed through the screaming church members, trying to get to Queenie.

Kevin and Queenie joined hands. "While we walk the pilgrim pathway, clouds will overspread the sky—"A plank of wood snapped from an old beam and careened downward. Downward and downward and downward…

Slicing Queenie Masters's head clean off her shoulders.


Akasha fell into a fetal position, terrified her sister was about to fire another round.

Nakoya spun back to Hector, realizing what she had done. She dropped the gun and sprinted to Hector, flipping him over.

"Hector! Oh my God! I'm so sorry! Stay with me!" Nakoya yelled to Akasha, "Call an ambulance!"

The late Oscar Lopez had always been the point of contact with The Man and everyone at the 141 Corona warehouse. Oscar didn't like talking on the phone, so he always texted Nakoya, who hated using what she referred to as "the phone app" on her company cell phone. Oscar had the education of a sixth grader, and Nakoya spent a great deal of time sounding out his text messages to understand what he was writing. Oscar was saved in her phone under his codename, "Coyote Movers." Oscar was the transport, and was the one who collected the cash after the haul.

Hector began working for The Man nearly two years earlier after leaving a life of body harvesting behind in Mathis, Texas. He considered going into business by himself, but a tip from Dolly Peavey at Athens State College led him to work as a "butcher" for Donald Dobkins. Because of his years of experience in Texas, Hector was hired by Donald to train other butchers in the field before being permanently assigned to work with Oscar full-time on their regular route.

Oscar would pick up Hector every morning in the Coyote Movers van (unless they were away for a few nights and staying in a rundown motel). Oscar would drop off Hector every night before making his delivery to the warehouse, and he would give Hector's cut the next morning at breakfast.

Hector met Akasha at The Coffee Cup (a few doors down from her shop on Main Street) one morning before they drove back to Atlanta after an overnight haul. Hector was smitten by Akasha but far too nervous about what she would say or do if she knew he was a body snatcher. It would be almost a year later before Akasha would coyly inform him she already knew, thanks to the fact she had a vast psychic knowledge. The only person Akasha could never read was her own sister, Nakoya.

Nakoya told Akasha she worked at a bank in Atlanta. She didn't think Akasha could handle the truth. Not only was she working for a company that distributed human remains on the black market, but she was also working with two individuals planning to take over the entire American territory of an international operation on a much larger scale.

After faking their deaths, Stephen and Stuart Lockhart had changed their names and, as of Christmas, their faces. They were living in Florence,

Italy, and were mere weeks away from throwing the switch, effectively shutting down all the processing plants in America and rebranding as a new company.

Nakoya's desk had been in the back of the warehouse, near Donald's office, away from the smell of the bodies and the sounds of the saw blades and snapping limbs. Nakoya kept small plants and pictures of Akasha and herself as children on her desk.

Hector met Nakoya for the very first time at Frances's Thanksgiving dinner three months earlier. Neither had any idea they had been working for the same company. Nakoya had no idea Hector's actions made him unintentionally a part of the demise of 141 Corona. Hector had no idea Nakoya had been The Man's right-hand woman for the past three years and that she had been working with the Lockhart Brothers to change the game forever.

Hector had no communication with the office. Nakoya never questioned that "Hector from Thanksgiving" was "Hector from Receivables" on her Excel sheet.

Blood freely poured from Hector's stomach. Nakoya slammed her hand over it, applying pressure as Hector gasped for breath.

"You shot me…" he said, spitting blood.

"My bad, don't die! Stay with me! Akasha is calling the ambulance!" Nakoya looked up to see Akasha staring at the burning church, frozen by fear as the screaming church members fled the building. "Call the damn ambulance, Kash!"

Akasha dug into her purse for her phone. "Siri, call 911," she shakingly said into the phone.

Hector closed his eyes, and his entire body went still. Nakoya slapped his face several times. "Stay with me, Hector! You have to stay with me!" Nakoya shouted to the fleeing church members, "Is anyone a doctor! We need help!"

Inside the church fellowship hall, Delores and Sissy looked over the tables of pies and cookies. "It smells so good in here," Delores mused.

"Do you smell smoke?" Sissy asked.

"We don't got nothin' cookin' in the oven, Sis."

"Is that screamin'? I hear screamin'," Sissy said.

Delores turned, her awareness tuning into the noise and commotion from outside in the parking lot. "Well, now that you mention it," she said, throwing back the curtains to see the roof of the church on fire and dozens of people running for their lives. "Call 911! Lord of mercy, Sissy! The church is on fire!"

Cooper Delaney blinked. He took a sip of his iced coffee, shaking it a few times, while staring out the window at some children playing on the swings behind the Catfish Cabin.

Frances took a deep breath and slowly let it out. "I gotta tell you, Coop. I feel so much better now that you know everything."

"I mean… That is quite a story, Frances."

"You can understand why I've been a little on edge the past few months."

"Frances, I can't be involved with someone like you. You've committed dozens of crimes. Maybe hundreds."

"We took an escaped killer off the streets!"

"You killed him!"

"*I* didn't kill him. And it was an accident!"

"You took over his business!"

"We needed the money, and I'm now out of the business!"

"You could have started an OnlyFans if you needed the money! Frances, this is bad! This is like, really, really, really bad! Did you kill the sheriff, too!?"

"I ain't seen Ray Jackson since the day I told him to get off my property. It ain't my fault he disappeared. And good riddance."

"And Sissy murdered her husband?"

"Hey! You're the one using the word 'accidental death,' and as far as I'm concerned, that's what happened. I ain't askin' her what really happened. It's very entirely possible he did, in fact, slip in the tub."

Cooper shook his head.

"Coop, I had to get out. I'm tryin' to get my life in order. I'm helpin' old people." She shook the check. "And look! God is rewardin' me for it!"

"You said you didn't believe in God."

"I did not! I never said that! I said we was in a fight. And look at him now! God *is* bigger!"

"How can you make light of this!?"

"I'm not makin' light of anything! Coop, we took down a massive dead body black market industry!"

"But according to you, the others are still doin' it! And you guys stole a casket out of the cemetery?! Who does that!?"

"Their hearts are in the right place. They think they're helpin' and bein' of service. People need these bodies and parts, and what they're doin' is helpin' save lives. Can't you see that?"

"No. I can't. Because it's completely illegal, Frances! It's wrong, Frances. How can you justify this for them?"

"I'm not justifyin' anything."

"And this man? 'The Man?' What about him? What happens when you two come face to face?"

"Well, let me ask you this. What would you do, Coop? You come face to face with someone who wants to kill you? What would you do?" Frances pulled the switchblade from her coat pocket.

"Oh, good Lord Jesus, Frances Hunt."

The police scanner on Cooper's dash squawked to life. "All units report to Liberty Baptist Church! There's a fire and a man shot with other possible fatalities!"

Frances's eyes widened as she slammed her hands on the dash. "Oh my God! Drive! Drive right now! That's Kevin's church!"


Kevin and Edie screamed loud, long, and in harmony like two cats being tortured by a psychopathic six-year-old as they watched Queenie Masters's head snap back and rip from her neck, landing on the new cobalt blue carpet. Her head spun around, blinking twice before rolling on its side.

Queenie's body crashed backward against a pew before falling to the ground, where it landed upright as if sitting by a campfire. Once settled, her arm fell from her lap to the ground beside her.

Kevin and Edie's bodies shuddered in fright. Edie's eyes rolled into the back of her head, her body went stiff, and she fainted dead away, landing atop Queenie's outstretched legs.

Kevin continued to scream, wildly flailing his arms to the parishioners running from the falling ceiling. Kevin couldn't formulate words and instead emitted guttural cries while aggressively indicating to the decapitated body and the old woman who had just passed out from shock.

Juanita White had just reached the door when she turned back to look for Edie and Queenie. She saw Kevin screaming, with tears shooting horizontally out of his eyes. He locked eyes with Juanita, erratically flinging his arms, gesturing as if to say, "Please come! One woman has lost her head, and the other has passed out! Please come now! Please! I beg of thee! Now! For the love of God and all that is holy! Help!"

Kevin looked up, slinging his arms toward the heavens like a blow-up person outside a car wash, begging for his Higher Power to lift him out of the church or raise up the dead woman and her head. Begging the way one would plead for a helicopter to lower a mountain rescue team to a group of missionaries turned cannibals who had been stuck in the cold for weeks. Begging as if life itself depended on it.

"Kevin! Boy, you need to get up on out of here before the ceiling falls down on top of you!" Juanita cried.

Kevin stomped his feet like an insolent child, still screaming, pitching his arms to the two women below him, who Juanita could not see from her vantage point. Juanita pushed around the rushing crowd and made her way to the clear center aisle, where she saw Edie, Queenie's body, and Queenie's head.

Juanita began howling as well. She jumped up and down twice before turning and plowing through the crowd with such force and speed that she knocked ten people to the ground. Just as Juanita found herself outside and in the pouring rain, a massive chunk of ceiling fell, silencing the squalls of about a dozen parishioners inside the church.

Kevin stopped shrieking long enough to take a deep, full breath. He stared at a large piece of the black shingled roof, which had collapsed near the door, crushing God only knows how many people. Kevin stood alone as the flames engulfed the ceiling. The only sounds he could hear were the cascading rain, the slowly falling debris softly crashing to the ground, and the distant cries and screams from the congregation in the parking lot.

Kevin closed his eyes, calmly looked to the sky, and peacefully prayed, "Lord, into your hands, I commend my spirit. It is finished. Take me now."

Kevin heard a voice from everywhere and nowhere. A voice that seemed to come from within him and outside of him at the same time. A genderless and all-powerful voice. That voice said, "What are you, boy? Stupid?"

Kevin opened one eye and looked around.

Flames crackled. Rain poured. Pieces of the roof continued to fall around him.

"Get the old woman and run, dummy," spoke the voice.

A strength and confidence filled Kevin. His body felt powerful, like a superhero in a comic book movie. He crouched, scooping up Edie Trussell in his frail, thin arms, heaving her upright.

He coolly walked to the rear of the church, where the doors had jammed moments earlier. He kicked the center of the doors, and they blew wide open.

The congregation outside the church watched as Kevin emerged, holding Edie in his arms. He triumphantly marched down the steps and handed her to a burly man three times his size. "Take her, she's in shock," he serenely stated. "She might need medical attention."

Kevin turned, marching back toward the church.

"Son, you can't go back in there!" the man shouted back.

But Kevin did go back in there, striding down the aisle and heroically lifting the body of Queenie Masters over his shoulder like a fireman and clutching her head by her hair.

"Don't you worry, Ms. Masters. We gonna give you a real nice funeral," he said to her disembodied head. He marched back down the aisle as the remains of the ceiling collapsed behind him.

Kevin emerged from the church. All the eyes of the congregation turned in horrified silence. Kevin raised Queenie's skull high into the air and proudly, boldly proclaimed, "God is bigger!"

Cooper and Frances couldn't pull into the church parking lot due to all the cars racing away with injured people, but they could see the flames from the roof all the way back to the town square.

Firetrucks sped down Main Street, honking for cars to move out of the way.

"I have to get to him," Frances said, jumping out of Cooper's Escalade and running toward the church. "Kevin!? Kevin, where are you!?" she wailed, rounding the main driveway into the parking lot.

She stopped in her tracks. The scene was like something out of a post-apocalyptic Spielberg movie. Cars fought their way out of parking spaces as parishioners honked, shouting very unchristian things to one another. The roof of the church was ablaze while the rain continued to pierce through the smoke, engulfing the ground like a thick fog.

"Frances!" screamed a voice behind her. She turned to see Nakoya soaked to the bone from rain and covered in what looked like blood. "Can you drive!? My hands are shaking, and I can't see straight!"

"Have you seen Kevin?" Frances cried.

"He's alive. He's got Queenie Masters's head somewhere over there and won't let it go," she said, tossing the keys to Frances. "We have to get Hector to the hospital right now!"

Frances saw Akasha with her hand pressed to Hector's chest in the backseat of the car. "Drive, Frances, drive!" she shouted.

Frances quickly jumped into the car as Nakoya ran to the passenger side. Frances started the engine. "What happened to Hector!?"

"It was an accident! I can't do questions right now! Drive! We have to get there before everyone else does! Drive like hell!"

Frances threw the car into reverse, speeding out of the space before throwing the stick into drive. She punched the horn of the car, hit the accelerator, raced around other cars, drove over through the grass, over the sidewalk (nearly killing three people), and made a hard right on Main Street.

Frances exhaled quickly, then looked into the rearview mirror at the chaos behind them. "What do you mean Kevin had Queenie Masters's head and wouldn't let it go?"

It's less than a five-minute drive from Liberty Baptist Church to Liberty Memorial Hospital. Liberty Memorial had never seen so much mayhem. Less than fifteen minutes after the chain of events that led everyone here, the halls were packed with crying, cold, soaking-wet people screaming in pain. Doctors and nurses didn't know where to start and began to physically number people with a black marker in order of priority.

Dozens of trucks and cars pulled to the emergency room entrance, one right after another, with bleeding and injured people, each driver insisting to a nurse or orderly, "I've got hurt person!" Horns honked, and drivers demanded other drivers to move out of the way.

Frances drove Akasha's car right onto the sidewalk in front of the emergency room doors and slammed the palm of her hand onto the horn. "I need some help over here!"

A young orderly, covered in blood, threw up his hand to Frances as she leaped from the car. "Everyone needs help here, ma'am! And I'm going to need you to move your car because this is a—"

Frances charged the young orderly, grabbing him by his scrub top and shoving him into a column. "He's about to die, and I don't give a flying duck about anyone else in there! You hear me!? Now get me a stretcher—"

Nakoya grabbed the orderly by his arm, pulling him toward the car. "He's been shot!"

"Shot!?" Frances and the young orderly screamed in unison, turning to the backseat.

The orderly pried himself from Frances. "I'll be right back. I'm going to get a stretcher and a team." He raced back inside.

"Who shot Hector?" Frances demanded, opening the door to Akasha and an unconscious Hector.

"It's a long story."

"Make it short and fast, Nakoya!"

"There was a man at the church, and he was following me," she began.

"Who was that person!?" Akasha bellowed from the backseat.

"Someone I used to work with! I was running out of the church, and lightning struck the steeple and the roof, and the steeple fell down and crushed him flat like a pancake, but I'd already pulled my gun out to protect myself, and Hector called out my name, and I got spooked, and I spun around, and I accidentally pulled the trigger and then the fire started and…" Nakoya burst into tears and fell to the ground like a sack of rocks.

"Ms. Hunt? Gosh dang it… I mean, Kevin's mom?" called a voice behind Frances. She turned to see Clint Peppers in pure white scrubs that unnecessarily filled out nearly every inch of his body.

"Clint?!" Frances softly whispered in bewilderment.

"Are you okay?" he asked. "I was just volunteering like I do every other Sunday and…" he raised his arms at the bedlam. He saw Hector. "Is he okay?"

"He's been shot!" Frances blurted out.

Clint dove into the car and lifted Hector into his massive arms, rushing him into the emergency room. "I need a bed! This man's been shot!"


Kevin sat on the grave of Brandy Lynn James in the center of the Liberty Baptist Church Cemetery. The rain continued to pour, and the ground was still covered in a light layer of smoke. The racket of people and honking horns in the distance was barely a low hum.

Kevin pulled stands of grass from the ground, rolling them in his hands. "Baby, did you see that? Did you see all that? That was some wild crap, right? Could you see it from heaven, or could you see it from here, like on the ground?" He looked around, expecting to see her full-bodied apparition round the corner.

"Baby, was that you who told me what to do? Or was that Jesus? I'm just dyin' to know. How wild would it be to get an actual message from our Lord and Savior to tell me to get Ms. Edie up out of there and run?" He paused, his face dropping. "But if it was Jesus, why did he call me a dummy? That's not very nice. Not very Christian."

Kevin laughed. "I mean, I guess I'd have to be pretty stupid to stand there while the roof was collapsin' all around me. But we all thought it really was the rapture and not a fire caused by lightnin'." Kevin looked around. "Baby, I didn't like the way those people were lookin' at me when I brought out Ms. Queenie and her head."

Kevin kissed her tombstone. "I love you, baby." Kevin noticed the rain was letting up for a moment. "Did you do that too!?" He smiled. "No, that was probably Jesus too."

Nearly an hour later, the rain continued, but the wind died down. Firefighters had extinguished the fire atop the roof of the church. The Reverend Bill White stood under an umbrella before local news cameras and announced, "We will rebuild! God is good!" When asked about the causalities of the day, Reverend Bill White solemnly bowed his head and stated, "They're all with Jesus now." He closed his eyes as he did a mental roll count of who had died. "Well, most of 'em."

Sissy and Delores carried past trays of cookies and desserts to the firemen. Sissy noticed Ben Camden, the Country Medical Examiner, arrive in his Kia. "Oh, look. Ben's here."

"Mornin', Ben! How you doin'?" Delores asked as she sauntered over to him with her outstretched tray of brownies.

He threw up his hands at the entire situation. "Well… This!" He griped, slamming the trunk of his car and shouldering his examination bag. "Never seen such a mess in all my whole entire life! I heard there's about twenty dead people. Or more."

Sissy and Delores gasped. In all the commotion, neither had heard about fatalities.

"Twenty dead people!?" Sissy whispered. "We ain't heard about any dead… That's…" Sissy turned her head as her smile grew exponentially. "Just awful."

"We only got six morgue drawers down at the morgue! Never had so many dead people all at once. Never! Where am I supposed to put 'em all!?"

Sissy and Frances exchanged a quick look. "We can take some of them over at the funeral home if you need.”

“I wish!” Ben shook his head. “But I need a space to work in silence. I don’t know what I’m gonna do. Might have to rent one of them mobile morgue trucks they used back durin’ COVID. Where do you even rent a mobile morgue truck!?”

“Google?” Sissy offered.

“Shouldn’t take you that long, right?” Delores asked. “I mean, if they died from the roof fallin’ in—”

“Each body still has to be examined. I have to make a detailed report of each decedent,” he said, walking toward the church. He paused at the fallen cross on the ground and saw Donald Dobkins’s arm, which extended out from underneath.

“Oh, good Lord! The blasted cross done crushed someone to death!” he yelped, jumping backward. He called to some resting firemen in the distance, “Can one of y’all help move this cross before y’all get goin’!? We got a body under this thing.”

The firemen slowly meandered over as Delores and Sissy approached to get a closer look.

It was at that moment, from underneath the rubble, the outstretched hand moved, jutting to life.

“Oh my God! He’s still alive!”


Frances’s eyes shifted from one injured person to the next. She clutched her phone, scanning the dozens of unanswered texts to Kevin which were all variations of **“Where are you?!”**

Akasha and Nakoya sat a few chairs away, numbly staring at the blood on their hands, arms, and clothes. Every time the bathroom door opened, Akasha would watch another waiting church member spring from their seat and race inside.

The doors to the emergency room entrance loudly banged open, and Clint Peppers strutted out, making his way to Frances. Blood soaked through his white scrubs. “They’re working on him now.”

“Thank God for you,” Frances said, grabbing his forearms. “You’re covered in blood.”

"He's lost a lot. Not gonna lie… It's not looking good. Do you know who shot him? Did you file a police report yet?"

"It was an accident."

"You sure about that?" Clint quietly whispered.

Frances looked at Nakoya. "It was an accident."

"How'd you know him?"

Frances shook her head. "He's a friend. He works with Sissy, Delores, and Kevin down at the funeral home. I met him last fall."

"Ah," Clint said, nodding. "Maintenance guy?"

"He's gonna live, right?" Frances pushed, dismissing his question.

"They got the best ER doc working on him right now. You should see what that guy can do. It's freaking awesome. He's like my hero." Frances and Clint's heads turned to the sound of a siren of an ambulance peeling around the corner of the hospital. "So many bodies."

The automatic doors at the entrance swooshed open. Sissy and Delores raced toward Frances. Frances stepped closer to Clint. "Here comes trouble."

"I thought y'all were friends," Clint said.

"Not anymore."

"Franny! Franny, we gotta talk to you! Right now!" Delores shouted from halfway down the hall, waving her hands in the air as if Frances couldn't see her.

"Is it about Kevin?" she asked, checking her phone again.

"No, it's about Ben Camden!" Sissy yelled from the distance.

Frances narrowed her eyes and motioned with her hands to "keep it down." "What's the Medical Examiner gotta do with me? I ain't no friends with Ben Camden."

Clint crossed his massive arms, locked his jaw, and stepped into a wide-legged fighting stance. "The Medical Examiner?"

"They's got like twenty dead people down at the church. Maybe more," Delores said, trying to catch her breath. "Wow, I am really out of shape! I really thought my cardio was improvin'."

Frances turned to Clint. "I'm all good. You got places to be and people to help."

"You said twenty dead people?" Clint asked Delores. "The morgue can only handle about a half dozen. I know because we did a field trip in school last year for an anti-drinking thing."

"That's exactly right!" Delores exclaimed. "What he said!"

Sissy looked over at Clint like a piece of meat. "You need to come work for us."

The doors to the emergency room entrance flew open again. This time, it was Sheriff Pembrook and Ben Camden rushing down the hallway. "Franny!" Ben cried out from the distance.

"What did you two do?" Frances quietly seethed. "What did you do!?" she demanded a second time, only louder, with spittle flying out of her mouth.

Camden and Pembrook landed at the foursome in the hallway. Ben wiped his brow with a handkerchief. "Franny, is it true you've got big coolers down at your old folks center big enough to hold about two dozen dead bodies?"

Frances stiffened. "I… I mean… I…" Frances turned to Sissy and Delores. She wanted to murder them both where they stood.

"Why do you have all them freezers, Franny?" Pembrook innocently asked.

"We bought 'em during a fire sale. Remember, we was startin' a cupcake bakery and"— Frances turned, pointing at Delores and Sissy— "these two morons thought we needed a bunch of freezers." Frances forced a laugh. "We didn't know what we were doin'! And I just listened to these two stupid fools and bought up a bunch of freezers! These two dumb, stupid, frickin' fools. Been tryin' to sell 'em on Facebook Marketplace for months!"

"I don't remember seein' any freezers out there when I visited with old lady Meyer for her birthday party last month," Ben said.

"Well, we don't keep 'em out in the main room, Ben Camden. It's a long story. We knocked out a wall. Found an old bar back behind it that used to be a speakeasy. I keep the freezers back there so they're out of the way." Frances felt her face get hot. "Anyways, I'd love to help, but we got arts and crafts tomorrow morning startin' at nine, and I think it'd just be bad taste to have a bunch of dead bodies in the next room. At least bad for business, if you know what I mean."

"Franny, I'm in a real pickle! Now I know you got your little senior citizen thing, but I need your building for a week to do all these autopsies. We have to make sure that everyone has an accurate and full reporting of how they died."

"A week!? But don't you already know how they died!? I mean, I wasn't even there, and I can tell you! And ain't there like dozens of witnesses!? The roof fell in—"

"That ain't how medical examination works, Franny." Pembrook put his hand on Frances's shoulder. "We really need your help on this one. All of Liberty needs you. Your momma would want you to help these dead people and their families, right?"

Frances's eyes darted from Delores to Sissy. Her rage grew even hotter. She had cut all ties with her past mistakes. Hadn't the universe even supported her great strides over the past three months with a million-dollar check and a neighboring property? Hadn't she been through enough?

*If I open this door, what else am I inviting inside? Is there any way my past could come back to bite me?* Frances wondered.

Frances closed her eyes. She clasped her hands and brought them to her forehead. "Fine. Fine. You win," she said, thrusting her hands into her purse and fishing for the keys. "I hate everything."

Nakoya walked over to see what the commotion was about. "What's going on?"

"Nakoya, we gonna have to close down for a few days," Frances started to say before correcting herself. "Or a week. This is Ben Camden. He's our Medical Examiner. He's gotta use our building for some autopsies. Not enough room at the inn."

"Where are you gonna put all them bodies?" Nakoya asked. "Why our place?"

Frances shook her head with a look that said, "Drop it." Frances pulled a key from the key chain and handed it to Ben. "Building code is one-two-three-four, number sign." Frances turned to Clint. "You want a cup of coffee? Or some rock cocaine? I'm buyin'."

"Coming through! Please move!" screamed a voice as a stretcher was rushed down the hall. Frances, Sissy, Delores, Nakoya, Pembrook, Ben, and Clint all split the hallway, hugging the walls.

Normally an individual afraid of looking at hurt people, curiosity got the better of Frances. She looked down to see the small man on the stretcher. "Oh… my… ducking… God," she breathlessly said as her heart began to pound through her shirt.

Nakoya gasped so hard she hurt her throat. Delores and Sissy looked down as the stretcher passed.

Pembrook's brow furrowed, noticing the reaction from all the women. "Do y'all know him?" he asked.

"No," said all the women in unison.

# CHAPTER FOUR

# THE BITCH IS BACK

Frances spit her nicotine gum into a bush and thrust her hand at Sissy. "Give me a cigarette," she demanded. "I can smell it on you."

"I thought you—"

Frances grabbed Sissy by her shoulders and shook her. "Give me a fuckin' cigarette right now, you scrawny old bitch!"

Delores pried Frances away from Sissy. Frances elbowed Delores in her chest. Delores grabbed her right breast. "White devil, watch the titty!"

Frances yanked Sissy's purse from her shoulder and riffled to find a pack of cigarettes in a leather case with a lighter. She lit one, dropped the purse to the wet ground, and walked in a large circle. "What did you two tell 'em?" she said, exhaling a long drag of smoke.

"They need a place to store bodies, and we need some bodies to finish a shipment later this week."

"You ain't stealin' no dead bodies out of my bakery, slash old folks recreational center, slash kill room!"

"Kill room!?" Delores shrieked.

"That's what it's gonna be when I get done with the two of you!" Frances took another long drag off her cigarette. "And where the fuck is Kevin!?"

"Don't know. We was passin' out cookies when Ben and them arrived and found him," Delores said, wringing her hands. "Franny, that steeple fell on top of him and crushed him! Look at God!"

"How is he alive!?" Frances screamed.

"He's the least of our worries right now," Sissy spat. "He ain't talkin', and there ain't no way he's gonna survive that cross. He probably dead already. You and us need to talk about the business."

"Nope. Nuh-uh. I don't want no part of your business."

"Franny, we just need this one shipment, and then we'll never ask you for anything again," Delores bleated.

"What do you expect me to do!? I ain't gonna pack up a bunch of dead Baptists and haul 'em down to your funeral home!"

"We just need a key, and we'll take them."

"I have security cameras! Ben will see you!"

"Not if you turn the cameras off," Delores said. "You just turn the cameras off, and we'll get Hector to go in tonight."

Mid-drag, Frances coughed, realizing Sissy and Delores were missing a huge piece of information. "Hector's been shot!"

Delores and Sissy looked at one another. "Come again?" Sissy said.

"Nakoya shot him! Apparently, it was an accident. I don't know what happened. He spooked her and, 'Bam!' And now Kevin's missin'! So, unless you two have been workin' out real hard with your Silver Sneakers recently, y'all are on your own. I ain't snatchin'."

"What about that boy you was just talkin' to in there?"

"Clint Peppers ain't gonna help you tomb raid! He's a good kid! A decent kid. A smart kid." Frances took another long drag from her cigarette and exhaled. She closed her eyes to calm herself. When she opened her eyes again, she had a better sense of clarity and a stronger hatred for the two women in front of her. "Why am I even talkin' to you two!? Kick rocks!"

Frances stormed away, pulling her hair into a ponytail. She took another long drag from her cigarette and exhaled. She looked at the cigarette like a long-lost lover. "Why did I ever quit you?"

"I'll tell Pembrook it was you who pressured us into the body harvestin' business," Sissy cried out from behind her.

Frances froze. She slowly turned around.

"Kind of suspicious Ray Jackson went missin', don't you think? Right after your momma died? Right after he found that warehouse in Atlanta? Almost looks like he knew somethin'. And after all, it was you who told him that was an address on the side of the van, right? Where that whole investigation started?" Sissy sneered. "Did you kill the sheriff, Frances? I think you might have killed the sheriff."

"I didn't kill Ray Jackson!" Frances screamed, stepping closer to Sissy. "And you don't have any proof."

"No, but I've got security camera footage of all of us down at the funeral home the night Oscar Lopez pulled a gun on us. Security footage of you loadin' up old Oscar into his van and drivin' it away. That same van that wound up at the bottom of Lake Briarwood with Dean Gilbertson's arm inside it."

"Oh, I forgot about Dean's arm!" Delores added excitedly.

"I'll tell Pembrook you killed Carl," Frances retaliated.

"I didn't kill Carl," Sissy said.

"We all know you killed Carl, Sissy! We were there! We saw him! We carried his dead body out of your house!"

"And where's his body now? It was your idea to deliver him to that college. You needed a body."

"*We* needed a body."

Sissy took a step closer. "You think you can fuck me?"

Delores stepped back, afraid to get in the crosshairs of the standoff. "I wish y'all would stop cussin'."

Sissy slowly lit a cigarette. "New deal, 'cause now you done pissed me off," she said, stepping closer. "This is what's gonna happen. *You* are gonna help us get this shipment. And then you're gonna help us get the next shipment. And the shipment after that. And the shipment after that. We invested in *you*, remember? We invested in this company you wanted to start. Remember? It was you. It was all you. You get out when I tell you you can get out. Do you understand, little girl?"

Frances flicked the ash at Sissy. "What if I buy myself out? Huh? I can give you all the land out back behind the bakery. Dusty Dingle's land. I own all that now. Like dozens of acres. Ella signed it over to me. It's probably worth a half million dollars."

Delores nodded. "I think that's a great idea, don't you, Sis? Franny can just buy herself out."

"I think that's a nice start. A good little place for us to expand," Sissy mused. "I'll take it. But you ain't gettin' out."

"Expand?" Frances asked.

"Not enough room at the funeral home. Too many eyes. And I got big plans for the business."

"Why are you doing this to me?" Frances pushed. "Why don't you just go travel? Get a hobby? Go on a cruise? Drop dead?"

Sissy reared back and slapped Frances hard across her face. "A cruise? Like the one my brother went out on and drowned!? Oh, you'd like that, wouldn't you?"

"More than you would ever know." Frances massaged her slapped face. "*Why* are you doing this?"

"Because we's helpin' people, Franny. We're savin' lives. We are out here doin' the Lord's work."

"I must've missed the chapter in the Bible where Jesus sold the head of John the Baptist to a pharmaceutical company in Jerusalem."

"Jesus raised Lazarus from the dead."

"You ain't raisin' anyone from the dead, Sissy Stone."

"You remember the story about The Sermon on the Mount? How there wasn't enough food, so Jesus prayed, and there was enough fish and bread for everyone?" Sissy waved her hand back to the hospital. "Dinner's up!"

"You're psychotic."

"We're givin' life. We are givin' people more time." Sissy smiled and patted Frances's shoulder. "Welcome back, old girl. We gots work to do."


Akasha returned from the cafeteria with two cups of coffee. She handed one to Nakoya. Nakoya took it without any words.

"Why did you shoot Hector?" Akasha calmly and quietly asked. She looked around the waiting room, and there were only five other non-white people in the room—out of about a hundred.

"It was an accident," Nakoya replied.

"Why do you have a gun? Why did you pull a gun from your purse? Why were you running away from that man in the church?"

Nakoya took a deep breath, snapping her head from side to side. She was going to have to dig deep into this story. "I knew that man. I worked with him at the bank. He was my supervisor."

"You said the bank went under. What did he do to you that was so bad you were going to shoot him dead in the church parking lot?"

"Kash, that man was the reason I left Atlanta. He… Kash, he stole a lot of money from some very important people. And I knew about it, and I didn't do anything."

"Did he give you any of the money?"

"No, nothing like that. But… There were some other men. They wanted me to come work for them. More money. Better title. And I was like… Okay, don't judge me, but I was slowly taking company secrets. And one day, that man up in there got in trouble and left the company. Just walked out one day. And I don't know what he knows about me or what I did. I ain't seen that man in nearly three months. But him? Here in Liberty? Sis, that's a bad, bad man. And I got scared. That's why I ran."

"I had no idea there was so much drama working at a bank." Akasha hugged Nakoya tightly. "It's okay. I mean, the stealing secrets bit ain't cool. But you're going to be okay." Akasha released her sister and scooted closer. "But what about those other guys? Whatever happened to them? Why didn't you go work for them instead of coming to Liberty to babysit old white people?"

Nakoya growled, grinding her teeth. "We don't talk about them. It's been months. They ain't told me shit. They ghosted me. I think they were lying this entire time about starting up a new… bank."


Stephen and Stuart Lockhart sat at a small café table outside a quaint restaurant in Florence, Italy. Stephen rubbed his chin, and Stuart quickly swatted his hand away.

"Don't touch it! The doctor said you need to be careful!" Stuart spat.

It had only been a few days since Stephen and Stuart had both undergone their facial reconstruction surgeries. "The swelling is just monstrous. I didn't expect this much swelling," Stephen insisted, staring into the screen of his phone, reflecting his new face. "I don't even look like myself."

"For what we paid, I would hope not."

"Don't you worry? That we'll be walking down the Arno or be standing in a museum and suddenly run into someone from home, and they'll recognize us?"

"I don't think anyone from Liberty is going to show up on the Arno or even a museum, for that matter. Besides, that's why we have hats and sunglasses." Stuart waved to the waiter and made a motion, indicating for the check.

"They hate that, Stuart. You seem like a dumb American when you do that."

Stuart checked his watch. "We need to get back to the hotel. The video call is in a half hour," he said, pulling out his wallet and dropping Euros onto the table. "Let's just go. I'll over tip."

"Oh, sure. Over tip. They love that, too."

They stood, popping open their umbrellas for the walk back to the hotel. Rain made Stephen depressed, but Stuart loved the chill.

"Any word back from Lily?" Stuart asked, watching as Stephen scrolled through emails on his phone.

"None. And it's been three months. How hard is it to find a midget in Georgia?"

"Little person. We don't use that word, Stephen. It's derogatory."

"All this damn woke language nowadays. In ten years, 'little person' will be the new word we're not allowed to say because it'll be considered offensive to tall people."

"Midget was a bad word before all this woke stuff," Stuart lamented. "But you're right. It shouldn't be that hard to trace him." Stuart's brows furrowed. "You know what? Where is Lily? Call her right now. We haven't had a proper update from her in weeks, and she's on retainer. What are we paying her for?"

Stephen pulled his Facetime and dialed for Lily. The name **"Tiger Lily"** appeared on his phone, and a few seconds later, a beautiful Asian woman appeared on the screen, wearing a leather jacket.

Lily squinted into the screen, then pulled back. "Who are you?" she asked.

"It's us!" Stephen excitedly said, pulling the camera back to include Stuart. "It's Stephen and Stuart!"

"Why are you using a filter?"

"It's not a filter!" he exclaimed, gleeful she had not recognized them.

"What did you do to your face?"

Stuart grabbed the phone from Stephen. "Lily?! It's Stuart! Where's Donald? It's been three months, and I'm running out of patience," he shouted as if she couldn't hear him because he was in Europe. "We're paying you good money!"

"Look, man, I don't know what to tell you. I've been trying to find him, but he just vanished. Can't locate anyone from Corona. It's like they were all raptured. And there's a lot of crazy shit happening down here. Seems like every day there's a missing or dead funeral director on the news."

"What are you talking about?"

"I did like you said, and I've been hitting up the list you sent me, but it's just a trail of dead bodies. It's like crazy, man."

"A trail of dead bodies!?" Stephen shrieked. "What… You don't think Donald is killing off our former clients, do you? Why would he do that!?"

"I'm not saying all of them are dead. But there's this one area. It's weird, man. Like out where you guys used to live."

"Out where we used to live!? What about our funeral home!? Is Christopher okay? Who's running the place now?"

"Yo, I'm heading to Liberty tomorrow. Next on my list. Chill out. I told you, I'm workin' on it."

"Why haven't you been there already?" Stuart screamed, shaking the phone.

"I got COVID. It knocked me out, man. That was no joke. Are you staying up on your shots, or are you guys…?" Her voice trailed off.

"Are we what!?"

"You know, like anti-jabby?"

"We have the vaccine," Stephen cooly insisted. "We might be

Republicans, but we're not stupid."

"Cool, cool. You can never tell with old people."

"Call our funeral home and ask for Christopher. Make sure he's okay. And maybe recommend he investigate getting some better security."

"Sure, man, whatever. Look, I gotta go. I just pulled over to pee at this gas station."

"Call Christopher! And call us back right away! And when you get to Liberty…" Stephen's voice trailed off.

"When I get to Liberty, what?"

Stephen and Stuart shared a quick look. They realized with Stephen "missing," Christopher was completely in the dark about body snatching operation. Of course, neither one had any idea their sister was running her own game after accidentally stumbling into it.

"Stay with Sissy. Pretend you're a funeral director, and you're looking for a job."

"Isn't your funeral home the Lockhart Brothers? Don't you think I might… I don't know… Not blend?"

"Figure it out! We're paying you good money!"

"You're gonna have to pay me more if you want me to pretend to have a job while I'm already doing a job!"

"Call Christopher!" Stephen ended the call.

Stuart sighed. "This investor call has to go well."

Stephen nodded nervously. "It will."

"We put everything on the line for this. We were promised millions of dollars. Millions of dollars that a con artist didn't—"

"I'm aware."

"We can't have any more con artists. We need a real investor. Someone who knows what they're doing."


Frances sat on the cold curb of the hospital, rocking from side to side. The doors to the emergency room opened, and Clint walked out, zipping up his hoodie. "Why are you sitting on the curb? It's freezing out here."

Clint unzipped and took off his hoodie. He wrapped it around Frances's shoulders. "Eye of the storm, you know?" he said, pointing to the sky. "We don't get the real brunt of hurricanes here in middle Georgia, but the worst is yet to come. Lots more rain, they're sayin'."

"I don't know what to do."

"About what?"

"Everything, Clint," she said, fighting back hot tears. "And no one knows where Kevin is. He ain't answerin' his phone." She shook her phone for emphasis. "And I'm still not sure what the hell he was doing with Queenie Masters's head! Did you hear about that!?"

Clint nodded. "I heard he walked out of the church with her body over one shoulder and held her skull up by her hair like it was Medusa in that old movie *Clash of the Titans.*"

Frances nodded. "Yeah… Yeah, I heard, too." She shook her head, trying to understand the events that would lead to Kevin heaving a disembodied head triumphantly in the air high atop the steps of the Liberty Baptist Church. "But, like, did they tackle him? Or did he run away? Why was he holding her head!? And most importantly, what in God's holy name made her headless?"

"Those are real good questions, Ms. Frances," Clint said, his attention turning to the distance. He pointed, "Why don't you ask him?"

Frances turned and saw a soaking-wet Kevin walking toward the hospital. He stopped, waving broadly as if he'd never been happier. Frances leaped to her feet, running to him, screaming his name over and over.

"Kevin!? Where have you been!?" She grabbed him in a tight embrace, nearly tackling him to the ground, then grabbed his arms, hands, chest, and face, checking him. Her hands moved from his forehead to his cheeks, to his chin and throat. "Kevin, what the hell happened!?"

"Momma, I think Jesus talked to me today!"

"Kevin Ryan Hunt, why were you holding Queenie Masters's head!?" she shrieked, shaking him.

"Because she got decapitated, Momma! Duh! I had to get her out of there so we could bury her!"

"How!?"

"I picked her up and threw her over my shoulder—"

"How did she get decapitated!?"

"A big piece of wood went like *mrrrowrr*," he said, mimicking the sound of a piece of wood hurtling through the air, "and then *kaaaaaa!* And it clean cut off her head like a buzz saw. And her eyes blinked twice. It was crazy. I mean, like, super scary but crazy. I didn't know eyes did that."

Frances gaped in horrified silence.

"Well, damn," Clint said, bouncing his shoulders as he thrust his fists into the pockets of his hoodie. Clint nodded to Kevin, and Kevin nodded back.

"Why haven't you been answerin' your phone!? I've been calling you for hours!"

"I always leave my phone in the choir room, so I'm not distracted by Pastor's message," he said. "I was talkin' to some of the firemen, and I thought I should come down here to pray over the injured and maybe donate as much blood as possible."

Frances turned back to Clint and held up her finger. "Clint, would you mind givin' us a minute here? I just need to talk to Kevin about some family business."

Clint nodded once, turned, and walked back inside.

Frances shook Kevin by his shoulders again. "Don't ever do that again!"

"Do what?!"

"Scare me like that! I thought you were dead!"

"I'm not dead! Ms. Masters is dead! And a lot of other people, from what I heard."

"About twenty-somethin' other people! And The Man's here! In the hospital! He got flattened by that damn steeple of yours!"

"Well, if that don't sound like the Lord's work—"

"And Hector was shot! He might not make it! That the Lord's work, too? If so, He sucks!"

"Shot!? Who shot Hector!?"

"And Sissy done lost her damned mind! She's blackmailin' me into working with all y'all again! She offered up my bakery to store all them damned dead Baptists so Ben Camden can do his autopsies!  And she needs bodies for a shipment comin' up, and she thinks she can just steal 'em up out of my rec center!"

Kevin clasped his hands and took a deep breath. "Okay, we'll let's look for God's blessin' in this—"

"Kevin! They're gonna poke around and figure out what those coolers were really used for, and Sissy's gonna slip up and blab about everything!"

"What do you suggest we do?"

"I dunno, Kevin!" Frances screamed, completely lost for words. "Maybe we should kill her."

"Momma, you really were the brains behind this operation. Maybe that's why God put you in this situation."

Frances pointed to the hospital. "The Man is right in there! If he wakes up, he's gonna spill the beans!"

"Spills the beans about what?"

"About everything! Too many people know too much! Five can keep a secret if four are dead! We gonna have to start killin' everyone in our circle!"

"Donald Dobkins has only *seen* you. He don't know you were workin' with Sissy and Delores. For all he knows, you were a lone wolf, workin' with Hector, who, by the way, can we circle back to that for a minute? Who shot Hector!?"

"Nakoya."

"Nakoya who works for you down at the old folks' place?!"

"Kevin, I've got like a whole list of questions right now, and why Nakoya shot Hector ain't in the top thirty."

"Well, it dang well should be!"

"Donald Dobkins is in Liberty because he's tracking Oscar's old route. That's why he had Duane's phone."

"So, let's go talk to him."

"We can't talk to him. He's in surgery."

"Woman, you really need to learn how to start prioritizin' your concerns," Kevin insisted. "First, we go deal with the bakery. We'll make sure there's nothing that can lead anything insidious back to you once Ben gets in there. Then we talk with Sissy and figure out this shipment."

"We gotta do something about her, Kevin. She's evil. She's gone off her rocker. It's like she's possessed by the devil. We can't trust her. I ain't never seen anything like it."

Kevin nodded. "We could turn ourselves in," he started.

Frances growled and pushed him away. "No, Kevin! We can't just turn ourselves in!"

"What if we made a deal? Like, what if we go down to the police station and say, 'Hey! We got some information on Dean Gilbertson, but we want to sign an agreement that we won't get in trouble.'"

"Police don't work like that, Kevin."

Pembrook and Ben Camden walked out of the hospital, finding Frances and Kevin on the curb. "See you found your son!" Pembrook cheered from the distance.

Frances and Kevin straightened up, locking eyes with one another. "Let me do all the talkin'," Frances insisted. "Keep your mouth shut."

"I just want to thank you so much for the use of your space, Frances," Ben Camden said.

"Yeah, we was just about to go over and clean up everything and get it ready for y'all. Wanna say tomorrow around noon?" Frances asked.

"We need the space today, Franny. They're already loadin' up bodies as we speak."

"Not a problem, sir!" Kevin said with a smile. "I'll just head over and check the rat traps."

Ben, Pembrook, and even Frances made a face. "Rat traps?" Ben asked.

"Yes, sir! We got rats in there the size of tigers! Most of my traps been catchin' 'em. That shouldn't be a problem, right?"

Ben shook his head, thinking. "I mean, it's not ideal. I used to hear stories about the coroner's office in Los Angeles. They'd store bodies in a unit outside because of lack of space, and the rats tried pullin' the bodies down the drains by pullin' the rope with their little teeth."

"Yep! They got little mouths and real strong teeth! Must've got that Obamacare! I'll head on over right now." Kevin turned to Pembrook. "Can you give me a ride back to the church? Left my car and my phone there."

"Sure. That's fine," Pembrook said, motioning to his sheriff's car in the lot.

"Always wanted to ride in a cop car!" Kevin said, sauntering over to the car.

Pembrook whispered to Frances, "Is he okay?"

"Yeah, you know. He's fine." Frances said, rolling her eyes. "Kids."

"You heard about Queenie Masters's head?"

"The kid's fine. Sure, he's got a loose screw or two, but he's fine," Frances said, walking back into the hospital.


"Hello, is 'dis de Lockhart Brothers Funeral Home?" Lily asked, laying on a thick Japanese accent and finishing with a giggle.

"Yes, ma'am, it is," Christopher said, seated at his desk in the main office. "How may I help you today?"

"Oh, how you say?" she said, giggling again. "I want to know. Is dis where the Lockhart family own?"

"Yes, ma'am. This here is the Lockhart Brothers. Mr. Stuart and Mr. Stephen are deceased now, but I'm helpin' run things here. Along with their sister, Sissy."

Lily sat up. "Ohhhh! Mrs. Sissy is working at the funeral home! Oh," she said again, realizing Sissy could be in danger. "Oh, no."

"What's that? Is something wrong?" Christopher asked.

Lily contemplated hanging up, then asked, "Is she there? May I speak with her?"

"No, ma'am, she is not. I don't know if you heard, but there was a big fire down at our church this morning, and a whole bunch of people died."

"Oh, no!"

"Oh, yes! We gonna have a bunch of people up in here soon. I'm sorry, ma'am. Did you need to plan a funeral?"

"Okay, bye!" Lily said, hanging up. Her head dropped to her chest. "Dammit. I gotta go to Mayberry."

Frances stood in the doorway to Hector's room, watching the machines keeping him alive beep. The elevator opened at the end of the hall, and Delores and Sissy emerged with a plate of cookies. Sissy dropped them off at the nurse's station, making small talk while Delores hurried ahead to Frances.

"How is he?" Delores asked.

"How could you possibly let her blackmail me like this!?" Frances hissed. "You just sat there! Momma is rollin' in her grave right now!"

"We just really need to get this shipment out. It's an important client—"

"I don't care, Delores! I don't care! It's bad enough y'all got Kevin wrapped up in this!"

"I'll work on Sissy, but the drop is happening tomorrow."

"So, what are y'all gonna do? Just rob the bakery in the middle of the night!? This ain't like slidin' Dean Gilbertson's coffin out a mausoleum."

Sissy's heels clicked and clacked on the tiled floor as she approached Frances and Delores. "Did you know from where you guys are standing, I can hear every word down at the end of the hall? The acoustics in this place are just marvelous." Sissy leaned closer to Frances.

"You're Shakespearean," Frances seethed.

"Don't worry your pretty little head about the bodies. We've been doin' this for months. We don't need your helpful leadership anymore."

"So, what do you need? I ain't cuttin' up any bodies."

Sissy grabbed Frances by her biceps. "Your muscle." She slapped her hands around her cheeks. "And your face. Everyone in town knows you're still grievin' the death of your momma. You know better than anyone how important a closed casket funeral can be."

"You evil…" Frances shook her head, then changed the subject. "Why was Hector in the church parking lot?"

"The Man came by the funeral home yesterday. We invited him to church. We thought it best to get him out in public," Delores said.

"And do what?!" Frances quietly shrieked.

"Bring him in. Think about it. Donald Dobkins was running an entire operation all over the Southeast. He has the contacts."

"Hello!?" Frances said, framing her own face with her hands. "We know he wants to kill me!"

"Yes, Franny! He wants to kill *you!* Not us! What are you not understanding about this?" Sissy asked, circling her hands about herself and Delores. "This ain't about *you.*"

Delores put her hands between the two feuding women. "But look at God! He done flattened Donald Dobkins with his own cross! Look at God!"

"He's still in surgery, Delores! He might live!"

"Looked like that cross broke damn nearly every bone in his body and probably flattened every organ in his body the size of a pancake! He ain't comin' out of surgery," Sissy said.

Frances pulled the strap of her purse over her shoulder. "I guess we'll see about that. And I'm sure if he does, he won't mind at all that you two were also involved in the take-down of his very successful southeastern operation. You remember *this?*" she said, circling her hands about the whole group.

"I'll tell him it was all your idea."

"My idea? You're the one who owns the funeral home. The one formerly owned by your brothers, who mysteriously disappeared." Frances took a step closer. "Want to know what the most dangerous poison in the world is, Sis?"

Sissy glared back, unflinching.

Frances leaned into Sissy's face and spat, "Doubt."

After a major storm in the South, one can always count on vibrant, beautiful skies. As the sun began to set over Liberty, the horizon was filled with orange, red, and amber clouds.

Ben Camden stood in the church parking lot, overseeing the removal of the bodies, all lined up under a privacy tent outside the church fellowship hall.

Sheriff Pembrook removed his Stetson, leaning against the door to his vehicle, watching the firefighters, EMTs, and coroner techs do their jobs. "What an awful day," he quietly said to himself.

Akasha drove Nakoya home. They were only allowed to visit Hector's room for a minute. Only allowed to stand at a distance and watch the machines attempt to keep him alive. Akasha furiously rubbed at a fleck of blood from her chin. Nakoya never moved the entire twenty-minute ride back to the house.

Kevin meticulously surveyed the entire bakery for anything that looked remotely of death. He found a box of body bags under the counter and laughed, "Dang, man! That could have been real bad!"

The Reverend Bill White visited with the remaining parishioners in the waiting room. Edie and Juanita catatonically watched from chairs on the other side of the room.

"He don't seem too sad," Edie quietly said. Edie had cried all day over the death of Queenie, while Juanita seemed to be forcing tears. "Queenie's dead, Juanita."

"I know. I saw her," she said.

"But you don't seem that sad, Juanita. Are you in shock?"

"People grieve in different ways. Besides, she's with Jesus now."

"I know, but I want her here with us!"

"Well, that's just selfish, Edie. She's up in heaven now singing in God's choir."

Exhausted and numb, Edie clasped the purse shut and walked away.

"Where are you going, Edie?"

"Home, Juanita. I'm goin' home because my friend is dead. Because I watched a two-by-four from the roof of our church slice off my friend's head. In church. You'd think church would be a safe space. But apparently it is not. Apparently, in the Lord's house, you can lose your life." She took a few steps, stopped, and turned back to Juanita. "And your head."

"I'll be praying for you, Edie."

"You'll be… Juanita, Queenie is dead. She's dead!"

The small crowd in the waiting room turned to watch Edie Trussell slowly lose her ever-loving mind.

"You understand me, right? Juanita? She's dead! She's real dead! She died in God's house! She wasn't doin' anything but praisin' his name and—"

"And God took her home, Edie. What are you not understandin' about any of this? She's home now. I wish I could go with her."

"I wish you could too," Edie quietly said, feeling betrayed by Juanita. "I don't even know you anymore."

Edie staggered out of the hospital, feeling her world falling apart. Feeling, for the first time, a question of her faith.

Edie gripped the handle of her leather purse, realizing Queenie had no surviving family. All Queenie had in this world was Edie and Juanita. Edie looked to the sky and cried aloud, "Guess I'm gonna have to plan your funeral myself, old girl!"


Frances walked away from the hospital, thrusting her hands into her leather duster. She felt a wad of paper and pulled it out. It was the check from Cooper. *Oh, that's right. I'm a millionaire.* Frances heard the motor of a car pull up behind her. She didn't have to turn around to know it was Clint Peppers. She heard the rap music get louder as he rolled down the window.

"We have to stop meeting like this!" Clint shouted, his torso half-hanging out the window.

Frances stopped walking. She turned around. "You stalkin' me, Clint Peppers?"

"Depends. You want me to stalk you?"

"I've had a long day, Clint Peppers."

"You don't think I haven't? Do you know how many people bled, pissed, and shat on me today?"

"You had a shower?"

"I've had four."

Frances strolled to the passenger side of the car, climbing in. "It's warm in here," she said, spinning the passenger vents onto her face.

Clint hit the accelerator. He turned the music down, and they rode in silence for a good three minutes, each seemingly daring the other to speak first.

They passed the Dairy King. Frances shook her head, remembering she was just slightly younger than Clint when she worked there and had very inappropriate relations with the manager.

"What?" Clint asked, catching her smirk.

"I used to work there," she said, pointing to the shop and tapping on the window. Other than a slap of paint from ten years ago, nothing had changed in the years since she had been an employee. "Back when I was your age."

Clint nodded.

"Did you do anything for your birthday?"

He shook his head. "Nope. Had cake with my parents and watched a movie on the TV. Had to get up early to run ten miles."

Clint let off the accelerator as they approached the church. They both peered at the winding-down chaos of the day. "You wanna?" he asked.

Frances nodded. Clint pulled his car to the side of the road and parked. They approached the police line. Denny Brewster, one of Liberty's finest, walked over, tipping his hat to Frances.

"Howdy-do, Frances. How you doin'?"

"You know, I think we've all had better days. How many dead people?" she asked.

"Last count was twenty-four." He pointed to the tent in the distance. "Twenty-four here. Not sure how many have passed since the hospital."

"We lost three so far," Clint offered.

"Twenty-seven," Denny mused. "That's like the size of a single Sunday School class, just gone."

"What about that little person you guys found? The one under the cross?" Frances asked. "Know anything about him? Like why he was here?"

Denny started to speak, but Clint cut him off. "I can't believe he survived that. That cross must have weighed nearly two tons!"

"That was God!" Denny said, smiling.

"That was something," Frances replied. "It's just awful. Imagine having to go through life with everyone making fun of you, and then you get killed by a falling cross in a Baptist church parking lot," Frances said, shaking her head.

"You know he broke so many damn bones in his body, but not a single organ was damaged? How is that even possible? They were putting his body in a cast when I left. But yeah, damnedest thing. Looks like he's gonna live. It's a miracle."

"He's gonna… He's gonna live?" Frances shook her head. "That's just great," she said under her breath, with a slight laugh.

"What was that?" Clint asked.

"I said, that's just great. It's a miracle," she said, looking to the sky. "A miracle from heaven. Look at God." Frances looked skyward, then softly growled, "Just look at Him."

Denny leaned in. "Them firefighter boys over there? Damn near pissed themselves when they pulled that cross of him. They seen a little person underneath, and one of 'em thought it was a leprechaun! Thought a portal from hell had opened up here in Liberty!"

Frances nodded. "Maybe there is a portal to hell here in Liberty. That would explain so much."

Denny laughed. "We're all about to head over to your place with the first load. Thanks again for letting Ben set up in there."

"Don't mention it. Not like I had much of a choice, right?" Frances said, surveying the destruction. She turned back to Clint. "Can we go?"

"Where you wanna go?" he asked.

She wanted a drink. She wanted to down an entire bottle of vodka and run through the cold, dead crops out behind the old chicken houses on the family farm. She wanted to scream at the moon and cry till it hurt. She wanted to punch a hole in a wall. She wanted to drive a hundred miles an hour and end it all, plowing into a tree.

"Take me home."


Clint's Mustang slowly made its way down to the long, gravel driveway to the farmhouse. He parked, pointing to Frances's daddy's truck parked near the house. "Any word on the truck?"

"Nope, but I recently came into some money, so I'm just gonna get on the internet and see if I can find a new engine."

"Why don't you just buy a new truck?"

"Because it was my daddy's. You wouldn't understand." She opened the door. "Thanks for the ride."

Clint tightly grabbed her forearm, and Frances stopped. "You want me to walk you to your door?"

She looked at his large hand, gently circling her tiny wrist. "Sure."

"I mean, psycho killers, right?"

"Totally. Psycho killers. Portal to hell. Who knows what's in that house right now?"

He followed her up the steps to the front door. Frances turned the doorknob and pushed open the door.

"You don't lock your door?" Clint asked.

"Nobody locks their door in Liberty," she replied, taking a step closer to him. "Remember?"

"You want me to come in?" he asked.

"Do you want to come in?"

"Do you want me to want to come in?"

"Do you want me to want you to want to come in?" she asked, cocking her head and taking a step closer.

"I just want to make sure you're safe."

"I'm always safe."

Frances pushed open the door and walked inside, the screen door bouncing twice, lightly bouncing before settling. She walked into the pitch-black living room. Clint stood outside the screened door.

"You're gonna have to invite me in if you want me to come," he said, lowering his voice.

"Why? You a vampire or somethin', and I don't know it?"

"Consent."

"Consent," Frances whispered back in the dark.

Frances stood in the dark. Clint couldn't see her, but she could see all of him, backlit from the moonlight, as he stood on the porch. She placed her hand on her chest, feeling her heart beat wildly through her cotton blouse. She pulled her hand up to her neck, feeling her pulse beat in time.

She took a breath and held it. "Come."

Clint threw back the screened door so fast and so furious it broke the top hinge. He kicked the door closed behind him as he bounded into the living room, finding Frances standing in the center of the living room.

His giant hands engulfed her face and neck as he pulled her toward him, kissing her.

Frances had to break the kiss to breathe. She took a deep breath, then devoured him as she pushed him backward. He grabbed her wrists as he lost his balance, and they both toppled onto the sofa. Clint hit first, and she straddled his lap.

She grabbed his face and neck, kissing him. He moved down her neck as she comedically fought to free herself from her heavy leather duster.

"Want me to—" Clint asked.

"I got it!" she insisted as she yanked it off her body and slammed it on the ground.

He spun her around, slamming her back onto the sofa, pulling himself on top of her.

He ripped open her blouse as buttons hit the wood floor. Frances laughed, kissing him harder. *I've always wanted someone to do that!* she thought. *And now, this eighteen-year-old*—"I can sew those back on," he offered.

Frances slammed her hands into his chest and pushed him off. Clint sat up with his hands in the air like someone on the other side of a gun in a hold-up.

"What's up? You good?" Clint asked.

"You're eighteen."

"I'm legal."

"I'm not eighteen."

Clint's eyes adjusted in the dark. From a sliver of moonlight through a window, he saw Frances resting on her elbows. "I don't care."

They stared at each other, panting. Frances's eyes adjusted, following every muscle bulging through his clothes.

Clint repeated, "I don't care."

"Well, this is awkward," said a deep voice in the dark.

Clint jumped off the sofa, and Frances reached under the sofa, pulling the shotgun out with the precision of a military assassin, cocking it, and aiming it into the corner.

"I've got a gun!" Frances screamed, aiming in the direction of the voice.

"I'm gonna turn on the lights, and I'm going to ask you to lower the gun," the voice calmly said.

Clint stood up, ready to attack whoever sat watching them in the dark. "Motherfucker, I've been lookin' for you all day," he growled, snapping his neck from side to side. The long-suppressed redneck had finally come out, and Clint was hungry for a fight.

The lamp in the corner switched on, revealing Ray Jackson dressed in a very expensive black suit.

Frances's eyes widened. She stood up, taking two steps closer to get a better look. "Ray Jackson… What are you doin' in my house?"

"I'm here because your life is in danger." He turned and looked Kevin up and down. "And who the fuck are you?"

# CHAPTER FIVE

# WHAT REALLY HAPPENED TO RAY JACKSON

The day after Birdie Hunt's funeral, Sheriff Ray Jackson moved his entire life into a storage unit in Athens, Georgia, and put his house on the market.

Sheriff Ray Jackson left a short, handwritten note on his desk, along with his gun, his work phone, and his Stetson, informing Pembrook and the other officers at the station he was officially resigning.

His house was sold three weeks later to a young lawyer who graduated from Georgia State University the previous spring. It was sold by the same real estate firm who had swindled Frances over the bakery.

The morning after he resigned, Ray Jackson drove his Range Rover to the Hartsfield-Jackson (no relation, obviously) International Airport in Atlanta, where he walked up to the Southwest counter and bought a one-way ticket to Palm Springs, California.

Ray had never been to Palm Springs, but Leland Peters and Mark Jones-Peters (the gay couple who owned the pricey coffee house, bakery, and boxed lunch shop in a Victorian house just off the square) raved about the weather and hiking a giant mountain overlooking the desert paradise. "The vibes are just magical," Leland had said.

"There's just an energy there," Mark insisted. "It resets you. It transforms you."

Ray landed at the small airport clutching one suitcase with shorts, one pair of khakis, and a few nice, short-sleeved shirts. He figured that he could buy anything else he needed at the nearby Cabazon Outlets, which he had read about in a magazine on the plane. The sun was warm. The energy bouncing off Mount San Jacinto had a buzz. It *was* magic.

"Dang, man," Ray said under his breath, taking in his new environment as he strolled out of the airport. Ray had never been past Texas. Ray caught a taxi to the Hyatt on North Palm Canyon and checked into a room overlooking the main thoroughfare. The room was nice to Ray, but most of the locals would tell their visiting friends to stay at The Ace or The Parker.

Ray unpacked, changed shirts, and threw on his sunglasses before taking a walk down the street to get his bearings.

He found himself at a hip restaurant called Lulu's, where he sat at the bar, ordering a beer on tap and a flatbread pizza.

*Ding!* went the phone in his pocket. It was a text from Pembrook. **"Call me right now, buddy. You can't resign. Been calling. We need to talk."**

*I gotta get rid of this damn phone,* he thought. He'd had this phone number since he was in high school, but now it was the time to change it. To start a new life. He blocked Pembrook's number. He scrolled through his Most Recent Calls and blocked them as well.

He paused at **"Hunt, Fran."** He didn't block her.

While Ray waited for his flatbread, he nursed his beer and opened the internet app on his phone. He searched the words **"Body Parts Selling, Georgia."** Before the actual links appeared on the page, a factoid appeared: **"Georgia law criminalizes attempts to buy and sell body parts unless they are for medical or scientific purposes. The punishment, if convicted, will be a felony conviction."**

The first link was **"Charged with Buying and Selling Human Body Parts in Georgia? We Can Help."**

"Dang, man," he whispered, sipping his beer. The first page of the results covered the law in Georgia, informing the reader that selling body parts was illegal. Following those results, local news stories appeared about people who had purchased stolen body parts for personal collections. He found links about people purchasing human skulls on Instagram for their decorative art projects. He found stories about people selling body parts to people in other states, which brought additional charges of mail fraud, wire fraud, and interstate transportation of stolen property.

He found Facebook groups of people selling brains from crematories out in the open. He found Reddit threads of users speaking in code to acquire remains.

Ray Jackson knew the situation in Liberty was much bigger than Facebook Marketplace and an Esty shop from hell. If Melody Wang and the FBI were involved, there was clearly an already much bigger web. The way Melody Wang spoke to him convinced him this was an ongoing investigation. He had discovered a massive warehouse, big enough to employ dozens of individuals. But what had happened to those employees and their equipment? Why leave just the one headless body? How were they tipped off? And more importantly, exactly how was Frances involved?

The warehouse was over two hours from Liberty. If someone was acquiring human body parts from funeral homes in Liberty, might they be doing it all over the state of Georgia? And was it just Georgia? Was this a regional business operating illegally?

Could there be other "body farms?"

Ray Jackson downed his beer. Just as the flatbread arrived, he pointed to his empty glass. The bartender asked, "Another?"

 Ray nodded.

An older woman slid into an empty seat next to Ray. The bar area was practically empty, and Ray wasn't looking for company or conversation.

"This seat taken?" she asked with a thick New York accent.

Ray shook his head. The woman ordered a house martini before the bartender could slide her a menu. "And I'll just have the spaghetti special."

*Spaghetti.* The plate Frances had ordered the night of their date. He shook his head. *The night she used me for information.* The night she ordered the removal of Dean Gilbertson's casket from his eternal resting place.

"You like spaghetti?" the woman asked Ray.

"I hate it. It's literally the one thing I hate more than any other food known to man."

The woman rolled her eyes and pulled a novel from her very expensive bag. Ray didn't know much about bags, but he knew that bag cost more than a few thousand dollars. She plopped the book on the counter. Ray's eyes peeked at the title: "***The Story of Her Bones—Written by Libby Meyer.***" The cover art was a skeletal woman in a box.

She opened the book, took the red marker holding her place,

and uncapped it with her teeth. She set the reading glasses from the chain around her neck onto the bridge of her nose and began reading, occasionally scratching out a word or making notes.

Ray's eyes darted from articles on his phone to the bloody notes the woman was making in the book. "Sorry, I have to ask, do you really not like that book?" he asked. "You're just bloodying up them pages. You a teacher?"

"No, it's the galley version. It's just easier for me to make changes when I see them in print. Writer. Used to be a teacher many years ago."

"Ah," Ray responded, immediately searching "Libby Meyer" on his phone. He shifted away from the woman as the results popped up.

The woman he was seated next to looked like an older, less glamorous version of "Libby Meyer" from the images on the internet. Wikipedia informed him Libby Meyer had published over forty crime novels, and her current worth was over ten million dollars.

"You know, I was just kiddin' about the spaghetti. Penne pasta is the worst. Hate them little tubes."


Over the next three days, Ray and Libby became fast friends. He purchased all the books of hers The Best Bookstore on Tahquitz Canyon had on hand, and the staff were only too eager to order other books they didn't have in the store. He tore through them during the day by the pool and at night on his balcony overlooking North Palm Canyon, usually following a dinner shared with Libby.

Libby was probably fifteen, maybe twenty years older than Ray. There was no romantic spark between the two. Without speaking extensively to one another about the collective elephants in their rooms, they each knew the other was working through some sadness and loss.

Libby owned a home in the Movie Colony area of Palm Springs. Her husband had died of cancer a few months earlier, and she was behind on her deadlines. While her editors tried to be as understanding as possible, "Libby Meyer" was a brand with rabid fans. Her editor had flown to Palm Springs a week earlier from New York, insisting *The Story of Her Bones* hit bookstands before Memorial Day. The book was practically finished and just needed a final polish.

Libby joked that Ray was taking up all her time, but the truth was, Libby saw in Ray a new character for her next book: a small-town sheriff who walks away from the woman he loved because she never loved him back. When he spoke of Liberty, he spoke with pride and great affection.

"I've got to visit this Liberty someday. Sounds lovely," she said over a house martini at a restaurant called Eight4Nine (for the address of the street, 849 N. Palm Canyon.)

Libby called Eight4Nine her "office." She would arrive Monday through Friday at 11:30 a.m., about a half hour after they opened, and order a house martini and rotate her meals throughout the week with the cobb salad, the carne asada flatbread, the burger, the cheese quesadilla, and the cauliflower steak. Her usual spot was the high-top next to the bar, under the photos of Michael Jackson and Elizabeth Taylor, shot by the owner, John Paschal.

"It was a great place to grow up," Ray said. "But I'm looking for a new adventure now. New place to put down roots."

"I don't think Palm Springs is a great place for you to put down roots, Ray. It's the desert. Not a lot of great soil. Doesn't rain a lot. Palm Springs isn't for everyone. But for those of us who she calls to, it's an oasis," Libby said, waving to the owner as he waved back. "It's like a small town. Everyone knows everyone. But your dating options would be terrible."

"I'm hoping Palm Springs will tell me what to do. Some friends told me this place 'resets' you."

"Oh, it definitely does that."

One afternoon, Ray and Libby took the tram to the top of San Jacinto Peak, overlooking Palm Springs and the miles and miles of desert.

"You ever heard of body parts being sold on the black market, Libby?"

"Sure. It's a pretty big deal. Very underground."

"People steal 'em out of funeral homes?"

"Depends. Some of the brokerage companies have deals with the local funeral homes and hospitals. And prisons. Bodies have to be recently deceased. No disease. No embalming. A lot of crematories are involved."

"Right… Because you could just say you burned 'em up—"

"And give them fake cremains."

"Why don't we just legalize it?"

"You can only donate your body to science. You can't sell it."

"Why not?"

"I don't make the rules!" she said with a laugh.

"Is that what your new book is about?"

"Oh, no. My book is about a woman who gets hit by a car so hard that basically her body explodes and goes in all directions." Libby's eyes shifted to the mountain landscape as the tram ascended into the sky. "But that's a good idea for a story."

"Yeah, I think it is, too," Ray said. "It's something I've been kicking around myself."

Ray and Libby arrived at the mountain station, high above the desert. Snow was still on the ground. Ray asked Libby if she wanted to take a small hike around the top of the mountain, and she laughed. "We only came up here for a drink and enjoy the view. It's forty degrees colder up here, and we'd freeze to death. Maybe in the summer. You'll have to come back then. It's perfect."

Ray took in the beauty of the horizon from the Lookout Lounge as the sun began to set in the distance. "I gonna step outside for a second. Be right back."

He pushed onto the lookout while Libby ordered another drink. He pulled his personal cell phone from his jacket pocket and hurled it over the side of the mountaintop, watching it bounce on a few rocks before disappearing from view.

Ray spent nearly ten days in Palm Springs before booking a one-way ticket to Washington, DC. He marched into the FBI headquarters and asked to speak with Melody Wang. The front desk attendant informed him, "Sir, the FBI doesn't work like that."

Ray leaned over the desk and said, "You can tell her she's got a walk-in."

Nearly an hour later, Melody Wang floated into the lobby. "What do you need?" she asked. "Why are you here? This is weird."

"I want a job."

"We're not hiring. And you're not qualified." She cocked her head slightly. "Do you know something?"

"I can be like a consultant. I know you're investigatin' them body snatchers, and I want to help. I want in."

"Why?"

"Because I believe in justice."

Melody crossed her arms. "Go home, cowboy. Let the professionals handle this. We don't need your help." Melody spun on her Stiletto and walked away. She threw a "Have a safe flight back to Georgia" over her shoulder as she badged herself back beyond security.

He knew the disappearance of Stephen Lockhart was suspicious from the day Delores told him at the Counter. *Two brothers missing? Where did the insurance money go?*

Ray hadn't expected to get shut down by Melody Wang. He had nowhere to go. He had nothing to lose.

He realized what he had to do. He embraced his purpose in life.

Ray heaved himself from the leather chair and walked out the front door of the FBI headquarters. As he stepped onto the cold but sunny Pennsylvania Avenue sidewalk, he slid his sunglasses around his eyes and whispered under his breath, "I'll do it myself."

Frances lowered the shotgun, and Clint relaxed his kung-fu stance.

"Sheriff Jackson?" Clint asked.

"Clint Peppers? Is that you?!" Ray asked.

"Sheriff Jackson?" Clint asked again, trying to understand why the sheriff had broken into Frances's home and was sitting in the dark of her living room.

"Clint, Ray. Ray, Clint," Frances quickly fired, adjusting her skirt.

"Ain't you like a minor?" Ray asked.

"He's legal."

"Wow," is all Ray could weakly scoff.

"My life *was* in danger. I'm aware. You can leave now," Frances said.

"Why was your life in danger?" Clint asked.

"Baby, you should probably head on home. I'll call you tomorrow." Frances turned to Ray, then added, "Or maybe you could just come over after school."

"But if your life—"

"Son, get your ass out of here before I toss it out," Ray insisted.

Clint adjusted himself and nodded to Ray. "Y'all have a good night."

Clint left.

Ray and Frances glared long and hard at each other in growing contempt. Frances stood, walking into the kitchen. "You want some coffee?"

"Gonna need something stronger than that," he said, following her.

"Well, I think Kevin's got an energy drink in here," she said, opening the refrigerator. "You want sour apple or unicorn flavor? But warning, these things might kill you." She placed both drinks in front of him. "On second thought, why don't you just have both of 'em. Knock yourself out."

"Frances Hunt, why are you screwin' a teenager?"

"I am not screwin' a teenager."

"What would have happened if I wasn't sittin' there!?"

"I dunno, dad," she snapped back. "I remember tellin' you to get off my property three months ago. If anything, I could call your friends down at the station and have you arrested for breakin' and enterin'." She ran water into the antique kettle.

"Clint Peppers—"

"Let it go, Ray! Who I sleep with is not and never has been any of your business."

"You used me."

"You drove my momma to blow her brains out. I think that makes us even."

Ray's head dropped. "You don't know that," he quietly retorted.

"I know you know what happened out there in that barn! I know you know I knew about ol' Oscar's van! I know you know my life was in danger. How's that? How did you know my life was in danger, Ray Jackson? You gone psychic all the sudden?"

Ray took a chair at the kitchen table with the sour apple energy drink. "You're not drinkin'."

"I'm literally makin' tea right in front of you."

"Alcohol. Your face is clear. Your eyes are bright." He pointed to the kettle. "Tea."

"What do you want, Ray?"

"I know you're involved in all this. I'm just missing some pieces. And I want to know the truth." Ray popped the energy drink and took a big swig. "Here's what I got. You somehow become a human remains broker, seemingly by accident because your momma and them was lookin' for shoes. You met Oscar, and he threatened y'all, but y'all managed to get the gun away from him and bring him back here, where he was accidentally killed. But you… You're smart. You figured out a way to drop off Oscar's corpse with the guy he was workin' for. How, if you don't mind me askin'? How did you get the address to his warehouse?"

Frances glowered at Ray. He was no longer *Sheriff* Ray Jackson. She didn't have to answer his questions. But he knew *something*. And judging from the nice suit, he knew a lot.

"Phone was ringin' in his pants. I answered it. Guy was lookin' for his delivery. I told him I had it. He gave me his address."

"His phone. Duh. That's… That seems almost too easy—"

"That's what happened, Ray!"

"I'm just sayin' I spent months tryin' to figure out how you found your way to that warehouse, and it was just a phone call."

"I asked for his address, and I told him I'd deliver Oscar's haul to him. And I did."

"His nightly haul?"

Frances shrugged. "I guess. We didn't do a lot of talkin'."

"Guy on the phone didn't ask why you was the one droppin' everything off at his warehouse?"

"He's a man, Jackson. History has taught me as long they get what they want, they usually don't ask a lot of unnecessary questions. Unlike you."

Ray laughed. "And you just decided to write the address on the side of the van

because…"

"Because there weren't no paper out in the barn, and I needed somethin' to write on! You

want me to tell this story or not?! I don't like it when people interrupt me!" Frances pulled a coffee mug from the cabinet and a box of tea from the pantry. "Got back to Liberty. Kevin and I sank the van to get rid of it. And you know… Whoopsie."

"If that one container hadn't surfaced, you'd have gotten away with it. Why'd you leave one container in the van?"

"I guess one of them workers missed it. I saw it back there, but I didn't think that one damned box was going to find its way to you in your little boat while you was out fishin'. And I sure as shit didn't think you was gonna go all *Hardy Boys and the Case of the Disembodied Arm* on it."

"You got greedy. You decided to strike out on your own."

"Hector showed up looking for Oscar. Lo-Jack on the van, before you ask. I told him what happened. We teamed up. We took Sissy and Delores's investment—"

Ray held up his hands, and his eyes went wide. "Hold up. Hold up. Wait. No." Ray gathered himself, taking in the news. "Sissy Stone and Delores Rogers are involved in all this insanity!? What are those two sweet old ladies doin' in all this mess!? How could you get them involved!?"

Frances growled. "Ray, interrupt me one more damned time." He pretended to zip his lips. "We rented the old Womack Bakery. We bought a bunch of freezers. We started reachin' out to colleges and universities. We got Athens State. That's when Delores and you had a little chat, and you told her about findin' the van."

"I told her that in private."

"You told an old woman a secret in Liberty and thought it was gonna stay a secret? Boy, you're a special kind of stupid. And then you asked me out. We went on a date. You told me about Dean. I had the boys steal his casket because I knew if you questioned Jim Jennings at Memorial Gardens, he'd sing, and I couldn't risk him giving us up."

"You were workin' with Jim by that time?"

"We was workin' with everyone, Ray. We was working with everyone Oscar and Hector sourced in the zone."

"That didn't answer my question."

"Yes, asshole, I was workin' with Jim. But we didn't tell him we was stealin' the casket in the middle of the night. We figured the less he knew, the more convincin' he'd be when you rolled in. And then I slipped up when I suggested '141 Corona' was an address."

"But did you?"

"Huh?"

"We was in the war room, and you said, 'That's an address.' You knew what you was doin'. You set up Donald Dobkins."

"Wow. Cool. So, you know the evil munchkin's name? You really have done all your research."

"Donald Dobkins, also known as The Man. And you sent me in there blind."

"I didn't send you anywhere! I tried to stop you! I called Donald the second you told me you were goin' to Atlanta. I told him to clear out of there. I was tryin' to protect him. *He* set *me* up by leaving ol' Oscar's body behind for *you* to find!"

The kettle on the stove began to lightly whistle. Frances poured water into her mug. "Wait, all this time, you thought *I* was settin' *him* up to take over his business? If you got in there and caught him red-handed, he'd have rolled on me! Do you think I'm stupid!?"

"So, he gets away, leaves the body."

Frances held up a finger. "Quid pro quo. How did you know headless Oscar was *my* Oscar?" Frances asked.

"Fingerprints from the crime lab came back with your prints and his prints on the van."

"Nope. You had a headless corpse and a fake ID. How did you know headless Oscar was *my* Oscar?"

Ray looked down at the table. Frances scoffed. "Momma told you. Of course." Frances dunked a teabag into her mug, exhaling her rage. "Did she tell you here? At the table?"

"You really want me to answer that question?"

"Where were you when she did it? When she shot herself in the head?"

"In the barn. I heard the gun. I ran in and found her in her room."

"I hate you."

"I know."

Frances spit in his face. Ray wiped the spit from his face with the back of his hand, then wiped his hand on his pants.

"Why'd you do it, Frances?" he asked. "Why would you take up a life of crime? Stealin' dead people and selling 'em illegally? You could go to jail."

"I needed the money. We needed the money. We was gonna lose everything." Frances fought back a stray tear, rubbing her eyes furiously. "We was days away from losin' the farm. And that money saved us. It was just enough to get my life back on track. It afforded me a new opportunity to save my life. Save Kevin's life. And I'd do it again if I was in that same situation."

A silence fell over the kitchen for what seemed like an eternity. Frances and Ray waited for the other to speak or make a move. Ray would sip his drink. Frances would blow on her tea.

Ray unclipped a set of keys on his belt and slammed them on the table.

"This is a keyring with keys to every funeral home in the area. I've tested every key. In the past week, I've learned that most of the undertakers at each of these homes have either gone missin' or been murdered."

Frances's eyes widened. "Where'd you get those keys?"

"They was in the van. They don't look familiar?"

Frances shrugged. "Oscar's old route?"

Ray shrugged. "I assume so. Don't got Oscar around anymore to ask. You got a Ouija board up in here?"

Frances leaned against the counter and shook her head. "Hector went by Duane Brown's crematory and said somethin' felt off. He called Duane's phone, and Donald answered. We assume that's why he came here. He was lookin' for me."

"Because he thinks you set him up?"

"Who knows? Why don't you go down to the hospital and ask him yourself?"

Ray's eyebrows furrowed. "Huh?"

Frances laughed. "Oh, you're behind. He's in intensive care at Liberty Memorial. Guess you're not as good a detective as you think you are."

Ray's eyebrow raised. "Why's he in the hospital?"

"Jesus crushed him with Liberty Baptist Church's steeple this morning."

Ray blinked twice. "What?"

"Did you not see all the flames and smoke? Church caught on fire. Lightnin' hit it. Killed about twentysomething people. Decapitated Queenie Masters."

"This all happened today!?" he asked.

Frances nodded. "Ain't no way he's gonna live." Frances took a sip of her tea. "So, I guess that's how your little story ends, huh? You break into my house in a nice suit to tell me an evil goblin wants to kill me, and"—she pointed to the keys—"he might have been going on a killin' spree all over the tri-county area. How underwhelming."

Frances looked him up and down. He was in the best shape she'd ever seen him. He was tan. He had a little bit of stubble. She didn't know if she wanted to kiss him or kill him. "Why are you in a nice suit? Where the hell did you go? You holed up in some motel in Macon with a map on the walls and string connected to photos like a serial killer?"

"I had a business meeting with some investors for my next venture."

"And what, pray tell, is that?"

"I'm launching a podcast on the big business of black market body harvesting. You see, this is a whole world of evil that most Americans don't know anything about. And I'm going to expose it." Ray leaned over the table. "And you're gonna help me take it down."

Sissy and Delores sat in the front seat of Delores's Crown Vic, watching as Ben Camden's transport techs finished unloading bodies into the bakery. After a bit of small talk, they got into their separate vans and pulled out of the gravel lot.

Kevin sat in the backseat. "This feels so wrong," he stated, shaking his head.

"We just need to pick through the bodies and get us the three we need. Three people we don't like," Sissy said.

"We don't even know who they got in there!" Delores whispered.

"It's gonna be like Christmas mornin'!" Sissy giggled. "Remember when you didn't know what you were gonna get because Santa had wrapped everything up in little boxes!?"

"There's somethin' seriously wrong with you, Ms. Stone. You done gone off the deep end. You turned evil," Kevin said. "When we get this delivery done, I'm gettin' out."

"You ain't gettin' out anytime soon. We're down a man with Hector in the hospital."

"Oh, I'm gettin' out!  You can't tell me what to do—"

Sissy spun around in her seat, slapping him with a speed so fast he wasn't sure it was Sissy who hit him. She grabbed him by his shirt and yanked him close to her face. "I don't think so, buddy. You don't just get out. You know too much."

Kevin leaned forward, nose to nose with Sissy. "Or what? What are you gonna do? Kill me?"

Delores turned around in her seat. "Baby, it won't be that bad. Rusty'll be here in a bit. He said he was stoppin' at Buc-ee's to get you some jerky, and then he'll meet us. He's real mad he had to cut his trip to Disney World short, but he'll be here shortly."

Sissy turned away from Kevin, turning her attention to the brush behind the bakery. "Dee, pull up around yonder to Dusty Dingle's place while we wait on Rusty. I want to get a good look at it. See what we need to do to get it up to speed."

"Why are we goin' out there?" Kevin asked.

Sissy repeated what he said in her head twice, then laughed. "You don't know about… Kevin, your momma owns all this property now. She didn't tell you?"

"What do you mean my momma owns this? Momma don't got the money to buy up all this."

Sissy clicked her tongue against her teeth. "I can't believe your momma didn't tell you she owns all this back here. Dusty's daughter sold it to her. His house, all these acres, and even the bakery. It's all hers now."

"How?"

"Guess she must have made a small fortune on Birdie's life insurance. Maybe she's been holdin' out on you. Wonder what else she hasn't told you."

"You're lyin'."

"Call me a liar one more time and I'll knock you into the middle of next week," Sissy quietly warned.

Kevin crossed his arms, sinking even further into the seat. Did his mother have money? He had wondered if there was any life insurance money after Birdie died but was too afraid to ask. He assumed since she killed herself, a suicide would nullify any policy.

*How could she have afforded to buy a new house? And why?*Kevin had felt a major disconnect from his mother since Birdie's death. He knew she was grieving, and Hunt's weren't known for sharing their feelings. He knew she didn't understand his love of church. But more than anything, he pitied her. He knew her life would never get any better. After all, weren't her best years behind her? At her age, who would want to ever marry her? She would spend the rest of her life a spinster, living in fear of getting caught for all of the terrible, illegal things she had done. She had covered up a murder and sold human remains on the black market. She would live with that for the rest of her days. He would never want to be like her. He would never want her life.

Kevin worried about the truth getting out, and in Kevin's world, nothing was more important than repenting and telling the truth.

Kevin realized in the back seat of Delores's Crown Vic that the best way he could help his mother (and, by proxy, himself) was to expose the truth.

"Yeah, Ms. Dee, drive us around back. I wanna see Mr. Dingle's house. See what we got." Kevin sat up a little taller. "It'd be nice to expand things a bit. Have some more room to work. I think I've just been a little bitch-boy because we've been so cooped up."

Delores suspiciously eyed him through the rearview mirror.

"Drive," he insisted, dropping his voice an octave.

Delores slowly peeled around the corner of the bakery, down the dark dirt road, past all the overgrown weeds and trees that hid the abandoned cars near Dusty's house.

Sissy stepped out of the car, staring at the dilapidated home in front of her. "What a dump!" she proclaimed, doing her best Bette Davis.

Delores turned around, whispering to Kevin, "Boy, you need to be careful with her. She crazy."

"I turn eighteen in a few months."

"She's crazy, Kevin."

"I'm seventeen now. I'm a minor. I'm just a little baby. I can go to the police."

"You'd do that to your momma?"

Sissy slammed her hands on her hips. "Y'all comin' to check out our new headquarters or what?!"

Kevin leaned closer. "I mean this with the utmost respect, Ms. Dee. You do not want to mess with me. I ain't got nothin' to lose, and I got Jesus on my side." Kevin climbed out of the car, flipping on a smile. "Let's see it! I ain't never been in a house where someone died—" Kevin abruptly stopped, realizing he had, in fact, been living in the same house where his grandmother killed herself. A pang of sadness hit him, and he took a deep breath.

Sissy ripped down the police tape and kicked open the front door. She flipped the light switch three times before offering, "Guess old Dusty ain't paid the light bill in a while."

They walked through the house, careful where they stepped.

"This place is awful," Kevin whispered.

"Give it a month or two, and we can have wall-to-wall freezers in here," Sissy said. "We can do the butchery in the kitchen—"

"And what if someone comes a-knockin'!?" Delores asked.

"Dusty Dingle was dead for nearly three years, and no one came a-knockin', Dee."

Kevin sneered, nodding to Sissy. "You're right. You are absolutely right." He walked around, running his finger along the bookcase collecting dust. "She just needs a good cleanin', that's all."

Kevin tried the light switches on the lamps, but none came on. "You need to get the power turned back on. If you write me out a blank check, I'll take it down to the power company tomorrow."

"What makes you think they'll just turn it on like that?"

"You said momma owns this place, right?" He shrugged. "Shouldn't be that hard. Besides, everyone in Liberty knows Momma found Dusty."

Kevin pushed back the dust-filled curtains, coughing as sheets of dust flaked the air. "And them cars out there. We can sell them for parts." He laughed. "We can literally run everything right out in the open! Everyone would be none the wiser!"

"Chile…" Delores muttered under her breath.

"I knew you'd get on board," Sissy said.

"Oh, I'm on board. I am so on board. I've never been more on board. I am on board, my seat belt is fastened, and I'm waitin' for my snacks!"

Delores's phone dinged. She looked at the text. "It's Rusty. He's two minutes away."

"Tell him to meet us at the back of the bakery," Kevin said, taking a step closer to Sissy. "We're partners, right?"

"That's all I ever wanted, Kevin."

Kevin leaned closer to her ear and whispered, "If you ever slap me again, I will knock you so far into the middle of kingdom come, it will take ten NASA space missions to find you. You hear me?" Kevin rattled the keys to the bakery as he walked out the door. "Let's go get us some dead bodies! I got the keys!"

Delores stepped in front of Sissy. "Hear me now, Sissy. Do not push that boy. He had Queenie Masters's head in his hands just a few hours ago. He's nuttier than you are, and that's sayin' something. Don't mess with him."

Sissy pushed past Delores, still stinging from Kevin's insubordination. "I ain't afraid of a child."

Moments later, Rusty stepped out of his van, giving Kevin a fist bump and punching a bag of Buc-ee's beef jerky into his chest.

"You know I hate cuttin' my trip to Disney short. That's 'me' time," he told Sissy.

"With Hector in the hospital, you and Kevin are gonna have to step up. And we're workin' Frances back into the mix, too."

"Frances is back?" Rusty asked Kevin.

"Still working out her deal, I guess. She ain't told me shit," Kevin said.

"How'd Hector get shot?" Rusty asked before Sissy cut him off, clapping her hands.

"Enough talk!" Sissy waved to the door, indicating for Kevin to unlock it.

Moments later, they stood in the center of the room, eyeballing the dozens of body bags.

Sissy exhaled. "Well, let's dig in. Go for old people. They tend to have less families."

"Oh, my goodness, I didn't even think about that! What if people start askin' where their loved one is!?" Delores asked.

"Not our problem," Sissy said, unzipping a bag. "Oh, well, here's Celestine Fulbright. She ain't got no family. Load her up."

Kevin unzipped a bag. He took in the contents, and tears poured down his cheeks. "Oh, no! It's Mrs. Upshaw! She was my Sunday School teacher when I was in the third grade!"

"She got any family?" Sissy asked.

Kevin exasperatedly scoffed. "Yes! She has… had a big family! Like the biggest family of all the families in Liberty," he proclaimed, zipping her back up.

Rusty unzipped a bag and jumped back. "Jesus! Body missing a head!" They all gathered around Queenie Masters. "Where's her damn head?!"

Kevin felt around the bag and found it at her feet. "Down here."

Sissy nodded to Rusty. "Take her."

"Sissy, that's Quee—"

"Queenie Masters ain't got no family. She would have been a closed casket anyways," Sissy said, void of any emotion. "I'll tell everyone we personally took care of her since we knew her for so long."

"Sissy Stone, I'm overruling you here. We are giving Queenie Masters an open-casket funeral. It's a clean cut. We'll slap her in a turtleneck. Everyone will 'ooh and ah' about how good she looks," Delores insisted. She turned, pointing to an elderly man with a caved skull. "James Green ain't got no family. Take him."

Rusty wheeled James Green to the side as they continued to search the bags for a final catch.

As they rifled through the bodies, it became obvious that there were just too many descendants with family members who could open up conversations about "Wanting to see the body."

They settled on Delroy Richardson, an elderly man with a broken neck. His family didn't have a lot of money and relied on the church for donations. Sissy stated she would personally reach out to the family and offer a pro bono funeral for him because of "all the damage they just wouldn't want to see."

As they loaded the bodies into Rusty's truck, Kevin eyeballed the security camera in the corner. He dramatically mouthed the words "Help me" before turning around just in time to conceal the smile spreading across his lips.


Four cups of tea, two energy drinks, and a pot of coffee later, Frances and Ray sat at the family kitchen table, numbed by their exchange. Frances bolted upright, searching the pantry.

"What are you lookin' for?" Ray asked.

"Cigarette."

"Thought you quit," he stated.

Frances rummaged through pockets of coats. She grabbed a lighter from her junk drawer before heading to the backdoor. Ray stood to follow, and she threw up a hand. "Stay here. I need a minute."

"To do what?"

"None of your damned business, Jackson," she said, pulling on a large, heavy coat from the hook near the door. She stormed outside, stalking toward the barn, before cutting around the side to her cinder block and smoking area.

She hadn't been out here in nearly three months, but she had hope. On her hands and knees, she searched the ground for cigarette butts through the moonlight and what little glimmer the stars offered. She lit one with about an inch of tobacco left, then spit it out. She sat on her cinder block and heard something fall next to her. A fresh pack of Marlboro Lights appeared on the ground.

"Well, how did you get there?" she asked the pack before slamming it several times into her fist. "Figures my guardian angel would be a redneck that leaves cigarettes as a gift. Much obliged!" she screamed, waving to the sky.

Opening the lid, she inhaled their aroma. "Oh, I've missed you, my precious," she said before plucking one and putting it in her mouth. She lit it, inhaled, and fell against the wall of the barn, completely relaxed.

She looked to the sky. She listened to the quiet of the farm, save the sound of bullfrogs in the distance.

"Daddy… Momma… God if you're… Daddy," she called out again. "God, I'm still mad at you, and I don't really wanna talk to you, so you can just send me someone else. I'm still mad. But thanks for the cigarettes if that was you."

She waited in silence. "I tried to be good. I tried to make my life right. I tried to get out. And now, I'm being held hostage by an old lady gang and a sheriff with delusions of grandeur. What exactly am I supposed to be doin' here? I have nary a clue.

"Hector's in the hospital. Dobkins is in the hospital. By the way, could you just take that evil little troll doll home tonight? That'd make my life a lot easier. Kevin's… I'm still not clear what happened with him today and Clint Peppers… Oh my God, Clint Peppers.

"Look, I got no idea what I'm supposed to be doin' here." Her eyes fell on the rotten corn fields in the distance, taking another drag off her cigarette. "I'm tired of tryin' to save everyone and then everyone turnin' around and demandin' more from me. And somehow, it's all my fault. What did I do to deserve this hand? I got dealt a real shitty hand. And I want to fold."

Frances leaned forward on her elbows and began to cry. She realized she hadn't had a good cry in a long time. She missed her mother. Missing her mother made her miss her father as well, even though he had been dead for years. She worried about Kevin. She worried about what this new influx of cash could mean for optics, and she was terrified she would be found out for her previous work as a body snatcher."

She cried harder. She clutched the cigarette tighter between her fingers as she watched tears hit the dirt. "What am I supposed to do?"

She loudly sobbed as her bellows echoed through the farmland. She took another drag of her cigarette and exhaled it, leaning against the barn again.

She heard the soft screech of her childhood swing gently rock on the large oak tree next to the barn. The same tree from which she tried to hang herself when she was a teenager, before the weight of her body snapped the branch and sent her body crashing to the earth, where she broke an arm.

She watched as that swing hauntingly swung back and forth ever so softly. She remembered the day her daddy hung that swing in the tree. She remembered how he used to push her, and how she would cry out, "Higher! Higher!"

She took another drag off her cigarette and whispered to herself, "You're still here, Sarah Frances. You're still here."

Through everything she had experienced in the last few months, she was a survivor. She was smart. She was tenacious. She was a leader. She was the righter of wrongs. She wasn't the kind of person to be pushed around by a man or two old women.

She was Frances freaking Hunt.

She wiped the tears from her face. She took another drag and quickly exhaled as she stamped out the cigarette. She held the mysterious pack of cigarettes in her outstretched hand. She looked up to the sky.

"Just remembered who I am."

# CHAPTER SIX

# THE HOSTAGE

Edie Trussell sat perfectly still on the steps of the Lockhart Brothers Funeral Home with her hands firmly clasped in her lap, staring at the pouring rain, which had returned overnight. She checked her watch. It was five minutes after eight o'clock, and their website said they opened at 8 a.m. She had been waiting for fifteen minutes, expecting someone to show up early. She was cold. She was wet. She was surly.

She sighed heavily, looking back to the door. Maybe someone came in the back, and she didn't see them drive around the building. Maybe they unlocked the door and didn't know she had been sitting out here the entire time.

The cold wind sent shivers through her body.

"Well, that's it," she announced to no one, standing up. She stomped to the front door and tried it. It was still locked. She slung open her umbrella and walked around to the side of the building, seeing the side door where, just three months earlier, Delores had disarmed and knocked Oscar unconscious with his own shotgun.

She tried that door. And it opened. She pushed it all the way open and squinted into the darkness.

"Hello?" she called down the dark hallway, shaking the rain from her umbrella. "Anyone in here?! It's Edie! I just want to come on in and plan Queenie's funeral!"

No response. Edie sighed again and walked inside, closing the door behind her. Her hand traced along the wall, turning on the hall lights.

Not one to be afraid of funeral homes or dead bodies, Edie strode down the hallway on her way to the lobby. Edie got a degree in cosmetology in the sixties and spent many years working at various beauty shops around town before she met her husband. After he died in the mid-nineties, Edie went back to working part-time for what she called her "mad money," setting hair and doing make-up at funeral homes all over the tri-county area. But never at Lockhart Brothers, because of Sissy.

Edie would simply wait in the lobby until someone showed up, and if they asked why she let herself in, she would explain she was old, cold, and the door was unlocked. She was about to drop good money in here, and she wasn't going to catch her own death waiting for the late Sissy Stone.

Queenie Masters had prepaid her funeral at Lockhart Brothers back in the early eighties when she had a small heart attack and was convinced she would be dead before turning fifty. Stuart Lockhart was running a special at the time that included the casket, embalming, the service, and all the bells and whistles. Queenie, Edie, and Juanita all knew exactly what music they would want played and which florist they would want to use. Some people plan weddings. Queenie, Edie, and Juanita planned funerals.

Edie was going to make sure Queenie's final wishes were handled to the T.

Edie paused outside the door that read "Employees Only." She looked both ways. *Wonder if they got any bodies just lying out on the table.* She pushed open the door.

She turned on the overhead lights and saw a spotless room.

*Just think about all the history in this room,* she wondered to herself. *So many fine citizens of Liberty spent their final days and hours in this room. Naked and their blood all pourin' down that drain.*She meandered to the cooling cabinets and heaved out a long drawer. A body was covered by a sheet. She lifted the sheet and saw the face of an old man. She gasped.

"Howard Fisher! I didn't know you had gone and died!" Howard Fisher had been a long-standing crush of Edie's. He was a senior at Liberty High when she was a freshman. To this day, he was one of the best-looking men in Liberty. He had owned a cattle ranch just on the edge of town, about fifty acres. He still had a full head of thick gray hair, and his skin was a leathery mocha from years in the sun. Still attractive. Still muscular. Still cool.

Howard had endured Edie's shameless and mostly harmless flirting for decades, but he was always forever faithful to his wife, Sue-Bobbie, who died of lung cancer about ten years earlier.

Curiosity got the better of her. She lifted and pushed the sheet down past his waist to get a quick look. She screamed a blood-curdling shriek so loud glass jars shook on the shelf.

Howard had no arms or legs.

She dropped the sheet and sprang backward, her back slamming into the embalming table. She grabbed her back in pain, watching as the sheet softly fell, covering Howard's body.

She shoved the drawer back into the wall and slammed the door shut.

"What in God's blessed Holy name…"

*Maybe he got in a terrible accident. Maybe it was diabetes.* Edie shook off her shock and gathered herself.

Her eyes fell to the drawer next to Howard. Dare she? She opened its door, gasping as she saw another covered body inside. "Our Father, who art in heaven, hallowed be Thy name…" She slowly pulled it halfway out as she had Howard. She paused for a moment, then steadied herself as she pulled the drawer entirely out.

She saw the covered torso and then saw the sheet drop just below the waist.

She lifted the sheet quickly and saw the side of a torso, yet again with no arms and no legs.

She thrust the drawer back inside and slammed the cabinet door shut. She stepped back, her eyes racing all over the entire room. "What is happening in here, Sissy Stone? This isn't normal!"

She threw back a set of curtains and saw a small storage unit in the corner of the parking lot, almost completely camouflaged by trees. A single key on a keychain with the word **"Shed"** written on it hung on a hook next to the door, which opened into the parking lot.

A minute later, under a downpour of rain, Edie slid that key into the padlock on the unit. She turned the key, and the lock popped open. She placed her hand on the door, and felt it gently vibrate. She placed her ear to the door and heard a low hum.

She removed the lock and opened the door. It was sealed tightly by a weather-stripping seal. *Probably to keep everything cold,* she thought.

Edie walked inside and saw four large freezers against the walls. A putrid smell hit her nose, and she instantaneously gagged. "Lord Jesus on high," she exclaimed. "Is that marijuana?"

She slowly approached the closest unit, placing her hand on the door of a freezer. She rattled her nails on the top before swiftly yanking it open. A gust of cold air wafted from the unit, smacking her in the face.

Inside were several white containers. The smell grew even more pungent.

"Sissy Stone… What in God's green earth are you doin'?" she whispered to herself.

She opened the lid of a small container.

Her knees buckled. She lost her balance.

As she fainted, she cracked her head on the edge of the freezer.


Ten minutes later, Rusty pulled his van into the Lockhart Brothers parking lot. He saw the shed door wide open. "I can't leave for five days without this whole damned place fallin' apart," he quietly lamented to himself.

The stink from within the unit was already sailing through the parking lot, mixed with the fragrance of fresh rain. He quickly looked around, checking to see if anyone was near, picking up his pace as he got closer.

He saw the padlock on the ground and stepped inside to see if someone had left the door wide open or if someone was working.

That's when he saw Edie.

"Well, shit."

He squatted down, checking for a pulse. She was still alive. He sighed in relief. He pulled the phone from his hip pocket. "Siri, call Sissy Stone," he said.


When Edie Trussell came to, she was lying on her back in pitch-black. She tried to raise up, but her head hit a soft wall.

"What the…" She attempted to raise her arms, and they, too, hit the satiny wall. Her hands felt around the pillowy encasement.

She was inside a casket.

Edie screamed. "Help! Help me! Help me! Let me out of here! Help! I have a heart condition! Do you hear me!? I have a heart condition!"

The entire casket jolted, slowly bouncing up and down. She could hear a soft hum outside the casket.

Edie screamed, cried, hyperventilated, and cursed during the fifteen-minute ride from Lockhart Brothers to Dusty Dingle's house. She felt the van pull onto gravel before coming to a stop.

Seconds later, she heard doors open and felt her encasement pull out of the vehicle. She cried and screamed, kicking and beating the casket with her fists.

"Let me out of here! I can't breathe! I'm gonna die in here! I don't got no air in here!"

Rusty and Kevin carried the casket up the stairs of Dusty Dingle's home. Delores offered a "Watch the steps. They look rotten," as she opened the screen door.

"And we ain't afraid the police are comin' back here?" Rusty asked as they maneuvered into the house.

"They done wrapped up their investigation. Drop her here," Sissy said, pointing to an empty space near the fireplace and a few feet from a large puddle of water caused by a leak in the roof.

Rusty and Kevin lowered the casket to the ground.

"Just so we're all clear, this is kidnappin'," Kevin softly noted.

"She knows too much," Delores reported, shaking her head. "Just be glad Sissy didn't kill her already."

"And your plan is to just tie her up here? And do what?" Kevin questioned.

"I'm tryin' to figure it out, boy. I don't got no plans at the moment," Sissy responded.

"Sissy Stone!?" Edie called from inside the casket. "Is that you!?"

Sissy shoved her hand into her purse and pulled out a pocket pistol.

Kevin grabbed his hair, yanking on it. "Did everyone just go out and buy guns at Christmas!? You, Nakoya..."

Delores reached into her purse and removed her small matching gun. "Sissy and I got a two-for-one deal down at Big Mack's Gun Shop out down near the interstate."

"Mine's in the truck," Rusty said. He turned to Kevin. "I got an extra if you want one."

"Open the casket, Rusty," Sissy demanded.

"What if she jumps out?" Rusty asked.

"Edie Trussell is nearly eighty years old with bad knees. What you think she gonna do?" Sissy said.

Rusty slid his coffin key into a slot and unlocked the casket. He nodded to Sissy.

Sissy cleared her throat, then shouted to the coffin, "All right, Edie, we gonna let you out now, but you gotta come out with your hands up."

"Why!?"

"Because I said so, gotdamn it!"

Rusty slowly opened the top drawer of the casket, and Edie popped up like a rabid raccoon, flailing her hands and arms above her head, dramatically gasping for air. She screamed again (louder, higher, and longer), seeing Delores and Sissy aiming guns at her skull.

"Why am I here!? Why do y'all have guns!?" Edie demanded before remembering. "Why have you got disembodied arms and legs in that freezer out back behind your funeral home, Sissy Stone!?" Edie looked around the room. "Where am I?"

"Your new home."

"You can't keep me here!"

"Copy that," Sissy said, pulling the hammer back on her gun.

"What in the hell is wrong with you!?"

"I am on a mission from God. We is savin' lives."

"By choppin' up dead people?!" Edie burst into tears. "Why are y'all doin' this!?"

"You shouldn't been snoopin' around my funeral home."

"It was cold and raining! I just went inside to wait for you! The door was unlocked!"

Sissy turned to Delores. "You didn't lock up last night?"

"I was just there to plan Queenie's funeral! She prepaid! She don't got no family! Sissy Stone, I lost one of my best friends and Juanita… She just…" Edie collapsed over the side of the casket in howling sobs.

"This is so messed up," Kevin said quietly under his breath.

Sissy motioned with her gun. "Get up, Edie." Sissy walked out of the room, shouldering a large burlap bag. Delores motioned to follow Sissy.

Sissy led her to the bathroom. She tried the light switch, and again, no power. "Keep forgettin' this place don't got no power. We'll see about getting you some light in here. Rusty can work on the toilet. It'll be like the Four Seasons in here if you're a good little girl."

"There's no heat in here!" Edie insisted.

"We'll get you some blankets. Maybe a space heater. We ain't monsters."

Delores held up a finger. "I don't like the idea of space heaters. Remember that old man who died in a house fire because of his space heater back in 1995?"

"Better not knock over any space heaters, Edie," Sissy said.

"I can't believe you are doin' this to me!" Edie wailed.

"You're lucky to be alive right now!"

Rusty stepped between Edie and Sissy. "Give me two minutes with her."

"To do what?" Sissy started.

"Two minutes."

Sissy, Delores, and Kevin stepped into the hallway. Rusty took the bag from Sissy and closed the door.

Sissy backed against the wall. "You're not gonna rape me, are you?"

"What? Ew. God, no."

"Ew!?"

"Listen to me. You're in a real bad situation, lady. You're lucky that old crazy woman hasn't killed you, hacked you, and taken you to market."

"What are you people doin'!?"

"We broker human remains for scientific research and development. We have a small but growing and thriving industry. We take limbs and bodies from those who no longer need them. We provide them to experts who need them for testing to advance medical science."

"That's… That's gotta be illegal!"

"It is. You are not wrong, sister. But the two senior citizens outside that door right now consider it a necessary evil, and there is nothing you can say that will change their minds. Our work helps save lives. It's frankly selfish to be buried without donating your body to science. Why not help others? For your friends to see you lying in a box, pumped full of chemicals, and your face spraypainted like an art exhibit? Shame on you, humanity. Shame. Your soul goes to heaven. Your body does not."

"That's not true. The Bible says there will come a day when we all hear a trumpet, and our graves will open up, and we'll all fly up to heaven—"

"You really want *that* old body?"

"Jesus could come tomorrow!"

"Could he?" he asked, his voice escalating a few octaves.

Edie relaxed slightly. "It's wrong." She shook her head. "What's gonna happen when Jesus raptures all them people up out of their graves and them people don't got no arms and legs!?"

"Jesus'll give them new legs and arms. Besides, think about it. You don't want decomposed arms and legs for all eternity, do you? And what about all them skulls and bones down in the catacombs in Paris? Jesus is gonna give us all new bodies. I think you're oversimplifying the decomposition process here."

Edie collapsed a little more. "I don't like it."

"Our work saves lives. We are saving people."

Edie sat quietly for nearly two minutes. She narrowed her eyes on Rusty. "You're saving people?"

"We're saving people." Rusty opened the bag and wrapped a chain around the back of a toilet pipe. He pulled out a set of handcuffs.

"I'm going to treat you right, and we'll figure this out, okay?" he said, motioning his head to the people behind the door.

"Just let me go," she quietly whined.

"Sissy ain't gonna do that," he whispered. "I'll take good care of you. Just try to take it easy."

Edie looked at her wrists as he cuffed them through the chain. "You'll get me some food and blankets?"

"I'll keep you comfortable. But if you want to get out of here, you need to play the game with Sissy."

"You're looking at Liberty's best checker player."

Rusty leaned closer to her ear and whispered, "You're not playing checkers, sister. You're playing chess."


Frances sat on a plush leopard sofa in Akasha's shop, sipping a latte from The Coffee Cup. Akasha sat across from Frances in a big leather chair, draping a blanket over her legs.

Frances turned, looking out the window. "Is it ever gonna stop raining?" she asked.

"I barely made it to work this morning. Main Street is flooding down near the square. I heard all them dirt roads are washed out, too."

Frances nodded. "I had to hitch a ride with Kevin this mornin' into town on his way to school. I thought we were gonna float here." Frances took a deep breath. "I'm in trouble, Akasha, and I... I need to get myself out of it. I've done some bad things. But I'm ready to get right. But I've done bad."

"I know." Akasha nodded. Frances looked up, puzzled. Akasha pointed to her head. "Psychic, remember?"

"I'm afraid to ask. How much do you know?"

"I know your sheriff is back in your life, and a younger man is vying for your attention. I know you're worried about Kevin. I know you came into a lot of money recently. And for some reason, I see you around a lot of dead people."

Frances closed her eyes. "You're gonna think I'm the most awful person on the planet."

Akasha giggled. "Girl, I know about you and Hector and the whole body harvesting thing."

"What? How—" Frances said, amazed by Akasha's gift. "You saw all that?"

"I've known Hector a long time. He told me. I know all about it. I know them brothers of Sissy are still alive."

Frances blinked, stunned.

Akasha realized Hector hadn't told Frances. "You didn't know."

Frances shook her head, shrugging. "Hector and I ain't really talked since I left the grave robbin' business. Since I pushed him away. I told him we can't be friends, and I…" Her voice trailed. "I wish he'd told me about that. Like… Damn. They really are alive?"

"They faked their deaths."

Frances nodded. "Hector and I just knew something was weird about those two. They both went missin', and no bodies to be found? Sketch. Real ducking sketch. And like… Why?"

"Why are there a bunch of dead people in your bakery?"

"Geez, Akasha," Frances gasped, taking a sip of her latte. "They's using it for autopsies from the church. Not enough space at the morgue. Ain't nothin' insidious there."

"Why is there a woman tied up in your house?"

"I can assure you, I don't got a woman tied up in my house!" Frances laughed. "Oh, God. Does Kevin have a woman tied up in his bedroom? That would definitely track."

"Maybe I'm seeing something else."

"I don't know what to do. I need help. Sissy and Delores are blackmailin' me back into the business, Ray Jackson is blackmailin' me to help him bring down some international black market body harvestin' operation, and a little person is tryin' to kill me. I'm damned all the way around. I just know I'm the only one who can save myself at this point."

"You thought about just going to the police?"

Frances nodded. "But it would destroy Kevin's future. Destroy his entire life. I thought I was doin' the right thing by gettin' out." Frances ran her hands down her face and neck. "But I gotta figure this out. I'm the only one who can save myself."

The bell over the door jingled as it opened, and Nakoya rushed inside, slapping her umbrella against the ground and shaking the rainwater from it. "Damn rain! I hate the rain!"

Akasha motioned to Frances. "Got your boss in here this morning."

Frances spun on Nakoya, taking a moment to shift the conversation. "Why you got a gun? Why'd you shoot Hector? Somethin' ain't right about your story in all of this."

"I'm a Black woman in a predominately white, small Southern town with a number of racist bigots. Why wouldn't I have a gun? And I done told you that Hector was an accident!"

"Nakoya knew that guy the steeple fell on," Akasha casually dropped.

Nakoya grabbed a pillow and slammed it across Akasha's chest. "Akasha, oh my gah! Don't be spreading my business!"

Frances gently sat her latte on the coffee table and slowly snapped her head from side to side. She opened and closed her fists several times. "You… You know that guy? How? How do you know that guy that the steeple fell on?"

Akasha nodded. Nakoya shrugged.

"How do you know Donald Dobkins?" Frances coolly asked.

Nakoya froze. Her entire energy shifted. Her nose flared, and she pursed her lips. "How do *you* know Donald Dobkins?"

"Asked you first."

They stared at each other, rage building behind both of their eyes.

"They worked together at a bank in Atlanta," Akasha said, breaking the silence.

"You worked together at a *bank* in Atlanta? And you arrived in Liberty right before Thanksgiving—"

"Because the bank closed," Nakoya ardently stated to Frances, clearly trying to shut down the conversation in front of Akasha.

"You worked for The Man."

Nakoya stared at Frances, emotionless. She popped her tongue and laughed. "Yeah, I've been working for the man all my life! Ain't that right, Akasha!"

Frances didn't laugh. "Yeah, that's funny. That's hilarious. You been workin' for The Man." Frances leaned closer and very softly whispered with a gleam of fire in her eyes, "Hey bitch… I'm Big Momma."

Nakoya's entire body tensed. Everything went silent around her. She balled her fingers into fists. All she could see in front of her was an angry bumpkin in cheap clothes and unkempt hair. An angry bumpkin who had ruined Nakoya's life.

"Yooooouu…!" Nakoya gutturally growled, leaping through the air. Her fingers retracted like a cheetah about to slash into its prey. She soared across the coffee table, slamming into Frances. They both hit the sofa, toppling it over. They rolled over twice before Nakoya straddled Frances and began punching her in the face with both fists.

"Nakoya!" Akasha screamed. "What in the hell is wrong with you!?"

"This bitch ruined everything!" Nakoya screamed, wailing away on Frances.

Frances managed to free a leg, kneeing Nakoya square in the center of her ass, sending her careening over Frances's chest and head, landing flat on her stomach.

Frances rolled to her knees, grabbed Nakoya by her legs, and yanked her full force until Frances had ahold of her hair.

"Not the hair!" Akasha screamed, but it was too late.

Frances had a fist full of Nakoya's wig, ripping it from her scalp as Nakoya screamed in pain. "You wear a wig!?" Frances exclaimed.

"Bitch, you really thought I had long, thick, luxurious straight hair all this time!?" Nakoya punched Frances square in the nose and straight in the throat. Frances dropped to her knees, gasping for air. Nakoya roundhouse kicked her in the face. Frances flew backward, slamming into a display case, exploding glass, and sending jewelry in all directions.

Akasha jumped in between them, shoving Nakoya into a wall. "Stop it! Both of you! Right now! You break it, you bought it!" Everyone tried to catch their breath. "Now, what in the holy name of Halle Berry is going on here!?"

"Your sister works for the guy who was runnin' everything! So was Hector! Everyone was working for The Man!"

Nakoya spat blood and hissed like a hurt cat. "Everyone but you! You got greedy, and decided to start your own operation, and you dropped a dime on us and called the FBI! You shut us down! You destroyed my life!"

"I did no such thing! The sheriff here in Liberty figured it all out on his own! He found Oscar's van! It led him to the warehouse! I called Donald to *warn* him! To warn you guys to get out before he got there! If it wasn't for me, your ass would be in the clink right now!"

Akasha pushed her sister against the wall. "*You're* tied up in all this dead people stuff, too!? You've been lying to me all this time!? How long!? How long have you been working in dead people parts!?"

"How do you know about—" Nakoya started to ask.

"Answer the damned question, Nakoya! How long!?" Akasha demanded, shaking her sister by her shoulders.

Nakoya thrust her hand toward Frances, demanding her wig. Frances tossed it to her. "Five years," Nakoya quietly announced.

"Five years!?"

Frances checked her face in the mirror. "You're fired, by the way."

"Oh, I fucking quit, you dumb whore!" Nakoya screamed. "You ruined everything! You ruined my life!"

"*Oscar* ruined your life, little girl! If Oscar hadn't pulled a gun on us, Delores wouldn't have knocked him out. If Imagene Bohanon hadn't died of brain cancer, Sissy wouldn't have had her marijuana that got me high. If Stephen and Stuart hadn't been runnin' dead people parts out of Lockhart Brothers, Ruth Chambers wouldn't have been sliced and diced. If Delores hadn't gone to Vegas, she wouldn't have bought those damned shoes. If Michael Kors hadn't opened a shop…" Frances clapped her hands in Nakoya's face. "Every moment in life has a consequence."

Nakoya wheezed, trying to catch her breath, taking in this new information. "Every moment in life has a consequence," Frances repeated, clapping her hands for effect. "I was just a woman trying to get rid of a dead Mexican my momma killed."

"*Your mother* killed Oscar!?"

"And the sheriff spooked her, and she killed herself. Every moment in life has a consequence." Frances picked up her knocked-over latte, grateful the top stayed on. She swirled it around and took a sip. "Sure. Yeah, I got greedy. I did one run. But I got out. And right now, I got everyone in town trying to blackmail me or kill me."

Frances paced aimlessly around the shop, trying to catch her breath. She rotated her shoulder, trying to work out the pain from the fight. She felt a sudden pain in her chest. "Dammit, I think you broke a rib."

Frances took another sip of her latte. "The Lockharts's sister's tryin' to take over the whole gotdamned body snatchin' market here in the Southeast now that y'all are out of business. Ray Jackson wants to take down the whole industry, and Donald Dobkins is in the hospital."

"And Hector," Akasha interjected, narrowing her eyes on Nakoya.

"And Hector," Frances nodded, pointing at Akasha. "What do you want, Nakoya?"

"What do you mean, 'What do I want?'"

"Don't play with me. What's your endgame in this? Everyone else has one. What's yours? Just put it on the table so I can keep everyone straight."

"I wanted to run the American syndicate of the brokerage business. What they're planning on doing could bring in billions of dollars a year. It's a way of brokering human bodies on a larger, international scale. But it's not just science. It's collectors."

"Jesus," Frances seethed as she continued pacing. She stopped, turning back to Nakoya. "Hold up, wait…" Frances caught her breath and realized, "You know who's behind all of this?"

"Behind all of what?"

Frances waved her hands in all directions. "This! Everything! You know who's the man behind all of this!? The man behind The Man."

Nakoya's head rolled with indignation. "The Men."

Frances shook her hands with a "Spit it out!"

"Duh, girl. It's Stephen and Stuart Lockhart."

Frances collapsed against a desk from another bout of vertigo. She held her head, squeezing her eyes shut. It was a sharp pain that felt like a needle going through her brain.

How did she not even consider the brothers Lockhart? Everything that had happened over the past three months… The answer had been staring her in the face the entire time.

*It was Stephen and Stuart all along.*

The bell over the door chimed, and all three heads of the women inside spun to see a small woman walk inside, dressed in black leather pants, a black leather jacket, and a large helmet. She brushed the rain off her sleeves, then removed her helmet.

Lily's hair beautifully cascaded over her shoulders as she smiled at all three women and giggled. "Oh, hello! I buy dress," she announced with her terribly bad accent.

After their quick jaunt to Dusty Dingle's house with Edie in tow, Sissy, Delores, Kevin, and Rusty stood over the conference room table, shuffling the Polaroids of their deceased bodies, which were prepared to be shipped.

"That's the last of them. You two should move on out to get ahead of the afternoon traffic."

"Nope." Kevin shook his head. "Y'all already kept me long enough! You're just lucky I wasn't already in class before you called! I've done missed three classes this mornin'! I have a history test at one. I ain't missin' it."

Rusty shrugged. "It's fine. I can handle it. Not that big of a deal."

Kevin nodded to Rusty and went to leave, just as the door flew open and Christopher rushed in. Sissy quickly scooped the Polaroids into her hands as Christopher ogled the group in a rage.

"Where have y'all been!? Do none of you people answer your phones!?" Christopher asked.

"We've been busy!" Delores fired back.

"Doing what, exactly?" he demanded.

"Why you got your panties in a wad?" Sissy asked, shoving the Polaroids into her purse.

"The phone has not stopped ringing this morning! We've got appointments all afternoon!"

"Appointments? For what?" Sissy asked. "Why?"

"Why!? Because two dozen Baptists went home to be with their blessed Lord and Savior yesterday and left their earthly vessels behind!" Christopher screamed at the gobsmacked crew before him.

They all stared in bewilderment. "We're a funeral home, remember!? We do funerals here! And apparently, no other funeral homes in town are answering their damned phones either!"

After his morning classes, Clint Peppers raced into the hospital, ripping off his t-shirt and pulling over his scrub top. Clint was proud of his uniform but was quick to remind everyone he was just a volunteer.

Liberty Memorial was happy to have someone like Clint, who didn't shy away from the cleaning detail and helping lift patients. He liked to make patients laugh, and he lived to charm all the doctors and nurses.

Clint jogged to the nurses' station, checking the charts for Hector's room. A nurse looked up and asked if he needed help.

"Checking on Hector Ramirez," he said.

"They moved him down to 402."

"He's out of ICU?" he asked.

"He's improving. Fortunately for him, the bullet went right through him."

"He awake?"

"He's been stirrin', but ain't opened his eyes yet."

Clint raced to Hector's room. Hector's eyes were closed. According to the chart, his blood pressure and heart rate were improving. Clint pulled up a chair next to Hector.

"Hey, mister. My name is Clint Peppers, and I'm friends with your friend, Frances Hunt. She's real worried about you. And I just wanted to know if you knew who shot you so I can tell the authorities, and we can arrest this monster."

Hector's hand moved. His lips began to curl. His eyes fluttered.

"Can I get some water?" he raspily asked.

Clint ran a cup of water in the nearby sink and held it to Hector's lips. "You're alive!" Clint exclaimed. "Look at you! You didn't look so good yesterday when you came in! You're alive!"

"Am I?" Hector said with a raised eyebrow.

"Yes, you are! Frances got you here just in time!"

"I love her," Hector said, closing his eyes again.

Clint froze, sitting up straighter. "You… Love her? What do you mean you love her? Like a friend?"

"She doesn't know. I can't tell her."

Clint took the water away from Hector's mouth.

"Maybe you should just keep that a little secret. Keep that under your hat," Clint quietly insisted. "Do you know who shot you? Let me get justice for you."

"It was Nakoya. Nakoya shot me."

"Who is this Nakoya person, and why did they shoot you?"

"I don't know. It was an accident. She was running away from The Man."

"What man?"

"The guy at the—" Hector turned his head to get a better look at Clint. "Are you an orderly? You look like a child."

"I'm a volunteer."

Hector tried to focus on Clint. "Can you go get me a real doctor?"

Clint leaned in closer. "I'll get you a real doctor as soon as you tell me Nakoya's last name."

Hector shook his head. "Was an accident. She didn't mean to. She was scared. No need to get the law involved." Hector relaxed back into the pillow. "I'll take that real doctor now, buddy."

Clint walked out. He spotted a doctor at the nurses' station and tapped him on the shoulder. "Gunshot dude in 402 is awake and asking for you."

The puzzled doctor watched Clint as he continued marching down the hall.

The elevator doors opened, and Ray Jackson stepped out, coming face-to-face with Clint.

"You're just everywhere," Ray stated, bowing up a bit.

"I work here. You don't."

"What's up with you and Frances?"

"You ain't the sheriff no more, so I don't have to answer any of your stupid questions, coward."

Ray stepped forward, trying to intimidate Clint, and Clint snapped his neck from side to side. "I wish you would, boomer," he quietly growled. "I wish you would."

Ray stood down. "You work here," Ray said aloud, wondering how he could use Clint's access for his needs.

"F you," Clint spat, continuing down the hall. Ray followed him.

"Do you know about a man who was crushed by a cross yesterday? A little fella?"

"Bruh, I done told you, I don't have to answer any of your questions."

"Listen to me, you little twink! Frances's life is in danger. And if you want to help her, you're going help me."

Clint stopped walking. "How is she in danger? And what were you doin' in her house last night?"

Ray hated how much he saw of himself in Clint Peppers. He also knew the best way to get Clint on his side was to tell him the truth.

"There are bad people out there who want to hurt Frances. Now I'll tell you some of what I know, but I'm gonna need your help, and I'm gonna have to swear you to secrecy," Ray said, pleading with Clint. "I need help, and as much as it pains me to say, I need your help."

"Who wants to hurt Frances? I'll mess 'em up."

Ray motioned for Clint to follow him into a private waiting room. He closed the door and leaned against it.

"You have to swear to me you won't tell anyone what I'm about to tell you. Especially Hunt."

"I swear," Clint said.

Ray picked up a Bible on a nearby table. "Swear on the Bible."

"I'm not swearing on the Bible. You have my word."

Ray sighed, unsure if he could trust Clint, but knew he was out of options. "There are a lot of bad people doin' bad things to dead people in this town. But not just here. All over the place. I've been tracking this for the past few months."

Clint's brow furrowed. "Come again?"

"There's an underground market for stolen dead human body parts and bodies. There are people here in Liberty involved with this trade. And I'm gonna put a stop to it."

"Girl, please," Clint moaned.

"You think Dean Gilbertson's body bein' stolen out of his grave was a prank?"

Clint widened his stance and folded his arms. "Mister, Dean Gilbertson was murdered."

Ray did a double-take, completely thrown. "What… What are you talkin' about?"

"I am one hundred million percent convinced Coach Gilbertson was murdered so his wife could get the insurance money."

"What… No, that's… No."

"Why else would that she-devil wife of his have him cremated after his body showed back up!?"

"No." Ray shook his head.

"Dean Gilbertson was murdered!"

"His body was stolen by people who had chopped off his arms and legs, and they sold them on the black market. I know because I found his arm in a container that came out of a van that was sunk at the bottom of Lake Briarwood."

"Must have been a different arm." Clint laughed. "People saw Coach in his casket. Ain't nobody said anything about him missing arms and legs."

"The people who did this replaced his arms and legs with piping in his clothes to make it look realistic. They put fake latex and plastic hands on the pipe. This is what they do."

Clint shook his head, not wanting to believe Ray Jackson because it would mean Coach was mutilated and it would also mean Ray Jackson was right. "So, you're… You're saying all this was done to him after he was murdered?"

"Sure. After he was murdered. Whatever you want to tell yourself, Clint. My concern is bringin' the people behind all of this to justice."

"Because I'm going to find out who killed Coach if it's the last thing I do."

"Cool story. In the meantime, someone is killing funeral directors in the area."

"Frances ain't a funeral director."

"Clint, listen to me. If you want to help Frances, you need to listen to me and shut your piehole. Frances upset a bad man. A very bad man. He's a dwarf. A little person. A very bad little person. And that man came to Liberty lookin' for Frances to kill her. And that's the exact same guy that got flattened by the steeple at Liberty Baptist."

"Well, newsflash, bub, little guy is wrapped up like the mummy upstairs with broken bones all over his body. He ain't gonna be tryin' to kill no one any time soon. And that's even if he survives. Last I heard, he was in critical condition. Frances is fine. I know what you're tryin' to do here, and it ain't gonna work. Not on my watch."

"And what exactly do you think I'm tryin' to do?"

"Take your white horse act and go back to wherever you came from. Frances ain't in no danger. You're just tryin' to win her back."

"I am not in love with France Hunt."

"You are a terrible liar."

"We have to bring this guy to justice, Clint. He's running an illegal operation that has desecrated thousands of bodies."

"That ain't my monkey. That ain't my zoo. And apparently, that ain't yours either, anymore."

"I need to see him."

"No visitors. Intensive care."

Ray took in this information and shook his head. "Peppers, I really need your help here."

Clint took a deep breath, his mind racing, contemplating his next move. If this really was so important, if Frances really was in danger, he was going to be the one to bring this man to justice. "Fine. I'll help you. But you gotta give me his name."

"His name don't matter to you. He's a ghost."

"He's literally still alive."

"I mean, he doesn't exist. He's wiped himself clean. Burner phones, no credit cards. Cash only, fake IDs. They call him 'The Man.'"

"Give me… His real name."

Ray cursed under his breath and spat a sigh. "Donald."

"What's his last name—"

"I ain't givin' you his last name! You didn't ask for his last name! I gave you his first name, and that probably ain't even really his first name! You can call him 'Ryan Reynolds' for what it's worth! The man in your hospital bed doesn't exist in society!"

"What does he have to do with Frances?" Clint asked, his patience waning quickly. "She doesn't work in a funeral home."

"Are you gonna help me?"

"He's unconscious, bruh! What do you want me to do!? Run some smellin' salts under his nose and ask him to stop bein' a bad guy!? You know what, screw you." Clint pushed around Ray, heading to the door. "Besides, for someone who used to be a cop, I can't believe you ain't going after the bigger fish to fry, which is staring you right in the face. At least that fish can talk and answer your dumb questions."

"What fish?"

"*What fish?* Bruh."

"What are you talking about?" Ray asked, completely frustrated by this child.

"Let me lay it out for you, old timer… Donald No-Last-Name was chasing a woman out of the church before Jesus Christ decided to drop a two-ton on his ass. *That chick* was the person who shot Frances's friend, Hector. If you're lookin' for dangerous people, why don't you start with her? You should be looking for Nakoya."

"Nakoya?" Ray asked, narrowing his eyes intensely. Ray widened his stance. He was a mirror image of Clint Pepper, nearly thirty years older. "Nakoya Whittler?"

*So that's her last name.* Clint smiled. "I got my rounds," Clint walked out.

Ray chased Clint out of the room. "Nakoya Whittler!? Are you sure?

How do you know it was her?!"

"Said her name was Nakoya."

"He who!?"

"Fuckin' Hector! Gotdamn, you are slow on the uptick."

"So, he's awake! I need to talk to him!"

"No visitors, and you ain't the sheriff anymore! You really don't get it, do you!? Now get out of my hospital before I have you thrown out. You don't have no business here."

"Nakoya Whittler?" Ray desperately asked one last time. "She was here in Liberty? Do you know where I can find her?"

Clint raised his eyebrows and shrugged his arms. "I dunno," he said, mocking Ray.

Ray grunted, realizing what Clint wanted. "What difference does his last name mean to you, Peppers? I done told you he's a dead end."

Clint tapped his foot.

"Fine! Dobkins. His last name is Dobkins."

"Whittler's sister owns a vintage shop on Main Street. Next to The Coffee Cup." Clint turned, walking away from him. "And we're not a team, Jackson!"


Sissy shook the stack of pink "While You Were Out" notes Christopher had carefully taken while her group was busy kidnapping and tethering Edie Trussell. "Twenty messages!? How are we gonna bury twenty people, Christopher!?"

"One at a time," he compassionately responded. "And they're going to start showing up shortly."

"Why are they showing up!?"

"I told them it would be easier on them if everyone came in at once, so they could grieve as a community, and I thought it would—"

"Are you fucking stupid!?" Sissy railed. "You move so gotdamn slow, it'll be Christmas before we get 'em all out of here! In all our years, we've never had more than six bodies in the back at one time, and that was during COVID! Twenty!? Two-zero!?" The phone rang on the desk.

"Don't you dare answer that!"

Delores chewed on a cuticle. "I have a question. Why is no one else answering their phones?" Delores shook her head. "Is it a holiday?"

"They're bringin' everyone here because we go to church with 'em! Dammit!" Sissy tossed the pile across the desk and closed her eyes. "This is exactly why I never wanted my picture and phone number in the fuckin' church directory!"

"Calm down! We'll just have to keep them at Frances's place until we can move 'em here. A few at a time. And we still got those two in the back to do," Delores said.

Christopher nodded. "Mr. Fisher's funeral is set for tomorrow morning, and the other one is a graveside tomorrow in Athens," Christopher said, nodding to Rusty, who would be transporting the body."

Sissy clapped her hands. "Chop, chop! Get on it! Battle stations!"

Christopher left Sissy and Delores as two more lines began to ring on the office phone.

"Call Frances and tell her what's happenin'. And call over to Baron Medical and see if they need any parts for later in the week. Maybe we can ship 'em some legs for that orthopedic convention they got comin' up."

"That's some good thinkin'!" Delores exclaimed.

 Sissy flipped through the messages. "Let's do James Green. He don't have any family. We can go ahead and do his funeral tomorrow afternoon. Go ahead and get that out of the way. Closed empty casket. Call Jethro to get his hole dug down at Liberty." She found messages from Delroy's family. "And Delroy. We'll tell them he has to be closed casket. Just get them out of the way and give us some more time."

Delores launched herself out of the chair, clapping her hands. "We're gonna make more money this week on funerals than we are body parts!"

"Well, I will," Sissy said. Delores shot her a look. "Lockhart Brothers is a family funeral home, remember?"

"Ain't I your family?"

"Just because we have all this work don't mean everyone is working on a commission. I don't remember cuttin' any bonuses to you for Lockhart business. Do you?"

Lily looked herself over in the mirror, admiring the simple blue skirt and floral top Akasha had chosen for her.

"You like it?" Akasha asked from the hallway. "Does is fit okay?"

"Oh, yes. Very nice!" she shouted over the curtain. "Damn, I look cute," Lily quietly whispered to herself, admiring the cut over her hips.

Akasha kept an eye on Nakoya and Frances, speaking in hushed tones on the other side of the store. "I'll be right back," Akasha called to Lily. "You just holler if you need anything!"

Akasha quickly made her way to her sister and friend, who had cooled on the in-store hand-to-hand combat. "What is going on?" she quietly asked. "What's the plan here?"

Frances closed her eyes, feeling her vertigo or another headache about to hit again. "I just keep getting dizzy! It started a few weeks ago." Frances sat on the couch, massaging her temples. "Donald's in the hospital. No way he survives this, right?" She shook her head. "He's not the priority right now. Our priority is findin' Stephen and Stuart and exposin' them."

"And just kiss my dreams goodbye?" Nakoya asked. "Yeah, no."

"Ray Jackson don't know it's Stephen and Stuart behind this whole thing. You need to hand Ray the villain he's lookin' for. Expose Stephen and Stuart for fakin' their deaths. We expose the fraud, and it could also shut down Lockhart Brothers completely, taking out Sissy. Two birds, one stone."

"Shut down the Lockhart Brothers?"

"Sissy Stone took over the game when I got out."

"That old white woman from church!?"

"That's Stephen and Stuart's sister. She's running with Delores Rogers."

"Oh, I like her. She's cute."

"Unless Sissy has known this entire time that Stephen and Stuart are alive, we can assume they don't know she's running things now. If we hand Stephen and Stuart to Ray, it would be the answer to all my prayers. I could finally end all of this on my end," she pleaded. "Let's just hand that story to Ray. And you can do whatever the frick you want to do with your dead body empire. Ray is just lookin' for a story. Give him those two, and then you can do whatever you want to do."

"One problem. I don't know where they are."

"What do you mean?"

"All I know is they were somewhere in Europe. And the phone number I had for him stopped working right after the raid. He told me to 'stand by' and then ghosted me."

"Don't matter. As long as Ray thinks they're alive, he's got a new lead to chase. Again, Nakoya, the only way you and I make it out of this without spending the rest of our lives in orange jumpsuits is to get the heat off us."

"How did Ray know about Donald?"

"A few weeks after the raid, Ray tracked down the landlord at the warehouse. The landlord gave him a description of Donald. The FBI had been asking questions for weeks, so the landlord just assumed Ray was just another agent. Ray spent weeks tryin' to track down Donald in Atlanta. Anyone who might have known anything."

"And why is he here now? Why did he come back?"

"Ray figured out headless Oscar was the owner of the van in the lake. He had Oscar's keys. Knowin' Oscar had worked in the area, stealin' from funeral homes, he started goin' around to the funeral homes a few days ago. He started finding dead morticians."

"Ray didn't want to come back," Akasha said knowingly. "He didn't want to see you. He was afraid he would fall in love with you again."

"Yeah, well, I think that spell has been broken, Madame Leota." Frances took a deep breath, trying to focus from her dizzy spell. "He found the body of a dead mortician out in Madison, and when he pulled the security footage, he saw Donald stab her to death. Apparently, he was on a revenge tour all over the Southeast."

"Why isn't this in the news?" Akasha asked. "This should be news."

"Because it just started three days ago. And Ray didn't tell anyone because technically, he was breakin' and enterin'. And besides, he's gonna wanna be the hero." Frances took a deep breath. "Nakoya, we got a man in the hospital who's in a coma and hopefully gonna stop breathin' soon. But you and I both also got a bulldog named Ray who is hellbent on making himself a star."

"How?" Akasha asked.

"His… podcast."

The two sisters looked at her, bewildered.

"His what?"

"He's doin' a podcast."

"Jesus," Nakoya whispered. "Ain't that the most white people shit you ever heard?"

Akasha raised a hand. "Even if Nakoya gives up Stephen and Stuart, there's nothing linking them to Donald Dobkins. Unless they go around and start exhuming the bodies of everyone all over Liberty who were laid out at Lockhart's."

The curtain slid open in the back of the store, and Lily emerged with her old clothes over her shoulder. "I wear these out?" she asked, pulling cash from her leather jacket pocket.

"Sure!" Akasha said, taking the tags from Lily's hands. "Why don't we just call it forty?"

Lily handed her the cash, looking out the window to the pounding rain. "Oh, and do you have an umbrella?" she asked.

Akasha pointed to a few umbrellas on a side table. "Let's call it forty-five," as Lily picked out a black umbrella. "You new in town?" Akasha asked.

"Yes." Lily giggled. "Hopefully job interview."

"Oh, fun. Where at?" Akasha asked.

"A funeral home," she said.

Nakoya, Frances, and Akasha all slowly looked up at the same time.

"Did you say… a funeral home?" Frances asked.

Lily giggled and nodded. "I work on dead bodies."

# CHAPTER SEVEN

# BRING OUT YOUR DEAD

**B**en Camden began his autopsies at the former Womack Bakery, and currently, the home to the Birdie Hunt Memorial Recreational Center and Senior Fun Day Center, by hitting a Celine Dion playlist from his Spotify.

Ben's gloved hands were deep in the chest cavity of Logan Voss when Kevin burst through the side door, soaking wet, rushing across the floor to Frances's office.

"Son, you can't be in here while I'm doin' the autopsies!" Ben shouted at Kevin.

"It's all good! I just gotta get somethin' for my momma!"

"But I'm in here working!" Ben insisted.

"And how much are you payin' my momma to commandeer her building for the week with all these dead people? Is it a lot? Or did you just ask her, and she gave it to you for free because she has a heart and a love of her community? Are you payin' to keep the lights on in here?!"

Ben sighed. "Make it quick."

Kevin rushed into the office and locked the door. He powered up the desktop computer and located the security footage from the night before, containing shots of the outside of the bakery and the view inside the main room.

He watched as the images glitched but clearly showed Sissy, Delores, Rusty, and himself removing the bodies. He downloaded the files and emailed them to himself.

While the files loaded, he looked around the room. *Was anything out of place?* Anything different that would indicate his mother had recently acquired a massive amount of land? And if she had, why hadn't she told him?

When the files finished uploading, the computer made a small "ding." Kevin kissed the wooden crucifix around his neck and whispered, "God is good all the time."

He closed out of the email program and walked back into the main room. He continued his tear across the room. "Have a good one!" he called out to Ben.

"Kevin, was anyone in here last night?" Ben asked.

Kevin froze. "What? Why would you ask that?"

"Just wondering if someone came in last night. I feel like some of the bodies got moved around, and I swear I'm missing a few."

"Maybe they weren't really dead and woke up. I've heard that can happen."

Ben shrugged, laughing. "Guess I can't count. Who's gonna come in here and steal a dead body in the middle of the night?"

"Not me!" Kevin laughed. "Not duckin' me! You locked the doors, right?"

Ben nodded. "Yeah… Yeah, sure, we locked all the doors. I remember checkin' all the doors."

"There you have it." Kevin nodded a final, "See-ya" and headed for the door.

"But just to be safe, is there any security footage?" Ben asked, pointing to the camera in the corner.

"Security footage? Uh, no, sir, Mr. Camden. Them cameras ain't never worked. I think they were left up there by the last people who had this place. Momma don't need security for old people daycare."

"Right."

"But if you're worried, maybe you should get you one of them Ring cameras and set it up."

"I'll be fine. Just wonderin'."

"Have a blessed day!" Kevin screamed over his shoulder as he pushed open the side door and ran back into the rain.

Frances stood by the door, watching Lily roll her leather pants and shove them into the tailpack on her motorcycle outside Akasha's shop. She managed to stay dry by wedging the umbrella between her neck and shoulder.

"I'll call you later," Frances called out to Akasha, never taking her eyes off Lily.

"What are you gonna do?" Nakoya asked. "Do you know something?"

"Tiny Asian woman shows up in Liberty looking like Catwoman in a black leather bodysuit to work on dead bodies. Are you dense or somethin'? She's gotta be workin' with Dobkins." Frances said. Frances grabbed her purse, tossed her latte into the trash, and rushed out of the shop and under an awning.

Lily stopped, standing still like an animal being hunted in the jungle. She spun around.

"Hello," she said, smiling broadly.

"Nice bike," Frances said, pointing to the Harley. "Was admirin' it."

"Thank you."

"Nice boots, too! Them DSW?" Frances asked of Lily's knee-high black, high-heeled boots."

"They're Michael Kors."

Frances burst out laughing at the irony. *"All roads lead back to Michael Kors footwear in this damn town."* "How are you gonna ride in that skirt?"

"Oh, I'm not riding it right now. This rain! I'm just leaving my clothes here before I go to my interview."

"At the funeral home."

"At the funeral home."

"Which funeral home?"

Lily forced a smile. Frances recognized that look. That was the look of a smart woman done playing games.

"Which funeral home?" Frances asked again. "If you don't have one in mind, I can happily recommend one." *This woman had to be an assassin,* Frances thought. Donald couldn't have killed all those people by himself. That didn't make sense, right? Donald was working with this woman. *Was she about to kill Sissy?* "You know a funeral home?" Lily asked.

"I do. Oh, sister, I do. Old family business. Run by an old woman. She lost both of her brothers. They just up and went missin'."

"That's sad," Lily said, swallowing a little harder. *Is this bitch onto me?* "Mmm-hmm." Frances rifled through her purse, looking for her cigarettes. "So, what kind of work do you do? In funeral homes."

"Embalming."

"That's fun. Where'd you study?"

Lily looked down at the rain collecting around her boots, trying to decide whether Frances was super smart or just another racist Southern Karen like the ones Lily had met over the years while playing the heavy for Stephen and Stuart.

"Mortuary School," Lily responded.

"You know a Donald Dobkins?" Frances unflinchingly asked, lighting her cigarette.

Lily stared back at Frances for a beat too long, and Frances laughed. "Who are you?"

"Why are you asking me all these questions?" Lily asked, making her fake accent a little thicker. "You drama."

"Drop the accent, sweetheart. I know a bad Japanese accent a million miles away."

"It's Chinese!"

"Is it?" Frances asked. "Besides, I got a good look at your hands and nails in there. Them hands ain't never touched no embalmin' fluids unless you're about to tell me it's an ancient Chinese secret."

Frances offered Lily a cigarette. Lily rushed under the awning, collapsing her umbrella. She took the cigarette suspiciously.

"What's your name?" Frances asked.

"What's your name?" Lily asked back.

Frances lit Lily's cigarette. "Welp, my Christian name is Frances Hunt, but some people call me Big Momma."

Lily's ever-so-slightly raised eyebrow gave herself away. Frances laughed. "Cool, so you're a fan. Cool, cool." Frances paced the sidewalk for a bit. "What am I supposed to call you?"

"My mother calls me Ching-Li. Stephen and Stuart call me Tiger Lily," Lily said, dropping all traces of her fake accent.

The two women sized each other up, taking drags from their cigarettes.

"Tiger Lily? Like from *Peter Pan?* Wasn't she an Indian?"

"Native American."

"Same difference."

"Not even remotely close, but now you see why those two old farts nicknamed me after a character in a Disney movie." Lily rolled her eyes. "Call me whatever you want."

"Stephen and Stuart…" Frances said, letting it hang in the air. "This story just keeps getting freakin' weirder every hour. You're workin' with them and not with Donald?"

Lily exhaled and waved her cigarette. "No, let's go back to you."

"Long story short: I fell into body snatchin' by accident. Killed a Mexican. Pissed off a dwarf. Sheriff got my momma killed. Quit grave robbin'. Hired a girl to help me run my old folks' rec center. Turns out she was in Stephen and Stuart's pocket all this time, and she just beat the shit out of me. Literally just fired her in that store. And now the Lockharts's little sister is blackmailin' me back into the business, and the former sheriff is blackmailin' me to do his podcast."

"Oh! I love podcasts! I've always wanted to start one! I think I would be really good at them!"

"You got a nice voice. Real soothin'." Frances took a drag. "Anyways, that's me. I'm basically being held against my will by the Golden Girls and Barney Fife."

A mother and her toddler hurried along the sidewalk under the rain. Lily and Frances hid their cigarettes behind their backs. "Howdy-do!" Frances exclaimed as the woman kept walking.

Frances and Lily looked at each other. "Are we supposed to start fighting?" Lily asked.

"Rather not. I just got my ass handed to me in there, so I'd prefer not to," Frances responded, taking another drag from her cigarette. "First time meeting a… Whatever you are. Are you the person goin' around killin' all the funeral home directors?"

"Am I what?"

"Wow, that really was Donald!" Frances said, then remembered, snapping her fingers. "You know he's in a coma down at the hospital, right?"

Lily coughed, choking on the smoke. "Excuse me? Did you do that!?"

"I wish! No, that was Jesus. The Baptist Church steeple got zapped by thunder and lightnin' yesterday and fell on top of him." Frances made a "splat" with her hands.

"Are you serious?"

"As a heart attack."

"Oh! Wow! Great! So, I can just like… Go!"

"Beg pardon?"

"Stephen and Stuart sent me to watch after their sister and take out Donald if he ever showed up. But I can just like head the hospital and like…" Lily slid her index finger across her throat, then her eyes narrowed, realizing something Frances had said.

"I think that's a real great idea! I'd pull his plug myself, but I'm afraid I'd screw it up. Want me to call you a car so you don't get wet?" she asked, taking her phone from her pocket.

"Did you say you fell into body snatching and Sissy was blackmailing you?"

"I did." Frances blinked, realizing. "They don't know."

Lily shook her head. "I don't think so. They were worried about her safety."

"They don't know Sissy took over."

Lily stared off into the distance, thinking.

Frances looked into the distance to see what she was staring at, then asked, "What's goin' on?"

"You know, I've always wanted to start a podcast. And Stephen and Stuart don't know Donald's in a coma. I could buy myself some time. Squeeze out some more coin. Research the area. This could be my ticket out."

Frances nodded but tried to get Lily back on track. "If Donald goes to prison, he's going to sing like a canary in a coal mine. He'll spill all the tea. So, I like this idea of you killin' him."

"But if we keep him alive, we can use him on the podcast."

"I think that might be the dumbest reason I've ever heard to keep someone alive. Besides, Ray Jackson is doin' his podcasts, and you know… Competing podcasts…"

"Who's Ray Jackson?"

"The former sheriff, who's now makin' my life a livin' hell."

"This ain't a life, Big Momma. You know that. I'm getting too old to ride around the country on my bike, killing people for hire." Lily flicked her cigarette into the street. "This podcast idea could spin off into movies. Books. T-Shirts. I could be very, very rich." She took a deep breath. "You help me, I'll make you a silent partner. Split everything with you."

"I'm like a multimillionaire, so I don't really need the money."

Lily looked Frances up and down. "I like shopping at Wal-Mart to save my money."

"Stephen and Stuart want me to check in on their sister. I'm going to ask for a job. If they give me a job, I would be *inside* the operation. Learn everything that they are doing. And expose them. We have to get me this job!"

Frances couldn't deny having more people on Team Hunt at Lockhart's could only help her. Especially an assassin. Frances opened her large umbrella. "Funeral home's three blocks this way. I'll walk you in."


June Franks chased Sissy down the hallway with a crying baby strapped to her chest and five children ages two to nine trailing behind her. "Mrs. Sissy, I gotta get Hugh buried as soon as I can! His whole family is comin' in from all over the country, and I can't take his in-laws! Last time his momma visited, she rearranged my entire house!"

Sissy continued her march toward the lobby. "Workin' on it, June! Got a full house up in here myself!"

"But my family's been comin' to Lockhart Brothers for centuries! Don't that account for somethin'?'"

"Ain't been open for centuries, June, but we'll do our best."

The baby cried louder. The kids scattered into the empty, open parlors. Sissy spun around and pointed her finger in June's face. "I got like a hundred people down there in that lobby I have to deal with right now. Get your kids and that squallin' baby out of my funeral home, and I'll get you to the top of the list."

"I just really need to get him in the ground—"

"I got it, June! I got it! Talk to Delores and do the paperwork."

"I ain't good at readin' and writin'," she whined as tears began to roll down her face.

Sissy wanted to shake her. "June! Go see Delores! I don't got no time for this!"

Sissy pressed on into the lobby, where it looked like triage in an old war movie. Crying families huddled in groups. Christopher passed clipboards and tissue around. Delores waved Sissy waved over to the door to the office.

"We can't do this all on our own, Sissy!"

The main door opened. Dramatic thunder shook the building. Sissy groaned, seeing the door push open and the bell jingle overheard. She exhaled, seeing Frances walk through with a small Asian woman.

Frances made her way toward the office as she slung rainwater from her umbrella. Lily followed closely behind.

All four scurried into the office, and Delores closed the door.

"This is… Ching… Ching-la-la-ri," Frances muddled, half forgetting Lily's name and half grasping onto a name she remembered hearing on a television playing *RuPaul's Drag Race* down at the Tool Box.

"Ching-la-la-ri! That's a beautiful name!" exclaimed Delores.

"You can call me Lil," Lily said, affecting her accent from her previous performance at Akasha's.

"And who are you? We don't got no dead Asians," Sissy lamented.

"She's looking for a job. I met her down at Akasha's—"

"You're hired!" Delores screamed, speaking a little louder than necessary. She thrust a stack of clipboards into Lily's arms. "We'll work your pay out later. We got good dental, too. Need you to get out there and take care of all these intake forms. We got like twenty funerals to do, and do them fast."

"She's Chinese, not deaf, Delores." Frances did a delayed double-take, acknowledging the people on the other side of the door. "We've got what?"

"All them damned Baptists came here! We have to bury all of 'em," Sissy bemoaned. She turned to Lily. "See if you can get any of them to do a group rate. I don't know what that would be, but run some numbers, and I'll give you a 10 percent commission if you can."

"Oh, I don't do paperwork. I embalm," Lily said, handing the clipboards back to Delores.

"It's all hands on deck up in here," Sissy insisted, taking the clipboards from Delores and shoving them back at Lily.

"Lil was a mail-order bride, and she's not real good with English," Frances said, trying to get Lily out of administration.

Lily slowly turned her head to Frances and, through gritted teeth, whispered a contemptuous, "Dude."

"We can handle the form. Right now, your priority is finding caskets. We only got seven in stock, and we need to get as many options as possible," Sissy said.

Christopher poked his head into the office. "I need help right now!" he yelled, motioning for Sissy and Delores to follow him. "It's like a Trump rally out here!"

"Good. They should be leavin' soon," Frances insisted. "When is Ben Camden gonna start releasin' bodies?"

"Tonight," Delores said.

"Three parlors. Let's aim for two to three in the mornin', startin' at nine o'clock, and a few in the afternoon to night. I'm guessin' they'll want Bill White doin' all the funerals. We need to get him in here. Let's suggest visitations here with a graveside service. We've only got the one chapel, but don't got a lot of parking. And since they all know each other, they'll probably go from parlor to parlor. Offer cremations at a discount."

"Them old Southern Baptists ain't gonna do no cremations! They're gonna want to fly to glory in their bodies out of their caskets when the Rapture happens!" Delores exclaimed.

"Offer cremations at a discount," Frances insisted. "Tell them if their loved one's bodies are broken and tore up, they don't want an open casket. Ask for photos, and we can blow them up and put them up on easels."

"We might need bodies," Sissy said, catching herself in front of Lily. "I mean, we might need to prepare as many bodies as we can."

"Can't we just focus on gettin' these people in the ground without focusin' on your side job?" Delores groaned.

"My side job?" Sissy hissed.

"It's 'Lockhart business,' ain't it?" Delores said, mocking Sissy.

"I'm tired of your mouth, Delores! I'm tired of you talkin' back at me!"

Delores punched her in the breast. "You get meaner every day! I ain't takin' your crap much longer, Sissy Stone! Pretty soon, it's gonna be just you runnin' dead people parts!"

"What kind of parts?" Lily asked.

"None of your business," Sissy said, slapping Delores across the chest with a file. "If we're gonna pull this off—"

"All y'all just shut up!" Frances threw her hands, shutting Sissy up. Frances sighed, realizing she was going to have to take the bull by the horns in order for everything to move smoothly. "I'm the captain now! You hear me? The only way we're going to get through this is if I'm in charge."

"I—" Sissy started before Frances cut her off.

"Don't open your piehole! You're the face of the Lockhart Brothers Funeral Home. You get out there and shake hands and kiss babies. Delores and Kevin will handle the paperwork. Christopher and Lil will prepare the bodies."

"And what exactly will you be doin'?" Sissy curtly asked.

"Runnin' the gotdamn show."

Frances turned, threw open the office door, and pushed back into the chaos of the lobby. Frances put two fingers in her mouth and loudly whistled. Everyone in the lobby got quiet.

"Hey, y'all. Most of y'all know me. I'm Buddy and Birdie Hunt's daughter. I ain't been to church in a while. And… Well, I guess I picked a good day to miss, right?"

No one laughed.

"I'm here helpin' Sissy and them get everyone squared away, so this is what we need y'all to do." Frances nodded to Delores and Christopher. They began passing out clipboards.

"We need everyone to fill out these clipboards with as much information as you can provide. Ben Camden's hard at work on gettin' everyone squared away. Now, I don't want to sugarcoat this, but y'all might want to consider cremations. Or closed caskets. Because there was some pretty significant damage when the roof…"

A few cries and wails erupted through the crowd.

"Yeah, it ain't good. And when they're good here at Lockhart's, they're good. But let's face it… I know havin' an open casket is a way to have closure, but not when you're lookin' down at Daddy, and his jaw looks like an ashtray your granddaughter made in ceramics at Vacation Bible School. Christopher's good, but he ain't a sorcerer."

Sissy gasped and stomped her foot. "Frances!" she hissed.

"I'm just sayin', y'all might want to think about not havin' an open casket viewing. Maybe just do graveside. Course we can't do any funerals at the church on account of… Well, you know, the whole new sunroof. And I know everyone's gonna be tired of funerals by the end of the week."

She looked at the forlorn faces throughout the lobby. "I hate that y'all are goin' through this. But we'll get you taken care of."

A hand went up. "How will we know?" he asked. Frances's brow furrowed an "about what?" and he cleared his throat, asking, "If we need to do a closed casket."

Frances nodded. "Once Ben releases the bodies, we'll go pick 'em up, and we can help you decide."

Another hand when up. "Is that why you had a closed casket for your momma?"

Frances locked her jaw. A headache pain darted in her skull. She thrust her hand into her purse and took the ibuprofen bottle, shaking four tablets in her hand, before swallowing them dry.

"We did a closed casket because my momma shot herself in the head, and she was missin' part of her skull and apparently most of the side of her face."

The room fell silent.

"Is that a good enough answer for you?"

Frances refocused. "Should be getting some of the bodies tonight. They got three suites in here, and they can do two to three in the morning and two to three in the afternoon."

"What about the rain?" someone shouted out.

"The rain?"

"We can't do graveside if it's raining, can we?"

"I mean… They can still dig the hole. I don't see why that would be a problem, right?"

Rusty stopped at a truck stop to fill up his van and grab an energy drink. He had just delivered all the bodies to the drop point. He sniffed his hands as he stood in line to pay and smelled the stench of decomposition on his hands. He gagged, placed the drink on the counter, and retreated to the bathroom to wash his hands.

**"The bitch is back,"** came a text from Frances on Rusty's phone, followed by **"Shoot me."** Rusty checked his phone and saw several missed calls from Sissy and a text message insisting he call her right away.

He smiled and called Frances.

She answered. "Boy, you might want to keep on truckin' to South Carolina and never look back."

"You said you were 'back.' Back where?"

"I'm at Lockhart's."

Rusty laughed, confused. "I'm sorry, what? Thought you retired from tomb raidin'."

"Long story. Tell you later. It's like one of them movies where the hero thinks they're out, and they get yanked back in for one last score."

"Like *Unforgiven!*"

"More like *The Wild Bunch.*" Frances massaged her temples, trying to rub her

headache away. All them dead church members are here because they all went to church together, and no one in town is answerin' their phones. And the Lockharts are Baptists. I just had to give a speech to all of 'em so we could lower their expectations."

"How many so far?"

"Last I counted, we got fifteen families out there right now, and they just keep comin'."

"Holy crap," he responded, adding extra soap to his hands.

"I'm runnin' the show, otherwise, Sissy is gonna screw up. Also, you need to know Ray Jackson's back in town, and he's goin' in. He's connectin' dots. We have to stay ahead of him again."

"How much does he know?"

"He knows about me. He knows about Donald. He missin' pieces, but he's got enough to see a picture."

"Understood. What do you need from me?"

"I'm gonna need your help in here the next few days as backup. We're gonna have back-to-back funerals and need you to help stage. We just gotta get all these people buried, and then we can deal with Ray. You got a suit?"

"I have a suit."

"Cool. Startin' tomorrow, if you wouldn't mind wearin' it, that'd be great."

Rusty looked at himself in the mirror. He pulled on his beard and his long hair. *Maybe it's time for a haircut and a buzz.* "I'll be back in about an hour. Just did the drop. Want me to pick you up anything?"

Frances laughed. "I'm beyond help at this point. Let's just get through this week and get ahead of Jackson."

"Done. See you in an hour." He hung up.

Rusty dried his hands, paid for the drink, and ran back to the van in the rain.

When he climbed inside, he sat in silence, just listening to the rain hit the roof. He listened to the total silence of the van and just the patter of nature above him.

*You might want to keep on truckin' to South Carolina and never look back!* Rusty contemplated that a lot recently. He thought about his next move. He had felt a stirring in his heart that it was time for him to find something new in life to explore. But he also couldn't help but think that maybe there was something keeping him in Liberty.


*KA-BOW* went the thunder outside Hector's hospital room as Dr. Morales pulled his stethoscope away from Hector's chest. "Thought for sure we had lost you. You lost a lot of blood. But it was a miracle. Bullet was a clean shot."

Hector pulled his hospital gown back up around his shoulder. "Have I had any visitors?" he asked.

"Several. A few women friends," Dr. Morales said with a smile. "I think they brought you in and threatened the lives of everyone here if we didn't save you."

"Do you have my phone?"

"We'll hunt it down. Get some rest."

"I need to get out of here."

"And it will be a few days before we consider that. Rest."

Dr. Morales stood up and turned to leave, seeing Clint standing in the doorway.

"I was just checkin' in on him," Clint said as Morales stepped out.

"Remember me? Clint said, walking to the bed. "We had a little chat when you came to. You told me you were in love with Frances Hunt."

"I… I don't remember saying that."

"Then I guess I'm a mind reader."

"Who are you?" Hector asked.

"Clint Peppers. Candy striper. I know most people here don't like that term, but I'm bringing it back. This will only take a minute. Why is ex-sheriff Ray Jackson pokin' his head around Liberty again, and why is he tryin' to get me to team up as Robin to his Batman? He's claimin' Ms. Hunt's life's in danger and seein' as how she's the one who dropped you off, and you had a hole in your tummy when she did… Shit ain't addin' up."

"What do you know?" Hector asked.

"I know I don't like Ray Jackson. That's for damn sure."

"He's back in town?"

Clint pulled Dr. Morales' stool closer and straddled it. "Start talking."

Hector sat up and motioned for his water cup. Clint handed it to him. Hector took a long sip.

"What does Ray want?" Hector asked, shaking his cup for more water.

"He wants information on the man that got hit by the cross. He was brought in as a John Doe with no identification. But I know he goes by Donald Dobkins. Seems like a shifty individual, and Ray Jackson wants access to him. Ray claims Frances got messed up with him."

"Wants access to him? Are you saying he survived? He's alive!? How is he alive!? I saw that thing fall on top of him!"

"Barely alive. But yes. Alive."

"Can you go and… kill him?"

"Not really protocol, paco."

"How do you know his name?"

"I'm resourceful."

"He wants to kill Frances. He said he was going to cut out her heart. I'm pretty sure he killed an asshole I knew. I think he's on a murder spree. What did you tell the sheriff?"

"One, he ain't on any more sprees. He's in a coma. Two, Ray ain't the sheriff anymore. I told him he can't see him, and he's got no visitors. Ray's claimin' there's a body harvestin' operation all over the Southeast, and he wouldn't tell me what Frances did. How do you fit in this puzzle?"

"So that's what he's been doing since he left town. He's been fishing. I need you to help me get out of here."

"Bruh, you were shot in the stomach. You ain't gettin' out of here for a hot second."

Hector grabbed Clint by his scrubs. "I need you to get me out of here. Frances is in danger."

"Donald Dobkins is in a coma. He can't hurt Frances."

"You have to pull his plug," Hector said, pleading.

Dr. Morales walked back. "Left my pen." He stopped when he saw Hector holding Clint by his scrubs. "Is there a problem?" he asked as he grabbed his pen from the corner of Hector's bed."

"No problem. I was just leaving," Clint said.

Hector grabbed Clint's hand. "Do it."


Ray stepped inside Akasha's shop and looked around, admiring her small but tasteful boutique.

"Be right there!" she called from the back of the store as Ray checked his reflection in a full-length mirror.

"Take your time!" he hollered back, taking a seat on the leopard sofa Frances and Nakoya tumbled over less than an hour earlier.

Akasha rounded the corner with her arms draped in dresses. She jolted with surprise upon looking up to see Ray. "Oh, hi. Can I help you find something?" *This can't be good,* she thought.

*She looks familiar.* "Have we met before?" he asked.

"Yes, sir, we have. We met briefly at Mrs. Hunt's funeral out at the churchyard. It was raining something awful that day." She looked out the window. "Just like today. It's never gonna stop raining, is it?"

Ray stood, shaking his head. He remembered the entire day. He remembered her with a man. A Hispanic man? "I'm sorry, I do remember that now. Yes, you're right."

Akasha read Ray and knew he was looking for Nakoya. "You were the sheriff, right? We got all worried when you disappeared. I know Mrs. Hunt's daughter was worried something sick about you."

"I doubt that," he barked.

"Oh, she was. She was very worried. I know you guys had a falling out."

"She tell you why?"

Akasha didn't know the full story, but she knew Ray had been involved in some way with Birdie's suicide. "She did," Akasha said, placing the clothes over her arms on a rack. Akasha folded her arms. She snapped her head to the side and dug in a heel. "You looking for a dress? I don't carry any men's clothing."

Ray looked down at his hands and looked back up Akasha, letting out a little laugh. "You're Akasha Whittler, right?" Ray asked, taking a stab that her last name matched Nakoya's.

"Whittler?" Akasha said with a laugh. "Yeah, I ain't used that last name in a good ten years. Had it legally changed because of my daddy." Akasha walked around the corner and appeared seconds later with a bottle of tequila. "You want to start talking straight now?" She plopped the bottle in front of him. "I'm all out of limes."

Ray unscrewed the top and took a large swig. He handed it to Akasha. She took a bigger swig.

Akasha sat in the leather chair across from Ray. "You're looking for Nakoya."

Ray's head dropped down to his feet.

"I don't think the answer is on those discount shoes you bought on the Amazon," Akasha said, crossing her legs.

"You didn't ask a question," Ray shot back.

"Are you looking for Nakoya Whittler?"

"I am. You know where I can find her?"

Akasha closed her eyes, attempting to read Ray.

Ray grew uncomfortable. Seconds went by. A moment went by.

"Hello?" Ray asked.

Akasha held up a finger. She saw he wanted answers. She saw that he wanted justice, but the justice was selfish. The justice was for himself.

"What are you doin'?" Ray asked.

"Reading you," Akasha quietly responded.

"Readin' me how?"

Akasha opened her eyes and stared into his eyes. He wasn't a serious threat to Nakoya or Frances. His quest felt self-righteous. But one that felt like it was exacting revenge. This was a hurt man. A very hurt man.

"Tell me what you think you want, former Sheriff Jackson," she asked.

Ray looked into her dark eyes. She was warm but just slightly defensive. She was confident. Not at all afraid of him. She wasn't someone he could intimidate. "I want the truth," he said, taking another shot of tequila. "You ever met someone who you fell madly in love with the moment you saw them, but they used you and broke your heart? I just want the truth."

Akasha nodded. "This is more than Frances. You let something slip through your fingers on your watch. You want justice."

"I need to talk to your sister. I think she can help me fill in some holes."


Clint Peppers leaned his chest over the desk at the nurses' station, flirting with Nurse Angie. She was the hospital hard ass, but he knew a smile and any bit of attention, and she would be eating out his palm.

"You know that little person we got in here? How's he doin'?" he asked, flexing his biceps as he squeezed the lip of the counter.

"He's still hangin' in there," she said with a small grin. "Can you believe it?"

"You think he's gonna live?" he asked.

"Broke damn nearly every bone in his body!"

"Can I poke my head in and see him?"

She raised an eyebrow and shot him an annoyed look. She grabbed her keycard and heaved herself off her stool, motioning for him to follow. "I need to check in on him anyways," she said, rounding the desk and walking toward his room. "Do a proof of life check."

They walked in to see Donald Dobkins wiggling his fingers through his arm casts and quietly moaning.

"Holy crap cakes! He's awake!" Clint screamed. "He's alive!"

Angie ran out of the room and back to her desk, shouting to Dr.

Morales down the hall, "The man that got crushed by the cross is awake! He's awake! Come quick!"

Clint got closer, whispering in Donald's ear, "It's gonna be okay, sir. I'm gonna take real good care of you."

Donald murmured quietly but loud enough to hear, "Where am I?"

"You're at Liberty Memorial. A big old cross fell on top of you at the Liberty Baptist Church. We thought you were a goner."

Donald stared back at him as Dr. Morales and Nurse Angie raced back into the room. "Step aside, son," Morales instructed before shoving him out of the way. When he saw it was Clint, he indignantly asked, "What are you doin' in here?!"

"Buddy, I'm like your coma whisperer at this point. You're welcome."

"I'm Dr. Morales," Morales stated in a loud voice over Donald. "You're in a hospital. Can you tell us your name?" he shouted, pulling a pad from his coat.

"I... I..."

"Sir, can you tell me your name?" Dr. Morales asked again.

"I don't know... I don't know... What is happening to me?"


Frances and Lily smoked cigarettes under their umbrellas in the parking lot behind Lockhart Brothers, pacing in a circle.

"I don't know the first thing about dealing with dead bodies other than making them dead bodies!" Lily exclaimed. "What was I thinking!? I should have come up with a better cover story. Stupid, Lily! Stupid!"

"To be fair, you didn't think you'd be walking into a bazillion funerals on your first day. But now you see why I need your help, right? She's nuts."

"Those two are bonkers," Lily said, indicating to Delores and Sissy inside the funeral home with her cigarette. This is crazy, Frances," Lily said, exhaling a long drag of her cigarette before squashing it under her boot. "I quit smoking. You're a bad influence."

Frances flicked an ash. "I've been thinking about this podcast idea of yours. I'll help you with it, but I'm gonna need something in exchange."

"What's that?"

"Where are Stephen and Stuart? I need to hand Ray Jackson a new suspect to go after."

"Not sure I want to give that information up so soon. And they've never done me wrong."

"What they are doing is wrong! It's illegal!"

"You were doin' it yourself!"

"I am aware, and I got out. I was desperate. I needed the money."

"I'm a bounty hunter. I don't ask questions. You're either finding people, watching people, protecting people, or killing people. My moral compass is real loose."

"You don't have any sort of emotional qualms about this line of work?"

"Oh, no. Nope. I'm on the spectrum," she said bluntly.

"Then you're lucky," Frances said. "If you want to do this podcast, you're gonna be askin' a lot of questions. And I'm the only person who can connect you to all the people involved. I know the entire story." Frances begged. "I want out of this, Lily. I need help. I need your help. I need to give Ray something," Frances said, pulling back the door and opening it for Lily. "After you."

"I'll think about it," Lily said. She collapsed her umbrella and filed inside. Frances collapsed her umbrella as the phone rang in her duster. She pulled it out to see: **"HECTOR CALLING."**


Nakoya returned to Akasha's shop with a bag of takeout from Leland Peters and Mark Jones-Peters sandwich shoppe. While Akasha was a huge fan of Leland and Mark's sandwiches, Nakoya was not a fan of the café run by Liberty's most famous and openly gay couple. She thought their food was bland and pretentious.

Nakoya didn't see Ray Jackson sitting on the sofa as she rushed in underneath her umbrella. "They were out of chicken salad, so I told them to just give you the tuna melt. You like their tuna melt, right?"

"Nakoya, this is Ray Jackson," Akasha said, patiently waiting for her sister to turn around and acknowledge the man in her shop.

Nakoya spun around and spotted him. Handsome, tall. Just her type. "Oh, hey there!" she said, rushing over and extending her hand. "I'm Nakoya. Kash's sister. How do you two know each other?"

Ray and Akasha shared a look. "We have mutual friends in common," Ray stated.

"Oh, that's nice," she laughed. "I know how Kash likes having white friends."

"Koya!" Akasha fired back. "Stop acting a fool." She said again, emphasizing, "This is Ray Jackson."

"I'm just kidding, gah." Nakoya threw the bag with Akasha's sandwich at her, and she plopped down on the sofa next to Ray.

"Y'all saw that incident down at the church yesterday?" Ray asked.

Nakoya glanced at Akasha. "Yeah, we were there. That's Akasha's church. She practically dragged me. It ain't like Black church. Black church is all day. The thing about them white Baptists is as long as no one gets up on the third verse of the call to invitation, then we might make it out of there in time to beat the Episcopals to brunch. I keep trying to get her to check out a Methodist church. Them people are out at noon on the dot."

"I'm a… reporter, and I'm doing a story about something that happened in this town," Ray lightly offered.

Nakoya slowly unwrapped her French dip. "Oh," she said blasély. She noticed Akasha sitting rigidly, not making eye contact. Something was off.

"What kind of story?" Nakoya asked.

"You see, I used to live here in Liberty. But I fell in love with a woman who didn't love me, and she used me. She told me a bunch of lies and threw off my—"

Nakoya slapped Ray across the face with her hoagie. "Are you the fucking sheriff!?" She turned to Akasha. "He's the fucking sheriff, ain't he!?"

"How did you—" Ray started to ask.

"This day just keeps getting—" Nakoya stood, pulling off her earrings and snapping her knuckles. "Ooooh, I'm so ready to fight everyone in this town!"

Akasha leaped to her feet. "No fighting! No more fighting in my store!"

"You got this damned podcast, don't you!?" Nakoya asked, her voice getting louder by the moment. "Is that what this is about? You want me to do your damned podcast!?"

"How did you know about my podcast?"

"Frances told us about it!" Nakoya bellowed. "She done told us about how you got a podcast, and you're trying to shut down this game. Well guess what, mister!? That ain't happening! You ain't shutting down shit!"

"You worked for Donald Dobkins. I've been trying to track you down for months. The landlord for the warehouse in Atlanta gave me your name. Told me you were the business manager. Told me you were a piece of work. Told me you were smart. All this time, I thought if I could find you, I'd find Donald Dobkins. And wouldn't you know, found you and found Donald Dobkins."

"Sounds to me like Donald Dobkins was only in town to kill your lady friend, who you can't seem to get over. The business is done. There's no story here for you. I haven't talked to Donald Dobkins since the day of the raid. The day he left me in there and left me to clear the place in less than ten minutes! You have any idea how hard it is to pack up over a hundred dead body parts in ten minutes with two dozen ex-cons who are stoned out of their minds!? It wasn't great!"

"Why did you shoot the guy in the parking lot?"

Akasha and Nakoya looked at each other. Akasha raised an eyebrow. "How did you know that was Nakoya? Frances wouldn't tell you that."

"Because Hector told a kid at the hospital a few hours ago it was someone named 'Nakoya,' and you might find this hard to believe, but there's not many Nakoyas in Liberty."

It took a few seconds for the news to register, then Nakoya fell to her knees, and Akasha gasped for breath. "Hector's awake!? He's talking!? He's okay!?"

Akasha grabbed her purse and her umbrella, rushing to the door. "Nakoya, lock up when you leave! Spare key's in the cash register!"

Nakoya grabbed her purse. "I'm coming with you!"

"I need to talk to you," Ray said, leaping to his feet.

"I don't want to talk to you! I'm *not* talking to you! Because of you and Frances, you put me out of work. I don't expect you to understand what we were doing on some moral level, but what we were doing was saving lives. We were helping people."

"You were robbing dead people."

"They were already dead! And last time I checked, you aren't in law enforcement, and there's no proof I was ever there. So you don't got shit on me! Your only hope is a man on life support."

Akasha shook her head and rushed out of her store.

"Just give me a name, please, Nakoya. First and last would be very helpful. I know Donald Dobkins wasn't the man behind the curtain. You're out of a job. Please help me get justice for the victims."

"There are no victims here."

"You desecrated the body of my friend, Dean Gilbertson. I saw what you people did to his body when his casket mysteriously showed back up after it was liberated from its tomb."

"I didn't have anything to do with that. I was in administration."

"But you sold his arms and his legs. That was a good man. A man who was beloved by this entire community. And I went back over the death records of over two hundred people over the past year in Liberty. How many of them wound up in your chop shop? How many families out in that community believe their loved ones are resting in peace when you people cut them into pieces?"

Nakoya looked away from him, moving behind the counter and opening the cash register. She grabbed the key and pointed to the door. "You need to leave."

"Give me a name, Nakoya."

"I give you a name; you're going to want more information. And I can't do that."

"Just give me a name, and I promise I won't ask another thing from you. I won't tell the police what I know. I'll keep your name out of it. I promise." Ray put his hand on the cover of a Vogue magazine. "I swear on the Bible of Cindy Crawford. Please, Nakoya. Who's behind all of this?"

Nakoya took a deep breath and walked to the door. They walked outside as the rain seemed to pound harder. She closed and locked the door.

"Stephen Lockhart," she quietly said.

"Stephen Lockhart is dead."

"No, he's not. And neither is his brother. They're who you are looking for. Never contact me again." She opened her umbrella and raced into the rain.


Kevin carried a fresh bouquet of flowers as he walked through the Liberty Baptist Church cemetery. The rain pounded harder, and he found himself sinking into the thick mud with nearly every step. It took great effort with each step to pry his boots from the mud to take another step.

He could barely see through the downpour.

Kevin had practically memorized all the names, as well as the birth and death dates, on the fifteen markers leading up to Brandy Lynn James's grave. He nodded and said "Hello" to each passing gravestone.

As he approached Brandy's burial spot, he noticed something looked "off" about her grave. It was as if the ground had shifted.

Kevin rushed ahead and tripped, sailing through the air and landing face-down in a massive puddle of rainwater and mud. His flowers scattered ahead almost to Brandy's grave, and his umbrella went softly, bouncing away.

He looked back to see what caused him to trip.

A large stone seemed to jut out of the ground at the foot of Gilbert Tomlin's grave. Kevin squinted through the rain to see it wasn't a rock. It was the edge of Gilbert's vault.

Kevin's head swiveled back to Brandy's grave. He realized the mound at the top of Brandy's grave was the head of her casket, breaking out of her eternal resting place.

Kevin stood, looking in all directions: the flood of rainwater was causing the caskets and vaults to surface from their graves.

Kevin backed up in horror and ran for his umbrella, which had been picked up by the rain and wind and was now two rows to the north.

When he finally reached it, he found himself at the grave of his grandmother.

Birdie Hunt's casket had completely emerged from its hole and was gently floating in a body of water. Rocking ever so calmly, as it banged against her tombstone.

# CHAPTER EIGHT

# AND THE SEA WILL GIVE UP THE DEAD

Frances raced into Hector's room, pushing past two nurses. She threw her arms around Hector as they jumped in to pry her off him.

"No! Stop! Be careful!" a large nurse shrieked, pulling Frances's right arm away from his neck.

"I thought you were dead! We all thought you were dead!" she screamed.

"I'm okay. I'm going to be okay," Hector said, wincing in pain. "Clean shot, apparently."

Frances broke free of the nurses to grab him in another tight embrace.

Clint Peppers walked into the room with a tray of food. He saw Frances with her arms tightly around Hector. "Got you some food," he offered, pushing a cart into the room with Salisbury steak.

Frances and Clint exchanged a look. "He looks better than when you brought him in, right?" Clint asked.

"Much better," Frances said, beaming from ear to ear.

"I hate to break up this little love connection, but can I talk to you in the hall, Ms. Hunt?" Clint asked.

Frances turned back to Hector. "I'll be right back. Don't go anywhere."

Hector laughed. "I'm trying to. Trust me."

In the hallway, Frances punched Clint in the stomach. "Ms. Hunt? What was that about?"

"Just being professional."

Frances smirked. "What's up with you? You've got a whole thing going on here. What's with the attitude?"

"Ray Jackson says you're in danger for some dead body part bullshit. The dude in that room right there got shot. And the little guy, who the former sheriff is so interested in, is awake, and I'm just beginning to ask myself—"

"Ray told you—" Frances's head shook violently, as if she were glitching. "Awake!? What do you mean he's awake!? How is he *alive!?* Is he talking!? Did he say anything!?"

"He doesn't remember anything."

The elevator doors opened at the end of the hall. Akasha and Nakoya ran out and saw Frances and Clint in the distance.

"He's in there!" Clint yelled, pointing to Hector's room. Nakoya and Akasha ran down the hallway. Clint turned back to Frances. "Now, why is Hector's shooter coming to visit him?!"

"It's not like that," she replied. "How is he awake?"

Nakoya and Akasha ran inside Hector's room. As the door closed behind them, everyone in the hall could hear a nurse scream something incomprehensible. Nakoya retaliated with an even louder and less comprehensible response.

"Come here." Frances grabbed Clint by the arm and pulled him further down the hall. "Donald Dobkins is alive!?"

"You knew his name all this time? Cool. You know that would have been helpful information to the hospital staff trying to save his life."

"No one asked me, smartass. He didn't have a wallet or ID on him?"

"I'm gonna need some grown-ups to start telling me the truth because there's some crazy shit goin' on, and everyone in this damn town is full of secrets!"

"What do you mean he doesn't remember anything?"

"He doesn't know his name or remember anything."

"Bullshit!"

"That's what he says. They got him in brain tests right now."

"Donald Dobkins don't got no amnesia."

Frances's phone rang. **"KEVIN CALLING."**

"Ugh, not now, Kevin," Frances groaned, sending him to voicemail. "So, he could, like… live? This could actually happen?"

"We are a hospital. You understand that's our job? To keep people alive here?"

Frances froze. "Oh, boy. Gotta say this hits a little different now."

"What hits different?"

"I was relieved when I heard he might die, but now that y'all are actively tryin' to keep him from dyin'—"

"Why is a little person trying to kill you, and can we just go back to the far more mysterious question at hand? What in the holy name of Tim Tebow are you doin' with dead body parts!?"

"I accidentally got his illegal business shut down."

"The illegal business with dead body parts?"

"What did Ray tell you?"

"Don't matter what he told me. You tell me. What are doin' with dead people?"

"Clint, it's a super long story, and you don't need all the details right now. Right now, we've got that one waking up from a gunshot," Frances said, pointing to Hector's room. "And I've got two dozen funerals to cater, and I don't got time to tell you about how Ms. Hunt ended up in an illegal body shop and pull-a-part operation. It's a good story, and maybe I'll tell you over a drink one day when you're old enough to drink."

"I want to help you."

"I don't need your help."

Clint stepped back. "So… What are you saying here? You and I are done?"

"Done? Clint, you and I never started."

Clint took another step back. "Oh. Okay. I see how it is. You know what, crazy lady? You and your shooters and evil little people and gunshot victims and former sheriffs and old women and your messed up son and your dozens of dead people can all go f yourselves! I'm a good guy! And I was just trying to help you! But you don't want a good guy! Women like you never want the good guy! I hope you have the life you deserve!"

Clint turned and walked away, leaving Frances outside of Hector's door. Frances watched him go, waiting for him to turn around. But he never did.

**"KEVIN CALLING."**

Frances sent Kevin to voicemail again.

*Donald Dobkins is alive somewhere in this hospital.* Somehow, he had cheated death. She knew he was lying. There was no way Donald Dobkins had amnesia. *How long will it take for him to heal? How long before the authorities connect the dots? What is his next move? What is his endgame?***"RAY CALLING."**

She grunted and immediately sent him to voicemail. "I wish people would stop freakin' callin' me!" she spat under her breath, shaking her phone.

Frances leaned against the wall as a massive headache hit her again. She grimaced in pain and massaged her temples. She rummaged through her purse for an ibuprofen, groaning loudly in pain.

A nurse walked out of a room and saw her shaking. "Ma'am, you okay?"

"Headache. Massive headache. You got an aspirin?"

The nurse laughed. "That'll cost you fifteen hundred dollars. Debit or credit card?" she asked as she waved Frances to follow her to the nurse's station. She pulled her purse out of a drawer and handed Frances the bottle.

"Thanks," Frances said, popping two tablets into her palm and swallowing them whole. She handed the bottle back to the nurse.

"You know that guy in there?" the nurse asked, pointing to Hector's room.

Frances nodded.

"Crazy, right? Heard he got shot, and the church steeple fell on top of another fellow."

"Yeah. Crazy."

The nurse nodded. "He can't remember a thing. It's the saddest thing you ever saw. His little body in a cast. Like a sad little American Doll."

A day later, her troubles were growing by the minute. Frances took several deep breaths and closed her eyes. *Concentrate. What is important right now, in this very moment?* She needed to handle the funerals. With any luck, they would be done by the end of the week.

She needed a car. Then she remembered. She even laughed to herself. *Hunt, you've got an entire yard full of cars. Surely one of them still works.*

Soaking wet, Kevin wandered aimlessly down Main Street in a daze from the horrors he had witnessed. "The Rapture is coming," he mumbled to himself. "The Rapture is coming." Kevin knew it was only a matter of time until Jesus Christ Himself appeared in Liberty. *Maybe that's why Jesus blasted the steeple from the church! He was sending us a sign!* The graves were surely a sign. Jesus was starting with Liberty. *How much longer until we hear the great trumpets and the horns!?* The loud blast of a car horn behind him startled him so badly that he screamed and jumped out of the road.

"Kevin! Get in the van!" Rusty screamed, driving alongside him.

Kevin turned, pointing back in the direction of the cemetery about a half mile away. "The Rapture is comin'! The Rapture's comin', Rusty! It's time to get right with God!"

"Boy, what in the hell are you talkin' about?"

"The graves are openin' up, Rusty! Grandma and Brandy's graves! Their earthly vessels are comin' out of the ground! There are nearly fifteen caskets poppin' up out of their holes! That's Jesus!"

"Oh, Lord," Rusty said under his breath, realizing the flooding rains were forcing caskets and vaults out of the ground. Rusty had seen this before, when he went on a church mission trip with his then-girlfriend, Frida. Her church had organized a trip to help rebuild homes in New Orleans after Hurricane Katrina, and he witnessed firsthand the horrors of graves emptying their inhabitants.

"Get in the van! You're gonna catch your death!" Rusty insisted.

"Don't matter none, Rusty! Jesus is comin'!"

"Get in the damned van right now, Kevin!" Rusty demanded like an irate parent.

Kevin slowly ambled to the passenger's side and climbed inside. Rusty turned up the heat, reached behind the seat, and handed a blanket to Kevin. "Here. Wrap this around you."

Kevin sniffed the air. "You got Chick-fil-A in here?" he asked.

Rusty pointed to a sack in between the seats. "I got Ms. Edie somethin' to eat. I'll run this food out to her, and then I'll take you home so you can get changed. We got work to do. Ben Camden's got the first round of bodies ready to move."

Rusty pulled back onto the road, looking into his rearview. "Where's your car?"

"Don't matter no more, Rusty?"

"But if it were to matter, where'd you leave it?"

"Back at the church."

"Did your Saturn break down, too? You Hunts have terrible luck with cars."

"No, Rusty. I'm on a walkabout for Jesus."

Rusty shook his head. *I'm gettin' too old for this shit,* he thought.

Rusty realized he was old enough to be Kevin's father. Rusty never wanted kids. He'd had a half dozen significant relationships and was a serial monogamist, but the idea of putting down roots never appealed to him. Rusty liked to pick up and move with no notice.

After the raid in Atlanta, which rendered Rusty unemployed, Rusty moved out of the basement apartment he had rented from an elderly woman in Kennesaw. The apartment had been about a twenty-five-minute drive to the old warehouse, and Rusty rarely saw his landlord.

For the past three months, Rusty had lived with Hector in Stephen Lockhart's old house. Sissy had insisted Hector take over the home after Stephen's disappearance and presumed death. Sissy wasn't ready to deal with his estate.

After moving in with Hector and after Frances cut off all communication with the group, Rusty was hired by Sissy to assist Hector with transportation and deliveries. Kevin would occasionally update Frances on Rusty's latest musings about life. Rusty liked Frances because she was strong and stubborn. She was fearless.

But now Rusty was looking for his next move. He didn't trust Sissy. Not that he believed she would intentionally throw him under the bus, but he was afraid she would slip up and expose the entire operation. Since Frances had left the business, Sissy had turned into a mob boss. He didn't like her demands, insults, and screaming. And with Hector in the hospital, he would be handling all the heavy lifting for the foreseeable future.

"Do you believe in God?" Kevin asked Rusty.

"Sure, buddy."

"When did you give your heart to Jesus?" Kevin asked.

"Look, Kev, my faith is a private and sacred thing. I don't like talkin' about it."

"But the Bible says—"

Rusty turned up the radio, and Ed Sheeran's "Photograph" began to blast through the speakers.

Kevin immediately turned it off. "I don't want to listen to the Devil's music, thank you very much."

"Ed Sheeran ain't the Devil, Kevin. He's just a ginger."

"Why do all gingers smell like pennies?" Kevin asked.

Rusty hit the accelerator, driving faster. The faster he got Edie fed, the faster he could drop off Kevin. The faster he dropped off Kevin, the faster they could pick up the bodies from Ben Camden.

Ten minutes later, Rusty's van pulled past the Birdie Hunt Memorial Recreational Center and Senior Fun Day Center. Rusty slowed as they saw the medical examiner's van and other vehicles parked outside.

"You don't know anything about Momma comin' into some money, do you?" Kevin asked.

Rusty shook his head, slowly driving past the old bakery and down the dirt path to Dusty Dingle's old place. "Nope. Ain't really talked to your momma since everything went left last fall. She called me a few hours—" Rusty shot a quick glance to Kevin. "What do you mean, comin' into some money? Like life insurance money?"

"Just askin'," Kevin nonchalantly replied. He turned, staring out the window as they slowly approached Dusty Dingle's old house. "Oh, shit!" he screamed. "Look!"

Rusty hit the brakes hard and fast. The van skidded over the wet gravel and mud, sliding several feet, nearly slamming into the dilapidated mailbox.

Frances stood on the front porch under the awning. She cocked her head to the side, making the universal sign for "Roll down your window."

Kevin did.

"Well, howdy-do," she said curiously. "And just what brings you two out here? Out here to Dusty Dingle's?"

"How did you get here?" Kevin asked.

Frances held up her phone. "I used a car ride thing on my phone. You just push a button, and a car shows up and takes you wherever you want."

"*You* used a car share app?" Kevin asked accusingly. "You told me those are just run by rapists and psycho murderers!"

"Help me!" came Edie's scream from within the house, scaring Frances so badly she leaped from the porch, tripping and falling down the steps before slamming her ass onto the wet gravel driveway below.

"Shit," Rusty quietly seethed, sinking in his seat.

"What in the…" Frances gasped, climbing to her feet and massaging her sore behind. "Is there someone in there!?"

Kevin and Rusty looked at each other. "Maybe it's a ghost," Kevin suggested.

"Do you have a woman tied up in my house!?"

"Help me!" came Edie's hoarse crying scream again.

"Your house?" Kevin challenged, climbing out of the van. "Since when did you buy a house? And with what money!? Huh!?"

Frances stumbled backward in horror. Kevin Ryan Hunt had a woman tied up in "her" house, just as Akasha had foretold. "Why is there a woman tied up in *that* house!?" she cried, pointing to the front door.

Rusty jumped out of the van, carrying the bag of Chick-fil-A. "Just chill out a second, Frances."

"I'm chill! I'm chill as a flippin' cucumber! See how chill I am!?" Frances rushed to the van, threw open the passenger door, yanked Kevin out of his seat, and smacked him on his chest and arms. "What the Devil is wrong with you, boy!? And why do you look like you've been rollin' around in the mud like a pig!?"

"Me!? What's wrong with me?! Why don't you ever answer your damned phone!? I called you three times!"

"I've been busy!"

"Busy!? Doin' what!? Buyin' more houses!? Sissy told me about all the money you came up on!"

"I was gonna tell you!"

"When!?"

"When everything died down from the two dozen dead Baptists, the dwarf in a coma, Ray Jackson bein' back in town, and shortly after we had gotten a good explanation as to why you were hoistin' Queenie Masters head high aloft in the air like she was a gotdamn prize at the country fair!"

"Help me!" cried Edie from inside the house.

"Who is in that house!?" Frances demanded.

Rusty rushed up the stairs, flung open the door, and ran inside.

Frances grabbed Kevin by the shoulders and shook him. "What is wrong with you!?"

"Grandma's casket done rose up out of her grave!"

Frances blinked. "What?"

"Her casket! And Brandy's casket! They are all risin' up out of their graves, just like the Bible foretells us! The Rapture is comin'! It's time for you to prepare! And woman, you of all people have got a lot of repentin' to do, so I suggest you get started!"

Frances took a step back, circling her raised index finger all over Kevin as if rejecting a demonic spirit. "Whatever this is… I don't got time for this, Kevin Hunt," she said, turning and carefully walking up the termite-infested stairs.

"The Rapture is coming, Momma!" he shouted from below in the pouring rain. "You need to repent!"

Frances walked into the dark house, searching for Rusty. She heard muffled conversations coming from the bathroom. She tried the doorknob and found the door locked. "Open up, Rusty!"

"Help me!"

"Who is that?!" Frances asked, pounding her fist against the door and violently shaking the doorknob. "Who have you got in there!?" she screamed.

Rusty opened the door and poked his head out. "I'm gonna show you, but you can't react. This ain't Kevin. This ain't me. We didn't do this."

"Then who's responsible for the prisoner in my bathroom?"

"Sissy. This is all Sissy Stone."

Frances pushed the door open and saw Edie Trussell chained to the pipe on the back of the toilet. The room smelled of urine, mold, and feces.

"Frances! Oh, thank God! Oh, thank God for you!" Edie cried. "You have to help me! They got me tied up in here! They got me kidnapped, and they gonna kill me!"

Frances back up and slowly walked back into the living room, where she had found Dusty Dingle, dead as a doornail, just days earlier.

Rusty cautiously walked in, joining her.

"Yeah, I'm fine with that," Frances said quietly.

"What?"

"Momma hated her. Maybe we can starve her to death."

"Frances, we have to let her go."

"What does she know?"

"A lot. Maybe everything."

"Then let's kill her," Frances suggested.

"I'm not killin' that old woman in the bathroom."

Frances raised her arms and dropped them in defeat. "I need a car. I came here for a car, Rusty. I own all this now. Dusty's daughter sold it to me. This and all the land on it. All the cars out in the back. I just needed a car. I need an engine for my daddy's truck. That's the only reason I'm here. And you and my deranged son, got Momma's biggest life nemesis, tied up to the back of a toilet eating a spicy chicken sandwich." Frances shook her head. "Is this real life?"

"Your daddy's old Ford?"

"Yeah."

"I can help you with that. I know a guy."

"Rusty, I want to be done with all of this. I don't want to be in this bullshit dead body business anymore. I want Sissy Stone out of my life. I want Ray Jackson out of my life. I want Donald Dobkins out of my life. I just want to babysit old people and… Hey, you know what? I can run a respectable pull-a-part operation for people."

"You mean car parts and not dead people parts, right?"

"Yes, I mean car parts. Daddy always loved old cars. I got Momma's rec center out there. I can honor Daddy here with a car parts place. Look at me. Livin' the dream."

"Help me!" screamed Edie from the bathroom.

Rusty and Frances flinched at the same time. They stood in silence for nearly a minute. Frances broke it with, "Kevin said Momma's casket had—"

"It's the rain. It happens."

"It happens? Momma's casket's up out of the ground? Like it ain't down where it should be?"

"This is Liberty, Frances. They probably didn't bury the hole that deep. With all the rain… We'll get her reburied."

Frances plopped into the chair Dusty Dingle had expired in several years earlier. A plume of dust and God only knows what exploded around her. Frances paused for a moment, realizing she was most definitely inhaling dead Dusty Dingle dust.

Frances sneezed. Rusty sneezed.

"Is that where—" Rusty started to say, and Frances nodded.

"I just wanna be done, Rusty." She stared into his crystal blue eyes. "Stephen and Stuart Lockhart are still alive. Did you know that?"

He shrugged. "So?"

"So? They got some master plan for an international body racket.

They're the big bads in all of this." Frances shook her head. "I almost screwed a teenager last night."

"I think that's TMI," he said, pacing the room.

"Take it up with human resources. Maybe they'll fire me."

Rusty laughed. Frances laughed.

Frances looked around the living room, contemplating whether she should tear down the entire house or remodel. "Jackson's back in town. He's tryin' to take down all of this. And y'all got an old woman chained to the crapper in the bathroom."

"How did you know about that? About Edie in the bathroom?"

"Psychic friend told me."

"Sure," he said. "Of course. Makes sense."

Frances looked into Rusty's eyes again. Neither one dared to blink. "Rusty, what do you want?"

"What do you mean?"

"What's your endgame in all this? It's a question I'm askin' everyone these days. Just takin' a poll."

"I don't have an endgame."

"Help me!" cried Edie.

"Rusty, what do you want? Are you FBI? NSA? You playin' a long game here?"

"I'm just a cracker with a van and fluid loyalties. It ain't that deep, Frances." He laughed. "You know I used to be a nurse?"

Frances looked up at him in disbelief. "A what? You were a nurse?"

Rusty nodded. "That's how I got into all this. I went to nursing school right out of high school. My momma was a nurse."

"How did you end up drivin' a van for dead parts?"

"Had a small problem with pain pills. Stealin' 'em. Sellin' 'em."

"Oh, boy."

"I was lucky they only fired me. It could have been way worse. It should have been way worse."

"How long ago was that?"

"About ten years ago. I was one of Donald's first employees. We met in Tennessee. I started off as a butcher, but because of my size and because I don't got no problem drivin' long shifts, I moved to transport."

Frances looked down at her weathered hands. Hands that raised a child, worked in a chicken plant, and had helped move dead bodies. "I came here, thinkin' I could find a car. I just need wheels right now. To get around. But every time I make a move, I discover some new shit. Like I'm in the most unhinged "Choose Your Own Adventure" novel ever."

"What about Hector's truck? It's still at the church, right? He can't really use it right now. Once we bury all them dead Baptists, we can get you an engine for your daddy's truck. We just have to get through this week, Frances."

Frances rubbed her shoulder. "We gotta get Momma and them others buried again."

"Help me!" cried Edie.

Frances and Rusty stared at each other. "What are we supposed to do with her?" Frances asked. "Wait. How did she end up here?"

"She went snoopin' around the funeral home. Found the shed where we been storing parts that were ready to move. Passed out. Hit her head. I found her."

"And you just brought her here?"

"Sissy told me to."

Frances spat. "I'm so tired of that old prune. She's changed. She's gone funny. There's somethin' wrong with her. In the head. There's something wrong with her in the head. We gonna have to do somethin' about her."

"Like what?"

"I'm gonna ask you one more time. What do you want? Because I want out. And I'm gonna claw my way out and do whatever I have to do. And I need to know what side you're on. Frankly, you're the only sane person in this whole mix that I can trust right now, so I need to know what you want. Because if you get in my way… It's probably not gonna end well for you."

"I'm lookin' for a change."

"You ain't attached to all of this?"

"I can take it or leave it. Darlin', I drive a van. I'd probably make more money doin' Uber Eats at this point."

"Can I trust you?" Frances asked.

Rusty knelt down next to Frances and took her hand. "Frances, I would like to think you know me well enough at this point to know you can."

"I want out."

"I know."

"I want my life back."

"I'm aware."

"Help me!" cried Edie from the bathroom.

Rusty took a deep breath and put his hand on her shoulder. "If you want to watch the world burn, Frances, I'm in. Or if you just want to set a small housefire in Liberty… I'm in."

"I'm gonna end this. I'm gonna end all of this." Frances stood and walked to the bathroom. She paused, turning to Rusty. "Oh, and Hector's awake, and he's going to be okay."

Rusty shouted gleefully, "Oh, shit! That's great!" as he teared up. "Man, you really buried the lede there!"

Frances pushed open the door and looked down at Edie. "Edie, you were awful to my momma her entire life."

"Frances, you have to—"

Frances held her hand up, and Edie stopped groveling. "I know all the stories. I know you and your clan of mean girls tormented Sissy, Delores, and my momma for nearly eighty years, but this all ends today."

"Frances, if you let me go, I won't tell anyone."

"I don't believe you."

"Queenie's dead. Juanita don't care. I don't got anyone anymore."

Frances turned to Rusty. "Give me the key," she insisted.

"You're settin' me free!?" Edie cried.

"No, we're movin' you to the farm. There's no heat in here. You'd probably die overnight, and I done got plenty of people to bury without adding to the body count."

"Just let me go! I won't tell anyone!"

"I can't take that chance right now. I've got too many balls up in the air, and I can't have you out there until the dust has settled."

"Frances, I can help you. I promise I won't do anything to hurt you or Kevin," Edie pleaded. "I promise."

Frances unlocked the lock around the pipe and handed the chain to Rusty. "We'll take you back to the farm, and we'll treat you right. But right now, I won't be havin' any more complications."

Rusty nodded. Frances walked back down the dark, moldy hallway, out the front door, and found Kevin on the porch, rocking back and forth on an old, rusty swing.

"I'd sit on this with you, but I'm afraid my fat ass would break it," she said.

Kevin shook from the cold, soaked to his bones.

"Look," Frances started.

Kevin cut her off. "I want to go to seminary, and all this is gonna destroy my chances."

"I want you to have a normal life. Everything I've done has been for you. And when we get through all this, I'll send you to any college you want to go to in the world."

"How?"

"Your grandmomma had a big insurance policy. Cooper set it up. And Dusty's daughter unloaded all this to me. Turns out the land is worth a lot of money. So, you're gonna be set for the rest of your life. You never have to work another day if you didn't want to." Frances picked up her purse from the ground and searched for a cigarette but remembered she had finished her last one on her ride to the house. "This is all for you. And we'll get you through seminary if that's what you want. But Kevin, right now, we have to get through this week."

"It's okay for me to just take a handout?"

"It's not a handout, Kevin. It's a gift. You're my son."

"I'm supposed to lead people to Jesus."

"And you can still do that. But right now? Today? We have to deal with them dead people."

"We? Thought you got out."

"Long story. But we got too many funerals and not enough hands. We have to bury them. We have to get all this handled as soon as humanly possible."

"Sissy's just gonna sell 'em off in pieces."

"No. Absolutely not. We aren't cuttin' up any more dead people on my watch." Frances leaned against the doorframe. "We all make mistakes. And me and them... We made some big mistakes. But that's all over now. We're ending this. Today. Right here and now. No more body snatchin'. And if Sissy has somethin' to say about that... Well, she might find herself in the middle of an investigation, and I don't think she's gonna like that."

"Sissy will blame you."

"I'll set fire to that bridge when I get to it. I'm doin' everything I can think of so that doesn't happen, but if that's the way the cards fall, so be it. I'd rather go to prison than continue down this road another minute."

Rusty walked out the front door, holding the long chain attached to Edie's handcuffs.

"Great, we got a slave now?" Kevin asked.

"She's not a slave. She's our hostage."

"What's the difference?" Kevin asked.

"She don't gotta do no work."

"Frances!" Rusty gasped.

"I wasn't bein' racist, Rusty!" Frances balked.

Frances grabbed her umbrella and pointed to the van. "Kevin, you and Edie in the back."

They all raced out from the safety of the awning, through the rain to the van. Frances jumped into the passenger's seat as Rusty got Edie comfortable in the back.

Rusty reached into the glove compartment and handed Frances a small paper bag. She opened it and pulled out her favorite Carter Clusters.

"Remember you tellin' me these were your favorites."

"Thank you," she said, taking a big bite out of one.

"You're gonna have to make those for me some time," Rusty said.

Frances stole a look into the back of the van where Edie and Kevin sat on the floor. "Where did you get handcuffs?"

"You gonna call human resources if I tell you?" he asked, throwing the van into drive.

It was nearly five o'clock, and Lily found herself heavily contemplating all her life choices. She leaned against the back door of the Lockhart Brothers Funeral Home, smoking a cigarette and watching the last of the cars pull out of the parking lot. She hid her cigarette behind her back as she waved to the Preston family, pulling away in their SUV.

The phone rang in her breast pocket, and she pulled it out to see **"STEPHEN LOCKHART CALLING."**

She held the phone at a distance, considering hurling it as far as she could. Only hours earlier, a strange woman tried to convince her turning on Stephen and Stuart was the best course of action. But Stephen and Stuart were paying her handsomely to protect their sister. Lily wasn't clear what was the best thing for Lily.

She answered, "I'm here."

"Have you found Sissy?"

"She's fine. Her church, like, blew up or something, and a whole bunch of church members were killed. They're all here to get buried. She's busy. I want a raise."

"I'm sorry, what?" Stephen simply replied.

"A raise. I want a big raise."

"No, the church thing."

"Lightning, fire. It's crazy.

"What about Donald?" Stephen asked.

"Donald?"

"Dobkins! Have you seen him?"

"*I* have not seen Donald Dobkins," she said, choosing her words carefully.

Stephen sighed. "Stay in Liberty. Stay with Sissy."

"I'm going to need a raise if I have to stay here. Hotels are expensive, and I'm doing the work of two different jobs now. And these people are giving me the ick. Your evil little sister has me running intake on two dozen dead people and expects me to embalm them later. I don't know anything about embalming people, and I can't find anything on YouTube that's helpful! I don't know how much longer I can take these uneducated country folks. They feel racist, even though they say they're not. Know what I mean? They're giving me anxiety. I'm going to need more money."

In Florence, Stephen turned to his brother, Stuart, sitting on a sofa, watching *The Traitors* on their television.

"Hello?!" Lily shouted impatiently. "Stephen, I'm doing actual work here! I thought I was just going to be watching her from a distance. I'm doing *work*. A lot of work! Actual work. I need a raise!"

"Okay, let me think about this," he said.

"What's there to think about!?"

"Let me talk to Stuart. We have an issue with our investor."

"What issue?"

"They aren't calling back. We don't understand what happened. They went radio silent."

"That sounds like a Stephen problem. Not a Lily problem."

"If you haven't seen Donald yet, that means he's probably still on his way. When you see him, take him out." Stephen hung up.

Lily stared at her phone and screamed. The door behind her pushed open, and Sissy stuck her head out.

"What are you doin' back here!? I need you inside!"

"I'm on a break," Lily insisted.

"Break time's over! Rusty will be here with the bodies in a bit."

Lily checked her watch. "You've got me for another hour, and then I'm out of here."

"You'll get out of here when I let you go."

"You're going to have to pay me overtime, or I'm out of here. I want more money."

"People in hell want ice water!"


The rain was finally letting up as Rusty pulled down the long, gravel road of the Hunt family farm. He passed Buddy's dead truck, parked under a tree, and continued all the way down to the farmhouse.

He parked the van and looked into the rearview mirror to see a stoic Edie and a freezing Kevin seated on the floor of the van.

"Let's do this," Frances insisted, climbing out of the passenger's seat.

"Ms. Trussell, just try to make the best of it," Rusty quietly offered.

Edie's previous fear had shifted to a righteous, cool anger. Rusty opened the van door, and she stepped out. All four walked up the steps and into the house. Kevin stripped off his cold, wet clothes as he ran up the stairs.

"You know I've never been in this house before?" Edie offered, looking at the photos on the walls.

Rusty and Frances searched the living room for the best place to lock down Edie. "What about that pipe on the fireplace?" Rusty asked.

Frances nodded. Rusty began to loop the chain around the pipe, securing Edie to the fireplace with enough room for her to move around. Rusty moved the sofa closer, and Edie calmly sat.

"I will need clothes," Edie flatly stated. "Would you be so kind as to please lend me some fresh clothes?"

Frances nodded. "Right. That seems fair. You and I are about the same size. I'll get you somethin' to wear. You want some coffee?" Frances asked, "A cola? Tea?"

"Water. No ice. Thank you."

Frances didn't like or trust this passive and gentle version of Edie. Frances walked into the kitchen as Edie sat on the sofa. "How long do you expect to hold me here?"

"Ain't got that far yet. You're not exactly on the top ten list of my concerns right now. Besides, you're my first prisoner."

"You been up in your momma's room since she killed herself?"

"No," Frances quietly said.

"That's weird," Edie responded.

Frances grabbed the biggest butcher knife from the block and stomped back into the living room. She wielded the knife inches from Edie's unflinching face. "Don't you talk about my momma, Edie Trussell," Frances calmly stated. "No one knows you're out here. And I guess you already know by now I can make you disappear for good. Wouldn't be that hard. And I'd quite enjoy it."

Edie slowly raised her hands, surrendering. "I apologize. I'm sorry. That was out of line."

Rusty slowly stepped between the knife and Edie. "Fran, let's take this down a notch. We've all had a rough and stressful day."

Edie leaned back on the sofa, curling her legs under a quilt. "I'll take a robe if you've got one. It's a little drafty in here."

It was close to seven o'clock when Rusty and Kevin returned to Lockhart Brothers with the first load of bodies from the bakery. In the morning, Delores would call the contacts for Delroy Richardson to encourage them to either cremate or do a closed casket, as his body was already off to market. James Green had no family, so they would quietly bury an empty casket when there was time.

Christopher would get to work on the first four victims of the wreckage. Of the first four bodies released by Ben Camden, only one would be able to do an open casket. One of the others would require extensive work, and the other two were beyond help, but all four had large families in Liberty.

Sissy and Delores would explain to the families who required closed-casket funerals embalming would not be necessary. *And ain't that a blessing, because you're saving money!* While Sissy would normally always push for an open casket with full embalming to maximize profits, Sissy just wanted to get everyone out of the Lockhart Brothers doors as quickly as possible.

Sissy's butchery skills were improving over time, and she believed she had developed quite a special knack for the art. It crushed Sissy to know that there just wasn't enough time to harvest from her current bounty, but there just were not enough hours in the day.

"Did you call Barron Medical like I told you and ask them about needin' any bodies?" Sissy asked Delores.

Delores put her hands on her hips. "Now, when in the flyin' fuck would I have had time to call Barron Medical!? Huh!? You've been ten feet away from me all day. I ain't had time to shit! When do you think I would have had time to… You know what? No. We ain't doin' *that* business this week! I ain't got the time!"

Sissy sighed. "Fine. You're just flushin' money down the toilet. Leavin' money on the table."

"Well, which is it? Flushin' it or leavin' it? You're so damn smug."

"*I'm* smug."

"You call 'em! You wouldn't deign to lift a finger around here with the forms and the dealin' with the payment plans and doin' the actual work of runnin' your damn funeral home! Frances had to grab the bull by the horns, or nothin' would be happenin' around here!"Lily could hear every word of Sissy and Delores's fight outside the office door. She was ready for a glass of wine and a bath. She knocked on the door of Sissy and Delores's office. "I go now," she stated.

"We need you in here at eight in the morning," Sissy said. "We have to get started early."

Lily took a deep breath. Crazy Southern people are gold for podcasts. And Sissy Stone was basically a blue-haired Tony Soprano. "Okay," she said with a smile. "See you, bye!"

Lily walked out, and it was only then she realized she didn't have a place to stay for the night. She hadn't expected the day to go so late. Hours earlier, she expected to check in on Sissy, buy some essentials, and curl up with a chicken burrito. She never expected to actually go to work.

She opened her phone and searched her Hotels Right Now app. Lily used the app whenever she was in a new town and needed a place to stay for the night.

She was shocked to find an establishment in Liberty. The Farmer's Son seemed priced a little high for Liberty, but she read The Farmer's Son was a newly established bed and breakfast on Main Street, just east of the square. She quickly perused the listing and booked it. It was called "elegant" and had positive reviews. She walked out of the funeral home, grateful the rain had momentarily stopped. She lit another cigarette and walked back to her motorcycle, which was parked outside of Akasha's.

"Oh, dang it, I'm going to have to buy more clothes," she lamented, staring down at her "costume." "Dang it, I can even ride my motorcycle!"

She walked back to Akasha's and pulled some clothes to wear from her bag. She walked to the hotel and checked in.

"You're in luck!" the night manager exclaimed! "The owners are here, and they're just finishin' up their wine and cheese hour! You're just gonna love Leland and Mark!"


While it may have taken Ray Jackson nearly two months to dig up any information on Donald Dobkins, it took Clint Peppers less than thirty minutes to find out everything there is to know on the internet about Donald Dobkins.

Clint was able to uncover that Donald Dobkins was fifty-six years old and grew up in Memphis, Tennessee. He went to Elvis Presley High School and graduated with a B average. He was a member of the science club and attended several 4-H events. He attended the University of Tennessee, where he studied forensic anthropology, and he even worked at the world-famous "Body Farm" under the direction of Dr. William Bass, where human remains were placed openly in the elements to study decomposition.

Clint was able to trace Donald's graduation from the University of Tennessee to employment at the coroner's office in Knoxville, where he worked as a transport coordinator for nearly twenty years.

And that is where Donald's employment records went cold. Donald didn't have a LinkedIn, a Facebook, a Twitter, or an Instagram, but a search of Nakoya Whittler's Instagram found him tagged by his name with a hashtag (along with ten other people) and a caption, which read, **"Office Christmas Party"** in 2021. The location of the party was the rooftop bar at the Hotel Clermont in Atlanta. Donald is seen wearing a Santa hat and a scowl on his face. "So, they was workin' together," Clint said to himself. "Ain't that a kick in the pants."

The majority of Nakoya's social media was heavily filtered selfies and dance challenges. All of her postings were in Atlanta, except for a few trips with Akasha to Florida. Nakoya followed a lot of influencers but didn't seem to have a lot of friends.

Clint paid to search "Donald Dobkins" for any criminal records or legal issues. He was as clean as a whistle. Donald seemed to drop off the map just over ten years ago. There was one house that he was paying for in Ansley Park, a small community in Atlanta. He purchased the home in 2016 for six hundred thousand dollars. No spouse. No children. No liens. No open credit lines.

Clint went to the lockers and found the clothes and personal effects Donald came in with. There was no ID in his wallet, only two hundred dollars in cash. No credit cards. A few coffee punch cards. He found a set of keys and a car key with a fob. There were two cell phones, both out of power. Clint hooked both phones up to charge with chargers from lost and found.

Twenty minutes later, Clint walked through the open parking area of the Liberty Baptist Church. He clicked the car fob, and a Jeep beeped in the distance, flashing its lights.

He cautiously made his way to the car, checking to see if anyone was watching nearby.

Clint opened the driver's side door and noticed a block and pedal extensions for the brake, the accelerator, and the seat, which boosted Donald while driving. "Ain't that the cutest thing," he said to himself. He saw three plastic ducks sitting on the dashboard. "I will never understand Jeep owners and their ducks, but I admire the dedication."

He went through the glove box and found a gun. He also found a knife with what looked like dried blood. "Welp… That's something Ray Jackson would just love to get his hands on."

He found Donald's car insurance card and registration. The registration was to 141 Corona in Atlanta, Georgia. The car insurance was registered to Chrysalis Labs at the same address. "Got us a company car, Donnie. Not bad. Not bad."

He continued to rifle through the glove box and found a thick envelope. He opened it and gasped. Easily ten thousand dollars in cash. Clint contemplated, then put the envelope back into the box. "We ain't gonna start stealin' shit just because everyone else is."

"You've obviously done some very bad things, Donnie." He looked into the backseat and found a duffle bag. He opened it to find clothes. "You were just in town for a few days, huh? So, what was the game plan, buddy? You got cash. You got a body count. If you were lookin' for Frances, why didn't you just kill her? Why kill the others? That don't make no sense, you little chaos goblin."

Clint opened the sunglasses compartment above the rearview mirror. A small recorder-looking device fell out. Clint picked it up. "Now what are you supposed to do?" On the side of the box read **"Voix Effrayant."**

"Voix Effrayant? Wait, I know this… That's French. Voix is voice." Clint laughed. "Little buddy, you got yourself a voice changer!" He leaned back against the seat. "Now, who would you have been talkin' to?"

An hour later, Clint Peppers stood in the dark corner, staring at Donald Dobkins lying in his bed. The room was a cold, blue hue from the lights of the beeping monitors.

Clint crept along the wall, out of Donald's eyeline. Because of the body cast, Donald couldn't see anything but the ceiling. He couldn't turn his head from side to side. It was a miracle his skull hadn't completely shattered.

The brain scans determined that there was some minor swelling in his brain, but it was a miracle he was still alive.

"Hey, buddy. How's it goin'?" Clint asked in a deep voice that sounded a little like Batman and a little like a Spirit Halloween gremlin.

"Who's there?" Donald asked.

"What do you know about Frances Hunt?" Clint asked.

"Who's there?" Donald insisted again.

Clint crouched closer to the bed. "I asked you first," he hissed.

"I… I don't know a Frances Hunt," Donald replied.

"What's your name?" Clint asked.

"I don't know!"

"You're lying!" Clint barked just as the door to the room opened, and a nurse walked in.

"Evening, my friend," the nurse said, sauntering into the room and checking his fluids. "You doin' okay? I mean, all things considered, right?

You remember your name yet?"

"Who was that? In the room?" Donald asked.

Clint pressed his body closer to the ground on the other side of the bed.

"Only two people in this room are you and me, sugar. It's just you and me in here. You seein' people now? They tellin' you to come into the light?" she said, barely paying Donald any attention as she checked the levels in the bags hooked to a pole. "Can you tell me your name?"

"I… No. I can't."

The nurse finished making notes in his chart. "I'll be right back in a bit to give you some more pain medication." She left.

Clint raised up, putting his mouth near Donald's ear, but Donald couldn't turn to see Clint's face. "You know what you did."

"Who's there!?" Donald shouted a little louder.

"You know what you did. And I'm gonna make you pay for your crimes," Clint threatened. "A lot of people want you dead. And I can make that happen. Your death would bring peace to a lot of people."

Clint held Donald's two recently charged phones in his hands. He put the first one in Donald's face, and nothing happened. Clint shook the phone and tried again.

"What are you doing!?" Donald cried.

Clint tried the other phone, holding it to Donald's face, and this time it opened. "Let's just get in here and turn off these security settings," Clint growled. "We don't need any stinking security settings."

"I don't know what you want!" Donald cried.

"I got everything I need. For now," Clint said, turning to walk away. He stopped, reached into his scrub pants, and pulled out a yellow duck from the Jeep, setting it in Donald's home. "Brought you a duck," he whispered before quickly sneaking out of the room.

The clock on Ray's Range Rover said 6:02. Ray sat outside the police station for five minutes before finally, reluctantly climbing out and walking up the familiar steps. He took a deep breath and threw open the door, heading inside.

Roscoe White slammed his hands on his desk in disbelief. "Pembrook!" he screamed, loud enough for everyone who was still in the station to hear. "We got us an intruder!"

Ray went to shake Roscoe's hand as Roscoe rolled himself out of his chair, running around his desk and clutching Ray in a tight embrace. "We all thought you were dead!"

"I got seven lives left, I reckon," Ray said, turning to see the door to the sheriff's office open at the end of the hall. His old office. Now Pembrook's.

"Well, look what the cat dragged in," Pembrook flatly said, not moving from the doorway. "You lost or somethin'?"

Ray made his way down the hallway, and Pembrook held up his hand. "That's close enough. I got new batteries in my hearin' aids."

"I'm sorry, buddy. I just had to get out of town."

"Ain't good enough. We were family. You just up and left us all. We was all worried to death. Thought you might have gone and killed yourself or somethin'."

"My mental health—"

"Don't give me that woo-woo crap. You were the sheriff. This entire community looked up to you."

"And look at you now. Sheriff looks good on you." Ray's head dropped. This was going to be a lot harder than he expected. He didn't expect Pembrook to harbor such a deep resentment. "I knew somethin' about that arm we found. I went off, and I was tryin' to solve the case. But instead, I just ended up with a bigger web. Them murders around the area are all tied to the web."

"What murders?" Pembrook asked.

"The..." Ray's eyes squinted. "Y'all ain't been out to Sacred Lawn Funeral Home?"

"For what?" Pembrook asked, concerned. "Why would we be out at Sacred Lawn? Who's dead, Ray?"

Ray had found the body of Jules Lasser two days earlier when he popped in to interrogate Jules about his possible connection to The Man. As soon as he discovered the body, he fled the scene for fear of being seen and having to answer questions later. "Well, you might want to send a car out to Sacred Lawn."

"Why?"

"Pem, Dean Gilbertson's arm was just the beginning. There's an entire body farm operation happenin' here in the Southeast. They's cuttin' up dead people, and they is sellin' 'em on the black market. It's happenin' here in Liberty."

"Bullshit," Pembrook said, crossing his arm. When Ray didn't budge, Pembrook insisted, "Prove it."

Behind Ray, the door in the lobby opened, and a man's high-pitched voice could be heard excitedly shouting. Ray and Pembrook turned to see the commotion. Ray recognized the groundskeeper from Liberty Baptist Church from a routine traffic stop a few years ago, when Jethro Farnsworth was spotted weaving down Main Street in his car before crashing into the back of a parked Prius and sending it into the next yard.

"What in the world?" Pembrook asked, walking down the hallway, passing Ray without as much as a glance.

Roscoe attempted to calm Jethro's hysterics with no success. Jethro turned to see Ray and Pembrook approach.

"Y'all have to come right away!" Jethro cried. "It's somethin' awful!"

"What's wrong, Jethro?" Pembrook asked in a soft, calming voice. "Just tell us what happened. It's gonna be okay."

"I was out in the cemetery, workin' on trying to get those caskets back in the ground! And… you just have to see for yourself."

Pembrook raised his hand. "Jethro, I'm sorry… Why were you workin' on getting 'those caskets back in the ground?'"

"The damned rains! Everyone out in Liberty is risin' up out of their graves because of the flood waters! It's like *Night of the Living Dead!*"

Fifteen minutes later, Pembrook, Ray, Jethro, and several other police officers walked through the soft mud of the Liberty Baptist Church Cemetery.

"Careful where you step," Jethro warned. "Some of these graves got bigger holes than you can see, and you'll fall right in!"

Ray slowed, realizing the direction they were heading. He watched as the others continued to follow Jethro to a grave. "Oh, no. Please, no," he said under his breath. "Not hers."

"It's the most awful, damned thing I ever did see," Jethro cursed under his breath.

They approached the grave of Bernadette Amelia Hunt. "Birdie," to everyone in Liberty. Jethro had already pulled her entire casket completely above ground in order to re-dig the hole.

"This is why we tell people you need to buy a vault! But I mean, even then, with some of the rains and storms, they can still…Well, look over yonder at that one. Rain pushed the damn vault above ground."

Liberty's finest (and Ray) gathered around Birdie's casket. Jethro had covered the casket with a tarp. "Careful where you stand," Jethro warned.

Jethro removed the blue tarp. The top of Birdie's casket was cracked open. "Pressure from the mud and rocks and above-ground shit can crack a casket. Especially if you buy an inexpensive casket," he explained. "I turned it on its side to pour the water out that gathered from the rain. But… look."

Pembrook leaned over the opening, peering down. He recoiled backward, screaming a high-pitched, "Jesus Christ!" Pembrook gasped again and paced around in a circle.

The other officers peered inside, each retreating as quickly, shouting expletives as well.

Ray was the last to slowly approach and peer inside. But Ray didn't flinch. He had already seen Birdie's skull. He was the first person to see the damage caused by a shotgun. But still, he wasn't prepared to see the so badly decomposed head resting on the soft, satin pillow at the top of the casket.

He wasn't prepared to see only her skull.

Jethro pointed into the hole of the casket. "In all my years, I ain't ever seen anything like this, and I know this ain't right! This ain't right! Where's her damned body!? Why she just a head!?"

Ray turned, looking at the other caskets popping out of the ground. *How many other graves hold only partial human remains?* Pembrook caught Ray's eyes, searching the other graves.

Pembrook took a deep breath and quietly whispered, "You have my attention."

# CHAPTER NINE

# IT'S ABOUT TO GET LOUD

It was six o'clock in the morning when Frances lumbered down the back stairs into the kitchen, half awake and momentarily forgetting about the elderly inmate in her living room. "I have to go to the restroom, Frances," Edie quietly stated from the living room as Frances jumped, screaming and grabbing her chest.

Frances turned to see Edie standing in the middle of the living room, wearing Frances's old flannel nightgown and robe. Frances gasped again, seeing what looked like a nearly ghostly image of her dead mother in the living room.

"Do I have to go in a bucket or…?" Edie quietly asked.

Frances grabbed the handcuff keys from the kitchen table and uncuffed Edie. "I'm sorry. I plumb forgot you were down here."

"How didn't you forget you had a hostage, Frances? Got a lot on your mind?"

Frances pointed to the stairs. "Let's go. Move 'em out." They marched up the stairs, and Frances motioned to the open bathroom in the middle of the hall. Edie walked inside without a fight, gently closing the door behind her.

"I'm not gonna lock it," Edie quietly offered.

"All good. I ain't comin' in while you're doin' your business."

A megachurch choir version of "When We All See Jesus" suddenly burst from the speakers in Kevin's room so loud that both Frances and Edie screamed in fright. Picture frames on the wall began to vibrate and shake.

"Turn that damn racket down, Kevin!" Frances screamed, banging her fist on his door. "It's too early for that shit!"

"It's church music!" he screamed back.

"I don't care!" she replied as the music died down. "I'll make some breakfast, and then we need to get down to the funeral home. We got a long day."

Kevin opened his door, dressed in a button-down shirt and khakis. Frances did a double-take. "Did you mug a frat boy in there?" she asked.

"I have school. You remember school, right? It's that place where I have to go every single day?"

"Kevin, I couldn't get you to go to school for the first seventeen years of your life, and now, when I need you, you all of a sudden have to go. We need you at the funeral home. That's more important today. Got bodies comin' out our ears."

"I worked with Rusty until nearly ten! I have school! I have tests! I'm going to school because I have tests! I don't give a flip about all the bodies you guys got, and it still don't make no sense to me as to why you're back with them. You told me you didn't want anything to do with them. And now you're lending the rec center to the coroner and settin' up dog and pony shows down at Lockhart's!"

Frances's head dropped, embarrassed to speak the truth. "Sissy's blackmailin' me."

"Sure."

"You think I'd be doin' all this if she wasn't, you little shit?! She's threatenin' to tell everyone if I don't help her!"

"Why would she blackmail you?"

"Because I'm the only one in this entire operation who knows what the fuck I'm doin'!"

Kevin (and Edie from the bathroom) screamed, "Language!" at the same time.

"You know it's true! Those two wouldn't be able to find their asses if they weren't attached to them!"

"So, you're back full-time?"

"I'm a hostage."

"*I'm* a hostage," Edie bellowed from the bathroom.

"Momma, that don't make no sense. Sissy can't tell anyone! If she does, you just turn around and tell everybody she's in on it too! And it's *her* funeral home!”

“I need you at the funeral home the second you get out of school. Anyways, if the Rapture’s coming, what do you care?! You ain’t gonna need your education up in heaven, right?”

Kevin shouldered his backpack. “I’m tryin’ to better my life for the kingdom of God. I would think you, of all people, would appreciate that.” He pushed past her, calling back to Edie in the bathroom. “See you later, Ms. Trussell!”

The toilet flushed on the other side of the door, and Edie opened it.

“Did you wash your hands?” Frances asked.

Edie rolled her eyes and retreated to the sink to wash her hands. She saw Birdie’s very old, very dusty decorative soaps (always for presentation, never for use) in a dish and mischievously snatched two of them, rubbing them under the water and rolling them between her hands.

“Frances, you need my help down there. I don’t know why you think you can’t trust me. I’ve never done wrong to you. I done told you I don’t got Queenie no more.” Edie chose her words carefully as she dried her hands. “Let me do the make-up and set the hair on the deceased members of my church family. I’ve been doing that over the years all over town. You know I got my cosmetology degree. Don’t make me stay here. Besides, if it’s someone you need to take down Sissy Stone… You’re looking the gift horse in the face, old girl. I’d do that for free.”

“Edie,” Frances said with an exasperated building rage, but then she thought about it: *Why am I holding Edie Trussell hostage?* “You know what? Right. You’re right. You’re not *my* problem, and we need the help. Okay, here’s what we’re gonna do. Sure. You can come work with me. You doin’ hair and make-up ain’t a bad idea. But hear me, Edie Trussell… If you screw me, your misery will be my gotdamned mission in life.” Frances unlocked the handcuffs on Edie’s wrists.

“Truce,” Edie said, extending her freshly scrubbed hands. Frances shook her hand. Edie crossed her arms, leaning against the door frame. “How much money are y’all makin’?”

“I’m not even in this business anymore.”

“How much is Sissy makin’?”

“A lot. A whole lot. So much.”

"Who's idea was it?"

"It's a real long story."

"I've got the time."

"Coffee," Frances insisted as they walked down the stairs. "Regular or decaf?" Frances asked.

"Regular," Edie replied, sitting at Birdie's old seat at the kitchen table. She could not have known that was her spot, and Frances was too wound up to ask her to move.

"Remember Ruth Chambers's funeral? Momma and them discovered the Lockhart Brothers had chopped up Ruth's body and laid her out with PVC piping up her jacket sleeves and attached some plastic hands at the sleeves. They removed her arms and her legs. She was just a stump."

Edie didn't flinch. She showed no emotion. She nodded for Frances to continue.

"So, we went back that night because Delores was looking for a pair of shoes, again… This is a really long story, and I'm gonna skip some parts. Delores was on a mission to find them damned Michael Kors shoes. We get there, run into a guy named Oscar, who is stealin' dead body parts out of the back of the funeral home and puttin' them in his van in these Styrofoam containers. The other one is cuttin' up bodies in the prep room. Oscar pulled a shotgun on Momma, but Delores got it away from him and knocked him out. We brought him back here. Momma accidentally killed him, and I ended up deliverin' the dead guy along with the rest of his haul to The Man in Atlanta. Just know, The Man is the villain in this whole story, 'kay? We made a lot of money, and yes, we all lost our minds and got a little greedy. We made some calls, and we pulled some bodies. We made one, one single run of bodies to the college out in Athens. The Man got pissed we were stealin' his business, and he tried to have me killed. Ray Jackson got wind of everything and found the warehouse in Atlanta, where The Man was operatin'. The Man shut down his entire organization before Ray could nab him. Momma killed herself. I got out. Sissy and Delores kept goin'."

"They kept going?"

Frances nodded. "And a few days ago, The Man started killin' off funeral home owners because we can only assume he was lookin' for me. It was all people we were usin' for parts."

"Where is he now? Do you know?"

"Liberty Memorial. He's the guy that got crushed by the steeple."

"Look at God," Edie said with a smile.

"Look at God. So now all them Baptists are going to Lockhart's because everyone else in the area ain't answering their phones on the account they is dead."

"That's a pickle." Edie cleared her throat. "You said the Lockhart brothers chopped up Ruth."

"Well, they were in on it. I don't know for sure that they did the actual job, but they basically left the back door open, so to speak."

*Holy shit,* Frances realized for the first time: *Stephen Lockhart was behind Ruth Chambers's botched funeral. And he knew Ruth. They were friends.* In all the time that had passed, Frances never realized Stephen would have been the person to put Ruth's corpse up for the mutilation it received. Stephen wasn't the butcher, but Stephen flagged her for processing.

"Son of a bitch," Frances said under her breath. "That asshole. Stephen knew, didn't he? Never put that together."

"I didn't realize that was his big secret," Edie said, spreading a wrinkle out of the tablecloth.

"Didn't realize what secret? Who?"

"Stephen."

"Stephen's secret?" Frances asked, confused. "What was Stephen's secret?"

"Stephen told me he had a secret that he couldn't tell anyone. A secret so big that if it ever got out, it would destroy the lives of every single person in Liberty. I just thought he was being dramatic. I thought it was that they were overcharging for funerals."

"When did he tell you about this… secret?"

"Just a few weeks before he disappeared."

Frances poured coffee grounds into a filter. "Oh. I didn't realize you were so friendly with Sissy's brother."

"Oh, sweetheart. I was screwin' Stephen Lockhart since before Lincoln was in office."

Frances dropped the bag of coffee, and grounds spread all over the kitchen floor. "Dang it!" she screamed, looking at the massive mess. She looked back up at Edie, who sat resolutely in her seat.

"He was the love of my life. When he disappeared, it gutted me. Juanita never knew. Queenie never knew. We were very careful." Edie sat still for a moment, taking in this new information. *Was she angry? Did she feel betrayed?*

"It never bothered me," Edie quietly said. "But we could never be married. We could never tell the world."

Edie raised her index finger to wipe away a tear but stopped, realizing she wasn't crying. "I should be crying, shouldn't I? I should be upset. This is upsetting news. Frances, what is wrong with me? Has Sissy broken me?"

"You're not broken, Edie. Sissy's just a psychopath," Frances said, grabbing the broom from the closet, sweeping up the coffee grounds.

"You really think Stephen was behind this? Behind Ruth's… Ruth's situation?" Edie asked. "Are you certain? Beyond the shadow of a doubt?"

"I am certain he is involved."

Edie shook her head. "We could never be public."

"Why? Why could you not be public with Stephen Lockhart? This is Liberty, not Washington, DC. He was an undertaker. Not the President of the United States. Always seemed a little weird he never had a woman friend around, but I just assumed he was… You know."

"We couldn't be public because it would have killed Sissy."

*Because it would have killed Sissy.* "I'd be fine with that," Frances said.

Edie narrowed her eyes on Frances and pursed her lips. "You said, 'is.' You said, 'I am certain he *is* involved.' You didn't say *was*."

Frances stopped sweeping. This woman had been her mother's mortal enemy her entire life. Here she was sitting, seated at her mother's seat at her mother's table. She even resembled her mother in many ways. The same hair color. The same length.

Edie Trussell spent her entire life in everyone else's business. And because of that, Frances could use her.

"Your secret boyfriend's alive," Frances said.

Edie took a deep breath. Frances saw a rage building as Edie's face quietly transitioned from confusion to shock to disappointment to anger and to quiet rage. Frances had seen that same look happen in her own mirror.

"I'm puttin' together a team, Edie Trussell. You're gonna help me end all of this. And you're gonna help me kill Sissy Stone."


The Farmer's Son was a hospitality concept by Leland Peters and Mark Jones-Peters. They opened the establishment, hoping to land an HGTV deal from the reality show they had won a year before. Even though they didn't get the show, The Farmer's Son stayed consistently booked, thanks to their small band of rabid fans, who would come to visit their sandwich shop. The inn had only been opened a month.

Ray had seen the grand opening on his Instagram and called ahead to reserve a room when he landed back in Liberty. Leland insisted they comp his room when he said he'd only be in town for a few days. Leland and his husband, Mark, were big supporters of the Liberty Police Department and dropped off baskets of food to everyone at the station at least once a month.

As a very hungover Ray Jackson stood under the rainfall showerhead that morning, he let

out a simple, "Boy howdy," reliving the past fifteen hours.

After Pembrook and the others exhumed the disembodied head of Birdie Hunt in the Liberty Baptist Church cemetery, he found himself even more disillusioned with Frances. He was angry. He was disgusted.

He was humiliated he ever had feelings for Frances Hunt.

*How could she have cut her mother's own body up for harvesting? What kind of person would do that!?*Ben Camden's coroner techs were summoned to the cemetery to take the casket back to the morgue for further investigation. Ben Camden broke down in tears, close to a nervous breakdown, when he heard there was the potential of exhuming more bodies from the cemetery. "I'm just tryin' to get two dozen of these people *in* the ground, and now you're tellin' me they're comin' *back!*?"

Tarps were purchased and draped over the watery graves in the cemetery. A rookie officer was placed on fire watch at the cemetery until the next morning. Notes were made about the graves in question, and Jethro would spend most of the night trying to track down the next of kin to request permission for the police to open the caskets and exhume the bodies. Jethro would tell the families it was all part of the procedure to reinter the caskets. In reality, they were checking the available bodies from the unearthed coffins.

Pembrook turned to Ray and said, "We need food. We need sleep. Our work can wait till morning." Placing their investigation on hold till sunrise, Pembrook and Ray had gone for beers at The Hawk's Nest. It wasn't until the third beer that Ray told Pembrook about why he left Liberty. Not one to ever expose his vulnerability, Ray told Pembrook about his unrequited love for Frances, followed by his newfound deep-seated hatred of Frances and her ultimate betrayal.

Ray never told Pembrook that Frances was involved in any form of body harvesting. Pembrook was under the impression Frances's crime was not being interested in Ray Jackson. "You just need to get over her," Pembrook insisted. "She's not worth your time. Plenty of fish in Lake Briarwood!"

"Yeah. And probably more arms and legs, too," Ray quipped.

However, as much as Ray Jackson hated Frances Hunt, he also needed her. Frances was his key to this world. And Ray also knew she needed him in order to keep Pembrook from arresting her and everyone in her circle.

"Pem, there are some things I just can't tell you, but you have to trust me. There are some sources I need to protect."

"Who have you gotta protect, Ray? Why would you need to protect anyone? No one is above the law."

"I can't tell you who. But I can tell you there's a much bigger game at play than Dean Gilbertson's arm. It's a bigger story than that warehouse in Atlanta. This is a global operation. That's what Melody Wang was investigating in Atlanta. I handed her a major clue, and she don't want any of my help. So I'm gonna take it down. And I can."

"Ray, you ain't sheriff anymore," Pembrook said quietly.

"No, but I've got public opinion," he said. "Want to really make a change in this world? You gotta get people's interest. Kick a hornet's nest. Get people talkin'," he said proudly. "I'm gonna launch a podcast. And I'm going to expose everyone involved."

Pembrook was not interested in Ray's grand scheme. "Give me something. This is Liberty. I have to protect and serve Liberty." Pembrook leaned closer. "You do you. This ain't about who gets credit. If you've been workin' on this already, fine. But you need us. You need me. You know you do."

Ray took a sip of his beer. "That church incident? The fire and the whole steeple thing? The steeple fell on the man responsible for the warehouse in Atlanta. They literally call him 'The Man.' That's his code name. He was here in Liberty because he's been huntin' down funeral home morticians and killin' them."

Pembrook didn't flinch. "Why's he killin' funeral directors?"

"He's out for blood since his operation got shut down, I reckon. I'm assumin' he's lookin' for the person responsible."

"How do you know his operation got shut down? You said you found a headless body."

"I got intel. All the equipment was moved out. They got a heads-up I was on the way. I'm assuming they left one body behind, knowin' it would track back to the person who betrayed him. Or maybe they were just screwin' with me. But he got a heads-up that I was on my way. He split and left his second in command to clear out."

"Why was he at church?"

"I believe that he had tracked down Sissy Stone and was gonna kill her. She goes to Liberty, and she's the one runnin' Lockhart Brothers now."

Pembrook sat up a little taller. "Because you think he's been huntin' down funeral home directors who might have been involved with him?" he asked.

Pembrook's head dropped. "Birdie was laid out at Lockhart's. I was there. It was a closed casket, but… Ray, are you sayin' Lockhart Brothers is involved in all this choppin' up body parts? No. No, that don't make no sense. They was all friends. Sissy and Birdie were friends." Pembrook gripped his beer bottle and closed his eyes. "Jesus."

Ray nodded.

"You think Sissy Stone sold off Birdie's body?" Pembrook asked.

"I can't possibly imagine a world in which that would happen. But maybe someone is breakin' into the funeral homes and stealin' at night."

"Without the undertaker's knowing!? Ray, you and I both saw Birdie's body that day at the Hunt family farm. Clean shot to the head. No reason for them to just bury her skull."

"Remember when I had you pull those keys for me in the van we found? Before the FBI came to take the van? Those keys open doors to funeral homes. That's how I started finding bodies."

"Bad guys had keys?"

"Bad guys had keys."

"We gotta question Sissy Stone."

"We don't have any proof."

"We've got Birdie Hunt's head. That's good enough for me." Pembrook leaned back in his chair. "Oh, Lord. Sissy's burying all the Baptists who were killed at the church." Pembrook sighed, rubbing his eyes. "My God. Half of Liberty is gonna end up in a junk drawer. We have to bring her in—"

"No. No, we can't. Her service is to this community. To bury as many citizens of Liberty as soon as humanly possible. We can't do that to the city. Not yet, at least. Let's keep an eye on her."

"Even if most of them end up in to-go containers?" Pembrook argued. "You really think the little guy in the hospital is the one goin' around and killin' off morticians *just because* someone disrupted his business?"

Ray nodded.

"Do you have any evidence that the guy in the hospital is responsible?"

"I have witnesses who can ID him."

"I need to talk to them."

"I can't let you do that. It would implicate them."

Pembrook slammed his hands on the bar. "Gotdamn it, Ray. I need something. If you ain't gonna protect and serve Liberty, then I will. I have to. It's my job."

Ray wouldn't budge. He took another sip of his drink. "Pem, the investigation is finding the people responsible. The guy in the hospital was working for someone else. And that is the guy or the people we are lookin' for. Once he wakes up, if he wakes up, we have to arrest him and question him about everything he knows."

"Is Sissy Stone involved? Is she the one?" Pembrook asked.

"We shut down the business, Pem. There's no more business."

"You sure about that?"

"Yes," Ray confidently said. "We're gonna bring the people responsible for this to justice. We are gonna make them pay for what they did to our citizens."

"What are you not tellin' me?"

Ray leaned closer. He took a very long, dramatic pause, locking eyes with Pembrook. He drew closer to Pembrook's ear. "Stephen and Stuart Lockhart are alive. They're involved. Somehow, they are involved. I think they could be the ones pullin' all the strings. On an international level."

Pembrook looked at his beer, considering ordering another but realizing he was losing the battle against sobriety. "You sayin' they faked their deaths?"

Ray nodded. "They did."

"Why?"

"Insurance money, most probably. And if we have a forensic accountant run the books at Lockhart Brothers, we'll probably find a small, steady stream going to an offshore account."

"I ain't sober enough to continue this conversation any longer, Jackson."

"We follow Sissy."

"You think she knows where they are?"

"I don't know. But Stephen disappeared, what like a week before Birdie shot herself?"

Pembrook nodded.

"I have to believe Stephen was somehow still around. Someone was doin' something."

Pembrook's brows furrow, doing the math. "The raid was before Birdie shot herself."

Ray nodded. "So why cut up sweet ol' Birdie Hunt?"

The waitress came by with the check, and Pembrook handed her way more cash than necessary. "All you, darlin'. Have a good night."

"I need you. You need me. I've told you almost all of what I know. But just trust me, there are a few people I need to keep to myself. You'll get the credit for taking everything down. But I want to tell the story. I want to control the narrative. That's all I ask."

Ray and Pembrook drank too much to drive, so Pembrook called one of his officers to drive them home. When they dropped Ray off at The Farmer's Son, Pembrook told Ray to get a good night's sleep, because the following day would be a day that would turn Liberty upside down.

Ray stumbled up the steps of The Farmer's Son and into the lobby.

Lily looked up from the fireplace in the den area, seeing him catch himself at the stairs. "Rough night?" she called out, choosing to not employ her terrible accent for the evening.

Ray turned, seeing Lily in her usual night attire: a tank top and scrub pants. She had a throw over her feet and was nursing a large glass of wine.

"Evenin'!" he said a little too loud, drunkenly waving to her.

Lily held up the bottle of wine. "There was a wine and cheese tasting thing earlier tonight. One of the guys left me two bottles. Gays love Asians, I guess. Want some?"

Ray staggered, trying to walk as soberly as possible into the room. "What's the saying, 'wine after beer, no fear?'"

"Not sure. I think it's the other way around." She poured him a glass, and he took a seat across from her.

Ray smiled. It had been a long time since a woman had shown him any attention. He couldn't remember the last time a beautiful woman had asked him for a drink.

"How was your day?" Lily asked.

"Not great," he responded.

"I'm sorry to hear that! What happened?"

"Oh, I can't get into it. It's boring," he said, downing a sip of wine before stopping himself. "I'm sorry! Damn, where are my manners!? Cheers!" He thrust his drink to hers, and she clinked her glass with his.

"Cheers. How long you been here?"

"Just got into Liberty yesterday, but barely slept a wink last night. Catching up with…" Ray stopped himself. He wasn't going to ruin this. He wasn't going to talk about Frances. He drunkenly said, "Hey, you know what? Not gonna talk about her. That. Not gonna talk about that. Just hung out with someone I used to know. Someone I thought I knew. No one special."

Lily was loving this. *Hot guy making effort. I'm in.* "They changed?"

"Oh. They changed. That's for damn sure!" He laughed. "What about you?"

"Got in town this morning. Business trip. Was only supposed to be a day, but now it looks like I'm going to be here longer."

"Same."

Lily smiled. *This guy is sexy!* She wondered if it was his Southern drawl or his eyes. Or his body. It had been a hot minute since Lily had done anything like this. Normally, Lily felt awkward around men, but there was something simple about this guy. She knew he was a little drunk, but he was charming. And if he tried anything funny, she'd knock him out. Or snap his neck and kill him.

"What brings you to Liberty?" Ray asked.

"I work in finance," Lily said. "Finance" was Lily's go-to response when strangers asked her what she did for a living. Strangers never asked her to elaborate, even though Lily loved talking about numbers. "I'm helping downsize a local company before the buyer takes over the market."

"Ah. So, you're one of the bad guys," Ray said teasingly.

"I'm not a bad guy. I don't look at what I do as bad at all," Lily responded, slightly offended. "What I do is necessary. Sometimes, you have to get rid of the employees who aren't working. Eliminate them. If the company isn't producing to its full potential, it needs to be restructured. Otherwise, the profits are not being maximized for the investors."

"I'm so sorry, darlin'. I didn't mean to make you mad. Wasn't tryin' to be that deep."

"I'm not mad. I'm not an emotional person. I sometimes miss cues that most people wouldn't." Lily poured some more wine into her glass. "What about you?"

"I'm a… writer. I do books."

"Oh, fun," Lily said flatly. Lily was not a reader. Lily didn't understand why anyone would read a book when they could listen to an audio recording. She thought books were wasteful and bad for the environment.

"You like books?" Ray asked.

"Sure. Yeah. Yes," she said, doing her best to sound convincing, but Ray knew she was lying. "I love them. Books." Lily waved to the well-appointed bookshelf. "Yay. I've read, like, all of those."

"I write crime novels."

Lily took a large sip of her wine and checked her watch. "Is it already one? Where did the time go? I have to be at the office early."

She downed the rest of her wine and walked to the stairs. She turned back to see Ray still sitting in the den. "Hello? Are you coming?"

"Am I… Am I what?"

"Could you get a shower first? I have a thing about smells. And dirty socks. Not just socks but feet in general. I need clean feet. And armpits. And hair. You don't smoke, do you?"

"I'm sorry. What is happening right now?"

"I'm in the… I think it's a sheep or a lamb. It's kind of small. What room are you in? "

Ray finished his glass of wine. "I'm in Barn Suite."

"Fancy pants! You must be loaded. That room is the most expensive one here! Ten minutes? I'm going to go brush my teeth," she loudly whispered as she disappeared up the stairs.

Ray stood under the shower, turning the hot water a little higher. *Did I have sex with that woman last night?* he asked himself. He remembered her knocking on his door. He remembered her traipsing in. But he couldn't remember anything else that happened after. He woke up naked and with the worst cottonmouth he'd ever experienced. He had a pounding headache and was severely dehydrated.

Ray stepped out of the shower, wiping the steam away from the mirror. He stared at himself in the mirror, searching his face for any clue as to what had happened after that woman walked into his room.

*That woman.* Did he ever get her name? Ray shook his head. "You are a terrible person, Ray Jackson. You are a terrible, terrible person."

He searched around the bed for any clues as to what might have transpired. He found two empty wine glasses and four empty bottles of tequila in the minibar.

He ran to the toilet and vomited. And vomited again. Vomiting felt good and cathartic. It felt good to vomit. Beer, red wine, and tequila. Not a great mix.

When he was finished, he rinsed his mouth out with a cup of water. He brushed his teeth. He sprayed his usual Dolce Gabbana cologne against his chest and pulled on boxers, slacks, socks, and shoes. He went to the closet to pull out a fresh shirt and noticed that in the middle of the rack was one hanger hung alone in the center.

He looked around. *Did I already wear that shirt?* he asked himself.


Lily caught a glimpse of herself in the reflection of a storefront. She did a little spin, genuinely impressed with herself. Her boots and the skirt from yesterday paired nicely with the oversized men's shirt she had lifted from the drunk guy the night before. But she was going to need more clothes.

She tugged on the door to Akasha's shop, and it didn't budge. It was locked. The sign read "Closed," and it would be hours before Akasha would open. She would have to come back on her lunch break.

She continued to the funeral home, grateful the rain had stopped.

Her own words rang in her head. *This isn't a life.* She wanted stability, and she wanted to buy a home or at least rent an apartment. Her lifestyle between the brothers Lockhart and other employers always kept her on the road. She had a nice nest egg of cash stashed away to keep her afloat for several years.

Why not start a podcast? Why not negotiate movie rights? No one knows who Lily is in the real world. She could be anyone she wanted to be.

She skipped along to the funeral home, ready to deal with Sissy and the barrage of funerals and mourners the day would bring. "Today's going to be a great day!" she shouted to a red bird in a tree.

Frances sat at the kitchen table, dressed in a simple skirt and sweater she bought at Akasha's store last December. She heard Edie walk across the floor upstairs, then slowly descend the steps into the kitchen.

Frances gasped.

"How do I look?" Edie asked, dressed in a green suit of Birdie's. She looked like a vision of Kim Novack in *Vertigo*. Edie had even pulled her hair up like Birdie used to wear it.

Frances sat motionless. "It fits."

"It does," Edie said, admiring the fabric. "I don't remember ever seeing your momma wear this."

"She wore it to an Easter service once. And she wore it to Kevin's elementary school graduation." Frances stood, pushing in her chair. "Sissy helped her pick it out at the Outlet Mall. Momma called it her 'special occasion' outfit, and I think she only wore it twice. Maybe three times."

"I was surprised," Edie said, tactfully addressing the elephant in the room. "Her room is real clean. Real nice. Like nothing… I'm sorry. I was just surprised."

"You know Calvin Huber and John Richardson? They got a bio-hazard clean-up company. They did it. They cleaned everything up. I ain't been in there since. I can't."

"Has Kevin?" Edie asked.

Frances shook her head. "You're the first. I keep thinkin' I need to send someone in there and just take all her clothes to Good Will. It gets real hard just walkin' past it at night. In the mornin'."

"You feel her here?"

"Like a ghost?" Frances asked.

Edie shrugged.

"Yeah. I feel her. She don't seem scary. Just feels a little sad. Never felt my daddy here in the house. But I feel him in his truck. I feel him sittin' right beside me."

"It must have been hard for Delores and Sissy. Losin' Ruth and then losin' your momma just a few weeks later."

"You wouldn't know it, I guess."

"Why do you say that?"

"We got Ruth buried, and that night, we were all back at Lockhart's lookin' for shoes. I don't begin to understand why old people will cry at a funeral and ten hours later return to the scene of the crime for some footwear, but here we are."

"When you get to be our age, death just becomes a daily occurrence. It just becomes your life. You grieve, but Frances, you have to understand when we see our friends and people our age dyin' all around us, we don't want to dwell on it. We can't. We don't want to wonder if we're next."

"So just… 'sorry for your loss' and move on?"

Edie frowned and changed the subject. "After your momma died, were they not around for you? Sissy and Delores?"

"I pushed 'em away. I didn't want to be around them."

"They didn't check in on you?"

"I pushed them away."

"No, Frances."

"No, Frances, what?"

"You were in mourning. You'd just lost your momma. You can push me away, but I'm gonna let you know I'm still there for you. That I am holdin' space for you. That I honor you, and that I respected and loved your mother. That's what they should have done."

"How is that different from what we were just talkin' about? 'Sorry for your loss' and movin' on?"

"Death is an inevitable fact of life. We lose people, and we hold them in our hearts, and hopefully, they stay with us. I'm not sayin' you're expected to just get over it. I think as we get older, we just find different ways of dealin' with it. When you're younger and you lose someone, you think your entire life is gonna fall apart. That pain stays raw every single day. But then, as you get older, you realize it was their time. Or there was a reason. But when they die here on Earth, their soul goes to Heaven."

"What did you think when my momma died? When you heard the news? How did it make you feel?"

Edie let out a little laugh. "Frances, I loved your momma terribly. I can't explain it. There's a fine line between love and hate. Your momma was part of my fabric. I needed her. Your momma and them made me who I was. Your momma more than anyone. Hatin' on them girls was my entire personality!"

"You spent your entire life hatin' on my momma and keepin' your love affair secret for fear of hurtin' Sissy Stone. Edie, I feel sorry you sacrificed your entire happiness for… Sissy."

"You ever have someone you know you *need* to forgive?"

Frances didn't move. "I ain't big on forgivin'."

"You're gonna need to come around on that. Forgivin' people is the only way we get off this rock."

"Then I ain't leavin'. I'll never die." Frances poured coffee into a travel coffee cup. "We need to get goin'."

"I can't wait to see Sissy's face."

Frances steadied herself as another headache seared her head. She reached into the pantry and grabbed a bottle of aspirin. "Promise me you ain't gonna blow this."

"I promise."

"We just have to keep you in public view. Let everyone see you. Don't let on that you know anything. But write down anything you see that might be useful later. If we can expose Stephen and Stuart—"

Edie shook her head. "No, no, Frances. This is not about exposing them. It's about bringing them to justice."

"If you were in love with him—"

"Stephen Lockhart underestimated me. And I don't take too kindly to bein' underestimated. And after what he did to Ruth and possibly others? He's going to jail. He and Stuart. We're gettin' justice. You hear me?"

Edie walked into the living room, returning with her purse. She rummaged through it till she found a postcard. She handed it to Frances.

On the front was a picture of the Duomo in Florence, Italy. Frances flipped it over to read: **"I can't wait to bring you here one day. The light is different in Florence. – S"**

"That's from Stephen. Got it eight months ago." She tapped her finger on the return address. "That's the apartment he bought. The apartment he bought a little over four years ago. Right about the time Stuart disappeared."

Frances stared at the return address in the upper right corner: **"Via Ricasoli, 24, 50129 Firenze FI, Italy."**

"Do you trust me now?" Edie asked. "I'm joinin' the team, Frances. I need to know you trust me."


Ray left The Farmer's Son, grabbing a small coffee in the lobby. He looked around all the open spaces, hoping to see the stranger he met the night before. Hoping for any signs and answers as to what happened.

He walked a few blocks to the police station, where he left his Range Rover after traveling with Pembrook to Liberty Baptist cemetery.

He found Pembrook in the war room, organizing all the information they had on Dean Gilbertson's arm and the subsequent investigation when his casket reappeared after being stolen from the mausoleum.

"You look like shit," Pembrook said.

"I feel worse. Ain't done that much drinkin' in a while."

"I put a call into Jim Jennings at Memorial Gardens. Since that's where Dean was interred after his funeral, I want to interview him myself about what he knows. And if he's had any communication with possible murder suspects."

"Lord, I hope The Man didn't kill poor old Jim Jennings. I never really liked the guy, but he wouldn't deserve to die like that."

"Hoping he's still alive. We're gonna check and see if he's got any security footage." "He told me back in the day his cameras don't work. But maybe he added some."

Maybe he was lyin'," Ray said, looking over the photos. "He's gonna lawyer up fast."

"Also, sending a car out to Sacred Lawn. You sure we ain't gonna find your prints on Jules Lasser's body?"

Ray shook his head. "Ben Camden's gonna shit a brick when he finds out we're adding more bodies to his dance card."

"Any other dead undertakers I need to worry about? That you *know* about?"

"The others are outside our jurisdiction."

"Thank God for that. We're short on manpower."

Pembrook spread the photos of the embalmed Dean Gilbertson across the table. Photos of his casket after it was returned. They had opened his casket to discover Dean Gilbertson was indeed missing both arms and both legs. Ray and the other officers never released the information to the public out of fear of starting a panic.

After Ray vanished, Pembrook was content to believe Dean Gilbertson was an isolated case in Liberty. There was no other concern at the time. With the only other real evidence connected to the warehouse in Atlanta, the Liberty Police Department considered the case closed and quietly filed it away. The FBI didn't want their help, so they closed the file so as not to concern the community. With Ray's resignation and Pembrook's promotion, the department wanted to move on quickly and quietly.

Pembrook pointed to the photos of Dean. "I never should have just closed this up after you left. But we just didn't have any leads."

Ray nodded. "You ain't gonna exhume Dean again, are you? Maynelle's been through enough."

Pembrook shook his head. "Can't. Maynelle had him cremated when he showed back up again."

Ray was aghast. "Wait, what? Why?"

Pembrook shrugged. "Day after you left, she had Brown and Brown pick him up and cremate him."

Ray opened his own report on Dean Gilbertson. "Ben Camden said it was a heart attack, right?"

Pembrook nodded. "Yep." Pembrook's brows furrowed in curiosity. "Why do you ask that?"

"Kid at the hospital claims he was murdered."

Pembrook laughed. "Unless someone gave him a heart attack, it was a steady diet of beer, doughnuts, hamburgers, and fries that killed Dean Gilbertson, rest in peace. Anyways, Jim ain't answerin' his phone. I'm sending a car over there to knock on his door."

Pembrook put his hands on his hips. "I've got some of our officers reachin' out to other the families of deceased members who were buried about that same time Dean and Mrs. Hunt died. I'd rather have their cooperation than get tied up with red tape."

"What are you tellin' them?"

"Tell 'em we just want to make sure the casket is secure before reburying it."

Ray froze. He looked at the wall of photos from yesterday of caskets, which had risen out of the ground. "You ain't gonna open up everyone, are you? I mean, hashtag, 'rest in peace.'"

"Them caskets are already up and out of the ground. Anyone buried in the past year, I want to open up." Pembrook noticed Ray's hesitation. "I gotta do it. I'm not going to open up anyone older than a year. But this is an investigation. And if we find some of Lockhart's work, it gives me leverage when I question Sissy. Or anyone else we connect."

Ray couldn't argue. He also couldn't protect Frances, Sissy, or Delores. "How many of them buried about that time?"

"Four of 'em, including Birdie. I put a call into Brandy James's family myself. That whole tragedy was such a mess."

Ray nodded.

"Headin' out there now. Ben's still elbows deep in autopsies, so he's sending some techs out there. And we've got our best crime scene guys comin' in. You wanna come with?" Pembrook asked. "I'm gonna stop by Lockhart's first. Leavin' her a present."

"Only if you put the siren on," Ray smiled.

Pembrook laughed, grabbing his Stetson from a chair. "You're such a child, Jackson."

"I like the siren!"

It was the day of the show at Lockhart Brothers. Sissy and Delores adjusted the PVC pipe running through Howard Fisher's suit jacket. Sissy didn't expect a large crowd to gather for visitation an hour before the small service in the chapel. She expected a small group later that afternoon for the visitation of James Green, whose closed, empty casket would be the first church member to be buried. James didn't have any surviving family, but he was involved with a small men's prayer group. No one would ask questions about who made his arrangements. Sissy put the cheapest casket they had in stock in the Mary, Mother of God Suite. They would bury it later, and she planned to use it as a tax write-off.

Rusty trudged into the Cherub Suite with a clipboard. He had shaved his scraggly beard down to stubble and cut his own hair the night before. His suit fit perfectly. He looked like someone who had just gone through an extreme makeover.

Delores and Sissy both jumped, not recognizing him at first.

"Flag on the play and don't shoot the messenger, but we got a problem with the cemetery."

"What problem?" Sissy asked.

"They ain't diggin' any graves any time soon. The cemetery's flooded. Jethro just called."

"Well, what in the hell are we supposed to do with all of the caskets!?" Sissy screamed. "Everyone goes to Liberty! I'm sure almost all of them plan to be buried there!"

"That's not a Rusty question. That's a Sissy figure-out. Jethro said they can't even get the bodies reburied that came out of the ground yesterday. Right now, there's too much water."

Sissy's eyes glazed over. "Did you… Did you just say they are trying to rebury bodies that came out of the ground?"

"I did."

"How? How in God's holy name did they come up out of the ground?"

"The rain. I just told you. The cemetery's flooded. Water pushed them coffins up out of the ground."

Delores threw her head back and grabbed ahold of Howard's casket to steady herself. "Is there another cemetery we can put 'em in?"

"You know damn well all them people are gonna insist on bein' buried at Liberty Baptist!" Sissy bickered. "Decoration Day! The rapture! Use your brain! You can't just bury them anywhere!"

"Well, then they're just gonna have to wait, Sissy," Delores insisted.

Delores's phone rang, and all three jumped. "I need to get me a new ringer!" Delores insisted. "This damn ringer gives me such anxiety."

"Answer it!" Sissy demanded. "And tell whoever it is, we're full up!"

"It's the other business, and I can't figure out how to answer it. It's not like my flip phone—"

Rusty seized the phone away from her and slid the bar at the bottom. He handed the phone back to Delores.

"You've got Black Barbie," Delores cooed into the phone. "Black Barbie" was the moniker/code name Delores used for their harvesting business.

Sissy's eyes widened. "Oh Lord, are we gonna get an order in the middle of all of this!?" she whispered to Rusty. "I mean, I don't want to turn down any business, but—"

"I see. And when do you need all of this? Mmm-hmm. Well, let me ask you this, would you be in the market for some bodies that might have… How do I put this? Might be a little blemished?" The caller asked, "How blemished?" and Delores responded, "Let's just say a roof might have collapsed on top of 'em."

Sissy rolled her eyes, quickly weighing her list of problems. "Tell 'em we can't help 'em! Tell 'em we're too busy to be choppin' up people right now! Tell 'em to call back in a few weeks."

"Ten full bodies, you say?"

Sissy's eyebrows raised. "I mean, we can probably pull ten."

Rusty shook his head. "Nope. Frances ain't gonna allow that. Not while she's here."

"Frances don't run *my* business. And if it's full bodies and not pieces, it's less work. Besides, we got a good excuse to pitch closed caskets right now and move some bones before they start stinkin' up the place." The bell chimed above the door in the lobby. "They're startin' to arrive. Get the order, and we'll deal with it later. We just need to convince ten people to do closed caskets. That's easy."

Rusty followed Sissy out of the suite. "This is a bad idea. We're gonna have too many eyes on us this week."

"We don't even have the space to store all these bodies!" Delores exclaimed, following them out with her phone pressed against her chest. "We should turn this down!"

"We can't put people in the ground right now! We'd have to embalm everyone just to keep them from stinkin' to the high heavens before we could!" Sissy proclaimed. "We don't got time to embalm everyone! Throw 'em in the freezers out back as they come in, and get 'em out of here! Capiche?"

"We don't have enough room for ten full bodies out back," Rusty lamented.

Delores threw up her hands. "There ain't no way half them Baptists are gonna be okay with closed caskets. They're gonna want the full dog and pony show with all the trimmings. We need to turn it down, Sissy."

"We need the business."

"*We* need to get through this week!" Delores cried. "Sissy Stone, Lockhart's might be your family business, but I'm a full partner in the *other* business. And I say no."

Sissy snatched the phone from Delores's bosom. "Hey there, this is Lil' Momma." She listened and laughed. "Dolly! Hey, old friend! We'll get you your order. When do you need them?" Sissy listened, and her eyes went wide. "Tomorrow!? Okay, well, we'll make it work. You were our first. I appreciate your business. I'm gonna have Delores, I mean, Black Barbie'll call you back in a half hour. Tootles!"

She hung up. "You didn't tell me that was Dolly Peavey. She was our first run. Out at Athens State. We can't lose her. What's wrong with you?"

"Tomorrow!? Are you out of gotdamned mind!?" Delores shrieked.

"It's handled. Get with that Oriental girl and help her make calls out to families that we need closed caskets or cremations."

Sissy strutted into the lobby. Rusty and Delores looked at each other, perplexed. "She's gonna get us all in jail."

Reverend Beth Pitts walked into the lobby with Howard Fisher's sister, Iona. Beth smiled and waved to Sissy. Sissy quietly groaned to herself, seeing Beth's new hot pink hair. "I just love what you've done with your hair," Sissy teased. "It's just so… pink!"

"Well, thank you! Doin' pink for Valentine's Day!"

Sissy blinked. "That's like in two days, ain't it?" Sissy took a deep breath. "Oh, right," she said quietly. Sissy's head dropped back, realizing, "That means all the florists in town are gonna be busy."

Beth nodded. "Ms. Stone, this is Howard's sister, Geraldine. She's all the way up here from Tampa."

Geraldine fought back tears, tightly hugging Sissy. Sissy hated when strangers hugged her. Sissy patted her back twice.

"It's right nice to meet you. We got your brother lookin' all handsome in the Cherub Suite. Want to go have some alone time with him before everyone else arrives?"

Geraldine nodded, and Sissy pointed down the hallway. "Great! First set of double doors on the left!" and gently pushed her down the hall. She turned to Beth. "You gettin' any calls to help handle the funerals for Liberty Baptist?"

Beth laughed. "I think I'd be more likely to get invited to the Republican National Convention as a guest speaker on women's rights than I would to preach over a dead Baptist!" Beth laughed, following with, "No. No, I have not."

"Bill White's gonna have to bring a sleeping bag up in here, I reckon. He's probably gonna end up havin' to do twentysomething funerals this week. This is why we kept tellin' him it was time to look for an associate pastor, but he just wouldn't hear it!" Sissy looked around the lobby. "I wonder if we could just rent a big tent and do a mass funeral and revival at the same time."

"How is that going? How many bodies do you have so far?" Beth asked.

"We've got four in the back right now. James Green this afternoon, and then we'll start the others tomorrow." Sissy checked her watch. "Where is that dang girl?"

Beth raised an eyebrow.

"We hired a new Oriental girl, and she ain't here yet. I thought they were supposed to be on time."

"Asian," Beth quietly said.

"That's what I said."

"Oriental isn't the word you want to use. It's considered racist," she said with a reassuring nod.

"I don't have time for all this PC bullshit."

The bell over the door jingled, and Sissy and Beth turned to see Lily.

"Oh! Looks like we found your Asian!" Beth said.

"Your Asian? Excuse me?" she said, affecting her accent.

Beth extended her hand. "I'm Reverend Beth Pitts. I'm handling Howard's funeral," she said. "I'm with the Methodist Church down the street."

Sissy grabbed Lily by the other hand, pushing her toward the office. "You're late! I need you in the office and calling out to families. We need to start tellin' everyone to do a closed casket!" Sissy looked Lily up and down. "What are you wearin'!? You look like a slut!"

Half an hour later, Frances and Edie walked up the steps of the Lockhart Brothers Funeral Home. Frances took a deep breath, taking hold of the doorknob. She looked back at Edie with a *Please don't screw me.* "We're on the same side. I'm on your team, remember?"

Frances nodded.

"Sissy Stone thought she could leave me for dead in a house with no power and no food. It won't be today. It won't be tomorrow. But someday in the very, very near future, Sissy Stone is going to pay. Understand?"

"I understand, and I'm rootin' for you."

Frances threw open the door. A small crowd of about fifty people milled about in the lobby. The doors to the Cherub Suite were open, and Howard Fisher's casket rested at the other side of the room.

Delores rushed out of the office with a box of tissues, letting out a slight scream, stopping in her tracks when she saw Frances and Edie. "Edie! What the….? How did…?"

"Edie is gonna help us do make-up and hair on our decedents. You know she's been doin' that all over town for years, and we need the help."

Edie extended her hand to Delores. Delores apprehensively took it. Edie tightly squeezed it, then yanked Delores into a snug embrace. "Oh, Delores, it is just so good to see you!" she bellowed throughout the lobby. "How are you holdin' up, old girl?" she cried for effect. "My old girl! My very old girl!"

"I'm… I'm good," Delores offered, terrified and confused. "Does Sissy know—"

"Does Sissy know what?" Sissy asked, pushing her way through the crowd.

Sissy froze, gasping loudly as if she had seen a ghost. "Edie," she shrieked. "What are you…? How did…?"

"Weirdest thing," Frances said. "I went to check out the cars at Dusty Dingle's, and I found Edie chained to the back of a toilet. Can you imagine? And the damnedest thing? Edie can't remember how she ended up there!"

Edie turned, smiling. "It's true! I can't remember at all! Gettin' so old! But y'all know what I mean, right? One minute, you walk into another room and can't remember what you were lookin' for. Next minute, you find yourself handcuffed to a crapper in a house with no electricity."

"Isn't that just weird? Amnesia, I reckon. Seems to be goin' around," Frances laughed before her smile dropped, and she pulled Sissy and Delores's heads close to her mouth. "Here's what's gonna happen, you two dumb fucks… Edie is gonna do hair and make-up in the back, and she's not gonna tell the cops you fuckin' kidnapped her out of your murder shed out back. Got it?"

"But she—" Delores tried to say.

Frances dropped her hand around Delores's throat and squeezed. "We have got funerals comin' out our hoohas for the rest of the week, and I need as many hands on deck as possible. Do not mess with me. Do not question me. I can't believe you two were holdin' her hostage in my house!"

"Our house," Sissy tried to boldly exclaim.

Frances dropped her hand around Sissy's throat and squeezed. "*My* house. The only way we're survivin' this week is if you guys listen to me and stay out of my way. If you don't, you're either gonna find yourselves wrapped up like a burrito in the back of Rusty's van on your way to Cancun for a medical conference. Got it?"

The bell jingled as the doors opened behind them, and Sheriff Pembrook and Ray Jackson stepped inside, followed by Officer Misty Hill.

Ray and Frances locked eyes. Hers with surprise. His with anger.

Sissy pushed toward them, hugging Ray. "Ray Jackson! Oh, my goodness, you're alive! I'm so happy to see your face! What a miracle! We've been missin' you! Where you been!?"

"I've been tracking down bad guys, Ms. Stone," Ray flatly stated.

"Then why are you here!?" She giggled. But no one else laughed.

"That's a dang good question. Why're you here?" Frances asked Ray. "Pembrook is sheriff around here these days. Y'all here for Howard's visitation?" Frances asked, taking a quick glance at the old felt flannel announcement board with press-in letters.

"Ms. Stone wanted to leave you a little gift. I don't know if you've met Misty Hill, but she's one of Liberty's finest, and she's gonna be hangin' out here this week, if you don't mind."

Frances, Delores, Sissy, and Edie all stiffened at the same time.

"Why?" Frances asked.

"This is a private matter between us and the funeral home, Franny," Pembrook lightly said.

"Well, I've been asked by Ms. Stone here to represent her on matters of funeral business for the week as she's completely incompetent, goin' senile, and can't possibly handle all the dead bodies this week by herself."

"I did n—" Sissy gasped.

"I'm runnin' the show this week until Ms. Stone here can hire her some new management." She turned to Ray. "You lookin' for a job? You'd be great at it. As long as you don't accidentally talk someone into killin' themselves." She turned back to Pembrook. "Why you installin' a cop here?"

Pembrook gritted his teeth and put his hands on his hips. "We recently learned about the deaths of several funeral home directors in the nearby area, and for security purposes, I believe it is in your and our best interests to have some protection."

"I don't need no protection," Sissy retorted.

"With all due respect, I'm not asking you, Mrs. Stone," Pembrook replied. "It's my understanding that y'all gonna have back-to-back funerals in here over the next few days, and I don't need any incidents happenin' here in Liberty. Not on my watch. Not as sheriff."

"This is ridiculous!" Sissy seethed.

The awaiting mourners all turned to the commotion. Delores took it upon herself to lead everyone into the parlor. "Why don't we all just move into the parlor? We'll be closing Howard's casket up soon, so now is a good time for everyone to say their goodbyes. Cause y'all ain't ever gonna see Howard's face again. Last looks, everyone! As we say in the theater, five-minute warnin'!"

Frances shot Ray a quiet, "This is bullshit."

Ray didn't respond.

"I don't understand y'all reticence here. I'm givin' you free security for the week. You're welcome." Pembrook turned to Misty. "You let me know if you need anything."

Misty nodded. "Mrs. Stone, I'm just gonna stand in the corner. You won't even know I'm here."

"Oh, I'll know," she said. "I don't want her here! I have a business to run! She's gonna scare everyone!"

"The safety of Liberty's citizens is my business, Mrs. Stone," Pembrook said as he and Ray walked toward the Cherub Suite.

"Where are you goin'?" Sissy asked.

"Just want to pay my respects to Howard. He was a good man," Pembrook said.

"Yes, he was. But it's mainly just a family visitation today, you understand, right?"

Frances trailed Ray, whispering his name several times, trying to get his attention, but he ignored her.

There were about sixty mourners in chairs and pews along the walls.

A few sprays of flowers near the casket. Tim McGraw's "Live Like You Were Dying" played from a speaker above the casket.

Pembrook nodded to several citizens he recognized. Pembrook and Ray made their way to the open casket and looked down at the body of Howard Fisher.

Geraldine Fisher sobbed next to the casket, clutching a snotty tissue in one hand and the lid of Howard's casket with the other. "I just can't believe he's dead! Can you?" she asked Pembrook. "He was so young! He wasn't even eighty yet!"

Pembrook shook his head. "No, darlin', I can't. I'm so sorry for your loss. Are you family?" he asked. Pembrook turned to Jackson and gave a quick nod. Pembrook put his arm around Geraldine, leading her away from the casket. "You takin' good care of yourself?" he asked, leading her to the water pitcher on a table of funeral announcements. He poured a glass of water and handed her his own handkerchief.

Ray quickly looked around, noting the coast was clear. He reached into Howard's casket and pulled the sleeve of his suit jacket back. Sure enough, a plastic hand was connected to a PVC pipe.

Ray shook his head as he reset the sleeve. He nodded to Pembrook, who was awaiting confirmation from Ray.

Pembrook said his goodbyes to Geraldine, and they made their way to the lobby. Frances followed quickly behind them.

Pembrook walked outside, placing his Stetson atop his head. Ray followed behind about ten feet. Frances grabbed him by his shoulder to spin him around. He jerked his shoulder away and turned. "Keep your hands off me," he barked.

"What's goin' on?" she whispered.

Ray didn't respond.

Frances chased Ray down the steps. "Jackson!" she called out. "Come back here! What's goin' on!?"

Pembrook's phone rang, and he answered, "This is Pembrook." Pembrook turned to Ray. "Jim Jennings! Well, thank God you're alive! Thank God for some good news this morning! Look, Jim, I'm going to need to come by and talk to you right away. We've got some distressing news, and I want to tell you in person. You gonna be there about 11:30?

Great, we'll see you then." Pembrook hung up. "At least that's some good news."

"Jackson! Why you got your panties in a wad!?" Frances shrieked.

"Franny, walk away," Pembrook sternly warned.

"I don't think so, buddy! What's y'all's problem!?"

Ray turned around and shoved Frances two feet. She stumbled, catching herself. Horrified of his behavior, "Ray…" was all she could manage to eke out.

Pembrook bellowed a "Ray!" that scared them both. "Frances, go back inside!"

Ray leered over Frances. "You runnin' things here? And be real careful how you answer that question."

Frances scoffed. "I'm bein' forced to—"

"You runnin' things here!?" he loudly and terrifyingly growled.

Frances nodded, defeated. She didn't know what to say in front of Pembrook, and she certainly had no idea what they had in the works.

Ray took a step closer to Frances and whispered, "I know what you did."

"Ray! Leave her alone!" Pembrook called out. "Franny, go back inside."

Frances took a step back and studied his face. She whispered, "Ray, I told you everything. Everything. What do you think you know?"

"Ray, if you're comin' with me, get in the car! We need to get to our next stop and to the cemetery!" Pembrook demanded.

Ray opened the passenger's door and climbed inside, slamming it shut.

Pembrook nodded to Frances and climbed inside as well.

Frances stepped back and away so Pembrook could pull out. She watched as they drove away, having no idea what Ray meant.

Ray stared at his hands. He'd never laid hands on a woman like that before. His hands shook. He was embarrassed. He was horrified by his own actions.

"Don't you *ever* do that to a woman, ever again, in front of me. Got that?"

Ray nodded.

"Howard?"

Ray took a deep breath and nodded. "They cut him up."

# CHAPTER TEN

# THE INVITATION

Akasha and Nakoya sat at the breakfast table in silence. Akasha stirred her oatmeal. Nakoya finally couldn't take the silence any longer.

"Girl, it has been a full day! You gotta talk to me! Why are you so mad? You're not the one who's unemployed!"

"How could you have lied to me about working in a bank? You've been lying to me for years," Akasha calmly asked.

"Because I knew you wouldn't understand!"

"What they're doing… What *you did* is completely immoral. It's completely grotesque. And you had plans on running an *international* operation? You were talking about selling dead bodies as art yesterday. Who are you!?"

"Not bodies as art! Like skull and bones!"

"Help her, Lord," Akasha lamented.

"'Kash, in a hundred years, there's not going to be enough room for big old cemeteries on this planet to bury people. We must start finding new ways to source dead bodies. In some cultures, they eat the bodies—"

"We live in America, and we don't eat dead bodies. Listen to yourself. What is wrong with you? You need serious psychological help."

"You literally own a consignment store! It's basically the same thing!"

"People come into my shop to buy dead grandma clothes. They don't come into my shop to buy dead grandmas."

"It's the same thing! It's repurposing—"

Akasha slammed her hands on the table. "It is not even remotely close to the same thing! Don't even try me. You should be in jail! You should *all* be in jail!" Akasha shook her head. "You have no remorse, Nakoya! Frances had a lapse in judgment because she needed the money, but she got out! And I never judged Hector because I think, on some level, I still had feelings for him, and now I'm beginning to see how wrong—"

"Hold up. Hector?"

"I told you about Hector! We dated very briefly, but it was years ago."

"Not that!" Nakoya replayed, *I never judged Hector* in her head. "What does Hector have to do with…" She circled her arms. "This."

"What do you mean 'what does Hector have to do with this?'" Akasha said, mocking her by circling her arms.

"What does Hector have to do with harvesting dead body parts?"

"What does…" Akasha studied Nakoya's face. While she could never truly read her sister, she knew for sure, "You don't… How do you not know?"

"How do I not know what, Akasha!? You're starting to freak me out!"

Akasha shook her head and sneered. "Hector was Oscar Lopez's 'butcher.' Hector was the one helping Frances. When Frances got out, he went to work with Sissy and Delores, and they—"

Nakoya leaped out of her seat and began circling the table. "What are these words that are coming out of your mouth!?" Nakoya grabbed a bottle of vodka and did a full shot. She did another. "Oh my God, 'Kasha!"

"How did you not—"

"Hold up. Hold the freak up. You're telling me that sweet little Hector Ramirez is the same guy who was working with Oscar all that time!? Who was working for me and The Man!? That Hector was… *that* Hector!?"

"How did you guys never meet!?"

"Communication and payment were always with the driver! We never talked to the butchers! They worked in teams. We paid the butchers in cash when they dropped off the bodies! Most of the butchers never showed up at drop-off. Their jobs were done once they locked up and left the location."

Akasha rolled her eyes. "Anyway, after Frances's momma died, she got out, but Sissy and Delores kept going. Hector was working with them. Now that Hector's in the hospital, Sissy's blackmailing Frances into working with them."

"Sissy?' You mean Sissy Stone?!" Nakoya asked. Akasha nodded. "What does that old woman from church know about working with funeral homes!?"

Akasha stared, dumbfounded by the lack of intel her sister had regarding her own business. "Sissy Stone is Stephen and Stuart Lockhart's sister."

Nakoya threw back another shot of vodka.

"How did you not know any of this? I'm not even in your business, and I—"

"You're psychic, Akasha! And I intimidate people!"

Nakoya paced around the table. "Oh my God… Oh my God…" she rambled. "I shot Hector. So, he probably thinks I shot him on purpose."

"And you should really apologize to him—"

"I did apologize! Why didn't he say anything!?"

"Because, dummy… He doesn't know *you* were working for The Man… either."

Nakoya steadied herself. "You couldn't write this shit. You need, like, a chalkboard and flowcharts just to keep up."

"What did you tell Ray Jackson?"

"He wanted a name. He told me he'd leave me alone if I gave him a name, and I gave him Stephen and Stuart."

"'Koya," Akasha groaned.

"Frances begged me to give him up! That's what she wanted! So, Ray Jackson can go do a travel podcast for all I care on his world tour to find Stephen and Stuart Lockhart."

"Why didn't you just tell him they were in Italy."

"Why would I… Girl…" Nakoya grunted at her sister. "Girl, you better tell me it's because when you close your little eyes, you can see them two old men sipping cappuccinos in a cute little café in Europe," she said. "No. No, I did not tell Ray Jackson they were in Italy. Why would I tell him to go to Italy?"

Akasha pushed away from the table and went to her desk. She went through her email on her laptop. She spun the screen around. "Because they were last spotted in Italy. Florence, Italy."

"How'd you get this?"

"Computer hacker friend. I talk to his dead mom for him, and he did me a favor."

"And Hector knows about this?"

Akasha nodded. "But he didn't do anything about it because—"

"He was already in business with those two old raisins." Nakoya threw back another shot. She collected her thoughts, then turned and ran up the stairs.

Akasha called out, "What are you doing?!"

"I'm going to that damned funeral home, and I'm getting everything I need to find Stephen Lockhart!"

Akasha chased her up the stairs. "Sissy doesn't know her brothers are alive!"

"How do you know that!?"

Akasha pointed to her head.

"I don't believe psychic Akasha on this one! There's no way that old woman doesn't know her brothers are alive. Besides, when was that picture taken in Italy?"

"Three months ago."

"Them two could be in Siberia by now for all we know!"

"And what are you gonna do when you find them!? You said they ghosted you. You're just going to demand your job back? Newsflash, Nakoya… I don't think they're that into you!"

"I'm getting what is mine!"

Akasha raised her hands. "You do you, boo boo. You want to ruin your life? Go right ahead. Right now, I'm the only person in this entire damn town whose hands are clean."

"Except you know things, so that makes you an accessory. You need to decide which side you're on."

"I'm not on any side. You want to continue down a road of ruin, evil, and sin? You go right ahead, little sister." Akasha turned and stomped back down the stairs. "And I want you out of my house by the end of the week."

Christopher had finished embalming the body of Kayla Nugent and was finishing dressing her corpse when Edie walked into the room.

"Hi. We've never met. I'm Edie Trussell. You must be Christopher. I'm going to be helping with beauty," she said, picking up a reference photo of Kayla from prom. "Little whorish for all of eternity, but I can do it. This all the make-up y'all got?"

"I work alone," Christopher instructed.

"Take it up with management," Edie laughed, getting settled at the counter. Edie turned her attention back to Kayla. "Who is she?"

"She came in Saturday. Drug overdose. Kayla Nugent. Visitation is this afternoon, and her funeral will be at the Catholic Church."

"Catholics," Edie said, rolling her eyes.

Sissy pushed into the room, her eyes locked on Edie. "Christopher, take a walk."

Christopher looked between the two women. "I'm going to check on the Fisher family." He dipped out.

"When do you think we'll get Queenie?" Edie asked. "You know she prepaid years ago. I'll make sure all her final wishes are handled."

"Leave," Sissy ordered. "Just get out of here. We'll continue our decades-long feud next week. I don't got time for this right now."

"You held me hostage, you dumb bitch."

"You were breakin' and enterin'."

"The door was unlocked!"

"We should have Queenie tomorrow, according to Ben. Leave. I'll let you come back, and you can do her makeup and hair, but I want you out of here."

Edie laughed a loud, cackling laugh. "Oh, bless your heart. I'm not going anywhere. And you're cutting me in."

"I will do no such—"

"I will go to the police, and I will tell them everything. Do not think for one millisecond I won't. Do not test me. It will not end well for you. I know everything. One-third of whatever you and Delores are pulling in."

"Never." Sissy laughed, crossing her arms.

"One-third, with a retainer of ten thousand due at the end of the day. Or I'll tell Sheriff Pembrook he should do a welfare check on Carl. You remember Carl, right? Your husband? Ain't seen him in around in what… three months?"

Sissy's glare never waffled. "Five thousand."

"Eight thousand in cash. Figure it out. We've got work to do."


Frances walked back into the funeral home, massaging the pounding sensation in her skull as mourners began to slowly file into the chapel.

*Center yourself, Hunt. Snap out of it.*Lily slinked out of the office and rushed over to Frances. "Why are the police here?" she quietly asked. "I saw a sheriff's car outside through the window!"

"That was Ray—" Frances looked down at Lily's shirt. She sniffed the air.

"What?" Lily asked.

"Nothing. It's just I swear I can still smell Jackson in here." She pointed to the shirt. "Nice shirt."

"Stole it off the guy I slept with last night. I need to get more clothes today at lunch."

*There's no way. There's absolutely no way. You're smelling Ray Jackson because he was just here. You're projecting that's his shirt.* Frances shook it off, checking her watch. "It's time. We need to move Howard down to the chapel and start resetting the Cherub Suite."

Rusty rounded the corner, and Frances stepped back in shock. "Holy shit, Rusty! You look like a model!"

Rusty blushed.

"Seriously," Lily said, stunned, accidentally dropping her accident. "I'd do you."

Frances snapped her fingers and pointed to the office. Lily retreated.

"You told me to wear a suit."

"You look great."

"You look stressed."

"Ray was just here with Pembrook, and somethin' is really off. He was actin' super weird. More weird than normal for Ray."

"I saw they planted Misty Hill out there."

Frances turned, seeing Misty Hill standing in the corner. "I used to babysit that girl a million years ago. Before Kevin."

"I met her at a bingo thing a few months back," he said. "Remember what we're doin' here."

Frances's eyes squeezed shut, and she slammed her fists into her head. "I keep getting these sharp headaches."

"You need to hydrate. Did you hear about the cemetery?"

"Which part?"

"They ain't burying anyone till the ground is more stable."

"Well… What are we supposed to do?"

"Hold 'em. Nothing we can do. Store the caskets until we can get them in the ground."

"Where are we supposed to store twenty caskets!? We need all three suites round the clock!"

"And also, Sissy and Dee just got a call from Athens State. Sissy is pullin' ten bodies for a job to deliver tomorrow afternoon."

"Oh, hell no," she said, spinning on her heel in a rage. Rusty grabbed her arm. "We ain't doin' that, Rusty! Not on my watch!"

"It's not a bad idea, Fran. We do ten closed caskets. We knock these funerals out faster. We don't got the manpower and time to embalm everyone. And we don't exactly got neighbors we can call to help."

"We need to call Jim Jennings and outsource some of this work. He's alive. Pembrook and Ray are on their way to see him now."

Rusty frowned.

"We are not doing this, Rusty."

"We're not. Sissy is."

Frances lightly gasped with a realization. "You're right."

"What?" Rusty asked.

"That's it! This is it. This is how we sink her battleship."

"Come again?"

"How many do we have?"

"Three that we plan on doing as closed casket. Four more comin' in after noon. Four more will be ready at the end of the night."

"So, we'll have at least ten by tomorrow mornin'. Get with Sissy and pull the names as Ben releases them. Lily and I will deal with those families first and make sure they are all closed casket."

Delores broke up their conversation, bouncing in with an "I'm gonna help you guys reset the suite. I can't take Edie and Sissy fightin' anymore!"

"Rusty and I can do it," Frances said, but Delores shook her head and started cleaning herself. "James Green's funeral begins at one. We don't expect a big crowd. He's just got eight men in his prayer group. Bill White will say a few words."

In the lobby, the bell above the door jingled. Frances turned to see a beautiful Black woman she recognized but couldn't place.

"Howdy do," Frances said with a warm smile. "Can I help you? You here for Mr. Fisher's service? It's just startin'."

"I'm Cyreia Sandrock with Channel Four. Are you the funeral director?"

Cyreia Sandrock had won several Emmys and other awards for her investigation work. She had a manner that could comfort those in pain and make anyone who had broken the law wish they had never been born.

Frances's eyes widened. "Right! I watch you every night. I am not the funeral home director. I'm just helpin' here. What brings you here?" Frances's heart started pounding in her chest. "Why... Why are you here? Why are you here, Cyreia?"

"I'm doing a piece about all the victims at Liberty Baptist Church. Can you tell me who I should speak to?"

On cue, Sissy stormed through the hallway, cursing under her breath. She saw Frances before she saw Cyreia. "Thanks again for freeing Edie Trussell! Now she's in there demanding I cut her in, or she's goin' to the police!"

That's when she saw Cyreia. "Cyreia Sandrock! Oh, my land and stars! What are you doin' here in Liberty!?" Sissy shrieked.

"Going to the police about what?" Cyreia asked. "Is everything okay?"

"Oh, it's nothing. Just some disgruntled employee goin' on about what an awful slave driver I am around here!" she laughed.

"She did not just call herself a slave master to the Black journalist," Rusty said behind Frances.

"She did."

Cyreia's cameraman walked through the front door with his gear. "Is now a good time to do an interview? We just need a few minutes of your time."

"Interview!?" Sissy cried.

"Cyreia wants to interview the funeral home director about the devastation at the church," Frances said with a knowing look.

Sissy patted her hair and giggled. "Oh, I don't know. I don't think you want my old face on your camera. I might break it!"

"We just want to share with our viewers about the destruction from the roof collapse and what our viewers can do for the community. We understand there's going to be several hundred people here this afternoon."

Frances, Sissy, and Rusty's heads all cocked to the side at the same time. "Why... Why do you understand there might be several hundred people... here... this afternoon?" Frances cautiously asked. "We don't. Why do you?"

"The Facebook invitation that was put out last night."

"The what?" Sissy asked. "What invitation?"

Cyreia showed the invitation on her phone to Sissy. "Someone who went to the church set it up. A Kevin Hunt? There are already about three hundred confirmed people coming."

Clint Peppers helped Oscar with his very modest sponge bath. Neither said a word during the entire exchange. Clint dumped the water into the sink and shouted from the bathroom, "Must be good and ready to get out of here!"

"Docs say I can leave tomorrow morning if I keep improving."

"Clean shot. You're one of the lucky ones."

Hector sat up on the bed. "It's been wild, man."

Clint walked back into the room. "I know everything."

Hector shrugged his shoulders with an "About what?"

"You. Ms. Hunt. The dead body parts. The goblin in a coma who don't remember his name."

Hector held up his hand. "Who doesn't remember their name?"

"The little man that got squashed by the steeple. Keep up."

Since the moment Hector had regained consciousness, he had not had a single moment with another person in the room to ask the questions he needed answered. Akasha had been with Nakoya. Frances was in the room with the nurses. He was afraid to text or call anyone for fear his phone would be taken away.

He remembered their trap. He remembered seeing Nakoya run out of the church. He remembered the bolt of lightning hitting the church. He remembered the steeple careening toward the earth. He remembered it falling on top of Donald. He remembered Nakoya turning and firing the gun.

"He's not dead?! How is he not dead!?"

"He's alive. Can't remember his name."

"How!? How is that?"

"Amnesia and shit, I guess."

"No, how is he *alive!?* I saw a gigantic cross crush him!"

"The Lord works in mysterious ways, my hombre."

Hector tried to throw his legs over the side of the bed but winced in pain.

"Hold up, mister! You can't be doing that in here," Kevin screamed.

"I have to go see him."

"That is quite simply not gonna be happenin', my guy," Kevin responded.

"He's a monster," Hector insisted.

"Be that as it may, you have to stay in bed."

"We have to kill him."

"Whoa, buddy. We got this whole 'first do no harm' motto up in here."

"What's your name again?"

"Clint. My name is Clint. I've been wiping your ass and handling your piss for two days. My name is Clint. It says so right here on my badge," he said, pointing to his pass.

"Clint, we need to pull his cord. Or do whatever you do to pop off a demonic ogre."

Dr. Morales walked in with Hector's chart and nearly stumbled into Hector's tray upon seeing Clint and Hector struggling to get out of bed. "What are you doing!?"

"He's trying to get out of bed! I'm literally doin' my job! And every damn time we start talkin', someone walks in and interrupts us!"

"I have to go, Doctor. I have to go see my family," Hector insisted. "Right away."

"Absolutely not. You're improving, but the very earliest I would consider would be tomorrow."

"I work for the funeral home, and everyone is being buried. I have to help them." When Hector's pleas went wasted on Dr. Morales, he tried, "I have to feed my family."

"And I will consider that tomorrow morning. But today, stay in that bed. And even when I release you, you aren't going to be allowed to lift more than ten pounds for the next six weeks." Morales turned to Clint. "I think you're done in here."

Clint held up his hands. "Fine. Just tryin' to be helpful." Clint turned to leave.

"Clint!" Hector shouted. "Please tell my wife she has to take care of the business. Tell her she has to kill the deal."

Clint snarled. "She ain't your wife, amigo."

"Tell her this could be our only chance. Otherwise, we could lose everything."

Frances paced in the parking lot near the shed, calling Kevin repeatedly, only to have the calls go to voicemail. "I'm going to murder him with my bare hands!" she screamed.

Rusty followed while she paced. "Don't do that. We already got way too many bodies to bury at the moment."

"Kevin's not answering his phone. Why would he do this!? Why would he post this!?"

"Honestly, it's probably inevitable. We had a big crowd yesterday, and people get curious—"

"But now we're in the news! What if this picks up nationally!?"

"This doesn't change anything. We have to run these funerals through the next few days. Keep your head down and stay focused on getting the job done."

"Ray can't resist a spotlight. He'll show up, drop some nugget, and get everyone whipped into a frenzy. It's the perfect timing for him. Ray never met a camera he didn't like." She lit a cigarette. "Before they left for the cemetery, he kept goin' on about 'are you runnin' this place and be careful how you answer it.'"

Rusty froze. The color drained out of his face.

"What?"

"Did Jackson say anything about them bodies in the cemetery?"

"No. 'Bodies?' You said the caskets were comin' up out of the ground."

"Bodies. Caskets. Same thing," he said anxiously.

"What are you saying?"

"Those caskets coming out of the ground... They ain't exhuming bodies, are they? Because if they do, they gonna start finding a lot of limbless corpses."

"Which is great because it's more evidence to tie to Donald and the other funeral homes! Pembrook is lookin' for someone goin' around and poppin' off funeral home directors, and Ray knows Donald Dobkins is involved. Ray's been tracking him for three months."

"What evidence does Ray have to connect Dobkins?"

"The landlord at the warehouse and Nakoya. They'll both ID him. Oh, and probably Lily as well."

"The Chinese girl y'all hired yesterday? What has she got to do with all of this?"

Frances nodded, choking on her cigarette. "Right. Forgot to tell you. She's Stephen and Stuart's henchwoman. She's a bounty hunter slash assassin. She's workin' undercover."

Rusty stared at her, confused. "What?"

"She wants to do a podcast." Rusty made a face, and Frances responded, "Ray plans on doin' a podcast about all this, too. I'm helpin' her get the jump on it."

Rusty threw his arms up in disbelief and lit a cigarette. "Does everyone in this damned town need to do a podcast?"

"I told you I had a lot to tell you! And if they do exhume any of those bodies, it only helps us pin all this on Donald and the brothers Lockhart. This is a win-win!" She tried Kevin again. "But I'm gonna murder this son of mine! Tell you what, put him down as one of the ten you need for tomorrow."

Rusty exhaled, remembering, and circled his cigarette in Frances's face. "In the midst of all the insane things happening at the moment, can we go back to the part where you just freed Edie Trussell this morning and brought her *here!* That was not the plan."

"There never was a plan, but Edie knows shit. Edie's this magical present that landed in my lap. Edie's our secret weapon."

"How so?"

"Once we get Sissy Stone sent up the river, Edie's gonna lead us to Stephen and Stuart Lockhart. And then we're gonna hand-deliver them to the police."

"How you gonna hand the police two ghosts?"

"They're alive." Frances took a drag of her cigarette. "Edie knows where they live. They're in Florence."

"Alabama?!"

"Italy. Florence, Italy. Stephen bought a house there about four years ago."

"How does Edie know?"

"She's been screwin' Stephen for a couple of hundred years."

"I have to get out of this town," Rusty bemoaned. "This place is like *Twin Peaks* on Adderall."

The side door flew open, and Delores shook her fist at Rusty. "Funeral's over! I need you to help Christopher load him up the hearse, Rusty! And Frances, get in there and get with Sissy! They's about to interview her!"


Sissy sat in her chair while Edie applied make-up to her face. In the distance, Cyreia and her cameraman discussed the story as he finished setting his lights.

Edie quietly whispered to Sissy, "Your tell is when you giggle."

"What?" Sissy quietly asked.

"When you giggle, I know you're lyin'. What's the saddest thing you can think of?"

"Why?"

"Because you are not a likable person, Sissy Stone. And when that red light goes on, the camera is gonna see it. That camera is gonna see straight through to your soul. Think of something sad."

Sissy's eyes landed on a framed photograph on the wall. A photo of Stephen, Stuart, and herself about a decade ago at a park. All three beaming with huge smiles.

Edie followed her gaze. She saw the photo. "You miss them?"

"I miss them every day."

"What would you do if you could see them again?"

"I'd tell them how much I loved them."

Edie snapped the blush compact closed and shaped Sissy's hair with her hands while lightly spraying it with Aqua Net. "Just keep Stephen and Stuart in your mind while you're talking to Cyreia. Think about how you will never see your brothers again. Never ever. You'll never see them again."

"Well… I'll see them in Heaven."

"Oh, that's so sweet," Edie said. "You think you're going to Heaven." Edie turned to Cyreia and loudly announced, "She's all ready for her close-up!"

Frances stepped into the room as the lights came on. Sissy squinted.

"Oh, that's just so bright!" Sissy whined.

Cyreia took her spot and held the microphone in front of Sissy. "I'm just going to ask you a few questions, if you don't mind."

"What if I don't want to answer them?" Sissy giggled and caught herself. "I'm just teasin'." *Think sad things,* she thought.

Cyreia smiled. "Just start by telling me your name and spelling it for me."

"My name is Sissy Stone. S-I-S-S-Y, one word, and S-T-O-N-E, second word."

"Oh, you're not a Lockhart?"

"I married and changed my name. Lockhart Brothers is a family funeral home that goes back decades and decades. My daddy opened this place nearly eighty years ago."

"And where are the brothers now?"

"Italy," Frances grunted quietly under her breath.

"Deceased. I am the last of the family line."

"I'm sorry to hear that. I understand that most everyone from the church is coming here."

"They are." Sissy giggled and caught herself.

Edie shook her head. "She's so bad at this," she whispered to Frances.

"I'm a member of the Liberty Baptist Church. Been a member since before I left my momma's womb."

"And it's my understanding there were twenty-one victims the day of the roof collapse."

"Twenty-four."

"Oh," Cyreia said, checking her notes. "Right, there were three victims who died of injuries once they were taken to the hospital."

Sissy's eyes went wide, and her mouth hung open. "Yes, yes… No, you are… Yes. Right."

Frances turned to Edie. "Is she glitching?"

Edie shrugged.

"I'm sorry, Ms. Cyreia, would you give me just one minute? I'm gonna go grab me some water. Got a dry mouth." Sissy ran out of the room.

Cyreia turned to Edie and Frances.

"Her teeth probably came loose. I'm sure she'll be right back," Edie said.

Frances followed after Sissy and found her in the Mary, Mother of God Suite. "Dude, what the fuck?" she asked.

"We stole James Green."

Frances blinked. "What do you mean, you stole James Green."

"We stole him, Delroy Richardson, and Celestine Fulbright the night of the fire. We needed three bodies for a shipment Monday morning. We stole them because they don't got no families and we thought we could just quietly… You know…"

"Oh my God, you fucking moron! James Green's funeral is going to be all over the news!"

"I know, Frances! I know! I'm not the one who made a Facebook page invite! That would be your son!"

"What about the others?!" Frances demanded.

"We already called Delroy's family in Detroit and said we'd get him cremated. Celestine don't got no family, so we were planning on burying an empty casket."

"Where are they now?"

"The Bahamas, I reckon. A medical conference."

"And you can't get them back?"

"You really think we're gonna call a company that bought three illegal dead bodies and say, 'My bad, can you send those three back? Turns out we need 'em.'"

"This is going to be on the six o'clock news! You idiot!"

"Stop screamin' at me!"

"If Ben Camden sees this…"

"I know, Frances! I know! Ben's gonna know he didn't autopsy them! I know!"

Frances closed her eyes and reorganized her priorities. "I'll deal with Ben."

"How?"

"I don't fuckin' know! Maybe I'll go and seduce him! I'll figure it out! I have to figure everything out! Get back down there and handle that interview!"

They heard the bell jingle down the hall. Frances checked her watch. "Great. They're startin' to arrive. Oh my God, I want to kill you."

Frances clenched her jaw as another migraine-like pain hit her skull. "Interview! Now!"


Jim Jennings nervously shook as he sat across from Sheriff Pembrook and Ray Jackson. He was too nervous to speak.

"I know that's a lot of information, Jim, but we have reason to believe the suspect is currently in the hospital."

"You've seen footage of him killing morticians?" Jim asked.

Ray nodded.

"But it's all over?" Jim asked.

Pembrook leaned closer. "What's over?"

"His… His killing spree, if that's what he was doin'!"

"Do you have any reason to be concerned, Jim? You seem awfully upset."

"You come in here and tell me someone is going around killing funeral directors in the area. Sure, I'm going to be upset."

"Do you have any knowledge of someone breaking into your funeral home and stealing pieces of human remains from your decedents?" Pembrook asked.

Jim turned to Ray. "Is this about Dean Gilbertson again? I told you, I didn't know anything about him."

"Oh, I remember. I remember when we discovered Dean's body went missing the day after I told you we had an order to exhume him. I remember us rollin' up out back, and it was gone, and I remember how it showed back up mysteriously—"

"Ray, if I had anything to do with Dean Gilbertson's casket disappearing, why do you think I would bring it back?"

"Guilt," Ray said.

"I didn't know anything about Dean Gilbertson. I swear to you. I swear to you on the Bible, I didn't know anything about how his body parts went missing." Jim spun around in his chair, grabbed a massive Bible from the table behind him, and dropped it in front of Ray. He slammed his right hand on the Bible and raised his left hand. "I, Jim Jennings, do solemnly swear I have no idea what in the hell you are talkin' about."

Pembrook and Ray looked at each other.

"You a Godly man, Jim Jennings?" Pembrook asked. "You just swore on the Bible. You committin' perjury and a sin at the same time?"

"Ray, I told you when you came out here last year and interrogated me, we had had some break-ins!"

"You said some cash and a laptop went missin'. You didn't say anything about arms and legs!"

Ray slammed the keyring on Jim's desk. "What do you want to guess one of these keys unlocks a door here at Memorial Gardens?"

Jim straightened up. "I'd love to see you try them all."

Over the next twenty minutes, Ray tried every single key on every single lock on the property at Memorial Gardens. He checked every office, door, hearse, shed, and embalming room."

"At some point, you're probably gonna start believin' me, Ray. Now

I know you and I ain't always had the best times together growin' up. But I swear to you, I don't know anything about Dean Gilbertson. Or any other grave robbin' bullshit."

Ray didn't believe him, but he also had no evidence to hook to Jim.

"When his body showed back up, I called you. Ray, if I was involved in any shenanigans involving Dean Gilbertson's casket, why would I call you and tell you it was back? Make it make sense. I called you because I was tryin' to help."

Jim walked Pembrook and Ray back to the sheriff's car. "Look, I'm an open book, and you can slap me up to a lie detector if you want. And in full transparency, we changed the locks on all the doors after each break-in. So, I don't know where you got those keys or how long you've had 'em, but doors on the building were changed last a month ago."

"Why didn't you stop me?" Ray asked.

"It was fun to watch!" Jim said with a laugh. "Plus, I was damn curious myself!"

They stood in silence outside the funeral home, realizing the dead end at Memorial Gardens. "Get your damn security cameras fixed, Jim," Ray said, grabbing his shoulder.

They turned to see an old pickup truck pull into the parking lot. It parked alongside the fence. A worker in coveralls climbed out with a lunchbox.

Ray squinted, remembering him. "That's… That's, oh, what's his name?"

"Elvin. He's been here about twenty years."

Ray nodded. "He works the grounds, right?"

Jim nodded. "The grounds and…" Jim's voice faded.

"The grounds and what?" Pembrook asked.

"Elvin's brother, Dwight, died of a heart attack around Christmas. They both did maintenance on all the grounds," Jim said. "And the funeral home."

Pembrook's phone rang. He answered, "Pembrook."

Ray and Jim exchanged a look. "We're gonna need to talk to Elvin, Jim."

Jim nodded. "I completely understand, Ray."

Pembrook finished his call and turned to Ray. "We need to go. The techs are at the cemetery, and they're ready."

News crews lined the curb. Nearly a hundred and fifty people from the church, community, and curious looky-loos had already arrived.

Nakoya pushed her way through the arriving crowd for James Green's and Kayla Nugent's visitations.

Lily very much enjoyed helping usher everyone inside. Lily rarely had opportunities to engage with other people. She often felt awkward around other people, but she enjoyed comforting the mourners as they entered the building, nervous and anxious to say goodbye or to get a peak at the circus.

Part of Lily's job as a bounty hunter involved sizing up people immediately based on their body language, which didn't come easy for someone on the spectrum. When Nakoya burst through the doors, her head pivoting like a Terminator searching for Sarah Connor, Lily knew something was up.

"Hello!" Lily cheerfully cooed in her bad accent.

"I'm looking for Sissy."

"She very busy right now with a funeral. Can I help you?"

"I know you're in on all this! What's with the weird accent?!"

Lily's face dropped, as did her accent. "Did Frances tell you?"

"Frances didn't have to tell me. I'm just smart like that. You show up looking like Catwoman in a black leather bodysuit to go interview for a job in a funeral home? You think I'm stupid or something? Where's Sissy?"

"Doing an interview with the press. For real, now is not the time."

"Why are you here?"

"It's a long—"

"Cliff Notes!"

"I'm working for Stephen and Stuart."

Nakoya squinted. "Wait, are you Tiger Lily?"

"Lily," she said, groaning in disgust. "How did you know about—"

"Where are they!?"

"Italy."

"They're really in Italy? Do you have an address?"

"Just a phone number."

Nakoya looked around at the crowd.

Lily studied her face. "How did you know my name?"

"I was working with Stephen and Stuart on the takeover before everything got raided. I was working as Dobkins's assistant, sending all the buyers and all funeral home contact info to Stephen and Stuart. I was promised a territory once they took it live. But then Frances blew up everything. They told me about you."

"What do you want with Sissy?"

"I want to know where Stephen and Stuart are so I can beat the tar out of them. *And…* I just heard she's running the game now, and we gonna have words!"

Nakoya started pushing through the crowd, searching for Sissy. Lily followed closely behind her. Lily could barely contain her excitement, recognizing she had a new character for her podcast and someone she could use to get information about the Atlanta warehouse.

"Hold up," Lily cautioned. "Wait! No! Stop! She doesn't know her brothers are alive."

Nakoya froze. "What?"

"I can help you, but I need you to help me." Lily pulled Nakoya away from the crowd. "I'm doing a podcast."

"Oh my God, what is it with everybody and their damned podcasts!?"

"If you help me, I'll help you. And you really need my help because you're about to blow a major opportunity for yourself."

Nakoya considered her offer and realized she was short on options and could use any advice available. And she could use Lily's podcast to craft her own narrative. "Fine, but you have to alter my voice."

"Done!" Lily pulled Nakoya into the office and locked the door. "You're not going in there demanding addresses. You're going to play stupid about all things Stephen and Stuart. You don't know them. You worked for The Man. You have all the contacts. You have the experience."

Nakoya nodded. "Okay," she said, wondering where Lily was going with this idea.

"You go in there and demand to be cut in. A full partner. Use them to run your streets. Use them to do your work. Use them to grow your business."

Nakoya smiled. "You're a bad bitch."

"I just like to see successful women thrive."


Clint claimed he needed to run home to check on his sick dog, begging off his volunteering for the rest of the day. He slung his gym bag around his shoulder and threw a kiss to a few of the older nurses.

"Can you go visit Mr. Ramirez before you leave? He's been asking for you," Nurse Angie said.

"Can do, you cutie!" he enthusiastically said, rounding the corner into his room.

Hector was sitting up on the bed with his legs over the side of the bed. "I need you to find me some clothes. I need you to help me get out of here. I'm begging you."

"I'm not doing that. I can't do that."

"Then I need you to find me some clothes, and I'll crawl out of here."

"Just wait until tomorrow," Clint insisted. "What's so important you gotta leave right now?"

"I need to be with Frances. I need to be there. I know something is wrong. I can feel it in my soul."

"The big bad is in a body cast—"

"Something's wrong, Clint. You know that. You know Ray Jackson is snooping around."

Clint sighed. He opened his gym back and yanked out a sweatshirt and some shorts. "This is all I got, dude. But how are you going to walk out of here and not be noticed?"

"You might find this hard to believe, Clint. But I'm a Hispanic man, and most people don't notice me." Hector started changing. "Thank you for the clothes."

Clint considered his options. He knew if he got caught, he'd be fired, and that would place his entire future in jeopardy.

"I've got a Mustang. If you're not downstairs in ten minutes, you're on your own."

Six minutes later, Hector ambled out of the hospital, moving slowly but determined. He climbed into Clint's car and smiled. "Fly like the wind, brother."


Pembrook and Ray walked through the cemetery, approaching Brandy's grave. Pembrook had contacted Brandy's family, and they agreed to have the casket opened. They did not want to be there when it opened.

"Brandy was laid out at Beulah Memorial. Baron Hill's funeral home. Baron's alive and well. Just got off the phone with him," Pembrook said as Jethro and Ashlyn Drapper, a coroner tech from Ben's office, opened the casket.

As the lid unsealed, everyone recoiled from the smell. Pembrook and Ray took two steps back.

Brandy looked peaceful. Though she had only been dead for over three months, the embalming process was exceptional.

Pembrook took a few steps closer, peering the casket. "Ashlyn, we'll make this real fast. Can you confirm that her body has not been desecrated and that her arms and legs are attached?"

Ashlyn nodded, leaning into the casket to begin her examination.

Ray and Pembrook stepped away from the casket while Ashlyn began undressing Brandy's corpse. Jethro turned away.

"Never get used to seein' dead bodies," Ray said. "Never."

"After this, I want to run by the hospital and check out your little person. See if they'll let us talk to him."

Ray nodded. "Gonna be weird bein' in the same room with the man I've been chasin' for three months."

"How are you doin' with all of this?" Pembrook asked. "Bein' back here and goin' through all of this? With Frances?"

"It's just the job," Ray insisted.

"Last time I checked, you ain't on the payroll, hoss."

"You know what I mean."

"I really don't. You show back up here after three months hellbent on some sort of revenge—"

"Justice. I want justice."

"'Kay."

"She's good," Ashlyn called out. "Typical surgical scars from the surgery she had. Autopsy y-incision. But two arms, two legs, ten fingers, ten toes. Ashlyn finished dressing Brandy's corpse.

"Thank God for that. I can't imagine having to tell Brandy's parents after all they went through."

"Who's next?" Ashlyn asked as she closed Brandy's casket.

"Richard Foster," Pembrook said, checking his list.

Jethro pointed to the covered casket and began unlocking the casket with his key.

"Richard died in October of last year."

"Funeral home?" Ray asked.

"Sacred Lawn," Pembrook read, turning to Ray. "Jules Lassner's place. Denny's out there now with the guys."

Jethro opened the casket, and everyone recoiled again. Inside the casket lay the body of Richard Foster, a man in his early thirties. Good shape. Nice face.

"How did he die?" Ray asked.

"Suicide, sadly. He took a bottle of pills. He lost his job during the pandemic and just couldn't ever get his life back on track. Wife left him. Had a lot of debt."

"Any family?" Ray asked.

"I don't think so."

Ray stepped closer.

Ashlyn knocked on his shoulder. It slightly caved. "Um," she said. She felt his hand. She looked up at Ray. She grabbed his hand and pulled. His "arm" slid out of the jacket sleeve. His hand was made of plastic, and a long line of PVC pipe slid out of the jacket.

Ray and Pembrook looked at each other.

Ashlyn reached down to his pants and pulled. His entire lower half separated from his torso.

Pembrook screamed and jumped backward.

Ashley showed everyone: His legs were PVC piping, placed inside the pants legs.

"So, this is how they do it?" Pembrook asked.

Ray nodded. Ray's eyes landed on a tombstone a few graves over. **"Ruth Chambers. Beloved Wife."** Ruth's grave had not been disturbed by the rain.

"Pem," Ray said.

Pembrook followed his gaze. "Oh, that would kill Arlan Chambers."

"Arlan was sheriff. Arlan would want the truth. Ruth was laid out at Lockhart's."

"They wouldn't... Not to Ruth. Right?"

"You saw what they did to Birdie. Pem, they've probably been doin' everyone who went through there."

"Richard Foster gives us proof. Birdie gives us proof. I don't want to go around diggin' everyone up."

"We should have told Frances about Birdie."

"Frances is a suspect, hoss. And you know that."

# CHAPTER ELEVEN

# WOULD YOU LIKE TO FORM AN ALLIANCE?

The crowd was growing bigger by the minute. Delores had to open all three parlors to accommodate the crowd. "They just keep coming!" Delores grunted under her breath.

A closed casket sat at the Cherub Suite as dozens of people cried, pressing hands on the (unbeknownst to them) empty container. Some of the younger men from the church helped Delores set up folding chairs in the other two parlors.

Sissy staggered through the hallway in a daze, scanning the faces in the crowd. She saw Juanita White near the sign-in book. "Juanita! There are just so many people here! I never expected so many people."

"It's the social event of the year. Everyone had to RSVP on the invitation."

"You doin' okay?" Sissy asked.

"Oh, I'm fine. I didn't really know James," she said dismissively.

Sissy nodded and made her way toward the office. "There's just no flowers available in town!" someone cried to Sissy. "Valentine's Day! I can't imagine what this week is gonna be like with no flowers for these funerals!"

"I know, sweetie. I know."

Sissy was yanked three feet. "What in the world!?" she shrieked, realizing she was being pulled down the hallway by a Black woman. "Jesus," she lightly whispered, out of sorts as she tried to pry herself from Nakoya's grasp.

"I know about your game," Nakoya quietly shot back. "The game you and Delores are running. The game you guys ripped off from Donald Dobkins."

Nakoya spotted Delores. "Dee Rogers! Embalming room! Now!" she shouted over the dull roar of the crowd and canned organ music from the speakers.

Delores quickly filed in line, seeing the fear in Sissy's eyes.

Nakoya kicked through the swinging doors to the embalming room, spinning Sissy into a corner. Edie looked up from organizing her make-up, perplexed and confused.

"What's all this?" Edie asked.

"I was Donald Dobkins's right-hand woman. Y'all took everything from me. And now you're cutting me in, or I'm calling my ex-boyfriend at the FBI and telling him everything."

"Then I'll tell him that you—"

"I'm a *source* for the FBI," she said. "You know how they have drug dealer informants? That's me. Only with dead bodies. So good luck with that. And if you want to go to the local police, you have no proof of my past life, and I can pass a lie detector. It's something I'm very proud of."

"You're lying," Sissy spat.

"Try me."

"Who are you?" Edie asked cautiously, as Sissy and Delores were clearly upset. "Who is this woman? I kind of like her."

"Nakoya Whittler. These two got my office in Atlanta shut down. And I already know you're the newest team member on Project Slice and Dice here, so y'all are cutting me in."

All three women balked at the same time.

"Over my dead body!" Sissy screamed.

"I'll take a quarter. I have the contacts. I have the buyers. I have the sellers. I have all the working records before you two screwed it all up. You three don't know your ass from a hole in the ground."

Sissy's anger softened. Having a Nakoya *would* make her life exponentially easier.

"Why don't you just go run your own game?" Delores asked.

"Because I don't need any complications, and I need to take over whatever you think you've started because I don't trust you're not going to slip up and expose all of the work we've put into this," she said directly. "We need a new space."

"Frances has a lot of land—"

"Nope! She stays out of this. We cut her out as quickly as possible. Whatever deal you had with her, cut ties. She's fired. Her silence buys her freedom. I don't trust the relationship she has with that sheriff. She's out."

Sissy and Delores exchanged a look.

Sissy bristled. "You seem to have it all worked out, don't you? There's just one remaining problem. Donald Dobkins."

"He's back in play. Everything goes back to the way it was."

"Why bring him back? That means we are cutting in another person?" Sissy said.

"Because he's on a revenge tour. Unless you're going to kill him, we bring him back in. We can't trust a loose cannon."

Delores laughed. "That's exactly what we were planning on doing before the Lord Jesus dropped a cross on top of him."

Sissy sized up Nakoya. "How did you know about us? How did you know about… everything."

"The 'how' is of none of your concern. I'm going to take all of"— she flourished her own hands about the space—"this and turn it into an empire. You think about screwing me, and you're in the next box heading out to market. I'll handle Donald Dobkins," Nakoya said. She held out her hand to Sissy.

Sissy stared at her hand.

"Shake my hand, Sissy Stone. Otherwise, I'm opening a full residency at the Liberty Police Station, and I'll be singing my greatest hits."

Sissy reluctantly shook her hand.

Delores enthusiastically extended her hand, and Nakoya shook it. "I'm just so glad we got us someone with experience!"

Edie extended her hand. "If you're open to suggestions, I have an idea I'd like to pitch."

Kevin arrived at the visitation with a big grin on his face. He was proud he had pulled the community to mourn and fellowship together. He was proud everyone could gather and lift up the life of James Green in an act of love and celebration. *This whole week is gonna be like church, and we are gonna save so many lives.* "I am goin' to beat the ever-lovin' the shit out of you," Frances whispered, yanking him into the office by shirt. She locked the door and shoved him against it. "Have you lost your gotdamn mind, Kevin Ryan Hunt!?"

"The church needs to gather—"

She poked her finger millimeters from his nose. "That ain't the church out there, Kevin! That's a bunch of fuckin' ghouls who came to see a trainwreck! And not only that, but James Green wasn't on Ben Camden's list! If Ben Camden sees this on the news, he's gonna know he didn't autopsy him, but see that Lockhart's hosted his last clam bake!"

"It's gonna work out."

"How!? How's it gonna work out!?" she demanded. Tears ran down her face, and she wiped them away, refusing to let herself break. "Everything I have done, I have done for you. Everything I have done in my life was to keep you alive. And you have ruined everything! You put eyes on us, Kevin! You've exposed us! You've left us vulnerable!"

"I was trying to help," he squeaked.

"How!?"

"By celebrating Mr. Green's life! Everyone had forgotten about him while he was alive, momma! Ain't nobody called him in years. He don't got no family. He used to say in prayer group how lonely he was. But look at that crowd out there! They are speakin' his name now!"

"That ain't love out there, you foolish child!" she screamed, shaking him by his shirt. "That's just a curious mob, wantin' to see other people's suffering. 'If it bleeds, it leads,' Kevin." Frances collapsed into a chair. "Ray's closin' in, Kevin. They know something. He knows about Donald. The only way out of this for us is to expose Sissy."

The doorknob twisted and turned but couldn't open since Frances locked it.

"Go away!" Frances screamed.

"I need in," Rusty replied.

Frances opened the door. Rusty craned his neck to see why the door was locked.

"I'm just murderin' my son," she said.

"We need to go pick up at the bakery. Ben's got the next batch ready."

"I'll go," Kevin said.

"The fuck you will," Frances snapped her fingers and pointed to the lobby. "Get out there. I don't want to see your face. I'm so disappointed in you," she said.

Kevin's head dropped, and he went back into the crowd. Frances grabbed her purse from the desk.

"I'll go with you," she said, grunting from the pain between her ears.

They made their way through the crowd.

Reverend Bill White rushed up to Frances. "I'm just so overwhelmed. There are too many funerals, Frances. Too many—"

"I don't give a fuck, Bill. Deal with it," she said, pushing past him.

Rusty chuckled. "That was a mood."

"Never liked that man." Frances saw Juanita White in the distance, laughing with a group of women. "I feel bad for Edie. I really do. She spent over seventy years with those women and just realized how awful they are."

Rusty and Frances made their way to the van just as Clint's Mustang pulled up. He rolled down his window. "Hey baby, you lookin' for a date?" he flatly asked.

"Not now, Clint," she said.

"Wasn't talkin' to you. I was talkin' to this tall drink of water," he said, winking at Rusty.

Hector climbed out of the Mustang. Frances stammered.

"Hector! Oh my God, what are you doing here?" she said, running to him and lightly hugging him.

"I could feel something was wrong, and you weren't returning any of my calls."

"I ain't lookin' at my phone. Too much to deal with. I thought you got out tomorrow."

"He left," Clint said.

"Hector, you can't do that," Frances insisted.

"This is what's important. What's going on? Tell me everything."

Clint climbed out of the car as Frances, Rusty, and Hector made their way to the van. Frances turned her back on him. "Hey! Yo! I'm not sure what I did to you, but I want to help!" Clint shouted.

"How, Clint?" Frances asked. "How you think you're gonna help?"

"For starters, I got your little guy's phones." He pulled them out of his coat pockets. "I'm pretty sure one of 'em belongs to a very unattractive fat man who likes to send pictures of his small penis to random dudes. The other seems like a burner phone that's only made calls to a guy in Italy named Stephen."

Frances, Rusty, and Hector all stared at him, confounded.

"And how, pray tell, do you know his name is Stephen?" Frances asked.

"I texted him and asked his name. I said I was trying to find a friend and wondered if it was the right number."

"Why was Donald calling Stephen?"

"Also…" Clint said, going through his glove box, "I found this." He held up the voice changer. "I'm guessing whoever he was talkin' to, he was changin' his voice."

Frances and Rusty shared a look. "What was he doing?" she asked.

"Messing with Stephen. About something."

The phone beeped with a text message, and all four of them screamed, jumping.

"Did… Did he hear us?" Hector asked.

"What does it say?" Frances asked.

Clint read the message. **"What happened to you? Do you have the money? Do we have a deal or not?"**

"Donald was pretending to be an investor," Frances said. "Get in the van, Clint."

Fifteen minutes later, Rusty's van pulled to the back of the Birdie Hunt Memorial Recreational Center and Senior Fun Day Center.

"Hector, you stay in here," Frances instructed.

"I want to help," he insisted.

"Buddy, you can't lift anything that weighs more than five pounds for the next six weeks. You do, and your insides are gonna spill out like spaghetti on the floor at Amici's," Clint said. "I'll go."

Frances, Rusty, and Clint rolled two gurneys out of the back of the van and wheeled them to the door.

They heard laughter inside. "Sounds like a party's goin' on," Frances said, throwing open the door.

Ben Camden shoved a person with near superhuman strength about ten feet, hearing the door open. The person made a squeal as they scattered across the floor. Ben turned around, zipping and buttoning his clothes. "Who is it!?" he called out. "You shouldn't be in here! I'm doing autopsies!"

Frances, Rusty, and Clint stood still, realizing they had just walked in on Ben.

"Please tell me he ain't fuckin' a corpse," Rusty whispered.

"It's just us, Ben," Frances calmly said. "You… You good? We're just here to pick up the next four bodies."

"I'm… Yes… Just… Give me a minute."

"This is bullshit," Clint said, pushing a gurney into the space. "We need to get movin' here, buddy! We've got funerals comin' out our hot pockets!"

"Just a minute!" Ben demanded, turning around as he tucked his shirt in his pants. Ben turned to see if his partner had scurried from view, but not before Clint saw her.

Clint's face went pale. "You."

Frances saw him tense. "Clint? You okay? What is it?"

"What are you doin' in here?" Clint asked in a low voice.

Maynelle Gilbertson climbed to her feet, adjusting her dress. "Clint, it's not what you think."

"You've been screwin' the coroner?" Clint asked.

"It's not like that—" she insisted.

"How long!? How long you been screwin' the coroner!?" Clint hollered.

"Son, I'm gonna have to ask you to leave!" Ben shouted.

Clint shot an arm out, his hand flipped up, shutting Ben down. "How long, Maynelle?"

"You don't understand, Clint. You don't understand."

"Clint, wait outside," Rusty said.

Clint shoved the gurney clear across the room and stormed outside. Rusty watched him sprint, full force, down the street, away from the building.

Frances turned to Maynelle. "Need you to step outside, darlin'." Maynelle quickly grabbed her purse and ran outside. Frances slowly approached Ben. "Here's what's going to happen. I'm going to need whoever you got ready who can be closed casket. We need to move bodies as soon as possible, and we don't got time to embalm everybody. Also, I'm going to need to store some caskets over there in the corner because we can't bury anyone until the ground is settled. We don't got room at the funeral home. It's like we're the innkeepers and Mary and Joseph just rolled up, lookin' for a place to stay without a reservation."

Frances's eyes landed on the unmistakable bag that contained Queenie Masters. "And I'm going to need Queenie Masters. Edie wants to get her set, and I need to do her a solid."

Ben didn't move. Ben was too embarrassed.

"Did you hear me, Ben Camden?!" Frances barked.

"Yes, yes. Those three over there, and Queenie is ready."

"I'm going to need four more closed caskets at the end of the night." Frances stepped closer. "Also, I'm gonna need you to watch the news tonight. I'm gonna need you to watch Cyreia Sandrock do a story about the funeral of someone who died out there, and I'm gonna need you to check your records. And there will come a day in the very near future when you're gonna realize that's important information for the police to have. Do you understand me?"

"I literally don't have a fucking clue what you are—" Ben said, nearly crying.

"I'm just suggestin' watch the news. Because your testimony might become useful in the very near future." She slapped him on the ass.

Five minutes later, Hector met them at the back of the van as they loaded the first body. "What was all that about? Why did the kid take off like a whirling dervish?"

"Long story. Tell you later."

"Kid's gotta thing for older women?" Rusty teased.

"You jealous?"


Pembrook and Ray stood at the conference table examining all the evidence, both eating pizza from that one place that no one really loves but orders from when they're drunk.

"We need to exhume Ruth Chambers," Ray insisted.

"I don't want to put Arlan through that."

"Arlan was sheriff before me. Before you. Arlan would want to know the truth. Arlan would want justice if anything had happened to Ruthie. We can't just go around exhuming random residents over the past two to ten years. Ruth ties Donald to the timeline for Stephen."

"We have Dean for that."

"Dean was at Memorial. Not Lockhart's. And Mrs. Hunt was after Stephen went missing. Arlan would want to know the truth."

The doors banged open in the distance, and Clint Peppers stormed into the lobby and pounded his fists onto Roscoe's desk. "I need to talk to the sheriff! I need to talk to him right away! Right now! I have information on a murder!"

"Son, just calm your horses! What's wrong?" Roscoe asked.

"I know who killed Dean Gilbertson!"

Ray and Pembrook heard Clint's high-pitched screaming and saw him erratically pacing the lobby like a wild animal. "Clint, what's wrong?" Ray asked

Clint was in tears and grabbed Ray's sleeves, pleading. "It's the coroner! It's the gotdamn coroner, Ray Jackson! He killed Coach Gilbertson! He's screwin' Maynelle! I need you to believe me! I need you to believe me, bro!"

"How do you know?"

"We walked in on them! They was screwin' in Frances's senior citizen center!"

Ray put his arm around Clint's shoulder and led him to a bench. "It's okay, son." He turned to Roscoe. "Can you get Clint something to drink?"

"I saw them."

"What were you doin' out there?"

"I was helpin' Frances and Rusty move the bodies for the funerals. And we walked in."

"That's not proof Dean was murd—"

"It makes total sense! He would know how to kill Coach and get away with it! Think about it! Bro, you know I'm right!"

"I believe you, Clint. I do. But can you do me a favor? Can we wait on this till we get all this other stuff figured out? I think you could really be onto something, and he could really tie all this together. You did great work, Clint. Great work. But can I let you in on a little secret? You can't tell anyone, but everything I told you about? We're about to blow it all up. We're so close to getting the bad guys."

Roscoe handed Clint a bottle of Coke, and Clint downed it. "I was right, see?"

"I think you have made a very compelling case, yes."

Clint reached into his pocket and pulled out Donald's keys. "Donald Dobkins's Jeep is in the church parking lot. Found a gun, a knife, and an envelope of cash."

Ray was so stunned he grabbed Clint and kissed his forehead. "Clint! You found the literal smoking gun! Or smokin' knife!"

Pembrook walked out of the war room. "Arlan's meeting us at the cemetery."

Ray turned to Clint. "You want to come? We can check out the Jeep?"

"He can't be there when we exhume the body."

Ray dangled the keys. "Clint found the knife."

Hector stood guard in the parking lot, watching out for Rusty and Frances as they moved the bodies into the coolers in the shed.

"We can only fit three more in here. We've got four tonight."

"We've got the six drawers in the embalming room, right?"

Rusty nodded, heaving another body out of the van and onto the gurney to wheel closer to the shed. "That Athens drop has to happen in the morning. We don't have the space."

"Let's take Queenie in and do her open casket. That will keep Edie busy, at least for the rest of the day, once Christopher embalms her."

People started walking out of the side door. Frances gasped and turned to Rusty. "Two o'clock show is over! You done?"

Rusty pushed the last body into the shed and quickly placed it in the cooler. When he was done, he padlocked the shed. "Queenie's in the van. I'll wait till everyone leaves."

"I'm going to go see what the fallout is." Frances turned to Hector. "I wish you would go home and go to bed."

"I've been in bed long enough. Go do what you need to do."

Frances made her way to the front of the building and saw Delores and Sissy shaking hands and thanking the crowd for coming.

"Well?" Frances asked under her breath.

"It's fine," Sissy said. "Not my first rodeo."

"Bill did some good preachin'," Delores added.

"Once they all leave, we need to get Queenie started with Christopher and Edie. The three of us need to call out to the families out back and tell them about the closed caskets," Frances said. "Arrange the drop with Dolly at Athens State late morning, after we get the first funeral going in the chapel. Tell her eleven."

"I was thinking in the afternoon," Sissy said.

"When I want your opinion, you'll know it, because I'll be lookin' at you."

Pembrook dropped the knife and the gun from Donald's glove box into evidence bags. He dropped the cash envelope into another bag. "I'll get someone out here to drive it to the station to go through."

Ray patted Clint on the back. "Son, you did real good."

"What y'all doin' out here?" barked a familiar voice in a big truck behind them. Ray and Pembrook turned to see Arlan Chambers wearing his cowboy hat.

"Look what the cat dragged in!" Arlan exclaimed.

"You the cat, because you're the one who dragged me in." Arlan shook Pembrook's hand.

Clint threw a quick salute to Ray. "Leave you to it," Clint said, shaking his car keys and backing up to his Mustang.

"Hey buddy," Ray whispered, "When we get this all handled, I'll look into Ben Camden."

Clint nodded to Arlan. "It's real good to see you, sir. My daddy misses seein' you down The Counter. Said he used to see you there all the time before court."

"Clint Peppers!? Son, you grew ten feet! I didn't even recognize you!"

"See you soon, sir. I'll leave y'all to it," Clint said as he headed to his Mustang.

Arlan Chambers had lost a lot of weight since Ruth's death. He had managed to keep her African Violets alive despite Delores's insistence he would kill them all. He spent most of his days sitting in his chair at home watching television, mournfully missing Ruth.

He'd lost weight because he had stopped eating. Friends would drop by and insist he eat or take him to Pasquale's or Amici's. He liked the ham sandwich at Mark and Leland's café, but he didn't like climbing their steps. He missed Ruth. He didn't have much to live for without her.

Arlan slowly made his way to Ruth's grave. Jethro had already dug her casket from the ground, and it was resting near the lip of the grave.

"Sheriff, I gotta say I feel just awful not comin' around and checkin' in on you. I'm gonna change that," Pembrook said as Arlan waved him off.

"You're busy," he said. But he narrowed his eyes on Ray. "But you… Where did you go off to?"

"I got my heart broke. Lost my mind. And started chasin' bad guys on my own."

"You shouldn't be chasin' bad guys without a shield, Jacks. You abandoned your post."

"I know. And everyone just loves remindin' me."

Arlan kept walking, fighting tears as he saw Ruth's casket back out above ground. He leaned down, placing his hand on it, softly whispering, "Oh, Ruthie…. Oh, my Ruthie."

"Arlan, I hate to put you through this, but we have good reason to believe that Ruth might be one of the victims in this body-snatching operation I told you about," Pembrook said. "Based on the timing of her funeral, the van we recovered from Lake Briarwood, a body that was found in a warehouse in Atlanta, and security footage that links a man to the murder of Imelda Weathers, we have more than reason to believe this. We know you would want the truth, and we know you would want to bring justice."

Arlan shook his head. "I don't want to know," he said barely above a whisper. "You can open her up and get what you need. But I don't want to know. You hear?"

Pembrook and Ray nodded.

Ashlyn gave Arlan a hug. "It's good to see you again, sir. Been a while."

"How's your momma and them?" Arlan asked.

"They fine," she replied. "Daddy keeps sayin' he needs to take you fishin'."

"I'd like that. You tell your daddy I miss him. I miss his face."

Arlan stepped back and pointed his cane to Pembrook. "I'll leave y'all to it," he announced.

Pembrook squeezed Arlan's shoulder, and Arlan slowly meandered back toward his truck.

Jethro unlocked the casket and opened it. Everyone tried not to react to any smells, as Arlan was still nearby.

Ashlyn reached into the casket and took Ruth's hand. It slid off the PVC pipe in her jacket. Ashlyn held the hand inside the casket so Pembrook and Ray could see, trying her best not to make any sudden movements.

Pembrook stepped back as Jethro attempted to open the bottom door. "It's stuck," Jethro said.

Ashlyn reached past the fabric skirt, separating the bridge and the foot panel of the casket, and felt around the space. "She don't got no legs," Ashlyn said.

Ashlyn could not have known the acoustics in the cemetery or the fact Arlan had recently purchased new hearing aids. But Arlan Chambers heard her say, "She don't got no legs."

Ray was watching Arlan as his knees buckled and he slowly crumbled to the earth. "Call an ambulance!" Ray screamed as he ran to Arlan.

He flipped Arlan on his back. He was unconscious. He wasn't breathing.

Ray began chest compressions. "Come on, Arlan! Today is not your day, buddy!"

For a brief moment, Arlan's eyes flickered open. He looked over Ray's shoulder.

Ray stopped compressions. "Arlan! Gotdamn, you scared me! Help is on its way! Hang on, buddy!"

Arlan smiled. His mouth opened, and a soft but distinct "Ruthie" left his lips.

And then he was gone.


Dr. Ireland, a young-looking doctor, probably two years out of medical school, pushed out of the emergency room doors and walked directly to Pembrook and Ray. His face said it all.

"I'm sorry," he said. "There was just nothing we could do."

Ray fought his tears, wiping them away and rubbing his face vigorously. "Gotdamn it, no," he said through gritted teeth. "Fuck… No."

Pembrook grabbed his shoulder, and Ray shook him. "Arlan

Chambers was a good man," Pembrook stated.

"He didn't deserve this!" Ray spat. "It's my fault."

Dr. Ireland squeezed Ray's other shoulder. "If I may, and I hope you don't mind me saying this. I don't know if you're a spiritual person, but I've never seen a more peaceful man in all my life."

Dr. Ireland motioned, and they walked through the emergency room doors. They made their way behind a curtain.

Arlan lay peacefully in the bed. His eyes were now closed. He had a small but undeniably peaceful smile on his lips.

Ray took his hand. He was still warm. His body was still warm.

"He's with Ruth now, Ray. He's in a better place."

Ray's eyes went dark. A rage slowly coursed in his veins. "Dr. Ireland, I'd like to see one of the other patients here at your hospital."

Pembrook and Ray stood outside Donald's hospital room with Dr. Hoff, Donald's primary doctor. Dr. Hoff's pallor was a light green, having just heard the allegations stacked against the patient he was desperately trying to keep alive.

"While I completely understand and respect your desire to place Mr…"

"Dobkins. Donald Dobkins is his name," Pembrook said.

"Mr. Dobkins. I cannot allow you to place him under formal arrest at this time. We can't place any undue stress upon him due to the swelling around his brain. The swelling is decreasing, but I'm going to have to ask you to wait a few days. I can't allow any questioning. Do you understand me?"

Pembrook nodded. "We just want to see him, if you wouldn't mind. I promise we won't cause him any undue stress. He clearly can't get up and sneak out."

Dr. Hoff shook his head. "I still can't believe the other one got away."

Pembrook and Ray shared a look. "What do you mean, 'the other one?' What other one?"

"The man who got shot. He just up and walked out. No one knows what happened to him?"

"Hector Ramirez?" Ray asked.

"Name sounds familiar. He wasn't my patient."

Ray turned to Pembrook. "A million bucks says he's a Lockhart's' as we speak." Ray turned to Dr. Hoff. "We'll find him."

Dr. Hoff pushed open the door to Donald's room, and they slowly approached the bed.

"Are we awake?" Dr. Hoff asked.

Donald's eyes were wide open. He couldn't turn his head but eeked out a "Yes."

The three men approached his bed. Dr. Hoff invited them closer.

"It's a miracle he survived. It's a miracle he's awake."

"Sir, can you tell us your name?" Pembrook asked.

Donald's brows furrowed. "I don't know my name. Everyone keeps asking me."

"Your name is Donald Dobkins," Ray said. "Does that ring any bells for you?"

Donald's eyes shifted from Pembrook to Ray as they leaned over in the bed into his range of sight.

"Are you sure?"

"I'm Sheriff Pembrook. This is Ray Jackson. We understand you had a big day at church."

"You sure you can't tell us anything about what you remember?" Ray asked.

"I don't remember anything. I promise you," Donald lamented.

"Well, once your brain heals up a little more, we're gonna have some difficult conversations. But for right now, we just need you to get to feelin' better." Pembrook nodded to Dr. Hoff. He picked up the duck on his side table. "Someone brought you a duck? You know where this came from?"

"It was…" Donald said, then stopped. "No. I don't know where it came from."

"Do you know what kind of car you drive, Mr. Dobkins?"

"I don't."

"It's a Jeep," he said, placing the duck back down. "Don't worry. We've got it all safe for you down at the police station." Pembrook nodded to Dr. Hoff. "We'll be seein' you soon."

Frances gathered the trash from the men's bathroom as Hector carefully helped clean a toilet. "You should be in bed, Hector," Frances insisted.

"I've spent enough time in bed," he exclaimed. "How does this end?"

"The less you know at this point, the better. But buddy, it's time for you to start looking for a new plan. I appreciate your help here, but I'm out of this game. I'm out, and Sissy has forced me into a corner. I'm ending this game in Liberty. I love you like a brother, but you need to leave. Move. Get out. You understand?"

Hector nodded.

Frances shook her head. "Y'all were plannin' on bringin' him in. Y'all were plannin' to expand. I can't have that in my life, Hector. I made a mistake. But y'all… You know you're in the wrong. And you just kept doin' it."

"I don't think I'm doing the wrong thing, Frances. Without the work, doctors can't operate. Students can't train. Think about all the great minds out there who want to discover cures for cancer and other life-threatening diseases. The very first medical discoveries were from pillaged bodies. Is it wrong? I don't care. I don't care as long as we are saving the living."

Ray stormed through the doors of Lockhart's and bellowed, "Frances Hunt!"

He charged through the office doors and found Lily seated at her desk. Seeing her took his breath away. *She's a liar too!* "What are you…. Why are you…" *She has to be working with Frances. Of course, she is.* He saw her wearing his shirt. "Nice shirt," he boiled. "Where's Frances?"

"She's in the back," Lily said with her fake accent, then remembered she didn't use it the night before. "She's in the back."

"By the way, fuck you," he said, backing out and slamming the door.

Frances left the bathroom, having heard him scream her name. "What in the Hell—"

"I need to talk to you, Frances! Right now! Right fuckin' now!"

"Calm down!"

"This is me calm!" he screamed.

"I have people back there visiting their loved ones! Shut your gotdamned mouth!"

They stood in silence.

"Let's go for a walk," she said.

"I don't want to—"

Frances spun him around and shoved him toward the door. "I'll be back in an hour," she said to Lily, standing in the doorway.


Frances and Ray sat next to each other at the bar inside Pasquale's. They were the only people in the entire restaurant, other than the bartender, who stood at the other end of the bar while Ray and Frances fought in near silence.

Ray knocked back three of the seven tequila shots he had ordered, lined up on the counter. Frances took a sip of her sweet tea.

"Why ain't you drinkin'?" he asked her.

"I have a problem with drinkin'."

"What kind of problem?"

"When I start drinkin', I turn into a different person. When I start drinkin', I don't know when or how to stop. It ain't good for me. It ain't good for anyone," she said, lighting a cigarette.

"You can't smoke in here," Ray said, aghast.

"Hey, Prichard! Can I smoke in here?"

Prichard shrugged. "As long as it ain't the marijuana!" he shouted back.

"You should stop smokin'," Ray insisted.

"You should stop drinkin'."

"Arlan Chambers died today," he quietly said, doing everything in his ability to not cry.

Frances gasped and grabbed his arm. He pulled away. She grabbed his inner thigh. "What!? How!?"

"How? That's a good one. That there is a good story, Hunt. See, we called Arlan because we needed to exhume Ruth Chambers out of her grave to get proof she had been chopped up for body parts like you told me. And he wanted to be out there because he's a cop by nature, but he didn't want to know because he's like a man, right? He didn't want to know that his wife had been mutilated by body snatchers. Stop me when this sounds familiar to you."

"Ray…"

"Arlan said his goodbyes again to his wife. Gently touched her casket. Started walking away… and…" Ray's eyes filled with tears. "I saw his legs just buckle. And I saw him go down. Damn near peaceful. And I ran over, and I tried to save him, but he… He was just gone."

"Ray, I'm so sorry."

Ray turned, staring into the face of the woman he had loved and possibly still loved. But the face of the woman who held all the cards. "How does this end, Frances? Because I don't want any more people dyin' on my watch. I want Donald Dobkins in prison for the rest of his unnatural life. And I want to find Stephen and Stuart Lockhart, and I want them to suffer for what they did to Ruth. And I want that Hector guy—"

"Leave Hector out of this—"

"You told me he was working for Donald, and then he was working for Sissy. And I know he bounced from the hospital. I done know that y'all hacked up Howard Fisher. Saw that today with my own eyes."

"I ain't a part of this, Jackson. Sissy's blackmailing me to work with her. I swear to you. I swear to you on my life."

"I just got one question for you, Hunt—"

"Me first. You want to know how this is going to end? I'm gonna tell you exactly how this is gonna go down, Ray Jackson. You wanna grab a pen, because here is how it ends. Sissy and Delores are planning on doing a drop tomorrow at Athens State. She's got ten bodies set, and she's planning on pulling them from ten closed-casket funerals. Some of the caskets are going to be stored at the bakery. We don't got room anywhere else. You're going to set up a sting. People at the bakery. People at Athens State. People at Lockhart's. When she shows up for the drop, you arrest her."

Ray downed two more of his shots.

"Ray, I'm literally fuckin' handin' you Sissy Stone. Be grateful."

"What about Delores?"

"Delores is collateral damage in all of this. She don't deserve to go to prison."

"And what about you?"

"I want immunity. I want protection."

Ray laughed.

"I'm handing you everything you need to take all of this down. You're welcome, you stupid prick, and last time I checked, you ain't even sheriff. You want justice? You want your fuckin' podcast? You're welcome. Also, precious boy, I know where Stephen and Stuart are, so yeah, I want fuckin' immunity. You want to take down the whole gotdamn show? Do it. But I'm the final boss."

Ray downed another shot. "Sissy will name you. She'll say it was all your idea. I can't do anything after she names you."

Frances took a drag from her cigarette. "You said you had a question. What was your question?"

Ray downed another shot. "Why did you do it?"

"I done told you, Ray! Jesus! I needed the money. We've been over this."

"But your own mother."

Frances stared at Ray. *But your own mother.* She could see his mouth moving, but she couldn't hear anything he was saying. She went into a fugue-like state.

Ray finally snapped his fingers in her face. "Frances!"

She blinked. "But my own mother, what, Ray? What about my

mother? But my own mother, *what, Ray?!*" she screamed. "What are you tryin' to say!?"

It was very clear to Ray that Frances had no idea about Birdie's burial. She had no idea that her mother had been harvested. He quickly grabbed her in a tight embrace and clutched the back of her head.

"Franny, no.  I'm so sorry. I meant… I meant, but your own mother was involved in all of this, and I'm sorry, I shouldn't have brought that up. I'm so sorry, that was so wrong, and I—"

"Did you see something!? Did you see something in my momma's casket!? Is something wrong!?"

"No. No, Franny, nothing's wrong. She's at peace. She's at peace," he said, patting her head.

"I don't believe you, Ray," she said, fighting tears.

He grabbed her face and pulled it toward his. "Look at me. Look at me. Do you trust me?" She didn't answer. "Do you trust me, Hunt?" he said, pleading with her.

"No, I don't."

"Franny, I need you to trust me."

"I wanna see her," Frances said.

"No. No, you don't. You hold onto those memories you had of her. Your beautiful momma. She's with Buddy and Ruth and Arlan and…" Ray smiled. "You know, half her congregation! She's probably up there fightin' it out with Queenie Master's as we speak."

"She's probably using Queenie's head as a bowling ball."

"Your momma was an excellent bowler!"

"You're drunk," she said.

"Not yet, but I plan to be very quickly." He downed another shot. "Also, I'm pretty sure I fucked your new employee, and she stole my shirt."

Frances slapped him, half mockingly, half jealous. "Are you serious right now?!"

"She said she worked in finance. She said she did downsizing."

"Technically, she does. What do you mean you're pretty sure?"

"I was drunk."

"You need AA."

"I need the lovin' of a good woman," he said, the alcohol definitely starting to hit.

Frances reached into her purse and pulled out a hundred-dollar bill, placing it on the counter. "I need to get back."

"That's a C-note, Hunt."

"Thanks, Prichard! Say hi to your wife and kids for me!"

Prichard waved back.

Ray grabbed her hand. "What time is that drop goin' down?"

"Eleven. Athens State. Medical labs."

"Are you ready?"

"Am I ready for what, Ray? Ready for this nightmare to be over? Yes."

"I need justice."

"I need my life back. But if you want justice, you might want to circle the wagons at Lockhart's, the bakery, and Athens State at eleven o'clock tomorrow."

The clock on the wall read that it was 6:15. Edie was alone in the embalming room with Queenie's corpse. Christopher had embalmed and took great care in setting her body (and head) in the casket. She wore a high-neck royal blue blouse and a beautiful skirt she bought in New York on a girls' trip they took to see *Phantom of the Opera* several years earlier.

Edie smiled, waving Frances into the embalming room. Edie pulled Queenie's hair back into a high ponytail that looked classic and placed a headband on top of her head. Queenie looked peaceful.

"She looks beautiful, Edie."

Edie nodded.

"Edie, I think it's in your best interest to not come in tomorrow."

Edie nodded, understanding. "Tomorrow," she said, acknowledging the plan was in motion. Edie touched Queenie's hand. "I'm just afraid something's gonna happen to her after I leave. I'm afraid Sissy's gonna steal her or something."

"That's not going to happen, Edie. I promise you."

Edie took her hand. "Your mother would be proud of you."

"I'm most positive she was not."

"What you're doing now. You're righting the ship. You're doing the right thing."

Frances squeezed her hand. "I'm heading out."

"I won't see you tomorrow," Edie said.

"I'll call you when it's over," Frances said and walked out. "And when it's over, we'll give Queenie a proper burial."


Pembrook sat at his desk, compiling all his official findings from the day into a report. Roscoe knocked on his door. "Sheriff, you got a walk-in."

Pembrook looked up, taking off his readers to see Kevin Hunt standing behind Roscoe. "Come on in, son," he motioned to Kevin. "Roscoe, why don't you get us some Cokes? Maybe a moon pie if there's one in the cabinet?"

Kevin took the seat across from Pembrook and pulled his phone out of his coat. "What's your email, sir?" Kevin asked. "I need to send you something."

"It's sheriff at Liberty GA dot net."

Kevin entered the email into his phone, and a swoosh sound followed a second later. "Before you open that, I need you to know I'm just a kid."

Pembrook nodded. "You're under eighteen, right?"

Kevin nodded. "I've been helpin' Sissy Stone down at the funeral home and… And she's been doin' bad things. And she was forcin' me to do bad things. She threatened to tell everyone what I was doin'. And I want to go to seminary when I graduate."

Pembrook nodded, lightening up the conversation. "You gonna get your Bachelor's first? You gonna go to Athens State?"

"Reverend White is helping me apply to some schools where I don't need that. So I can start preachin' faster."

"I think that's great, Kev. And if you ever want to go back and get a full education, you can do that at any time. I just want what's best for you." Pembrook turned to his laptop and heard his email ding. "I've got mail," he said with a little laugh. "Let's see what we got here."

Pembrook opened the attachment and slid on his glasses. He watched the video of Sissy, Delores, Rusty, and Kevin moving the bodies in the back of the bakery. Pembrook leaned closer to the video. It was undeniable what he was watching. He did not react.

"I see. And this video is recent, right? Probably from Sunday night?" he asked. "This is your momma's place, right?"

Kevin nodded.

Pembrook watched as Kevin mouthed, "Help me" to the camera.

"They were makin' you do this against your will?" Pembrook asked.

"Yes, sir. I was only doin' it because I like helpin' people, but they made me do it. I didn't want to."

"And your momma?"

"Momma ain't involved in any of that, I swear," he said emphatically. "Momma's been tryin' to help with all them funerals down at Lockhart's because Sissy's so old and can't organize shit," he said, his face dropping. "Ms. Stone has been blackmailin' my momma into helping her."

"Blackmailing her how?"

"She was just makin' her do it."

"Kevin, do you know how long this has been going on?"

"A while, sir."

"Do you know if Stephen Lockhart was ever involved?"

Kevin nodded. "Yes, sir. I'm pretty sure he was involved."

"Do you know where Stephen is now?"

Kevin flinched, confused. "Dead, sir. He died on a cruise, right? Did you not hear about that?"

"With everything you know and your workin' with Ms. Stone, it never came up that he might still be alive?"

"No, sir. Never. I promise you. I've ain't ever heard that. And Sissy ain't that good of an actress."

"But Delores is," he said with a grin. "You see her when she did *Steel Magnolias* down at the Liberty Little Theater?"

"I don't go to plays, sir. They's borin'."

"She's a pretty darn good actress," Pembrook said. "Thank you for sharing this video, Kev."

"Am I gonna be in trouble?"

"You're not going to jail. I can promise you that. But we might need you to be a witness, and that's going to put some eyes on you."

"That would ruin my opportunities for seminary, sir."

Pembrook nodded. "I understand, Kevin. Thank you for this. I'll do everything in my power to protect you."

"You already know somethin', don't you? You got leads."

Pembrook slid his elbows across the desk, leaning closer to Kevin. "What do you know about Donald Dobkins?"


Frances made her way out of the back of the funeral home, seeing Rusty and Hector near the shed. She replayed the past nearly three months in her head. She felt like she had developed a true friendship with Hector, and she might have felt some small feelings for Rusty. It had been years since she felt comfortable around men.

"I think y'all need to take to higher ground," she said.

"What do you mean?" Rusty asked.

"It's goin' down tomorrow. All of it."

Hector stammered. "What… What does that mean?"

"It means you two should get out of town. While you can."

Rusty shook his head, realizing it was time to move again. "So… That's it?"

"It ain't goodbye forever. But you don't want to be here when heads start rollin'. No pun intended."

"What are we supposed to do?" Hector asked. He grabbed her hand.

"What are you going to do?"

"I want you to stop by the bank in the mornin'. Cooper'll have somethin' for you."

"I don't want a hand-out," Rusty said.

"It's not a hand-out."

Frances put her arms around Rusty and gave him a tight hug. She carefully hugged Hector. "I'll see you soon. I'll see you again. Someday."

Hector kissed her cheek. She pulled away from him.

She turned, walking away. "Y'all didn't… Y'all didn't do anything to my momma, did you?" she asked, locking eyes with Rusty.

Rusty never dropped her gaze, but he stared a beat too long before his voice cracked, and he responded, "No, Frances."

Frances's eyes shot to Hector, who looked to the ground.

Frances nodded. "Okay. Well, thank you for bein' honest."

She walked past the funeral home, past the cars, and turned on Main Street.

Edie had been watching Frances, Hector, and Rusty talk through the window in the embalming room. She had heard every word. She opened the door and moseyed over to them.

"You're a nurse, right?" she asked Rusty.

Rusty smirked inquisitively. "How did you—"

"I overheard you and Frances talking when I was tied up at Dusty Dingle's old place. I've got the hearing of an elephant."

"I'm a former nurse, yes."

Edie extended her hand to Hector. "Edie Trussell. I don't think we've ever met properly. I've seen you around town. Nice to meet you." Hector reluctantly shook her hand, wondering if they were in trouble.

Edie took a Sharpie from her purse and wrote "2428 Brookwood Lane" on Rusty's forearm.

"Meet me there tomorrow at noon."

Frances walked about half a mile before she heard the familiar roar of an engine behind her. It slowed as it pulled up alongside her. The window rolled down, and rap music blasted from the speakers.

"Get in the car," Clint said, turning down the music.

Frances opened the car door, climbed inside, and buckled the seatbelt. Neither Clint nor Frances said a word during the entire ride back to the farm.


Frances smoked a cigarette, sitting on her cinder block behind the barn, staring at the fire pit. Clint sat on the ground next to her.

"You should quit smoking," he said.

"You should mind your own business," she retorted, then looked at the cigarette. "You know what? You're right." She flicked the cigarette into the fire. "You want to talk about it? You want to talk about Maynelle?"

"I mean, it's pretty obvious, ain't it?"

Frances nodded. "They ain't gonna do anything till Ben gets everyone autopsied. You know that, right? And even then, they may not find any evidence."

Clint nodded. "Solving Coach's murder ain't even on a list of priorities right now."

"And you're also gonna have to resign yourself to the fact Dean Gilbertson might have just had a good old-fashioned heart attack, Maynelle got some insurance money, and she's now in a relationship with an age-appropriate man with a job."

Clint giggled. Frances scoffed, "What?"

"In another life, Hunt." They locked eyes. "Damn, that's all I gotta say. Just damn."

"You need to find you a little girlfriend. Date. Get engaged. Get married. Have kids. You got your whole life in front of you. Whatever you thought this is, or was… It ain't it, Clint."

"Another life," he repeated.

"We'll find each other in the next one, 'kay?"

They sat in silence for nearly a half hour. Neither moving. Just staring at the fire. They both heard the back door open and bang shut, snapping them out of their trances. They heard footsteps approaching.

"Kevin?" Clint asked.

"Or a psycho killer."

Clint rounded the back of the barn, surprised to see Kevin but not letting on. "Oh, that was your car," Kevin said. "Thought momma had bought her a new one with all her new money."

"Go to bed, Kevin. I don't want to see you," Frances said.

"Are you still mad about the invitation?"

Frances's eyes never left the fire. "I'm so terribly disappointed in you. You're such a massive disappointment in my life, Kevin. You know that? I did the best I could, and you just… You just don't get it. You just don't get it."

Kevin had never experienced such disdain from his mother. He tried to speak but couldn't. Between gasps of breath, he said, "I'm sorry."

Frances shook her head. "I don't want to see you, Kevin. Go away from me with this."

"I'm sorry," he said again.

"Go away, Kevin! I don't want to be around you!" she screamed as he spun and ran back to the house.

"I want a drink," Frances whispered.

"No, you don't," Clint said quietly.

"I do. I want a drink. I want to drown myself in a bottle of vodka right now," she said, pouring a bucket of water over the fire.

"Frances, you don't want a drink."

"I can't have a drink because I've got enough ibuprofen running through my veins to kill a cattle ranch." Frances spun around and grabbed Clint by the face. She pulled him close. "I want to do bad things to you, and I want to drink a bottle of alcohol and dance naked under the moon. I want to run away from here, and I want to fly through the air like a bird. I want to kill Sissy Stone, and I want to forget everything. I want to die, Clint Peppers. I want to die and be reborn so I can do this all over again in another life as someone who doesn't live in pain every single fuckin' day of my life. I want to know what real, true, deep love feels like for just one day, and I want to know what it feels like to have someone love me back. I want to know what it feels like to be someone other than Frances Hunt. Someone who gets to be selfish for just one day. Someone who's a bad girl because she wants to be. Not because that's the way she was created."

She pulled his face closer and lightly kissed his lips, and smacked his ass.

"But I'm gonna go inside. I'm gonna draw me a hot bath with my Calgon powders I've been savin' since 1994. I'm gonna make me a cup of hot chocolate with some whipped cream on top, and I'm gonna go to bed. Because tomorrow morning, I'm going to set fire to everything in this town. That disaster down at the Liberty Baptist Church is gonna look like a Saturday morning cartoon compared to the fury I'm gonna unleash tomorrow mornin'.

"It ends tomorrow, Clint. It ends tomorrow."

# CHAPTER TWELVE

# EVERYONE HAS AN ENDGAME

Frances stood in front of her full-length mirror in what she used to call her "one good black dress." The clock on her nightstand said 6:54. The sun wasn't up yet.

Her head snapped to the door, realizing the house was silent. Kevin must have already left for school, she realized, looking at her watch. Maybe he left early for breakfast at The Counter, where Delores used to work.

Frances walked into the hall, heading to the stairs. She paused at her mother's door.  She gently placed her hands on the knob and turned, gently pushing her shoulder against the door.

Dust danced in a ray of moonlight from the window. Everything in Birdie's room looked exactly as she last remembered it. Exactly as she remembered the morning she screamed at her mother, "I can't handle your crazy today, Momma!" slamming the door behind her, shutting her own mother in her room. Shutting her into her own home. Leaving Birdie behind while Frances and the others dealt with "the business."

The same bedding covered the bed. She could almost smell her mother's perfume lingering. Her favorite tea rose.  Frances sat on the bed and gently touched a pillow.

In the near dark, she saw her mother's cross on its gold chain resting on the bedside table. *Why didn't she put that on? She always wore that necklace,* Frances mused. Frances never considered her mother wasn't wearing the cross the day Ray came to visit. Frances certainly didn't request any of Birdie's personal effects from the coroner's office, and none were offered.

Frances took the cross and chain necklace and went to the mirror. She placed it around her neck and clasped it. For as long as Frances could remember, Birdie had always worn her cross.

"I'm sorry, Momma. For everything," she said to the room. "I thought I was doin' the right thing."

Frances sprayed Birdie's off-brand version of perfume onto her wrists and rubbed them under her neck.

She walked out of the room and started to close the door behind her but paused, pushing the door all the way open.

The grandfather clock clicked and clacked in time in the living room. Frances made herself a breakfast of coffee, two scrambled eggs, and a piece of toast. She went through all the motions with no television in the next room or video playing on her phone. Birds cawed and crowed outside. Boards creaked inside the house. Life slowly returned to the Hunt family farm as it did every morning at this hour.

She washed the dishes. She gently grasped the cross in her hand. "Hey God, it's me again. Frances Hunt. Reporting in live from Liberty, Georgia. I know we ain't talked in a hot minute. I'm still mad at you. I'm a little less mad now. Just so you know.

"Look, today's gonna be real bad day. I know it. You know it. I see it. I can feel it. And I know I did wrong. But I need a break here. Okay? I need you to… I need your help here. Okay? Please forgive me for my sins and all that crap, but I need you to help me here. Just tell me what I need to do. And I'm a little slow, so I'm gonna need you to be really, really clear. Like you're talking to a three-year-old."


Ray stood under the steady stream of hot water in his room at The Farmer's Son. He was hung over, but not as bad as the day before. "Maybe I do need to go to AA," he said to himself.

Ray wasn't a big drinker. He used to drink beers with Pembrook and the others a few nights a week, and he enjoyed a scotch when he was alone at home. He also visited wineries whenever he was invited by friends. And he enjoyed a fully stocked bar in his old home. But Ray didn't consider himself an alcoholic because he'd never driven drunk, and alcohol never ruined his life.

"I just need to cut back," he told himself. "I'm fine," he lied to himself.

Ray dressed quickly and grabbed a coffee to go from the common area downstairs.

"I didn't lie to you," came a voice behind him. He spun around to see Lily dressed in black slacks and a tight black sweater.

"Did we—"

She nodded.

"I am definitely going to visit an AA meeting this afternoon."

"It's okay, cowboy."

"No. No, it's not. That's not who I am, and I apologize for my actions."

"You have nothing to apologize for. I had a great time."

"I don't think I did."

"You did. You really did. Trust me."

"Well, I'm not havin' a good time right now, okay?" he insisted. "This, that ain't who I am. I respect women."

"Do you respect yourself?"

"Apparently not."

In another life, Ray and Lily might have had an incredible relationship. In another life, they might even be married. But in this life, Ray was anchored to Liberty. His heart and soul was here. And Lily was like a bird. Lily never stayed in the same town for too long.

Neither knew they were pieces in the other's puzzle. Ray didn't know she was a bounty hunter. She was oblivious to the fact that Ray was the former sheriff and "that guy" who was doing a podcast.

"Good luck with your funerals today," Ray fumed.

"Good luck with your writing," she said. "My name's Lily, by the way."

"That's a beautiful name," he said, walking out.


Pembrook and Ray stood near the edge of the field of Pembrook's farm, watching the sunrise on the horizon. Carrie Pembrook walked up with two Thermoses of coffee, handing one to each of them.

"You got a big day planned?" Pembrook asked his wife.

"Oh, sure. I ain't missin' any of the drama down at Lockhart's! You kiddin'!? I got my outfit planned out and everything."

Pembrook and his wife had been married for nearly thirty years, and never a morning passed where Carrie didn't worry about her husband's safety. Even in a town where crime was extremely low, she worried.

"Welp, Jackson. I hereby officially deputize you," he said, tapping his Thermos on both sides of Ray's shoulders.

"I think you just knighted him, honey," Carrie said.

"You ready to do this?" Ray asked Pembrook.

"You were a better sheriff than me, Ray, and you know that."

"Oh, I know," Ray joked. "But today… Today's gonna put Liberty on the map."

"But on your terms," Pembrook stated. "Ray, if the roles were reversed, what would you say? What would you think? You ain't tellin' me everything, and that don't sit right with me."

"Pem, I promise you, we're going to get all the bad guys. I promise you. And that's all that matters."


"This is a check for a hundred thousand dollars," Hector flatly stated, holding a check for one hundred thousand dollars made out in his name.

Cooper slid a check across the desk to Rusty, made out in his name as well for the same amount. "My client extends her appreciation," Cooper said apathetically.

"Much appreciated," Rusty responded in disbelief.

Cooper folded his hands. "This concludes our transaction for today, gentlemen. Please enjoy your day," Cooper said, extending his arm toward the door.

"Hey, Mr. Cooper, thank you," Rusty said, extending his hand.

"No need to thank me," Cooper replied, not shaking his hand.

"Please tell Frances we appreciate this," Hector said, realizing his entire life was unknown from the moment they stepped outside. Hector had always had a job, even as a teenager.

Cooper nodded. "Y'all have a good day, you hear?"

Frances paced the back parking lot of Lockhart's. She wanted a cigarette. She wanted a drink. She wanted today to be over. Her hand tightly grasped the cross around her neck.

She looked down at the cement driveway, where one night, just about three months earlier, she split her lip open and knocked out a tooth when she went flying out of Delores's Crown Vic, high as a kite. She looked to the spot where they had first seen the Coyote Movers van and then to the side door where they had snuck inside to find Hector cutting off an arm and the same door where Oscar had pulled a shotgun on the group.

She jumped, startled, as the door opened, and Delores and Sissy stormed out.

"I ain't seen Rusty this morning," Sissy said. "You talked to him? He's late."

"He ain't answerin' his phone," Frances said. "You gotta drive the van to Athens State, Sissy."

"I ain't never done a delivery before," Sissy stated.

"Nothin' to it. You just drive up, and they come and get the bodies out of the back. Easy-peasy."

"What happens if I get pulled over?" Sissy asked.

"Keep it at the speed limit, and you won't have any issues."

"I'll go with you," Delores said.

"No, I need you here with me," Frances insisted.

Sissy shook her head. "Frances, you should drive the van out there, and we'll handle—"

"We have three bodies on deck and three in the afternoon, along with a pickup at noon. I'm not asking for a vote here. Sissy, you're driving the van. You're makin' the delivery. End of story."


Lily sat at her desk, finalizing the paperwork on the afternoon decedents. Frances barreled through the door, closing and locking it behind her. "It's goin' down in an hour," she said.

"Okay," Lily calmly responded. "What do you need me to do?"

"I need you out back to help me load the bodies. Sissy's gonna drive 'em to Athens State."

Lily nodded.

"I don't know what this means for you when the clock strikes eleven. There are gonna be cops in here. Cops all over the place. If you got problematic fingerprints, you might want to hit the road."

"I'm a Scorpio," Lily said.

"What's that got to do with the cost of tea in China?"

"Scorpios don't get caught."

"All the same, you've done right by me, and I don't want to see any more people get caught up in all of this."

Lily snapped her head from side to side. "Let's go move some dead bodies," she said with a little laugh. "I haven't said in like five months!"


Frances handed the keys to Sissy. "Drive carefully," Frances said.

"I'll be back as soon as I can."

The side door flung open, and Delores waddled quickly toward the van. "Wait for me!"

"I need you inside with me," Frances insisted.

"Oh, you'll be fine," Delores proclaimed. "You got Lil and Christopher. Plus, a whole bunch of people from the choir. We'll be back in a jiffy."

Frances grabbed her arm, pleading, "Delores, I need you to stay here. With me."

"We'll pick you up a hamburger on your way back! Or some of them Carter Clusters you like out there on the interstate."

Delores threw open the passenger's door and climbed inside. "I ain't never been on a drop before!"

Sissy and Frances locked eyes. "Is something wrong?" Sissy asked.

"No. All good," Frances said, clearing her throat. "Hurry back, 'kay?"

Sissy climbed into the van and started the engine.

"Let's ride, Sis!" Delores said excitedly. "It's just like *Thelma and*

*Louise!”*

"Sissy!" Frances called out. Sissy rolled down the window.

Frances looked into the eyes of the woman who had helped raise her. The woman her mother considered one of her best friends. Frances wondered how their lives had grown so dramatically apart over the past three months. Frances wondered if she ever truly, really knew Sissy Stone.

"What?!" Sissy squawked.

"See you soon."


An hour later, an overflow crowd of cars could be seen all down Main Street. Mourners walked the sidewalk and onto the property at Lockhart's. Makeshift tables were set up with refreshments, coffee and pastries. The morning visitations for the next three victims of the Liberty Baptist Church were underway. Visitation would follow in the afternoon for three more victims. Of today's decedents, Rev. White would preach over three funerals between noon and the end of the day. One would be pushed to the following day. Two would be graveside funerals at a date to be determined.

Frances checked her watch. **10:55.**

Pembrook and three of his officers slowly made their way through the crowd and into the lobby area. Carrie Pembrook saw her husband charge through the lobby and moved to get a closer look.

The old felt flannel announcement board with press-in letters announced that Gina Chumley was in the Mary, Mother of God Suite, Logan Voss was in the Cherub Suite, and Adrian Gower was in the rarely used Little Lamb Suite.

Pembrook nodded to each of his officers.

Frances saw Pembrook while escorting individuals into the Cherub Suite. She lightly gasped and nodded to him. *This is it.*

"Franny, we good?" he asked, whispering in her ear.

She nodded. "We were just about to move Ms. Chumley into the chapel."

He checked his watch. "Move the crowd out, and we'll check her. We need to clear the parlors, Franny. We need to do it now."

Frances nodded to Lily. Lily made her way down to the Mary, Mother of God suite and asked everyone to step outside for some coffee. "We just need to make a small adjustment in the room. It's the air conditioning, and we just need a moment."

Five minutes later, the parlors were secure. Pembrook squeezed his walkie. "Do it," he whispered.

Pembrook opened Ms. Chumley's casket and found it was empty. Misty Hill opened Logan Voss's casket in his parlor at the same time Officer Shaw opened Adrian Gower's.

"Negative," Misty responded over her walkie.

"Empty," Officer Shaw responded over his.

They closed their caskets.

Pembrook texted Ray and Denny. **"All empty."**

At the bakery, Ben Camden watched as Officer Johnson and other officers opened the empty caskets of the next three funerals, which would take place at Lockhart's that afternoon, as well as James Green and Delroy Richardson's caskets.

They were all empty.

Officer Johnson texted back. **"All empty."**

Pembrook texted Ray, **"You're up."** He followed up with, **"And don't f it up."**

Sissy and Delores pulled to the back of Athens State's Medical Building right on time. She backed the van into the space, with the rear doors facing the loading dock. Sissy looked all around the building. "I thought they were supposed to have someone meet us here," she lamented.

"I'll call Dolly," Delores said.

Ray, who had been watching from his Range Rover in the corner of the parking lot, signaled to the other officers over his walkie. "They're here. Go, go, go."

On cue, six police cars raced down the streets, sirens blaring. They roared into the parking lot and surrounded the van.

Sissy white-knuckled the steering wheel, realizing what was happening. "She set us up," she calmly stated.

Delores watched as officers exited their vehicles and took cover behind their open doors with guns aimed at the van.

Ray climbed out of his Range Rover and placed a bullhorn to his mouth. "Sissy Stone," he paused, seeing Delores in the passenger's seat. *Dammit, Delores.* "I need y'all to come out with your hands above your head."

Delores panicked. "What are we gonna do!?"

Sissy revved the engine.

"Turn off the engine! I need you to come out of the van with your hands in the air."

"She set us up," Sissy repeated.

"Turn off the engine, Sissy!" Ray screamed through the bullhorn. "You don't want to do this. It's all over. There's nowhere to go!"

"I can't do this anymore, Dee. I can't take it anymore."

"Can't take what?"

"All I ever wanted to do was help people. All I ever wanted to do was be a good Christian." She thrust her hand into her purse and pulled out her gun.

"What are you doing?!"

Sissy turned to Delores, staring in her terrified eyes. "I'm not goin' to jail, Dee. I'm not ever goin' to jail."

"Come out of the van, Sissy!" Ray reiterated.

Sissy revved the engine again.

Delores ducked down in the seat. "Don't do this, Sissy! Turn off the van! We can talk to Ray. We can explain—"

Sissy closed her eyes. "I'll see you later, old girl." She opened the door and stepped out, tossing her hand with the gun behind her back.

"Put your hands in the air," Ray demanded.

"Hey, Ray!" Sissy called out.

Sissy raised the gun, aiming at Ray, and fired.

All the officers fired on Sissy.

Sissy's body took bullet after bullet until she finally fell to her knees and careened over, landing on her side. Her eyes were open and frozen as they stared at the sky. Dead.

"Hold your fire! Hold your fire!" Denny demanded. All the officers stopped firing. "Delores Rogers! Come out with your hands up! And there better not be a fuckin' gun in your hand when you do!"

The officers aimed their guns at the van.

Delores gently rose up in the seat and raised her hands above her head.

She opened the door and slowly stepped out.

Denny turned back to see Ray lying on the ground.

Officers rushed to clear Sissy's gun and confirmed she was dead. Officers rushed Delores to cuff her.

Denny rushed to Ray and flipped him over.

Ray's eyes were wide open. His face was immobile in horror.

Denny checked his body for bullet holes. "Ray! Ray, talk to me!"

Ray finally gasped and sat up. "I felt that bullet whiz right through my hair, Denny. A millimeter off, and I'd be dead."

Denny hugged Ray. "Thought for sure you were gone."


Pembrook made his way through the crowd as they filed back into the parlors. He found Frances at the entrance and whispered, "Can I talk to you in private somewhere?"

Frances motioned for him to follow her outside. They walked to the edge of the parking lot. "It's a pretty day out," she said.

Pembrook took her hand. "Franny, Sissy Stone is dead. Delores Rogers has been arrested. We found the empty caskets at your place and the empty caskets inside. Ray and Denny found the bodies in the back of the van at Athens State."

Frances didn't move. She waited for Pembrook to read her Miranda rights. She closed her eyes, waiting for him to arrest her.

"Thanks for your help, Frances. I know this had to have been hard for you," he said.

Frances nodded. Tears rolled down her cheeks. "It's over?"

Pembrook just nodded.

Frances's eyes rolled into the back of her head as she fell forward. Pembrook caught her before she hit the ground.


Hector and Rusty rang the doorbell of Edie Trussell's palatial home. Hector stepped back, taking in the enormous home. "I never pictured Edie Trussell living in a place this big," Hector said.

"How well do you know this woman?" Rusty asked.

Hector shrugged. "Not that well at all. I've seen her around town, and the way Delores and Sissy rant about her, Queenie and Juanita, I feel like I've known her forever."

A Hispanic woman appeared at the door. "Good morning, she said. I'm Maria, Ms. Trussell's estate manager."

*Estate manager?* Rusty shook his head. "She around?"

"Follow me," she said, leading them into the house. The house was enormous, with beautiful hardwood floors, expensive art, fresh flowers, antique furniture, and a gigantic staircase that curved up to the second floor. Classical music played from somewhere in the house.

"Are we still in Liberty?" Rusty asked as Maria led them further and further back into the house. Past the dining room. Past a massive kitchen. They arrived in a large room, which looked like it would have been used as a salon for writers and cigar smokers back in the day.

Rusty and Hector stopped in their tracks.

A small figure in a full body cast rested atop a bed.

"Please tell me that's a child. Please tell me that's a very small child."

"You made it," Edie exclaimed, sweeping into the room in what looked like a cross between a caftan and a business suit. Nakoya and Lily followed in behind her. "The gang's all here."

"What is going on?" Hector asked.

"Welcome to Bonaventure," Edie announced to the room. "Maria, get us some drinks!"

"Isn't it a little early for that?" Rusty asked.

"It's five o'clock somewhere!"

Hector approached the bed. He leaned over, coming face-to-face with Donald.

"Hello, stranger," Donald whispered. "When I get out of this cast, I'm going to slit your throat and drink your blood. You hear me, you greasy little beaner? I'm going to fry your rice. I'm going to stomp on your sombrero. I'm going to…" Donald began laughing, then winced in pain. "Hello, old friend. Wow. This has been a journey."

"You wanted to kill Frances."

"I did," Donald said. "But look at God."

Hector turned to Edie, Nakoya, and Lily. "What is happening here?"

"I'm rebooting the enterprise," Edie announced. "With your expertise, Donald's contacts, Nakoya's business brain, Lily's muscle, and my money, we'll be unstoppable."

"How do I fit in?" Rusty asked.

"You'll be the driver," Edie said flippantly. When she saw his face fall, she said, "Or the head of transportation. It's all up in the air at this point. There is room for growth. But for now, I need you to help me nurse Donald back to health."

"Is that what you see me as?" Rusty asked. "The driver?"

"I'm feeling some animosity," Edie stated. "I don't like it when people condescend to me."

"You're correct, sister. Good luck. This *is* animosity, condescension, and a big old bowl of 'go fuck yourself.'" Rusty gave Hector a quick hug, whispering, "Good luck, buddy. I'm out."

Rusty stalked through the house. Maria quickly followed behind him.

"You don't got to follow me, darlin'," he said. "I know my way out."

Rusty turned the doorknob, threw the door back, and walked outside.

For the first time in a long time, he felt free.

For the first time in a long time, he felt alive.

Stephen Lockhart sat on a park bench tossing bread to pigeons. Stuart sat next to him, anxiously chewing a cuticle. They sipped lattes Stephen had made at home.

"Why are you feeding those nasty birds?" Stuart asked.

"I don't think pigeons nasty at all. They're survivors. They're beautiful. They are messengers. They can travel over five hundred miles in a single day."

"What are we going to do, Stephen? We have no investor. We've lost everything. You realize that, right?"

"This was all your idea, Stuart. You were the one who wanted to do this. And I've been carrying you this entire time. I've been carrying this family my entire life. I took care of Mother. I took care of Father. I carried your workload for years. That's all I do, is carry everyone. You've not had a single idea. You just wait for me to do everything. I'm not getting any younger, Stuart.

"Did you know that I was in love with Edie Trussell? Ever since high school. But she was afraid of what Sissy would think. And I was weirdly worried about what you might think."

Stuart coughed. Stephen handed him a handkerchief. "Cover your mouth, little brother."

"I woke up this morning and realized, 'What am I living for?' Me. Stephen. I had this master plan to take our work on an international scale, and now I'm realizing I've wasted my entire life. Wasted it on other people."

Stuart coughed again into the handkerchief.

"I woke up and realized I need to cut out what is not serving me."

Stuart coughed again, pulling the handkerchief from his mouth, seeing it covered in blood.

"Tell Momma and Daddy I said hi when you see 'em," Stephen said, kissing his brother on his forehead. "I envy you, Stuart. Tonight, you will be in paradise."

Stephen reached into his brother's jacket, taking his wallet and passport.

Stuart coughed uncontrollably. "Don't make a scene, Stuart. Just look at the clouds. Look at the clouds, Stuart, and open your arms to God's beautiful and warm welcome home. You are welcome, little brother. You're welcome."

Stephen pulled Stuart back onto the bench so they could face the clouds. He began singing, "When we all get to Heaven, what a wonderful day of rejoicing that will be. When we all see Jesus, we'll sing and shout the victory."

Stephen finished his latte, taking Stuart's from his hand. "Don't worry about me, Stuart. I'm a survivor."


"It has been three days since officers with the Liberty Police Department stopped an illegal body parts operation that has quite possibly been going on for years." Cyreia Sandrock's face filled the television screen, cutting to images of Rusty's van in the parking lot at Athens State and a gruesome image of Sissy's body, covered by a sheet. "While there's no additional information available at this time, Channel Four has received exclusive information the investigation has been taken over by the Federal Bureau of Investigation." The news piece cut to images of Melody Wang and her agents disembarking vehicles.

"We understand Cecila Stone, also known as Sissy Stone to those who knew her in Liberty, was shot and killed in a firefight with police officers. Stone was running the Lockhart Brothers Funeral Home, a local family-operated mortuary. Her accomplice, Delores Rogers, is currently being held without bond.

"Social media stars all across the internet are vowing their support to Ms. Rogers, claiming that she was set up and simply at the wrong place at the wrong time."

The screen cut to a video of a young white girl, her screenname "@QueenAlly" in a lower third. "There's just no way that old grandma was involved in any of this body snatching! I'm going to break it down in my series on the Tragedy in Liberty. It's so obviously clearly a setup. They clearly set up this elderly Black woman to take the fall."

The screen cut to a Black creator named "@JamalATL" as he ranted into his phone. "This is Patty Hearst all over again! Don't know who she is? Look it up! They brainwashed that old woman into this! She's probably got dementia! I mean, look at her! She's got both feet dangling above her grave!"

Cyreia stood next to Pembrook, and her voiceover stated, "Sheriff Pembrook of the Liberty Police Department said he could not provide any additional details at this time, but he hopes to bring closure and healing to this community."

Pembrook looked into the camera and then back to Cyreia. "We lost about two dozen fine people here in Liberty due to a fire. My only priority is taking care of the loved ones and the families left behind. My department will support the FBI in any way we can. But right now, my concern is making sure those who have passed can rest in peace and those left behind have the resources they need to heal and move on."

Frances stirred, hearing Pembrook's voice. Akasha leaped from the chair next to Frances. "Oh my gah, hey momma. Take it easy, girl," she said, snatching the remote and turning off the news.

Frances was lying in a hospital bed, staring at the ceiling. She tried to rise up and immediately winced in pain.

"What happened?" Frances asked.

"Hang here for just a sec. I'm going to go get a doctor. Don't move, okay?"

"Where am I gonna go?"

"That's funny 'cause you don't know."

"I don't know what?"

"Little people and Mexicans just dip out of here. I'll be right back."

Akasha ran into the hall. She found a nurse and a doctor. She sent a text to Ray, **"She's awake."**

Moments later, Clint ran into the room, rushing to her bed. He grabbed her fingers, careful to not disturb any of the IVs in her arm and the top of her hand. "Welcome back," he said with a smile.

"Back? Where did I go?"

"They put you in a little time out."

"A what?"

Akasha and Dr. Hoff appeared in the doorway. He grabbed her chart from the door and clicked his pen. "Welcome back, Ms. Hunt."

"Why does everyone keep welcomin' me back? Where did I go?"

"You were in a small, induced coma."

"How small?"

"It's not like you were out for three years."

"How long? Where's Kevin?" she asked Clint.

"They're… um…"

"What's wrong?"

"They're still lookin' for him."

Frances tried to sit up again. Akasha and Dr. Hoff gently pressed her back down. "It's best if you stay lying down, Ms. Hunt."

"My name is Frances. Ms. Hunt was my mother. Where's Kevin?" she insisted again.

Everyone looked at Clint. "I went by your place. All his clothes were gone. His toothbrush, all his things."

"Have you called him?!"

"He ain't answerin' his phone."

"What happened?" Frances asked. "Where am I?" she said, pulling her arm to find an IV needle in her hand.

"You just need to rest," Akasha gently said. "You're a Liberty Memorial. Just relax, Frances. You just don't need to have any stress in your life right now," Akasha calmly stated.

"Have you met me?" she asked. "Why is everyone actin' like I died or something? Did I have a heart attack? Am I dead?"

"You are not dead. What's the last thing you remember?"

"I remember a lot of bad shit was goin' down."

"Frances, we've had you in an induced coma for the past three days. When they brought you in, we did a series of tests. We did a surgery."

"Three days? That's im… That's impossible. What surgery!?"

"Frances… You have a glioblastoma multiforme. Or a GBM for short."

Frances's heartbeat steadily increased. She searched his eyes for any good news. "What the fuck is that?"

"It's a form of brain cancer."

"Okay," she said. "Well, can't you just take it out? I've got insurance."

"We tried. I'm sorry to say that because of its size, I wouldn't advise it. The surgery could be quite dangerous."

Frances stared at Dr. Hoff in utter disbelief. "But without it, I'm gonna die, right?"

He nodded. "We can make you comfortable for the next few months."

"Do the fuckin' surgery!"

"I cannot advise it."

"Months!?" Frances stared at all the faces in the room. "Months!? No! No! I want to live! I want to live! I don't want months!"

"Ms. Hunt—"

"I fuckin' told you to call me Frances!"

"Frances. I'm very sorry to say this, but Frances, you are going to die. You need to start preparing for your end of life."


Clint, Akasha, and Ray sat around Frances's bed, listening to Joni Mitchell music from Akasha's phone.

"You got a passport, Hunt?" Ray asked.

Frances laughed. "Yeah. It's right next to my ball gown I was plannin' on wearin' to the Met Gala."

"We gonna have to get you a passport."

"Why is that?" she asked.

"Because we got bad guys to catch in Italy, Hunt. And I'm gonna need you there. We can't do it without you. It might be part of your immunity plea."

"Liberty Police payin' for my trip?"

"Oh, absolutely," he responded. "Yep. All expenses paid."

"I'm like a real special agent now, ain't I?"

A nurse walked in with a small manilla envelope. "I was asked to give this to you, but he wouldn't give me his name. But he was tall and hot." She handed it to Frances.

"That narrows it down," Frances said, opening the envelope and pulling out two Polaroid photos. One was of her daddy's truck parked under the tree in the front yard. The second photo was a snapshot of a new engine inside the truck with a tattooed man's arm and an enthusiastic thumbs-up. Frances smiled. "Rusty," she said.

She flipped the photo over to see a sticky note that read: **"Get out soon. You still got miles to go. – R"**

Frances laid back on her pillow. She felt calm. She felt at peace. But she wasn't ready to die. She stared at the ceiling.

"Hey Akasha, I got a question for you. When people start seeing dead people, how long before that person dies?"

"It could be months. It could be days. It could be hours," she said. "I've had customers see people almost a year before they passed," she said, grabbing Frances's hand, tears welling in her eyes.

"Why you cryin'?" Frances asked.

"These ain't sad tears, Frances. These are happy tears."

Clint and Ray looked at each other.

"Hunt? You good over there?" Ray asked.

"I'm good," she replied.

Akasha leaned close to Frances's ear and whispered, "Your momma's here, baby."

Frances whispered back, "I know. I can see her over your shoulder."

THE END

# SPECIAL THANKS

Thank you to my mother, who is a warrior and a survivor.

I'm mortified I didn't thank one of my very best friends, Cate Hill, in the last book! Cate, I'm so grateful for you and grateful for our friendship.

Thank you to my agent, Jason Lockhart, for telling me, "Okay, we'll you're not quitting acting. That's not on the table."

Thank you to Diana Bianchini, Libby Blake, Nora Clark, Amy Condon, Caila Cordwell, Andy Darnell, Gina Darnell, Rich Eldredge, Catie Boles-Finley, Bo Bowen, Sarah Carpenter, Christy. Clark, Amy Condon, Michael Cuddy, James Dean, Kerry Droll, Jim Farmer, Carol Green, Zen Grey, Drew Jackson, Madison Junod, Linc Hand, Alison Haselden, Mary Lambert, Alexis Leggett, Jessica Luza, Jasun Mark, Julie Martin, Thom Milam, Jill Melancon, Bill McKinney, Steve Murray, Kelly Nehman, Beth Nelson, Anthony Paderewski, James Rhine, Candice Rose, Nicole Sage, Matthew Sefick, JD Sobol, Anne Stainback Davis, Cynthia Stillwell, Haviland Stillwell, Mark Stephenson, Mike Szymanski, Elizabeth Wachsberg, Michael Weatherly, and Summer Wesson.

Thank you to Stephanie Osteen, for all the support and kindness. I look forward to many more projects together. (And catch MURDER QUEENS on the festival circuit!)

Thank you to all the bartenders at Blake's, who watched me write most of the book from my usual spot.

To those who have left me, but I speak your names every day: Pat Murray, Jennifer Jenkins, Kyle Oldham, Darren Nowell, and Curtis Schnell. I can't believe you guys are gone.

Thank you to Jimmy Howell, for keeping me out of prison.

Thank you to everyone at the LA County Coroner's Office and special thanks to the FBI.

And thank you to YOU, dear reader, for buying my little book and supporting an independent, self-published author. Are there typos? Absolutely. But this was self-published!

If I forgot to thank you, it's because I'm old. Or because I'm saving you for my book YOU SHOULD HAVE BEEN NICER TO ME.

Frances Hunt will ride again in 2025 – Ride or Die.

~ 312 ~

www.ingramcontent.com/pod-product-compliance
Lightning Source LLC
Chambersburg PA
CBHW022026310726
48972CB00006B/1822